VIGILANTE'S
LIGHT

"A Christian version of Christopher Nolan's Batman trilogy, complete with an exciting origin story, citywide corruption, and epic final battle."

—Jessica Joiner,
author of *Dare & JT Crime Dramas*

"Armed with conviction and cool equipment, an average man becomes a superhero to save his endangered community. Light-hearted action and faith-filled drama create an exciting debut!"

—D.A. Randall,
author of *The Red Rider*

"*Vigilante's Light* is an action-packed superhero story that shows the darkness so that the Light shines even brighter. The story builds to an explosive finale, and it leaves a satisfying tale of bravery and sacrifice in its wake. Superhero fans will be sure to enjoy it."

—Jason Joyner,
author of *Rise of the Anointed: Launch* and *Fractures*

VIGILANTE'S
LIGHT

JAKE TYSON

Ambassador International
GREENVILLE, SOUTH CAROLINA & BELFAST, NORTHERN IRELAND

www.ambassador-international.com

Vigilante's Light

© 2021 by Jake Tyson

ISBN: 978-1-64960-027-1
eISBN: 978-1-64960-028-8
Library of Congress Control Number: 2020951659

Ebook edition by Anna Riebe Raats
Edited by Daphne Self

AMBASSADOR INTERNATIONAL
Emerald House
411 University Ridge, Suite B14
Greenville, SC 29601, USA
www.ambassador-international.com

AMBASSADOR BOOKS
The Mount
2 Woodstock Link
Belfast, BT6 8DD, Northern Ireland, UK
www.ambassadormedia.co.uk

The colophon is a trademark of Ambassador, a Christian publishing company.

Dedicated to Jessica. You are my inspiration, always.

ACKNOWLEDGMENTS

So many people have been a huge help to me in preparing to write this book. I couldn't name all of them if I tried, but here are a few who particularly helped me.

Jessica, for always being there for me, listening to me, encouraging me, and being one of my first readers and my number one fan forever. I couldn't have done it without you. You're the best, babe.

My family—Dad, Mom, Zac, Hunter, and MaKayla—as well as my extended family, for always being supportive of my desire to write, encouraging me to do so, giving me feedback on my writing, and letting me bounce ideas off them.

All the members of the Realm Makers Consortium who helped me figure out things like character names, superpowers, motivation, costume design, and on and on. Specific thanks to Randall Allen Dunn, Jason Joyner, and Daniel Slusser.

Ambassador International, for being willing to publish *Vigilante's Light* and taking a chance on a first-time author.

The cast and crew of the TV show *Arrow*, my favorite show and one of the biggest inspirations for writing this story. You did not fail this author.

Most importantly, I couldn't have done this without the desire and the ability to write given to me by my Heavenly Father, and I couldn't have written anything honoring Him if He had not saved me through Christ. Thank you, God, for bringing me to this point.

CHAPTER 1

Six months ago

A bullet whizzed past Gideon Turner's ear and lodged into the trunk of a tree off to his left. Pushing off with his left foot, Gideon rolled right into a patch of bushes and belly-crawled for several meters. He spat leaves from his mouth as they kicked up from the dirt. Another gunshot sounded, but Gideon didn't hear the bullet pass by—or feel it strike him. He kept crawling.

The cover of darkness helped; the only lights for miles around were the flashlights on the ends of the guerrillas' gun barrels. As long as Gideon stayed out of the light, he'd be a difficult target to hit. The problem was, he also had no idea where he was going, and in the rainforests of Venezuela, that was a death sentence. Gideon forced two deep breaths—*in, two, three, four; out, two, three, four; repeat*—and advanced, crawling at a snail's pace to make as little noise as possible.

He was probably going to die. As soon as he'd made the escape attempt, he'd figured he wasn't long for the world. But he'd had to try anyway. Even if not for his own life, for the promise he'd made.

Someone shouted behind him in Spanish. The bushes rustled, and Gideon froze. There was no way he could move; they'd detect the motion by the noise it made. But if he stayed there, it could be seconds before one of the flashlights swept over him and he was caught—and then unceremoniously shot and left to die.

Lord, help me.

Gideon clenched his fists. If it came to it, he'd fight. He didn't want to. He was both a Christian and a doctor, and he felt that violence contradicted both of those things, but he had already killed since all this had started. It wouldn't make things any worse for him if he had to fight and even kill another.

"Volvamos," one voice said. *"El morira aqui."*

Gideon knew enough Spanish to know that at least one of the guerrillas had written him off. Fair enough; he was a city boy from a preacher's home who was lost in a rainforest with no weapons or supplies and no idea which direction to go to find help. His death wasn't just likely; it was all but certain.

But another guerrilla seemed determined to keep looking, because the footsteps kept getting closer. Gideon prepared himself to fight or run, his body tensing with each leaf that crunched.

"Aqui!"

Gideon jumped to his feet and spun around. Three flashlights pointed straight at him. His eyes watered as the lights pierced through the dense jungle. Gideon held his hands in front of his face, grimacing and preparing for the pain of bullets tearing through his skin . . .

But then the guerrillas screamed. Gideon opened his eyes, and stared out at . . . an impossible, blinding light, brighter than the flashlights had been. Coming from *his hands.*

"What the . . . ?"

"Over there!" That voice had spoken English!

Gunshots whizzed past and Gideon tensed again and squeezed his eyes shut. The jungle grew silent. He peeked through one eye. All three guerrillas lay on the ground before him. He ran his hands over his body and found himself free of injuries. His hands were not glowing anymore, either. He looked down at them, puzzled, and flexed his fingers. Not so much as a glimmer.

What happened to me?

"We've found him!" the English voice said.

Gideon turned. Three people, illuminated by the lights on the ends of their own guns, approached. They wore dark clothes and bulletproof vests.

"You Gideon Turner?" one asked.

"Yes . . ."

"We're federal agents. We're here to rescue you, son. You're going home."

Gideon slumped to his knees. One of the other agents approached and helped him to his feet. The one who'd spoken to him pulled a satellite phone from his pocket and began relaying instructions. Gideon didn't pay attention to what he was saying; he was too full of relief. God really had come through for him.

But . . . what had that light been about? What had those madmen done to him?

And how could he fix it?

CHAPTER 2

Six months ago

The perfect orange globe of the sun contrasted beautifully with the purple sky as it met with the horizon. Gideon admired the view from the window of the rescue plane with new appreciation. He had all but given up hope on ever seeing a sight like this again. It was all he could do not to stare at the sun.

His gaze wandered downward to the earth far below. Directly below, the lights of a small town fell into shadow as the sun sank ever lower. It was the largest sign of modern civilization he'd seen in months.

It was all so amazing, and he had taken it for granted his whole life. Not anymore.

Something moved next to Gideon, and he swung his head around. The agent who'd greeted him, the one who'd been on the radio, was kneeling beside Gideon's seat. He had introduced himself as Agent Ross.

"We'll be landing in about half an hour. Your parents are already waiting for you at the landing strip."

"Thank you." Agent Ross started to get up, and Gideon grabbed his arm. "Anyone else?"

"What's that?"

"Is anyone else there?"

"I'm not sure, son. I made sure there wouldn't be a whole crowd of people—there won't be any media or anything—but I don't know who your parents brought with them."

"Okay. Thank you."

Ross nodded and moved back to his seat. Gideon slowly let his gaze return to the window. He could just see his reflection in the Plexiglas. He needed a haircut and a shave. Even before his captivity, he'd had a beard, but it had always been neatly trimmed—Jolie had called it "attractively scruffy." It was way too bushy now. His blond hair was long past his shoulders, tangled and matted. His long-sleeved blue Henley shirt had a few holes in it, and his gray pants and black shoes were tattered and dirty.

He didn't care. Once, he would've died if Jolie had seen him like this. Now, he just wanted to hug her and never let her go. He hoped she had come to the landing strip with his parents.

Before he'd gone down to Venezuela, he'd bought an engagement ring. He'd planned to propose to her upon his return to the States. That had been a year ago.

Gideon sighed, closed his eyes, and leaned back in his seat. Shouts and gunfire echoed in his ears. Pinpricks crawled all over his skin, and he shivered. How long it would take to erase the memories of that awful year?

He opened his eyes. On the horizon, he could see Sojourn City, Michigan jutting out into Lake Superior. *Home.*

When Gideon had first been grabbed by the guerrillas on his third day in Venezuela, he'd been sure they were going to kill him. He'd mentally said his goodbyes to all his loved ones and prayed they would find peace and comfort after they heard about his death. He'd given up on ever seeing Sojourn City again. But the guerrillas hadn't killed him, and his prayers had changed to pleading God to send someone to rescue him.

Finally, he was coming home.

Memories of the past year rushed through Gideon's mind, and he struggled to push them out. *The end of a rifle cracked against his skull, and then he fell and felt another impact as his head hit the ground. Leather straps curled tightly around his wrists, holding him to the table. Tubes and needled pierced his arms; a strange device weighed down his head. A gunshot echoed.* "No!"

He snapped back to reality. All that was over.

The plane descended. Gideon took a deep breath, ran a hand through his hair, and tried to settle down. He should be able to relax now; he was free, and he was home. If only it were that easy. Every little sound or movement triggered his fight-or-flight reaction. Maybe a good night's sleep in his own bed would help. Maybe if he could pretend things were normal for long enough, he'd start to believe it.

Maybe.

The plane jolted as it touched the ground. Gideon jumped, but the federal agents were all relaxed, calmly waiting for the plane to stop. He sighed and forced himself to sit straight and still. It seemed like hours before the plane finally rolled to a complete stop. Gideon looked out the window. Several people stood on the landing strip, but it was almost completely dark now, so he couldn't tell who.

There was movement in Gideon's peripheral. He turned. Agent Ross was standing next to him again. The agent placed a hand on Gideon's shoulder.

"You're home, son. Let's go."

Gideon unbuckled his seatbelt and stood. He didn't have any luggage to grab and this wasn't a commercial airliner anyway. There was no line to the exit ramp; the other agents were still in their seats. He could go now, get off the plane, and run and hug his family. He took a deep breath, steadied himself, and took it one step at a time.

As he reached the ramp, the cool spring air washed over his face. He closed his eyes and smiled. It was so different from the hot, sticky air of Venezuela. He'd almost forgotten. He took one step down the ramp, then another. The figures on the strip were approaching at a brisk walk, and one of them—his mother, Tasha—sped up to almost a run. He took the last three steps down to the pavement.

And then she was on him. She embraced him, and the feeling of a warm, loving contact with another human being rushed through Gideon. He squeezed, hugging his mother as tightly as he ever had. Tears welled in his eyes and as he blinked, they streamed down his cheeks.

"Mom," he whispered.

"Thank God you're safe!"

"I am." He squeezed her again. "I love you."

"I love you, too."

Gideon looked up past her. There were four others behind her: his father, Matthew, younger brother, Wes, former youth pastor, Jeff, and best friend, Dean. *No Jolie?* Gideon pushed the disappointment aside; he would worry about her later. After another ten seconds, he released his mother and moved to his dad.

"Gideon," his father rumbled.

The breath rushed from Gideon's lungs as his dad grabbed him in a huge bear hug and squeezed. Gideon grinned and felt more tears on his face. He hugged back and cried onto his father's shoulder. He felt his brother, Wesley, move up beside him. Reluctantly, he released his father and turned to hug Wes.

"I knew you weren't dead," Wes said. "You're too tough!"

Gideon grinned and ruffled Wes' hair, which was a few shades darker than Gideon's own. As he stepped back from his brother, he turned to look at Dean. Gideon's best friend pushed his curly, out-of-control brown hair out of his face and stepped toward Gideon.

"What Wes said." Dean grinned and hugged Gideon.

Pastor Jeff stepped forward and put a hand on Gideon's shoulder. "I never stopped praying for you, Gideon. I'm so glad you're safe."

When Gideon finally stepped back out of the hug, he felt suddenly awkward. What now? Where did they go from here? Judging from the way Dad shuffled his feet, Wes kicked a pebble, and Mom looked down at her hands, none of them really knew, either.

"Can we go home?" Gideon asked. "I could sleep for a week."

"Right." Dad chuckled. "Let's go."

* * *

The ride back to the house was much more opulent than Gideon had expected. Dean's family business, Sterling Enterprises, had provided a limousine for the Turners' use. The four of them, along with Dean, had piled into the back seat, while Pastor Jeff left in his own car on church business. As the car pulled out of the airport parking lot, Gideon stared out the window, taking in the familiar sights of his home.

"What have I missed?" he asked.

There was a long silence. Gideon looked away from the window. Dad and Mom were looking at each other as if unsure who should answer. Finally, Dad turned to Gideon and leaned forward.

"A lot." His father put a hand on Gideon's shoulder. "For starters, the upper class have moved offshore completely and onto the lake."

Sojourn City had been an experiment of sorts: what if the wealthy and the destitute ran the city together—upper, middle, and lower classes alike living in harmony? The business center of Sojourn City, along with the high-rises and skyscrapers that the wealthy called home, had literally been built on the lake—a floating platform built by Sterling Enterprise's science division. But most of the upper class had lived on the shore of the lake, near to the lower class. They had done what they could to provide jobs, resources, and supplies for the poor.

Gideon had always felt it was a bad idea and would eventually go awry. It looked like he was right.

"What else?"

"There's been a lot of crime growing in the poorer parts of town—people have started calling it the Brooks because they're on the riverfront. That's led to the majority of the police force moving toward the shore to protect the upper class. They would deny it, of course, but they're being paid off."

Gideon clenched his jaw. "And Jolie?"

Again, Mom and Dad exchanged glances. "Jolie is one of the few officers who's remained in the Brooks. There's a handful of precincts left there; they're doing the best they can."

"That's why she wasn't here," Mom said. "She's on patrol."

That was a relief. At least she hadn't moved on. But at the same time, Gideon felt a sudden wave of nervousness and protectiveness. He wanted to go out and find her and drag her to safety. *She can take care of herself. Which one of us just spent a year in captivity, again?*

He thought back to the inexplicable blinding light blasting from his hands. He shoved the memory aside, unwilling to think about what he'd become.

"Is there any hope of recovery?" he asked.

"Right now, we're doing what we can for the poor," Dad said. "We've opened two new church campuses in the Brooks and we're using them to supply food and shelter. Pastor Jeff is the lead pastor at one of them, and he's doing great work. But to actually drive out the crime?" He sighed. "I'm afraid it's a slow process."

Gideon slammed his open palm against his knee. Couldn't *anything* go right? From captivity to a freak of nature to a city overrun by crime . . .

God, what can I do to stop it?

* * *

When Gideon woke up, the sun was shining through the window at his back and to the left of his bed. He inhaled, rolled onto his back, and slowly let his breath out. He felt . . . refreshed. He wondered how long he'd slept. It hadn't been later than eight or nine o' clock when he'd gotten home. What time it was now?

He'd dropped into bed as soon as he possibly could. He'd hardly waited for the car to stop before opening the door and trudging up the sidewalk toward the house. As his father had unlocked the door, Gideon had been tempted to just crash on the couch, but he ultimately decided that he needed his own bed. He forced himself upstairs, mumbling good night to everyone, and he barely remembered entering his room or collapsing onto his bed.

He tried to sit up—and pain racked his body. He grimaced. All the beatings and prodding he'd suffered had finally caught up to him. The adrenaline from running, followed by the relief of rescue, had dulled the pain. But now, it hit him full-force.

Slowly, he pushed himself upright. Every nerve in his body seemed to scream at him. He looked at the alarm clock beside his bed. It was just after noon. He took a breath to steady himself and swiveled to put his feet on the floor. The house was too big to call out and hope someone was nearby; he'd have to get downstairs himself.

Gideon grabbed the edge of his bed and pushed. When he was on his feet, he shuffled toward the door. He realized he hadn't even taken off his shoes before he'd fallen asleep. He was still in the same raggedy clothes he'd been rescued in. But he didn't feel like changing—not right now.

He reached for the door. The brass knob was cool on his hand—cooler than pretty much anything else he'd touched in the past year. He opened the door, went out, down the hall, and to the stairway. His mother was in the living room below, sitting on the couch facing the fireplace, her back to him, talking to . . .

He steadied himself on the banister.

"Jolie." He hardly recognized his own voice.

Her head swiveled around, and she beamed. "Gideon!"

"Are you okay?" Mom asked.

He gritted his teeth and nodded. "Yeah, but I . . . think I need a doctor."

Jolie's smile disappeared. Both women jumped off the couch and ran up the stairs to his side. Jolie got there first; as she reached him, he leaned into her for support.

"I'll call Doctor Edwin right now to let him know we're coming," Mom said. "Let's get you down to the car."

Gideon looked at Jolie as they walked down the stairs. Her dark hair and almost-black eyes contrasted beautifully with her pale skin. She was everything he'd remembered, and despite the pain, he wanted to just stand there and relish being in her presence again.

"Hi," he said.

"Hi." She smiled again. "I'm so glad you're home."

"Me . . . too."

The stairs were an agonizing affair, but finally, they reached the floor. Jolie helped Gideon out the door while his mother grabbed her cell phone and keys off one of the side tables. Gideon groaned as he stumbled out the door and to the car. Jolie sat beside him in the back seat, and he slumped against her.

"I love you," she said.

"I love you, too." He gingerly wrapped his arm around her and gave her the best hug he could manage. "I never thought I'd see you again."

"I knew I'd see you again." Jolie beamed. "I never doubted it."

Gideon smiled. As they drove to the hospital, the two of them just sat there, resting in each other's arms. Gideon tried to ignore the pain racking his body, but it seemed to keep reminding him, *I'm still here.*

It seemed like forever, but they finally reached East Regional Hospital, where Dr. Edwin worked—where Gideon himself had worked, before his trip. Carl Edwin was a member of Refuge Church, where Gideon's father pastored, and he had assured them that he was on call for them whenever they needed him. Jolie helped Gideon out of the car, while his mother ran to get a wheelchair.

Edwin was waiting for them just inside the hospital, and he led them back to an examination room.

"Let him lie down," Edwin said.

Gideon held out a hand, and Jolie helped him to his feet. She brought him over to the bed and he pulled himself up. Edwin stepped up beside Gideon and began his examination.

Suddenly, Gideon worried that somehow, Edwin would find out about the light that had come from Gideon's hands. Would that be the kind of thing that would show up on any scans the doctor did? Even as a doctor himself, Gideon had no idea what had happened to his body, and no idea how it would manifest itself.

"He's definitely sustained some serious bruising," Edwin said. "Not surprising, all things considered. There are no signs of internal bleeding, though. I'd like to do an x-ray to make sure he doesn't have any broken bones."

Gideon hoped that was all Edwin found.

* * *

Hours later, Gideon was able to go home. Dr. Edwin had prescribed him painkillers, but other than that he'd said Gideon would recover with time. None of his injuries should cause future problems, provided he didn't aggravate them before they had a chance to heal properly, and he didn't have any broken bones, miraculously.

And he hadn't said anything about any anomalies. As far as Gideon knew, Edwin hadn't discovered his secret—whatever it was.

Sitting on the couch back at his parents' house, leaning against Jolie's shoulder, Gideon thought that maybe his life could finally go back to having some semblance of normalcy now.

Maybe.

CHAPTER 3

Now

The Brooks had not improved in the six months Gideon had been home.

With hands tucked in the pockets of his favorite navy-blue bomber jacket, he strode down the sidewalk from the parking lot down the street from the West Brooks church campus. The weather was starting to turn cold, and more and more people needed help every day. They came to the aptly-named Refuge Church to receive what food and supplies were available.

Thanks to donations from many of the upper class who had not yet secluded themselves—including Dean's father, Edgar Sterling—the church was able to hand out flashlights and space heaters in addition to food. Each day, Gideon drove in from the apartment he and Dean shared at Lakeside Central Tower and volunteered at the church for an hour before heading into work.

He had tried returning to work at the hospital. But every day, walking down the halls of the hospital, guilt burdened him for the things he'd done in Venezuela. He'd broken a sacred creed among doctors, the Hippocratic Oath—he had intentionally harmed others, even taken lives. And in doing so, he was no longer worthy to be a doctor. Finally, with Dean's help, he had accepted a job at Sterling Labs as a bio-analyst.

It wasn't his dream job by any means, but it paid well enough and it kept him busy.

Trash littered the street around Gideon. The fence to his right was covered in graffiti, much of it obscene. He clenched his jaw at the sight. Ahead, two men warmed their hands by a fire. They looked up as Gideon approached. He recognized one—a black man with a kind gleam in his eye. His name was Wyatt Jonson; he and his family were regular attendees at West Brooks Refuge Church, the church Pastor Jeff led. Gideon didn't know him well; because the church had opened while Gideon was gone, and it wasn't the campus he normally attended, he was still getting to know most of the members. The man with Wyatt, whom Gideon did not recognize, stepped toward him.

"Excuse me, sir. Do you have any money? I lost my job last week, and my rent is due. If I don't pay, my family . . . "

"Come with me," Gideon said. "I can't promise money, but I can get you food and some other necessities that may help."

"Come on, man." He stepped closer. "My family will be out in the cold if I don't pay."

Gideon's fingertips brushed the twenty-dollar bill in his pocket. That wouldn't be enough to pay this man's rent.

"I'm sorry. Food and supplies are all I have to offer."

Wyatt stepped forward, his brow furrowing. He looked ready to intervene if his friend escalated. Gideon doubted it would come to that, though. He kept his expression calm and his attention on Wyatt's friend.

"You're lying," the first man said. "I saw that car you pulled up in. You're not hurting for cash."

Gideon closed his eyes and sighed. He did drive a brand-new navy-blue Mustang. He had worked hard to afford it. *Note to self, don't drive that around here.* The tension between classes was bad enough already; he didn't need to exacerbate it himself.

"I really don't have what you need on me. But come to the church and—"

"What has the church ever done for us?" the man snarled. "They pull in here after things start getting bad, trying to make it right. But we all know, this church has members at Lakeside that are well off enough to help us all out. Where are they?"

"Aw, leave him alone, Lionel." Wyatt grabbed his friend's shoulder. "It's not the boy's fault."

"No. I said, where are they? Hiding in their towers and their fancy houses, waiting for the crime to bust us in the Brooks down to dust."

"Sir, that—" Gideon started.

"Church won't help our families stay out of the cold! My landlord's in the mob's pocket, man. He'll kick us out the day I don't pay rent! He's not gonna give me a second chance cause if he does, the mob's gonna put a bullet in his brain instead of money in his wallet. My friend here, he just lost his job, too; how long until he's in the same situation?"

Gideon hadn't known about Wyatt's job. He tried to catch the man's eye, but Wyatt stared at the sidewalk, unwilling to meet Gideon's gaze.

"I understand, sir, it's an injustice—"

"Well then why don't somebody do something about it? Huh?" Lionel pushed Gideon's shoulder. Not hard, but hard enough to make a point. "Where's the cops? Oh, that's right, they're up at Lakeside defending the rich people that pay for this church while letting us rot."

Gideon took a step back and stumbled off the sidewalk into the street. He kept his footing, thankfully, and held up his hands in a placating gesture.

"I'm sorry." He took a step back onto the sidewalk. "I really am. If I could fix it by myself, I would, but . . . "

Lionel scoffed. "If everyone who said that would get together and actually do something about it, maybe things would get solved around here."

Gideon nodded and then hung his head. The members of Refuge Church *were* trying; that was why they'd opened the two new campuses. But he knew he'd never convince Lionel of that. The man's mind had been made up.

"You're right." Gideon reached into his pocket. "Here. I have twenty bucks on me. Not enough, but maybe if anyone else can help you, you can put it together and pay rent. Or at least give it to your landlord as a down payment or something."

Lionel shook his head. "Thanks. But he don't do down payments."

"You can still come to the church, you know."

"Nah." He returned to the fire. "I'm good."

Wyatt traded glances with Gideon, shrugged apologetically, and backed away. Gideon resumed his walk toward the church, sighing deeply as he passed the men. This was far from the first time he'd seen this kind of situation in the Brooks, though it was the first time he'd been confronted with it so directly. He really did want to do something about it. The Sojourn City experiment had been put together when he was only a year old, so he'd known the city for his whole life, basically. It was his home, and he hated seeing it like this.

But what could one man do?

A soft light glowed at the edge of Gideon's peripheral vision. Frowning, he looked down. His eyes widened, and he slowly drew his hands out of his pockets. They were glowing again—not as brightly as they had been in the jungle, but there was a definite luminescence. His heart rate accelerated, and as it did, they began to glow more brightly.

Calm down, calm down . . .

Gideon took several deep breaths. As his heart rate slowed, the glow began to fade. He sighed, relieved, when they returned to normal.

They had done something to him. But what?

* * *

After work, Gideon spent an hour each night working out. He'd taken martial arts as a hobby before he'd gone to Venezuela. He'd had a pretty severe temper, and it helped him channel it. Since he'd been back, he'd taken it because he now knew how important it was. It had saved his life. On Tuesdays, Thursdays, and Saturdays, he met with a sensei and practiced *aikido, tae kwondo,* and *eskrima.* On Mondays, Wednesdays, and Fridays, he went to a gym to build muscle mass.

Tonight, as he left the gym, he thought about Jolie. She was on patrol now, as she was almost every night. Their schedules were practically opposites, leaving very little time for them to see each other, but they made it work however they could.

He still had the ring he'd bought. It was at his apartment, hidden in his dresser. He was ready to propose . . . but was it the right time? He'd only been back for six months, and they'd both changed in the year he'd been gone. Maybe they needed to get to know each other again before he took a step like that.

Gideon unlocked his car and slid into the driver's seat. He quickly shut the door and turned on the heat; it was cold out. As the car heated up, Gideon turned his phone back on. He backed out of his parking spot and drove toward the road. As he angled out into traffic, his phone began vibrating. He glanced down at it. Dean. Probably just calling to see when he was going to be home and ask if he could pick up some pizza on the way, or something.

He brought the phone to his ear. "Hello?"

"Gid, you need to get to the church."

"What?"

"Someone hit the west campus. They broke a bunch of windows, spray-painted the walls, and stole food and supplies. It's a mess."

Gideon clenched his jaw. "Anyone hurt?"

Dean's voice broke—and he never broke. "Just get here."

Gideon hung up the phone, swung the car around the next corner, and sped toward the Brooks. They should've known this would happen eventually. They should've prepared for it. He just hoped that he wouldn't arrive to find anyone dead.

* * *

Gideon parked on the street half a block from the church. About half a dozen people were standing outside the church. As far as he could tell, none of them were police officers. He didn't see a single cruiser in the vicinity of the church—no flashing lights, no blue uniforms. It had taken him how long to get here, and he had still beaten the police? The only emergency vehicle he'd seen on his way here was an ambulance, going the opposite direction. Shaking his head, he turned off his car and jogged in the direction of the small group. As he approached, he made out the distinctly tall form of his father at the center of the gathering.

Dean was there, too. Gideon recognized the others as patrons of the church, though he couldn't call their names to mind. The only one he could put a name to instantly was Wyatt, the man he had encountered on the street the other day.

"Dad!" Gideon called. "Is everyone all right?"

His father looked up at him. Tears welled in his eyes. "All of us are fine, son. But Pastor Jeff . . . he . . . "

Oh, no.

"I barely recognized him," Wyatt murmured. "I was the one who discovered him—and I called 911 as soon as I did, and then your father. The ambulance just took him away."

The one Gideon had passed on his way here—it must've been taking Pastor Jeff to the hospital. Jeff had been like an uncle to Gideon; he was his father's best friend, and he'd taught Gideon much of what he knew about the Bible. A lump welled in Gideon's throat.

"Is he . . . ?"

"It's a coin toss whether he'll survive," Dad said. "EMTs said if Wyatt had arrived any later, they wouldn't have been able to do anything. Now, they may be able to save him, but it's going to be close."

"Where are the police?"

"On their way, I'm sure." Dean rolled his eyes. "It's not like the twelfth precinct is only a couple miles from here, or anything."

"I am sure they will get someone along as quickly as they possibly can," Dad interjected sternly. "There are many problems in the Brooks . . . the police may have to prioritize us lower than the more dangerous situations."

"Most dangerous?" Gideon snapped, his ears burning. "A man almost died. He still might. That's not considered dangerous?"

"There wasn't a present threat for the police to defuse. That's the way it is these days."

The allegations of corruption his father had inferred on the night Gideon had returned from Venezuela stuck in his mind. *Are they really busy, or are they just prioritizing the people who're padding their wallets?* Gideon wasn't inclined to trust any of the local police, save for Jolie.

"Let's head inside," Dad said. "Be careful not to touch anything that could be evidence, though. We wouldn't want to contaminate the crime scene."

As the others shuffled into the church, Gideon couldn't help but feel dumbfounded by the situation. Members of the church, downtrodden citizens, were being forced to be the first on-site to a crime scene while the police did who-knew-what. He started to fall in line behind the others, and Dean wound around to stand next to him.

"You made good time."

"I thought speeding was warranted, given the situation. How did you find out about this, if the police haven't even been here yet?"

"After Wyatt called your dad, your dad called me when he couldn't get a hold of you."

Gideon always turned his phone off while he was in the gym. That explained why Dad hadn't been able to get through to him and had called Dean instead. It was fortunate that Gideon had turned his phone back on when he had.

"Do we know who did this?"

"No idea yet. There should be security footage on one of the office computers."

The sanctuary was a wreck. Wooden pews had been smashed and cut—some of them so cleanly that it had to have been done with a chainsaw. Chairs had been overturned. Glass shards were everywhere, all the windows lining either side of the sanctuary completely smashed in, letting a chill breeze waft through the auditorium. Random patches of carpet had been torn up. Obscene graffiti covered three of the four walls. But the most ominous sign of vandalism, written along the fourth wall in bloodred paint, was a three-word message.

WE'LL BE BACK.

A siren crooned. Red and blue flashing lights illuminated the sanctuary. Gideon turned. A trio of police cars had pulled onto the curb in front of the church. Dad gestured for the other parishioners to stay inside. He strode through the sanctuary and back outside. Gideon caught Dean's eye and jerked his head toward the door. He and Dean followed in his father's wake. Four police officers, along with a single detective, approached the church.

"You the pastor?" the detective, a man in his early forties with a distinct Northern accent, asked.

"That's me. Matthew Turner."

"Detective Simon Walters." The detective held out his hand and shook Dad's. "I'm sorry about your church, Pastor. Rest assured, we'll do our best to get to the bottom of this and ensure no one gets hurt."

"Thank you, Detective Walters," Gideon's father said, "but I'm more concerned about the life that hangs in the balance tonight. Don't catch these criminals for the vandalism; catch them so no one has to suffer the same way Pastor Jeff is."

Not to mention to get justice for Pastor Jeff. Gideon eyed the detective. Walters wore a light gray dress shirt, a black and gray checkered tie, and a knee-length black trench coat over pressed black slacks and wing-tipped dress shoes. High-class for a detective. *I'd bet anything this guy's taking bribes.* He looked past Walters at the four cops. Two of them were young white men, probably only a year or two older than Gideon each.

The third was an older black man, probably around Wyatt's age, his skin hard and weathered. He was clearly a man of experience. Gideon wondered how long he'd been on the force.

And that man's partner . . . *Jolie*. She made brief eye contact with Gideon. Tears brimmed near the corners. She returned her attention to the church without further acknowledging him, all business. *Pastor Jeff was her friend, too.* Walters stepped inside the church with Matthew. The two younger cops began unrolling yellow crime scene tape, while Jolie and her partner ascended the steps to the church's porch.

"Is nothing sacred anymore?" the older cop groused. "In my day, even the worst criminals knew to leave the churches alone. And a pastor?"

Gideon nodded soberly. "This city's a mess."

"You can say that again." The man extended a hand. "Officer Paul Jordan. I know who you are; I've seen your picture on Jolie's desk enough times. Good to finally meet you, though, Mr. Turner."

"Nice to meet you, too, Officer Jordan."

"Paul, please. Let's go inside, shall we?"

Paul entered the church first, followed by Dean. Jolie brushed past Gideon and leaned close to him as he joined her in walking into the church.

"Should've known you'd be here," she whispered. "Can't stay out of trouble, can you?"

"How long have you known me?" Gideon smirked. "I'm glad you're one of the cops on the scene. At least you, I know we can trust."

"Paul, too," Jolie said. "He's as old and incorruptible as they come. And those two out there—Pulaski and Bates—they're good kids. Pulaski and I came in at the same time, and Bates is new blood, but he seems good. They're impressionable, so I'll have to keep an eye on them, but they're not on the take right now."

"What about Detective Fancy up there?"

Jolie turned her attention to Walters and clenched her jaw. "Him, I'm not so sure about."

Gideon closed his mouth as they came into hearing distance of his father and Walters.

"Pastor, maybe you should consider shutting down for a while," Walters said. "This is a clear threat of further violence."

"We can't," Dad said. "The people here need us."

"You won't do anyone any good if you're dead."

"I'm not afraid.

Walters cleared his throat. "This wasn't some group of young punks with a collective bad attitude and a few tools and cans of spray paint, Pastor. This was a message from the mob. They want you out of their neck of the woods, and they'll kill if they have to in order to get that across. They already have."

Gideon glanced at the him. "Isn't it your job to be what stops them from coming back?"

Out of the corner of his eye, he saw Jolie's surprised expression, but he ignored it. He wasn't sure if her surprise was at his anger or his boldness in speaking up, but his anger wasn't directed at her; she was only doing what she could. But the police force as a whole was falling down on their job.

"We're spread thin, kid," Walters said.

"And who's fault is that?" Gideon spread his hands. "Maybe if a few more officers were out here in the Brooks instead of clustering up at Lakeside, near the one percenters—which is already a safe part of town, I might add, and doesn't need additional protection—this wouldn't have happened."

"Gideon . . ." Jolie said.

"Watch yourself." The detective stepped toward Gideon. "Like I said, we're doing the best we can. I'm here, aren't I? There are other cops here. We didn't sell out for a cushy job by the shore. So be thankful we're here instead of whining about the ones who aren't. We're understaffed, undersupplied, and just plain tired. So when I say we can't, we really can't."

Gideon glanced down at Walters' shoes. *You may not have sold out to Lakeside, but you sold out to* somebody. That was probably worse.

"We understand, Detective." Dad put a hand on Gideon's shoulder. "Please let it go, son."

Gideon sighed deeply, nodded. "Fine."

"We'll keep this church closed until the spring," Dad said. "We can't repair in the winter anyway, and we still have the east campus."

Walters nodded. "I'll arrange for someone to come by and rope everything off if you can arrange for all the supplies that didn't get stolen to be moved to that church."

"We will. God bless you, Detective."

Walters and Paul filed out. Jolie remained a moment longer. Gideon looked at her and saw hurt and worry in her eyes.

"You're fine, Jolie. This isn't your fault."

"I know . . ." She hesitated, then nodded. "Don't worry, Gid. We'll catch these guys."

"You will." He hugged her. "I love you. Stay safe out there."

"I will. Love you, too."

She turned and walked out. Gideon glanced at the graffiti again. The letters, jagged and large, looked like they'd been written in blood. Maybe it had.

"They mean this," he said.

"I know." Dad pulled his jacket close and spoke to the rest of the congregants in the sanctuary. "Come on. There's nothing more we can do here tonight."

Gideon looked to Dean as Dad and the others left. "They're going to get away with this."

Dean raised an eyebrow. "Pessimist, much?"

"Sorry, but they will. Jolie's a good cop, and I'm sure some of the others are, too, but you heard Walters: they're spread thin. They won't find these guys. And that's not even considering the fact that Walters there is dirty as sin."

"When did you become so negative?"

Gideon shoved his hands in his jacket pockets and stormed toward the door. "Maybe when I spent a year rotting in a cell with no hope of rescue and returned to find that my city had gone to shambles."

He heard Dean's footsteps behind him as his friend rushed to keep up. "But you've got to believe God will work this out, right?"

"I do, but God works through people, and right now it seems like all the people in this city only care about serving themselves." He stopped on the sidewalk. "Someone has to do something about it."

"Like what?"

"I don't know yet." Gideon started walking again. "But something. Someone's got to get justice for Pastor Jeff. I'll see you at home, Dean."

"O . . . kay. See you there."

Gideon got in his car and tore down the road, his jaw set. He honestly had no idea how he could help, but he was sick of watching his city suffer. These people deserved better, and they were going to get it. He was going to see to that. One way or another, the Brooks were going to get cleaned up.

He would make sure of it.

CHAPTER 4

Last year

Gideon had only been in Venezuela for three days, and he already felt his heart changed. Oh, he didn't feel like God was calling him to move down here permanently, or anything, but he felt changed, nonetheless. For one thing, he had a renewed appreciation for the modern medical technology he'd had back in the States. For another, he felt his heart break for taking his own health and relative wealth for granted.

At the end of the third day, he was exhausted from all the work he'd done, but it was a good kind of exhausted. As the last patient left the small clinic, he stripped off his gloves and tossed them in the trashcan. He turned to Dr. Jameson, the head of the clinic. He was the one who'd invited Gideon down for the trip.

"Another good day's work, Doc."

"Amen." Jameson took off his white coat and hung it on a rack. "And now to head home and get a good night's sleep."

Gideon was hanging up his own lab coat when the door rattled.

"Didn't Lisa lock the door?" he asked.

"Gideon, don't move," Jameson said.

Gideon's heart skipped. He titled his head just enough to see what was going on behind him. Jameson had his hands in the air. Three men clad in camouflage and carrying AK-47s had entered the clinic.

"*Danos medicina,*" the front man said. "*Ahora!*"

"*Sí, señor,*" Jameson said. "Gideon, the medicine."

Gideon moved toward the medicine cabinet. What should he do? Should he just turn the medicine over to these men? Should he somehow try to fight back or protect Jameson? He didn't stand a chance against three armed men. He might know martial arts, but he wasn't close enough to them to disarm them before they could fire. They were on the other side of the counter that divided the clinic's small waiting area from the rest of the building.

He took several trays of medicine and rounded the counter. He extended the medicine to the leader. One of the two other men approached, lowered his rifle, and took the pallets. Gideon's blood grew hot as he thought about all this medicine, which could help so many innocents, being used by these criminals. Gideon considered trying to grab for the man's gun, but . . . *it's just medicine. It's not worth risking lives.* Besides, he'd sworn an oath as a doctor to never harm others.

"*Vienes con nosotros,*" the leader said.

"*Perdón*eme?"

The leader repeated the order and bashed Jameson on the head. The aging man fell to his knees.

That's enough. The anger Gideon had been containing burst free. They were threatening a good man's life. Gideon snapped out a kick at the man in front of him, knocking the medicine pallets from his hands and sending him stumbling backward. That man fell into the third man, who had been directly behind him. Gideon spun and grabbed the barrel of the leader's AK-47.

"Jameson, run!"

"Gideon—"

"Run!"

The doctor climbed to his feet and limped toward the back door. Gideon threw a punch at the leader's face. The guerrilla dodged it and jerked on his rifle. Gideon, still holding the barrel, stumbled forward and belatedly released his grip on the weapon. He tucked his head against his body and rolled off his shoulder, coming up in a crouch behind the leader.

He swiveled, extending his right leg in a sweeping kick that caught the leader on his ankles. The man fell, and his head smacked against the medicine cabinet. Gideon started to stand and found himself staring into a pair of gun barrels. The other two guerrillas had recovered and were standing right over him. He clenched his jaw. Any second now, they'd fire, and he'd be dead.

One of them leaned down to check on the leader. He shook his head at his colleague. Guilt flooded through Gideon like cold water in his veins. *I killed him.*

The guerrilla who'd been carrying the medicine grabbed Gideon by the arm and hoisted him up. He snapped instructions at his colleague, who bashed Gideon on the head. Gideon groaned and fell, hitting his head again on the floor. The two men dragged Gideon toward the door. He didn't resist. He wouldn't—couldn't—take another life.

He just hoped Jameson managed to call for rescue.

Now

The steady beat of the heart monitor was the only sound in the small, warmly lit hospital room. Gideon stood at the foot of the bed on the side closer to the door, while his father stood on the opposite side and closer to Pastor Jeff's head. Two wooden upholstered chairs sat in either corner near the window. Both were currently vacant. The blinds on the window had been drawn, but golden light from the streetlight shone through.

Pastor Jeff looked peaceful—his expression relaxed and his head resting against a well-fluffed pillow. A team of surgeons had managed to save Pastor Jeff's life, but he was holding on by force of will. Gideon had seen it before. If anyone could pull through, it was Pastor Jeff. He was one of the strongest men Gideon had ever had the privilege of knowing. And here he was, brought low by some arrogant mobster.

"This isn't right," Gideon said. "Someone should do something."

"The police are doing something, son." Dad didn't take his eyes off Jeff. "We can only pray that they catch the culprit before he hurts anyone else. But Jeff wouldn't want us to be consumed with anger on his account."

"The police. Dad, you were the one who told me that most of the police in Sojourn City are corrupt. I mean, did you see Detective Walters? The clothes he was wearing, you don't get on a detective's salary. The man's dirty."

"That's an unfair assumption. He could have wealthy family. Most people in the Brooks couldn't afford your clothes. Or many of mine, for that matter." Gideon grimaced at the accusation, and Dad pressed on. "And besides, I know what I said, but the police in the Brooks, they're doing the best they can. There are corrupt officers among them, but most of the corrupt are the ones who've moved outside the Brooks. The ones still there are working with what little resources they have. That includes Detective Walters."

Does it, though? Gideon didn't press the point. There was no reason to argue with his father, because neither of them was likely to relent on his viewpoint. But Gideon's original statement still stood—someone had to do something.

"How is he?"

Gideon turned. Jolie stood in the doorway, dressed in a white t-shirt, blue jeans, and black leather jacket, her dark hair tossed over her shoulder in a ponytail. She must've just gotten off duty. He smiled and held out a hand for her to join them. She crossed to his side, took his hand, and rested against his shoulder, looking down at Pastor Jeff.

"He's holding on," Dad said. "God didn't see fit to take him from us yet, so I believe Jeff will pull through. Thank you for coming to check on him, Jolie."

Had Jolie heard any of the conversation between Gideon and his father before she'd come in? If so, it would've been the second time that Jolie had heard Gideon badmouthing the police in the Brooks. He hoped she didn't take it personally. If she were a detective, Pastor Jeff's attacker would already be behind bars, Gideon was confident of that much.

"I can't stay long," Jolie said, "but I still wanted to drop in. I'm glad he has you here to watch over him. But don't forget to rest—both of you. You won't do Pastor Jeff any good if you can't function from sleep deprivation."

He wanted to ask her how the investigation was going—if Walters had found any leads on the attackers or if there had been an arrest. It didn't seem like the time, though. So he stood there with her in silence, staring down at Pastor Jeff's still form, and embraced the bubbling anger that expanded in his chest. His ears burned at the thought of the mobsters getting away with this. His words to Dean came back to him. *Someone's got to get justice for Pastor Jeff.*

Somebody, he added this time, *like me.*

* * *

Gideon had stopped going home at night.

The first night after the church vandalism, he'd gone straight from his martial arts practice to the Brooks and hidden out in an alleyway across from the church with a video camera and a powerful audio recorder. He pointed them at anyone who passed by, picking up snippets of conversation.

That hadn't borne any fruit. No one who'd passed the church that night had spoken about the vandalism. They all seemed consumed with their own problems.

The next night, he decided to see if he could track down some information himself. He took a bus to the Brooks and roamed the streets. Several times, he saw groups of people huddled around trashcan fires or outside drug stores and moved to talk to them. None of them seemed to be interested in discussing the vandalism. Either they didn't know anything, or they were too scared to tell him what they did know.

By the third night, Gideon was exhausted. He had hardly slept at all; he didn't go home until between three and four in the morning, and he woke up early to go help at the other church campus before work. But he was determined to figure this out.

He sat in his car, parked in an alley, and sipped hot chocolate to keep himself warm. He had decided to watch the church again. Maybe the vandals would return tonight.

His passenger door opened, and he jumped, nearly spilling his hot chocolate. He turned to find Jolie sitting in the passenger's seat, staring at him with a raised eyebrow and a frown.

"What are you doing?"

"I'm . . . watching the church."

"Gideon . . . " Jolie rolled her eyes and leaned back in the seat. "That's our job, Gideon. Sojourn PD. That's what we do. You should be at home sleeping."

"I know, but I also know you're spread thin and—"

"Did you ever think that no one's shown up to vandalize the church again because you're here? Maybe they noticed you and got spooked?"

"Well, then I guess I'm doing my job."

"No, you're not. You're doing my job." She huffed. "Actually, you're not; you're making my job harder because I'm supposed to catch these guys."

Gideon sighed. "Sorry, babe."

"Don't 'babe' me, Gid. I love you, but you need to go home. Please."

"Okay. Fine."

Jolie opened the door. "Look, I'm glad you want to help. But I'd rather know you're safe, so I don't have to worry about you, too."

"I can take care of myself, Jolie."

"I know. But this is coming dangerously close to impeding an investigation. We've already got the Crusader to deal with."

"The Crusader?"

Jolie sighed. "It's nothing. I'll see you tomorrow; I've got a day off."

Gideon smiled. "That'll be nice. Be careful, okay?"

"I will. You too." She stepped out and glanced back into the car. "Love you."

"Love you, too."

She shut the door and walked off. Gideon put his hot chocolate in a cup holder and leaned back in his seat. She was right. He was getting in the way. And besides, he hadn't even noticed her approaching the car. What if that had been some criminal? He would probably be dead, or at least bleeding out in an alley without a car or any money.

He put the car in drive and pulled out onto the street. As he drove, he prayed that God would protect Jolie out here. And he wondered who this "Crusader" was. Some civilian who'd gotten tired of the crime in the Brooks and decided to take matters into his own hands? That sounded all right to Gideon.

Just before he reached the on-ramp to the freeway, he reconsidered. Turning left instead, going under the overpass, he drove toward Wyatt's home. *Jolie said to go home . . .*

He just had to do his one thing. Driving as quickly as he could without getting in trouble—not there seemed to be any police around, as usual—Gideon passed through the Brooks to the older man's home. He parked on the curb, opened the fence to Wyatt's front yard, and walked up to the porch. Wyatt had three children—Gideon wasn't familiar with their names, but they came to church with him—all of whom were likely asleep at this point, so he approached the front door as quietly as he could and knocked on the door.

It was a long moment before there was an answer. Wyatt, clad in a black robe, poked his head out.

"Gideon?"

Gideon wasn't sure what to say, suddenly. "Are you okay?"

"Yeah. I'm good. Why?"

That was a relief. "It's just . . . the thing with the church has been bothering me. I haven't been able to take my mind off it. In fact, I've been parking out across from the church to keep watch in case the vandals come back. Doesn't seem like the police are doing anything about it."

Wyatt huffed. "Surprised?"

"Not particularly. Listen, I was just wondering, did you see anything? Anything that might hint at who did this?"

"Afraid not. They were long gone by the time I got there. And good luck getting anyone around here to talk. You snitch on the mob, you're asking for a bullet to the head. Trust me, kid, you're better off staying away and letting whatever good cops are left do their job."

"Right." *Ask how he's doing.* "You find a job yet?"

"Nothing yet." Wyatt smiled wanly. "Don't worry. I will."

"I know. I'll be praying for you. Good night, Wyatt."

He started to back away from the door . . .

He knows something. He knows exactly who did this.

Gideon frowned. Where had that come from? He shook his head. It was almost as if he'd been able to divine what Wyatt had been thinking. But it was nothing, right? Just a random thought. He turned and headed back for his car.

"Hey!" Wyatt called. "You know your flashlights are on?"

"Lights? I—" Gideon looked down.

His hands were glowing again and shining straight through his jacket pockets. Slowly, he pulled them free and held them up. They were brighter than any flashlight he'd ever seen—not as bright as they had been that night in the jungle, but certainly brighter than they'd been the last time he'd seen them glow.

"What the . . . ?" Wyatt slammed the door.

Gideon shook his head. What was this?

CHAPTER 5

Gideon crept down the hall to his apartment and turned the key to unlock the door as quietly as he could. The living room lights were off. Good. It wasn't as late as it had been the previous nights, but with any luck, Dean would already be asleep, and . . .

Slight amusement covered over by concern and frustration. Uh-oh.

"Well, well, well." The light flicked on. "If it isn't the Prodigal Roommate."

Gideon grimaced and scratched the back of his head, distracted by the fact that he seemed to have once again sensed someone else's feelings. "Hey, Dean."

Gideon's best friend sat on the arm of their couch with arms crossed and eyebrow raised like a disapproving parent. Gideon resisted the urge to laugh because he couldn't tell if Dean was really upset or not and he didn't want to make matters worse. He unzipped his jacket and took it off.

"'Hey, Dean'? That's all I get?" Dean hopped to his feet. "Three nights in a row you've disappeared into the night after work and haven't come home until Lord knows when. And this after you tell me you're going to 'do something' about the Brooks."

"Sorry to keep you up." Gideon draped his jacket over the recliner. "Do we have to talk about this tonight?"

"Um, yeah. If you're going all super-crazy vigilante on me, Gid, I need to know."

"I'm not 'going all super-crazy vigilante.' I was just doing some recon."

"Aha!" Dean jumped up and pointed at him. "So you were in the Brooks."

Gideon sighed and dropped down into the recliner. If they were actually going to have this conversation, he might as well get comfortable.

"Yes, I was. I've just been watching the church and asking a few questions."

"Do you have any idea how dangerous the Brooks are this late? No, of course you don't, you were gone for a year." Dean shook his head. "Gideon, I'm all for doing something. You know me; I'm a man of action! But I don't want you to get hurt, man."

"I can take care of myself. Black belt, remember? I'm strong and I'm a good fighter."

"Yeah, and you have anger issues. That could get you in a lot of trouble, and no martial arts skills are going to save you if a bunch of mobsters with guns corner you in an alleyway."

No, but my Flashlight Hands might. Gideon pushed the thought aside. He would figure out what was causing his glowing hands as soon as possible, but he had no desire to start thinking of them as a positive thing, let alone as a superpower to be used to fight crime in the Brooks.

"I know. Look, Jolie already read me the riot act. She saw me staking out the church and told me to go home because I was getting in the way."

"Good. Your girlfriend has sense." Dean ran a hand through his curly hair. "Just be careful, man. I lost you once already."

"I know."

"Is this about what happened there?"

"No."

"You never talk about it, Gid. A whole year of your life and you haven't said more than ten words to me about it."

"I'd prefer to forget it." *Pinpricks, crawling all through his skin.*

"Yeah, but that's the thing, man. You can't. Like it or not, that year will shape who you are now. Trying to block that out is dangerous. You won't be able to move on until you accept what happened."

Leather straps curled tightly around his wrists, holding him to the table. Tubes and needled pierced his arms; a strange device weighed down his head.

"And look, I respect that you came home to a screwed-up city and you're mad about it, Gid. But getting yourself killed won't fix the Brooks, so just be careful. And try to get some sleep once in a while, yeah?" Dean smirked. "You almost switched some samples in the lab today."

Gideon snapped back to the present and forced a laugh. "You noticed that? Okay, fine. I'll go to bed right now."

"Good man. I'll get the lights." Dean patted Gideon on the shoulder. "See you tomorrow, crime fighter."

Gideon rolled his eyes, chuckled, and walked down the hall to his room. Then he stopped.

"Hey, Dean?"

"Yeah?"

"Who's the Crusader?"

Dean chuckled. "Urban legend. Some guy in a mask who tears up thugs in the Brooks. He's done some good but he's only one guy, and some people actually say he makes matters worse by egging the criminals on. The cops definitely don't like him. Why?"

"Oh, Jolie mentioned him." Gideon shrugged. "Anyway, good night."

"Night."

Gideon put the Crusader out of his mind. It was the weekend now. Tomorrow, he'd see Jolie and spend the day with her. Then next week, he'd go to the lab and run some discreet tests on himself. He'd figure out where this light was coming from—what they'd done to him—and whether it had anything to do with his odd penchant for picking up other people's emotions. And then, he'd decide what to do about the Brooks.

* * *

Jolie Anderson was in a constant state of exhaustion.

Working nights in the Brooks was a cop's nightmare, and she was living it out every single day. She'd lost count of the number of domestic disturbances she'd had to deal with, the bodies she'd found in alleys with track marks in their arms, the gang fights she'd had to break up. She'd been shot at countless times.

The worst of it was that it didn't seem to be doing any good. No matter how many drug dealers, gang bangers, and mob enforcers she put behind bars, it seemed like there were more waiting in the wings to take over. It was so . . . pointless.

And now Gideon was trying to help, and it made her feel even worse. Not because he was her boyfriend, but because he was a civilian who didn't even live in the Brooks and he'd decided that enough was enough. If only more cops in her precinct had that attitude, the Brooks probably would've been cleaned up before things ever got this bad.

It scared her, too. Gideon had always struggled with anger. Not to the point of violence, although he used martial arts to channel that anger . . . but she feared what he could do if he ever snapped.

With her shift finally over, Jolie parked on the street outside her apartment and pulled her jacket tightly around her as she stepped into the cold. At least her home was outside the Brooks. She could come home and try to forget the misery she witnessed every night.

Shivering, she went inside, locked the door, and went straight to bed without even turning any lights on.

"You're a failure," Gideon said.

They stood on a street corner in the Brooks in the middle of a cloudy afternoon. Jolie was wearing her uniform and Gideon was looking at her with . . . such disgust.

"No, Gideon, don't say that!"

He sneered and shoved her away. He was wearing a leather jacket over a bulletproof vest and carrying a pistol in either hand. His blond hair had grown shaggy and fell over his eyes.

"It's my turn," he said.

He strode out into the street. Dozens of people rushed at him. Some were criminals, but others Jolie recognized as innocent residents of the Brooks— victims to the criminals they stood beside. But now, they all rushed Gideon, carrying baseball bats and guns and knives. Gideon raised his guns.

"No!" Jolie shouted.

Gideon mowed them down, firing bullet after bullet, indiscriminately killing criminals and civilians alike. The slaughter seemed to go on for endless minutes, but when it was finally over, Gideon lowered his guns and turned back to Jolie, a wicked grin on his face.

"Now the Brooks are clean," he said.

Jolie's eyes snapped open and she screamed. She sat up and looked around. This was her apartment. She was home, safe, and the sun was shining through the window.

"Heck of a dream," she muttered.

She rose and went to the bathroom. She remembered telling Gideon she didn't work today, so she needed to make good on her promise to see him. She quickly showered, dressed in jeans, a flannel shirt, and a denim jacket, and pulled her dark hair into a ponytail. She sent Gideon a text, *Lunch at noon?*

A few minutes later, he responded, *Sure. Wally's Diner?*

Their first date had been at Wally's. Jolie smiled at the memory.

See you there.

She sat down at her small dining room table and opened her Bible. After reading a Psalm about the Lord's protection, she prayed over the Brooks, the police department, and Gideon.

"Lord, please protect our city," she finished. "Amen."

CHAPTER 6

Wally's Diner was a classic Sojourn City locale, a street-corner restaurant almost as old as the city itself. Gideon's family had frequented it since he'd been a toddler, and old man Wally, the owner, still ran the old-fashioned ice cream bar built into the back wall, handing out samples to kids and mixing shakes and root beer floats with vigor. As Gideon grew older, he and Jolie had visited countless times after their first date. Walking into the diner was like stepping into the past.

As Gideon opened the door and walked in, nostalgia hit him like a tidal wave. The white-and-black checkered floors were spotless. The red, fifties-style tables and vinyl booths and chairs were crowded with customers. Servers in white, collared shirts and black aprons milled about behind the ice cream bar and between the lobby and the kitchen. It was the same as it had always been. It was as if he could, for a moment, forget about Venezuela, the Brooks, and his mysterious condition. He could just be Gideon Turner, here for another date with Jolie Anderson.

"Gideon!" Old Wally looked up from wiping down the counter and waved. "Ha-ha, long time no see, kid!"

"Hey, Wally." Gideon smiled. "Good to see you."

"I was so glad to hear that you made it home safely." Wally walked out from behind the bar and came over to Gideon. "I prayed for you every night."

"Thank you."

"So, you here for another date, eh?"

"That's right." Gideon smiled. "The usual booth?"

"Right this way." As Wally weaved through the diner, Gideon noticed a slight limp in his step. "You're lucky it's not the lunch rush yet; that booth would be taken!"

"Hey, Wally?" Gideon scooted between two tables. "What happened to your leg?"

"Oh, it's nothing." Wally chuckled. "Some punks broke in here one night during closing and I got knocked down in the ruckus."

Gideon frowned. "I'm sorry."

"It's no biggie. Hasn't happened since."

Was the crime wave really spreading so far into the middle-class part of Sojourn City? Gideon had practically never heard of crime in this part of town. It was almost a utopia. Or it had been . . . when he'd lived here before. *How much has really changed in a year?*

Worse was that it had happened to old Wally. The man was a local legend and practically untouchable. Even the worst local street thugs knew better than to hurt him. Gideon clenched his jaw. *Focus.* He didn't need to be thinking about this while he was supposed to be on a date with Jolie.

Wally stopped beside the booth and Gideon sat down. The old man dropped two menus on the table and, with one last smile, limped back toward the ice cream bar. Gideon looked out the window. Within moments, Jolie's car pulled up—a white, early-2000s Toyota Camry, nothing fancy but at least dependable.

As she often was when off-duty, she was dressed in flannel and denim. She walked in the diner and headed straight for Gideon without looking around. He smirked at that. There had been no question in her mind where he'd be sitting. Apparently, her memories of this place were as fond and as vivid as his.

"Hey, Gid."

"Hey, yourself." Gideon rose and hugged her. "Did you get some rest?"

She nodded. "Yeah, I slept pretty well." She sat down. "And you?"

"Yeah, not bad." Gideon sat, too. "I'm glad we're getting to do this. It's been too long. I know you're busy and I have work, too, but . . . "

"But it feels like we've grown apart even since you've been back."

"Yeah."

"Well, I don't want that anymore." She reached out a hand and put it on top of his. "I love you, Gideon."

"I love you, too."

Wally returned with two glasses of water, and Jolie greeted him. Gideon watched her, reliving how he'd felt when he'd first met her and when they'd first started to date. He studied her features and found her even more beautiful than she had been then.

After they'd put in their order, they discussed old times. Gideon reflected fondly on the times they'd shared before his trip to Venezuela. And as they talked, she seemed less and less a cop and more and more herself.

"I just wish things were different," she said. "Sometimes I just want a boring desk job, you know? Maybe even try my hand at journalism. I know what I'm doing is important, but it takes so much out of me."

"I'm sure. But I know I'm glad for what you're doing, and I bet the people in the Brooks are thankful for it."

"Are they?" She shrugged. "Sometimes it doesn't seem that way."

They paused as Wally approached again, carrying their food. They thanked him, blessed the food, and began eating.

"It'll get better," Gideon said. "I mean, there can only be so many criminals there, right?"

And just like that, she was the cop again. "You'd think so, but no matter how many we put away it seems like more of them trickle in. We think they're coming from out-of-town, but we don't know why."

"You mean they're not local?"

"No. In fact, a lot of them aren't even American."

"Really?"

She nodded. "We're beginning to suspect that the mob leadership might even be foreign. We're not sure exactly what their plan is, but . . . I'm sorry, we shouldn't be talking about this. It's not good date conversation and I could probably get in trouble for talking about it, anyway."

"No, it's fine." Gideon ate a fry. "But I've been meaning to ask you more about this 'Crusader' guy you mentioned. Dean told me he's some kind of legend in the Brooks, going out and stopping criminals by himself, but a lot of people consider him to be just as bad as the criminals he fights."

"Because he is. Criminals still have rights, Gideon. Just because they do bad things doesn't take that away. The Crusader is a vigilante who takes those rights away."

"Does he kill them?"

"No, but he beats them half to death and leaves them for us to find." She shook her head. "I can't deny he gets criminals off the streets, but it doesn't make what he's doing right."

"But if he's saving lives, doesn't it justify it?"

Jolie raised an eyebrow. "Seriously?"

"I don't know, I just . . . I mean, I guess I just respect that there's someone out there who's willing to protect his own city."

"But that's our job. And he's doing it illegally."

"I know, I know." Gideon shrugged. "I'm just saying, if it were my choice, I'd focus on getting all the other criminals rounded up and then when the really bad ones were gone, maybe then go after him. Or who knows? Maybe he'd just go away after they were gone."

"Doubtful. Whether he would admit it or not, I would guess that in some way, the Crusader enjoys what he does. He wouldn't stop. Look, can we talk about something else? This isn't my favorite thing to talk about."

"Sure. I'm sorry."

But even though they talked about a lot of other things, Gideon's mind stayed on the Crusader for the rest of the day.

* * *

On Monday morning, Gideon rolled out of bed and landed flat on the floor on his hands and feet. He began doing pushups before his mind had even awakened fully. He'd gotten into this habit when he first began training in martial arts; it allowed his body to become active as soon as he woke up. That, in turn, cleared his mind of any sleep fog.

. . . 21, 22, 23, 24 . . .

As he counted, his mind began to become alert, and while one part continued to count his pushups, another part began planning out his day. He'd go to the church first, as usual. When he had that settled, he would go down to the labs and, while he worked on one of Dean's projects, he would also surreptitiously run some tests on his own blood. He needed to know what was going on with him.

. . . 97, 98, 99, 100.

He jumped to his feet. His biceps burned with the effort, and it felt great. He walked out onto the landing that overlooked their living room and stood in the center of the circular mat he'd set out in the middle of the floor to practice on. He went through a series of crunches, jumping jacks, leg and arm stretches, rolls, and falls. Once he was certain his body was limber, he began going through his *katas.*

Gideon punched, kicked, and chopped quickly at the air. His fists and feet would "strike" and then immediately return to their ready position. He spun around, attacking imaginary foes and angling his blows. A side kick would've broken an opponent's ankle. The uppercut he swung with his left hand would've shattered teeth.

Without breaking his rhythm, he performed a back-flip midair, twirling around twice before he hit the ground in a crouch. He reached out and grabbed two eskrima sticks from his weapon rack and began swinging them in tight, deadly attacks. The batons whooshed through the air audibly.

When he'd completed all his daily exercises, he replaced the batons and breathed deeply. He fought to keep his breaths steady. He went to the bathroom and prepared a shower. The hot water pouring over his body calmed him and washed away his sweat, and the steam helped him slow his breathing. He dressed in a pair of black jeans, a gray Henley shirt, and a maroon jacket and went downstairs. Their apartment's living room was at the corner of their building, and it had two-story floor-to-ceiling windows on the south and west walls. The kitchen sat directly beneath the second-floor balcony. Gideon settled down with a plate of eggs and bacon. As he ate, he stared out the window at the city. From here, it was a glittering jewel. Someday, the streets would match that image. Gideon rinsed off his plate and headed out.

An hour later, he was parking down the street from the church. There was a line of people out the door of the church's food pantry. Gideon squeezed past them and went into the kitchen. His mother and brother were in the kitchen among the other church staff, handing out a bag of food and a space heater to each person. There was a Christmas tree set up in one corner of the room. Gideon smiled at the sight.

Gideon squeezed past his younger brother's muscular frame and began packing food. "Morning."

"Morning, Gid!" Wes said. "How's life?"

"Life's good. How about you?"

"Oh, you know." Wes shrugged. "Classes are out this week for Thanksgiving break, so that's nice. Doesn't stop the assignments from being due next week, of course."

"Of course." Gideon chuckled. "Hang in there, bro. One semester left. Then onto the big leagues."

"One semester to keep my grades as high as I can. Football scholarships don't impress law schools, you know."

After Gideon had finished an hour of handing out food and supplies, he told his brother and mom goodbye and weaved his way back outside. As he rounded the corner to where his car had been parked, he was surprised to see a familiar figure leaning up against his car, looking at him with a mix of bemusement and fear.

"Wyatt," he greeted.

The dark-skinned man stepped toward Gideon. "I just wanted to say I'm sorry for slamming the door like that the other night."

Gideon raised an eyebrow. "Really? Most people wouldn't apologize for being freaked out by a guy with glowing hands."

"Yeah . . . " Wyatt shrugged. "I've seen a lot of strange things in my life, kid. Who am I to judge?"

"I guess . . . "

"Anyway, I came by to tell you some good news. I was offered a job by one of the deacons of the Lakeside Refuge Church campus. I'll be working security—on the Platform, no less!"

"That's great! Who was it?"

"Don't know; I'd never met him before today. He was white, had dark hair and a beard. Wore a really nice suit, like he had a lot of money. Drove a nice car, too. But if he works on the Platform, he'd have to have money, I guess. He didn't offer his name, though."

Gideon scratched his chin. "Well, I'm happy for you. I wonder if you might come to the service here next week."

"I'll be here." Wyatt extended his hand. "Thanks, kid."

Gideon shook his hand. "You're welcome. And thank you—for not being so scared of me you didn't come back."

"Don't sweat it." Wyatt started to walk away. "But whatever you've got, kid, I'd like to give you some advice: learn how to use it. Something like that's got to be a gift."

Then Wyatt had rounded the corner. It didn't feel like a gift, especially since it had probably been bestowed by some . . . madman. But he was definitely going to figure out what it was, at least.

He climbed in his car. Time to get to work.

* * *

The four-story building sat on three acres of land in the middle of an immaculately-trimmed lawn. The sidewalk leading up to the front door was lined on either side by a long canal that constantly trickled water down to a pool in the middle of a courtyard. The front wall of the building was made up of floor-to-ceiling windows, and the other walls shone white in the morning sun. "Sterling Laboratories" was printed on the east wall in huge, dark gray letters. Below was the company symbol: a blue cross surrounded by an intricate, swirling red circle.

He slid out of the driver's seat and strode onto the sidewalk. The biology lab where Gideon worked was on the third floor and took up half that level. When he passed the waterfall in the center of the courtyard, he smiled at the sight of a little boy tossing a penny into the water and closing his eyes to make a wish. A few employees in white lab coats, the company emblem stitched on their left breast pocket, passed him. Gideon walked into the lobby and took the elevator.

He stepped out into the lab and breathed deeply. It smelled of antiseptic and a variety of chemicals. For most people, the smell wouldn't be pleasant. For Gideon, it screamed normalcy. He looked around. The lab had three white walls, a black floor and ceiling, and a great view of the courtyard. It was occupied by workbenches, half-completed devices, and whiteboards with equations and calculations written over them.

Four technicians and biologists scurried around, working on their own projects. Gideon walked past them to his own workstation. His desk was neat, everything arranged where it should be. He turned on his computer. Dean had him running simulated tests on a vaccine the lab was developing that would, hopefully, shrink and even break up tumors and regenerate normal tissue in their place.

Luckily, running the simulations was an automated process. All Gideon had to do was start the program, let it run, and check it on occasion to see the results. While the simulations ran, he could focus on testing his own blood and DNA. Surreptitiously, he pulled a needle and several glass slides and beakers from his desk.

As Gideon worked, the door to the lab opened again. He glanced up to see who was entering. It was Dean's father, Edgar Sterling, the owner and CEO of the company. He wore a three-piece dark blue suit and he had close-trimmed brown hair and a full beard.

Gideon blinked. Edgar Sterling perfectly matched the description of the "generous donor" that Wyatt had told him about. He was a deacon at Refuge Church's Lakeside campus, too. *No way.*

"Hello, Gideon." Edgar approached him and extended a hand.

"Hello, sir. Good to see you again."

"I'm sorry I haven't been able to pay you a visit since your miraculous return, but I was so glad when I heard you were safe." Edgar leaned forward and grinned conspiratorially. "I always thought you were a good influence on Dean."

Gideon chuckled. "Thank you, sir. And it's an honor to be working with your company."

"Glad to have you, son." He glanced at the needle. "What are you working on?"

"Ah . . . " Gideon blushed. "Something personal. Sorry, sir. The program's still running, so I thought . . . "

"Don't worry, Gideon." Edgar chuckled. "I'm not going to report you. Who would I tell? Me? Just don't let it distract from your work, and I don't care what personal tests you run."

"Thank you."

"Carry on, then!"

Edgar turned and walked to the next biologist's desk. Gideon exhaled and turned back to his desk. He inserted the needle into his arm, took the blood, and began his examination.

* * *

Gideon's accusing words rang in Jolie's ears as she walked through the precinct from the CSI lab back to her desk. As much as she hated to admit it, he was right. The police force in the Brooks, as a whole, was far too corrupt to be an effective deterrent to the ever-growing criminal presence. Certainly not to the career criminals like the mob. And because of that, innocent people like Pastor Jeff were getting hurt, and no one was doing anything about it. The corruption needed to be rooted out—and if IA wasn't going to stop sitting on their hands and do it, then Jolie would do something.

She could count on one hand the cops she knew were not corrupt, other than herself. She had told Gideon she was certain about Paul, Pulaski, and Bates at the church. She also had complete confidence in her immediate superior, Sergeant Andrews, as well as the leader of the twelfth precinct, Captain Cranston.

That wasn't to say that every other cop was corrupt, just that Jolie wasn't certain enough to place her bets one way or another. But the one man she was certain was taking bribes from the mob was Detective Walters. And that meant she had a place to start, albeit an unofficial one. She was a beat cop; she didn't have the authority to investigate Walters. But she could keep an eye on him, report any suspicious activity she saw.

As she dropped into her chair—which was probably ten years old, with torn brown leather padding that was beginning to fade toward tan and stuffing that was coming out more and more by the day—she glanced across the precinct to Walters' desk. The man wore a light blue dress shirt with a multicolored tie held down by a sterling silver tie clip. He was on the phone, the handset of his desk line tucked between his cheek and shoulder as he reclined in his chair—which was much nicer than Jolie's—and used his hands to peel an orange.

"What a guy."

Jolie looked up. Bates stood next to her desk, hands on his hips. The young officer was a welcome presence in the precinct; his constant upbeat attitude was a refresher from the otherwise gloomy setting. He was always ready with a joke to lighten the mood or an encouraging word for anyone who looked downcast.

"You think he makes payments on those shoes?" Bates continued. "Bet they cost more than my mortgage."

Jolie snorted. "On a detective's salary?"

"Yeah, you're right. Probably knockoffs." Bates winked. "See you later, Anderson. Have a good one."

As he walked away, Jolie returned her gaze to Walters, who was deep in conversation now. She studied his shoes. Bates was right; they were expensive shoes. And not knockoffs; the brand name was stamped just above the heel. Bates had to know that as well as she did. Just one more sliver of evidence that Walters might be less clean than he appeared to be.

"Uh-huh," Walters said. "See you soon."

Placing the half-peeled orange on his desk, Walters hung up the phone. Then retrieving his fruit, he rose and made for the door. Jolie looked around. *What am I doing?* Oh . . . screw it. She had to know. Jumping up from her own chair, Jolie weaved across the bullpen and kept an eye on Walters' back. The detective shrugged on his wrinkle-free black trench coat and ducked out the door.

Could she get in trouble for this? Probably. But Gideon's words wouldn't leave her mind. She had to know for sure. If Walters was corrupt, he needed to be taken down so he could be replaced. For Pastor Jeff.

Jolie slid into her Toyota Camry as Walters pulled away in his sleek black Charger. She had to be careful—if Walters was corrupt, and he caught her tailing him, he would likely cut his losses and put a bullet in her head. It would be easy enough to frame it on some local thugs. Or worse, he could say that Jolie was corrupt, and he'd been forced to shoot her to protect himself. It would be her word against his, and with her dead, there would be no counterargument.

If that happened, Gideon would probably track Walters down and shoot him dead. She half-smiled at the thought. Gideon was so sincere in his desire to help. It got him in trouble, and she was afraid it would again, but it was endearing. At the very least, it was better than being completely apathetic to the struggles of those poorer than him.

Jolie followed Walters until he drove out of the Brooks. He entered a suburban neighborhood and parked on a curb next to a small, idyllic house Jolie kept driving, keeping her head turned away from him as she passed. The road he'd stopped on was a gradual slope; if she parked up the hill from him, she could see down on whatever he was doing. She drove half a block and parked her car. Climbing out, she found a vantage point in a shop entrance where she wouldn't be visible to Walters.

The detective stood on the sidewalk outside the house rubbing his gloved hands together to ward off the cold. Jolie shivered, Walters' motion somehow reminding her of the chill in her own body. She crossed her arms and pressed them close to her body. With any luck, she'd only be here for a few minutes.

Walters strode up to the front door and knocked on it. Moments later, he was joined by a young woman—blonde-haired, lithe, and athletic but not skinny. She wore a tan leather coat and bright red gloves. Jolie inched as close as she could, but they were still too far for her to pick up on their conversation. But if she could identify the woman, that would be a start. Crouching, Jolie stepped out onto the sidewalk and crept closer to them, finally ducking behind a gray car.

When she came up again, she got a good look at the woman's face. She didn't recognize her. Was Walters paying a visit to a family member, or was there something more sinister behind all this? From here, she had no way to tell. Biting her lip in frustration, Jolie ducked back down behind the gray car and waited.

Moments passed, and finally, the indistinct murmur of conversation ended, replaced by the soft sound of a closing door. Jolie peered over the trunk of the car again. Walters stood alone next to his car. Whatever he and the woman had been talking about, they'd clearly finished. Jolie returned to her car as Walters pulled away.

She continued following him, in case the woman had given him a package to deliver or he had a second meeting. Finally, Walters parked again, this time outside a bodega. Jolie parked, too, but stayed in her car. Walters could've been going inside to shake down the owners for money, or to deliver a package . . . or, he may have just wanted to stop for a snack. Going in after him would surely get her discovered. She leaned back in her seat and waited.

Moments later, Walters exited the bodega, a plastic bag in one hand. With his other, he grabbed the handle of his car door—

A black-clad figure dropped onto the hood of the Charger. Walters reeled back, stumbling, and reached for his sidearm. Jolie placed her hand on the butt of her own gun. The figure wore a black leather jacket with a hood, which was raised to cover a head completely concealed by a black ski mask. The figure appeared unarmed, but Jolie knew that didn't make him any less dangerous. She would've recognized the description anywhere.

The Crusader.

The vigilante dropped from the hood of the car to the sidewalk. Walters got a grip on his gun, and the Crusader stepped forward and kicked out with a foot clad in a heavy black combat boot. Walters' hand recoiled, and his gun clattered to the sidewalk. The detective backed away from the vigilante, scrambled to his feet, and rushed down the alley behind him. The Crusader took off in pursuit.

Corrupt or not, Walters was a cop. The Crusader was a criminal, and Jolie wasn't going to let him hurt Walters. Especially infuriating was the fact that this attack would end her chances of continuing to investigate Walters; if she showed herself now to help him, he'd know she'd been following him. But she couldn't stand by and do nothing. Growling deep in her throat, Jolie jumped up and rushed into the alley after them.

Walters lay with his back against one of the alley walls, his formerly perfect pants soaked and resting in a muddy puddle. There was no sign of the Crusader. Jolie swept her gun across the alley, scanning for him. He had vanished. She lowered her gun and crossed over to Walters. He had a bright new shiner under his right eye, but he was alive. He looked up at Jolie in confusion as she approached.

"Anderson?" he asked. "What are you doing here?"

"I was in the neighborhood." Jolie knelt and helped Walters stand. "Saw the Crusader drop down and attack, so I came to help. Didn't even realize it was you he was after. Are you okay, Detective?"

"Yeah, uh . . . fine." Walters rubbed his head. "Thanks."

"Why did he come after you, Detective? Doesn't the Crusader normally go after the bad guys?"

"Who knows?" Walters half-smiled and lifted his shoulders in a shrug. "You'd have to ask him."

Mm-hmm. Jolie followed Walters out of the alley. Walters acted as though he'd bought her excuse, but she doubted it. The man was smart, and he had to suspect that she'd been watching him. He'd be keeping an eye on her now, which made her job more difficult. But if she couldn't investigate Walters directly, there were other avenues she could take. And she would—she wasn't going to rest until the truth came out.

* * *

Gideon didn't know what to think of the results. He had taken scans of everything he'd tested and emailed them to himself so he could look at them more in-depth once he got home. Now, sitting on the second-floor balcony with his laptop, he puzzled over the scans.

His blood test seemed normal. At least, at first glance. But when he enhanced it, zooming in to examine the smallest details, he could see that there was a faint glow to every cell. He'd never seen anything like this, let alone think of anything that could cause it.

Gideon put his laptop down on the floor beside him and stood. Dean wasn't home yet; maybe Gideon should do some more tests. Not lab tests, but actual, practical tests. He walked to the middle of his exercise mat, took several deep breaths, and held his arms out. They didn't seem to be glowing . . .

"How does this work?" he muttered.

He took another deep breath, held it, and focused. He imagined his hands getting brighter, shining like a flashlight. To his surprise, slowly, they began to light up. Not very brightly, but with a faint luminescence equivalent to a glowstick that had just been cracked. *Okay, so I can do this at will.* He took another breath and imagined himself pushing the light outward. His hands began to shine more and more brightly.

"Whoa." He imagined them fading, returning to normal. And slowly, they did. "Okay, that's . . . kinda cool."

Maybe it wasn't so bad, after all. He wondered if any other parts of his body glowed, or if it was just his hands. He closed his eyes and imagined his arms, shoulders to hands, glowing. He opened his eyes to find both arms shimmering. With a thought, the light faded away.

Wyatt might have been right. Maybe this could be a gift, after all.

CHAPTER 7

Last year

Gideon groaned and rubbed his head. It felt like a watermelon that had burst when it hit the ground. The moment he'd been hit, and the few seconds after it, was the last thing he remembered. He knew they'd dragged him out of the clinic, but he had no idea where he was now. He opened his eyes slowly and grimaced as sunlight pierced his pupils.

"Ow."

"Don't try to sit up," someone said.

Gideon turned his head. From what he could tell, he was lying on the ground—dirt and leaves were everywhere—inside some cage. Another man sat in one corner of the cage. He was a light-skinned man, bald, with a thick gray beard. He wore a jungle explorer's garb. When Gideon made eye contact with him, the man grinned, and it was the friendliest smile Gideon thought he had ever seen.

"Hi there."

"Hello," Gideon said.

The man rose to his haunches and came over to Gideon's side. "You took quite the hit, looks like."

"I did. Where are we?"

"In a cage." The man chuckled.

"I can see that."

"Of course. We're in a guerrilla camp. I'm not sure where, honestly, but I have a feeling it's pretty remote."

"Why's that?"

"Because I have been here for almost a year, and I haven't heard any sounds of civilization other than the guerrillas' own vehicles." The man returned to his corner, sat down, and shrugged. "May as well get comfortable. You'll be here awhile."

Now

The owner of the home that Detective Walters had visited was listed as Regina Langston. Jolie had never heard the name before and couldn't connect it to any known crime bosses. Maybe Walters' visit to the woman's house had nothing to do with his corruption, but Jolie wasn't willing to place bets on that. She needed to find out what Walters was doing, and that meant going to the source.

"What are we doing here?" Paul asked. "We didn't get a call."

Jolie pulled their cruiser up to the curb outside Langston's house. She was taking a risk, involving Paul in her behind the scenes investigation, but approaching Langston off the clock would be even more suspicious than doing so while in uniform. Right now, it would be easier for her to look into Langston than Walters; the detective would be keeping an eye on her now, and there was too great a risk that he'd catch her sniffing around. He was going to great lengths to keep something a secret, so he'd likely take action if he found out that Jolie knew.

"A . . . friend asked me to check into something," Jolie said. "It's all for legit purposes, I promise."

"I trust you, kid." Paul smirked. "I wouldn't have been your partner this long if I didn't. But you should tell me the truth. This isn't a favor for a friend, is it? It's a gut instinct thing. I know 'em when I see 'em."

Jolie nodded. "Yeah. Yeah, it is."

She put the car in park and opened the door. Glancing at Paul to confirm he would stay in the cruiser, she got out and shut the door behind her. A sidewalk sliced Langston's immaculate lawn cleanly in half, leading straight up to a small, square porch. *Stay casual.* Jolie strode up the sidewalk toward the front door. If she appeared on edge, it would put Regina on edge, too.

She stepped onto the porch and knocked on the door. The faint rustle of shuffling feet sounded from behind the door. A few seconds later, the door opened just enough for Jolie to glimpse Regina Langston's face.

"Can I help you . . . Officer?"

"Miss Langston?" Jolie cleared her throat. "I'm Officer Jolie Anderson of the twelfth precinct in the Brooks. Do you have a minute?"

"Um, sure." Regina frowned. "What's this about, Officer?"

"I need some information on a man you may know—Simon Walters."

"Of course! Could you give me a moment? I just need to get dressed, and then I'll be right out."

"All right."

The door closed. Jolie suspected that "get dressed" was an excuse, one to buy Langston some time, but Jolie couldn't push because she didn't have a warrant. She'd have to wait for the woman to cooperate. She glanced at her watch, back at Paul, and then at the door. Moments passed, with no sign that Langston was returning. Jolie leaned in close and pressed her ear to the door, listening for sounds of movement. There were none. She knocked.

"Ma'am?" she called. "Miss Langston, may I come in?"

There was no response. Jolie furrowed her brow and put her hand on the doorknob. She could get in a lot of trouble for this, she knew. Peering inside cautiously, holding her hand near her taser, Jolie pushed the door open. The living room was empty. She searched every room and couldn't find a single person. She went back to the living room. Through the kitchen, sunlight shone from a back door that hung wide open.

She walked out into the back yard. There were vague impressions of footprints in the grass, but they ended at the fence. She frowned. So, Langston had something to hide. Whatever her business with Walters was, it wasn't on the up-and-up. Jolie went back through the house into the front yard, closing the door behind her, and returned to the cruiser.

"The resident fled."

Paul frowned. "You got any idea why?"

"No clue. Something strange is going on here. I'm going to get to the bottom of it."

* * *

After a week of practicing, Gideon was almost confident enough in his abilities that he didn't consider them a problem anymore. He hadn't had any incidents of his hands lighting up without his consent. He still couldn't get them to light up as brightly as they had in Venezuela, though, and he'd also learned that if he tried to keep them lit for too long, it wore him out. And he still had no idea what their source was.

On Sunday night, Gideon and Dean attended church in the remaining Brooks campus so they could help with a special Thanksgiving dinner that was open to the public. As Gideon shoveled mashed pota-toes and gravy onto a teenage boy's plate, he glanced up at the doorway. A familiar figure entered. Gideon smiled. Wyatt.

The man and his family—a wife, two boys, and a girl—got in line with others who had flocked the church for a warm meal. As Wyatt passed, Gideon acknowledged him with a nod. The man nodded in return and led his family to an open table.

"Hey, Wes," Gideon said. "Take over for me for a minute."

"Sure thing."

Gideon stepped aside to let his brother take his place. He walked out into the dining area and weaved his way toward Wyatt's table. As he approached, the older man looked up from his meal, smiled, and rose.

"Hello again."

"Hello, Wyatt." Gideon shook his hand. "I'm glad you came."

"So am I." Wyatt gestured to his family. "My wife, Joanna. My sons, Carter and Ellis, and my daughter, Rhonda."

"Hello," Gideon said. "It's nice to meet you all."

"Thank you for putting this on," Joanna said. "It means so much to so many people."

"Glad we could help." Gideon glanced back at Wyatt. "So, that job you got. It wouldn't happen to be at Sterling Enterprises, would it?"

Wyatt blinked. "As a matter of fact, yes, it would. How did you know?"

"I work at Sterling Labs. I didn't realize it later, but the man you described is my boss, Edgar Sterling. I'm actually roommates with his son, Dean."

"Small world." Wyatt chuckled. "Yes, I work security at Sterling Enterprises."

"Well, I'm happy for you." Gideon looked back to his family. "And again, good to have you all here. Enjoy your dinner and feel free to come back for seconds."

Hours later, as Gideon and Dean walked out of church, Gideon took in a deep breath of the cool night air. It felt good to be helping people. The joy he'd seen on their faces as they'd eaten had filled a void he hadn't known was there. *Crack-crack-crack.* Gideon's head snapped up. Those were gunshots! Several church members cried out, and a few took cover.

Dean sighed. "What a mess."

"Someone's got to fix it," Gideon muttered.

"Someone is. Your buddy, the Crusader, remember? And of course, your girlfriend, the cop."

Gideon wasn't so sure. Where was the Crusader now? Even if he was out there, fighting for good, he was only one man. He couldn't possibly take down every single person who went out with malicious intent. Sojourn was a huge city, and the Brooks by themselves were massive.

He patted Dean on the shoulder. "Yeah, guess so."

The rest of the members broke up quickly and drove off. Dean and Gideon remained standing on the steps of the church. Gideon locked the front door.

"We shouldn't have to leave church the second we get done because we're afraid to get shot, Dean."

"I know, buddy. It'll turn around; sooner or later there'll be more bad guys in jail than on the streets. And then maybe there'll be some peace around here."

"Yeah, maybe. Or maybe this city needs more than one Crusader."

Dean laughed uproariously. "What? And you're going to do it? Gideon Turner, the doctor, the scientist, the vigilante!"

"Not me," Gideon replied. *I could, though, easily.* "No, I'm not the crime-fighter. I may be a fighter but at heart, that's not me. The Crusader's the vigilante; Jolie's the cop. And me, I'm the doctor."

"And I'm the looker."

I'm the doctor. Maybe that's what Gideon was missing. Being a doctor, he'd helped people all the time. As a scientist, he didn't feel the same. Even if the formulas and serums he worked on would eventually help people, he didn't get to witness it. Maybe that's why tonight had felt so good; he was seeing the results of doing good.

Could fighting crime provide that same feeling? He doubted it. Besides, he'd sworn to never kill again. Even if he could do vigilante work without killing, he'd be risking it every time he got into a fight. Did he really want that?

Dean patted Gideon on the shoulder. "I'm sure that tonight the Crusader's wishing he had some of your sick moves on his side."

"Maybe," Gideon grinned. "Have a good night, Dean. I'll see you back home."

"See you later, bro!"

Gideon drove away from the church, chased by the sounds of those gunshots and the words his friends had spoken: *Gideon Turner, the doctor, the scientist, the vigilante.*

He turned his car in the direction the gunfire had come from.

* * *

"You want to die?" one thug shouted. "No? Then hand over the money!"

The man he'd accosted trembled and took another step back into the alley. He bumped up against a dumpster. The thug fired his pistol up into the air. Those first three shots must've been warning shots, too. The shooter seemed content to scare his victim, for now.

Gideon watched from across the street. It took everything in him to not run in and help. But he was unarmed, and he'd never get close enough to take on the guy with the gun. Still, he couldn't just let them hurt the guy . . . he had to do something.

The man started to pull off his watch and remove his wallet from his pocket. The two thugs backing the one with the gun stepped forward to take them. The man trembled and tossed his valuables to the ground. One thug, who carried a crowbar, knelt to pick them up.

The gunman lowered his weapon, but before their victim could run away, someone dropped from the rooftop above onto the lid of the dumpster. The thugs looked up and raised their weapons. Gideon's eyes widened. *The Crusader*! He stepped away from his car and crept closer to the alleyway.

"Run!" the Crusader shouted.

The thugs' victim sprinted out of the alley in terror and nearly plowed over Gideon. Gideon moved aside and peered into the alley. The two backup thugs moved in, brandishing their weapons, while the leader pointed his gun at the Crusader.

"You've bought judgment on this city with your wicked ways," the Crusader said. His voice was a threatening baritone.

"Oh, is that so? What? You're God's judgment on crime? You know vigilantism is illegal, too, right, man?"

The Crusader ignored him. "Drop your weapons now!"

"No way. Unless I'm mistaken, I'm the one with the gun. Imagine the street cred my crew and I will get for being the guys who took down the Crusader."

"Better than you have tried. They've all failed."

The Crusader didn't seem in the least intimidated by the gun, but the thug definitely seemed scared of him. He used his other hand to steady the gun and trained it on the Crusader's chest. Gideon was impressed by the vigilante's steadiness. From here, he could see that the Crusader wore all black—jeans, boots, shirt, and a hooded leather jacket. He also had a mask under his hood that had some sort of design on it.

"All it takes is one lucky shot!" The thug fired.

By the time he'd pulled the trigger, the Crusader had already moved; he front-flipped off the dumpster and the bullet cracked harmlessly into the alley wall. Gideon cringed and pulled farther out of the alley. This would be a stupid way for him to die.

The Crusader landed in a crouch beside the crowbar-wielding thug and kicked out sideways, catching him in the knee. The man howled in pain and swung his crowbar at the Crusader's head. He missed, but by then the third thug had moved in, stabbing a switchblade at the Crusader's back. The Crusader, still crouched, reached back, grabbed his wrist with both hands, and hurled him over his head. Switchblade crashed into Crowbar and the two went down in a tangle of limbs.

Wow. Gideon detected hints of aikido and karate in the man's technique. He was good, whoever he was.

The gunman was now the last man standing, and he fired three more shots, but the Crusader had already ducked back behind the dumpster.

"You're stuck, Crusader!" the gunman shouted.

"You should surrender now. It would be less painful for you."

The gunman fired again. As soon as the bullet hit the dumpster, the Crusader picked up a length of pipe and hurled it. The pipe struck the gunman's hand. The thug dropped his gun and cursed. The Crusader rushed in and decked the guy.

Police sirens sounded in the distance. Gideon turned and rushed back to his car. He didn't need to be here when the cops arrived. Jolie would kill him, for one thing.

He pulled away from the alley and wondered if maybe he could do some good. The Crusader hadn't killed any of those guys. What if Gideon could do the same? And if he could use his light powers to his advantage . . .

Well, maybe *the doctor, the scientist, the vigilante* made sense, after all.

* * *

It was 6:00 a.m. and the sun had not yet risen. As Jolie and Paul patrolled the streets, Jolie kept thinking about Regina. She couldn't get her mind off the mystery. Who was she? A mistress of Walters'? But that was no reason for her to flee her home. But her name didn't come up in connection to any crimes. Things just didn't add up.

They took their usual route, Paul driving and Jolie scanning the streets and alleys for any sign of trouble. This morning, they'd already had to deal with several muggings. That wasn't at all unusual. Last week, they'd had a rape, an assault, and a B&E all within two hours. It was mind-boggling.

The radio squawked. "All units in the vicinity of Junction Park, please respond," the dispatcher said.

"We're close." Jolie picked up the radio. "This is Officer Anderson, responding. What's the situation?"

"ADW," the dispatcher replied. "Officers on the scene need assistance, Code 3."

"Roger that," Jolie said. She put the radio down. "Code 3, Paul. Go!"

Paul switched the lights and sirens on and gunned the engines. Jolie shook her head desperately. Junction Park was another neighborhood that was near the Brooks but had always been a nice, clean area. For its streets to dissolve into a gang war . . . how had it happened? Hundreds of people would be in danger.

When they got to Junction Park, they found three other cruisers already there, the officers out of their vehicles and pulling on bulletproof vests.

Jolie hopped out as soon as the car had stopped and pulled a vest of her own from the trunk. Officer Pulaski ran up to her and Paul, who was also putting on his vest. Jolie checked her sidearm as he approached.

"What's the situation?" Jolie asked.

"We've got a massive gang shootout," Pulaski said. "The Tyrants and the Red Dogs are having it out down there, and there are civilians caught in the crossfire."

Jolie groaned. This was bad. The Tyrants and the Red Dogs were two of the biggest gangs in the city. Every officer on the force dreaded the moment the gangs' leaders finally came to blows. It looked like that day had come. Paul pulled a shotgun from the back of the car.

"Let's go," he said.

"We're hitting them fast and hard," Pulaski told them. "SWAT's on the way but we need to act now, or innocent people are going to die. Sergeant Andrews is here, and he wants tear gas, riot batons, tasers—everything. But lethal force has been authorized if they won't stand down."

Paul's jaw tightened visibly, even under the dim light provided by the lampposts. Gunfire cracked in the distance. Things weren't going to quiet down anytime soon. Farther away, Jolie could hear more sirens—SWAT, she hoped.

As they approached the police checkpoint, Jolie, Paul, and Pulaski raised their firearms and ducked. They dashed toward the command post Sergeant Andrews had set up. The rest of the officers were already there, arming up with shotguns, pistols, and even a few submachine guns. Even with all the chaos in the past months, Jolie had never seen anything like this.

"We can't wait any longer," Andrews was saying. "We go in now. Stay with your partner and make all the noise you can. Scare them, intimidate them. Make them want to surrender rather than fight. If they don't lay their weapons down, don't hesitate to take them out. We have injured in the park, and we need to get them out fast."

Paul grabbed Jolie's arm. "We've got this. You stick with me and do what I do."

Jolie nodded, fueled by fear. Adrenaline pumped through her veins, as if she'd had one too many espressos and couldn't get herself under control. She tried to put on a brave face, but how could she be prepared for something like this? Minutes ago, her biggest problem had been a mysterious woman who had lied to her. Now, she was going into the midst of a gang war. It was insane.

God, please protect me and all my fellow officers tonight.

She took some tear gas grenades from an officer, clipped them to her belt, put on a gas mask, and nodded to Paul. They ran forward together, with Pulaski and his partner, Bates, right behind them.

As soon as they rounded the street corner, they emerged into the warzone. Guns flashed as the criminals fired automatics and semi-automatics back and forth. An officer lay behind some bushes and cradled a gunshot wound on his thigh. The gangs seemed to be ignoring him for now. A young couple, apparently out for an early morning stroll, hid in a back yard.

"Everybody down!" Sergeant Andrews shouted into a bullhorn. "Drop your weapons now, do it now!"

Jolie and the other officers started shouting for gang members to lay down their weapons and surrender. As soon as the first gang banger turned his gun on the police, officers began throwing tear gas grenades. Jolie was thankful for her mask as the criminals instantly began coughing and wiping their eyes. Most of them, however, did not lower their weapons.

Paul shoved Jolie to the ground as a guy with an AR-15 fired wildly. Two men with AK-47s opened up on the officers, too.

"Guess that's their response," Paul muttered.

He stood and fired his shotgun, taking out the guy with the AR-15. Officers opened fire or beat down the thugs with nightsticks. Those criminals who had dropped their weapons when the tear gas was dispersed began crawling for them now, ready to rejoin the fight since the officers had taken their eyes off them in the chaos.

Jolie fired her sidearm at a guy who was waving around two Uzis. The shot struck him square in the chest. He dropped instantly. Then a huge man wearing a leather vest stepped forward and trained a shotgun on Jolie. She swiveled to face him. If he got off even a single shot, that shotgun's blast would tear into her vest.

Suddenly, a black-clad figure appeared from between two houses, dived, and drop-kicked the big guy. He dropped his shotgun and stumbled back. The black-clad figure hopped back to his feet and took up a fighting stance. The big guy pulled out a knife.

It's the Crusader!

Jolie turned her attention elsewhere and shot a gang member who was swinging a long pipe at another man's head. The guy with the pipe dropped, and the man he'd been attacking picked up the weapon and charged. Paul took him out with a sweeping nightstick blow to the head. The criminal hit the ground hard.

Jolie looked back to the Crusader. He grappled onto the big guy's shoulders, kicked his knife from his hand, and pulled him to the ground. He took him in a chokehold and waited until he was unconscious before releasing him. Then he leapt at his next opponent, fists swinging like hammers.

Somewhere amidst the endless chaos, SWAT arrived, and after that it was over. Jolie holstered her gun and tried to still her trembling hands. She'd never killed anyone before. Tonight, she'd dropped multiple bodies.

The Crusader stood in the middle of the street, surrounded by a mass of unconscious gangsters. He stared down at them, as if deep in thought. Jolie wondered what he was doing. She started to take a step toward him, then stopped. What would she even do? Thank him, or slap him in handcuffs with the rest of them?

"It's the vigilante." Sergeant Andrews sounded awed.

"He assaulted me!" Walters snapped. "Anderson saw it. Arrest him!"

The Crusader looked up in surprise and dashed off. A few officers half-heartedly tried to pursue him, but he disappeared quickly. Andrews sighed heavily, and Jolie wondered if he'd thought bringing the vigilante in would've put him on the fast track to promotion.

Jolie couldn't find it in her to be disappointed that he'd escaped. He may have assaulted Walters and thus impeded her investigation, and she still didn't approve of vigilantism, but tonight, he'd saved her life. They could catch him some other time. He'd earned his freedom for now.

"Round them up," Andrews said. "We've got a lot of paperwork to do and a lot of bad guys to book."

Great. She looked at the sky. The sun was beginning to peek over the horizon. Somehow, the hints of orange in the sky made things a little better.

A new day, a new beginning. Maybe this one will be different.

CHAPTER 8

Gideon strode down the street toward the church, taking in the cool morning air with a smile. It was actually freezing; last week, the temperatures had dropped below thirty-two for the first time that season. He had learned that if he concentrated, he could flood his body with light—not enough to be visible, but enough to warm him. He couldn't do it for long periods of time, but the time it took for him to walk from his car to the church was now pleasantly cool instead of teeth-chattering cold.

"They went that way!" someone shouted.

"Call the police!"

More shouts punctuated the otherwise-silent neighborhood. Gideon frowned and picked up his pace. He rushed into the church's back lot. A huge crowd of people filled the lot, many of them shouting and scrambling about. The fellowship hall's windows had been busted out, graffiti covered the walls, and trash had been strewn all through the parking lot. Gideon's jaw clenched, and he sprinted toward the building.

Gideon paid the people around him no attention. They seemed to be okay, albeit confused. He needed to find out for himself what was going on.

He barged through the back door into the food pantry. The white walls had been tagged with blood red letters.

WE'RE BACK.

Gideon clenched his fists and fought to keep light energy from escaping them. Several people were leaning up against the walls, their faces scraped and bruised. Splotches of dark red spotted the gray carpet. Gideon was familiar enough with blood to know it when he saw it.

Over by the kitchen, a group of people huddled around one body. Gideon ran in that direction, his heart rate accelerating and blood pounding in his ears.

"Move aside!" he shouted.

Several people did. The body lying on the floor was Wes. *Tell me he's not dead.* Gideon dropped to his knees next to his brother, tears welling in his eyes and rage threatening to burst his heart through his ribs. Wes's chest moved a little. Gideon let out a shaky breath and leaned in close to his brother.

"Gid . . . " Wes said.

"We're going to get you help. Stay still."

Wes had a swollen eye and a busted lip, and there was a bloodstain on the right shoulder of his white hoodie. Gideon pulled the garment aside and found a shallow knife cut in Wes' shoulder. He grabbed a kitchen towel from the floor, balled it up, and pressed it against the cut.

He spent the next few minutes running through procedures he'd memorized as a doctor. He checked Wes' pulse, and once he was sure his brother was stable, went around the room to check on everyone else. When he was satisfied that the church's occupants were unharmed, he looked around for his mother. She stood a few feet away, her hand covering her mouth.

"Mom."

"Oh, Gideon . . . "

He hugged her. "It's okay. Everyone's alive, it looks like. EMTs and cops should be here soon, and you need to tell them everything you can. But Mom, I need to know. Who did this?"

"They . . . they all wore masks. Red ski masks. And they wore black leather jackets over white shirts, and . . . and they had ties on. It was so odd."

"That doesn't sound like any of the local gangs."

"No . . . I don't think so. One of them spoke and he had a strong accent of some kind. Foreign."

Jolie had been right, back at Wally's. These criminals, probably the mob, were from out of town. He wondered what they wanted in Sojourn City.

"Okay. Stay here, Mom." He brought her to Wes' side. "Keep pressure on the towel. The blood flow needs to be kept contained."

Mom pressed down on the reddening towel. "Where are you going? What are you going to do?"

"I'm going to help."

* * *

They hurt my brother.

That singular thought echoed through Gideon's mind, driving his feet as he ran from the church. They had nearly killed Pastor Jeff, and now they had injured Wes. They weren't getting away again. He returned to his car at a sprint and popped the trunk. Inside was the hodgepodge outfit he'd put together as he had begun to consider fighting crime like the Crusader. It was a pair of black jeans and boots, a gray shirt, a navy jacket, padded gloves, and a black ski mask. He had also brought along a pair of truncheons and a pocketknife.

He grabbed the outfit from the trunk and went to a nearby alley. As soon as he had changed, he pulled the mask over his face and ran back into the street. Police cars and ambulances had already pulled into the parking lot outside the church. He went around to the other side of the building; no one would be there right now. He slipped into the side door and crept down the hallway to the offices.

The church's security cameras could be accessed from the pastor's office. Gideon took out the pocketknife and used it to jimmy the door open. The lights were off. He flicked them on and snuck over to the computer. All Refuge Church pastors used the same password for the sake of accountability. Gideon entered it and logged into the security system. He rewound the feed until he found the footage of the attack.

Don't have much time. Cops will want to check this soon, too.

He found his mother's description accurate. The men—four of them—had come in, fired guns in the air, and shoved people against the walls. A few tried to resist, and the masked men had beaten them to submission. One had taken out a can of spray paint, while the others began taking people's valuables. Wes grabbed a kitchen knife and lunged at the nearest assailant; the thug punched him in the face twice, jerked the knife away, and rammed it into Wes' shoulder. It looked like he was about to finish him off, but the leader grabbed his shoulder and shook his head.

When they ran out the door, Gideon switched the feed to the outside cameras. The men piled into a black van and drove away. Gideon zoomed in the best he could to check the van's make and model. Once he had it, he closed out the program, turned off the computer, and snuck back out the door, locking it behind him.

Time to find these guys. He wondered if he'd get them before the Crusader did.

* * *

The black van hadn't been special in any way—no different from any other of its make and model—but Gideon drove through the streets searching for it because it was his only lead. He hadn't been able to make out its license plate on the feed, but he'd be able to recognize it anyway . . . probably. As he drove, he considered that he might need a new, less recognizable vehicle if he was going to keep doing this. He didn't need to get arrested by the cops because they knew the vigilante drove a navy-blue Mustang.

It took him an hour to spot the van. It was parked in an alley behind a rundown apartment building. Gideon drove down the street two blocks and parked his car. Sticking to alleys as much as he could, he made his way toward the apartment. He kept his eskrima sticks tucked away under his jacket, ready to pull them out and use them at a moment's notice. He wasn't confident enough in his powers yet to use them in a fight, but at least he was a skilled enough martial artist to take these guys. If the Crusader could do it, he could too.

The building was old, made of brick, with no exterior access to the individual apartments. It looked abandoned. If the attackers were in there, they'd likely be alone. That was good. Gideon found a back door and tried the handle. It was unlocked. He went inside and pulled out his fighting sticks. Then he made his way down the hallway, checking the floor room by room. The few lights that were still working flickered, giving the hall an eerie ambiance.

He reached the stairwell without encountering anybody. He went up the stairs, stepping as softly as he could, peering up to check for any watchers on the upper floors. He still didn't see any sign of occupants.

As he reached the threshold of the second floor, he heard voices. They weren't being quiet, either. Why should they be? They thought they were alone. Gideon smirked under his mask. That would be their mistake. He crept down the hall and stepped into the room the voices were emanating from.

They didn't notice him at first. Three were gathered around a table in the middle of a studio apartment. The fourth was off to the right in a kitchen area, apparently making himself some lunch. The walls were brick and bare; the floor, concrete. The room was lit only by a dim hanging lamp above the table and a row of fluorescent lights in the kitchen.

The thugs spoke rapidly in some foreign language.

"Who are you?" Gideon growled.

The three men at the table jumped to their feet. The man in the kitchen reached for the gun tucked into his belt. Gideon hurled one of his truncheons. It smacked into the man's hand and he shouted and dropped the gun.

"I said, who are you?"

"Kill him!" one of the men at the table said.

The two men next to him rushed Gideon first. Gideon charged in and ducked under a punch, swinging his baton inside the man's guard and slamming it hard into his solar plexus. His assailant wheezed and staggered back. Gideon spun around and kicked high, catching the second man's chin. By then, the man in the kitchen was on him. He grabbed Gideon and tackled him. Gideon wheezed as his back hit the concrete floor.

Gideon grabbed the man's face and tried to shove him off, but he was significantly bigger than Gideon. He pressed Gideon down and got his hands around his throat. Gideon brought his right knee up hard into his attacker's groin. The man groaned and loosened his grip. Gideon bucked his waist and angled himself to roll out from under the attacker.

Now the first attacker was back up, holding his chest—his ribs had to be cracked—and brandishing a knife. The second attacker climbed to his feet and picked up a chair.

The window shattered. A black-clad figure rolled into the room.

"It's the Crusader!" the fourth man, who seemed to be the leader, said. "Get him!"

The attacker with the knife rushed the Crusader, while the one with the chair came at Gideon. Gideon spun out of the way of the brutish, wooden weapon with ease. He smacked the butt of his baton in between the man's shoulder blades and then kicked him in the small of his back. He stumbled and fell on top of the chair, shattering it.

Now the fourth man, the leader, rushed Gideon. In his peripheral vision, Gideon saw the man who'd pinned him get up and join his knife-wielding buddy in attacking the Crusader.

Gideon blocked a punch from the leader, but this guy was fierce. With his other hand, he grabbed the end of Gideon's baton and jerked forward. Off-balance, Gideon stumbled toward the man. He brought his head forward into Gideon's face. Blood filled the inside of Gideon's ski mask. He bit his lip and pulled away from the attacker.

The leader reached into his jacket and pulled out a pair of knives. He charged at Gideon again, spinning the knives in carefully-crafted arcs. Gideon held up his truncheon to block the blades. As he did, he angled himself so that he was backing toward the kitchen. He needed to get his other baton back.

A gun crackled across the room. Gideon hoped it wasn't the Crusader who'd been shot. But right now, he had to focus on the guy in front of him. The moment's distraction allowed the man to score a shallow cut across Gideon's left forearm. Gideon tried to suck in a breath, but the blood inside his mask was sticking around his nose, making it difficult. He grabbed the edge of the mask and jerked it up, so it was only covering the top half of his head. He snorted as hard as he could to free the blood, still trying to focus on blocking the knives.

"This city doesn't need two vigilantes!" The leader brandished his blades. "After today, it will have none!"

Gideon turned his body to the side as the leader changed his attack pattern, stabbing with his right-hand knife. Gideon took the opportunity to bring his baton down hard on the inside of the man's elbow. The foreigner cried out and dropped the knife in that hand. Gideon quickly reached down and scooped up his other baton.

"We'll see about that," he said.

Now he had the leader on the retreat. He spun through a series of intricate attack patterns, striking the man across the body and on the shoulders and arms. Occasionally, the man was able to use his remaining knife to block a strike, but he was weakening. Gideon finished him with a roundhouse kick that struck him full in the chest and knocked him back into the table. He crashed down on top of it, destroying it, and lay still on the floor.

The room was quiet. Gideon looked at the window. The Crusader stood over the crumpled forms of the other two men. He kicked a gun away from them and looked up at Gideon.

"Who are you?" he asked.

"I'm just someone who's trying to help."

"I don't need help. I—ah!" The Crusader stumbled.

"What's wrong?"

Gideon moved in closer. The Crusader brought a hand up to his side and touched it. Blood glistening on his fingers.

"You were shot," he said.

"Guess so." The Crusader huffed. "Maybe I do need help."

"I'm a doctor," Gideon said. "Come with me."

Sirens sounded from outside the building. The Crusader limped over to Gideon and leaned on his shoulder. Gideon helped him out and down the stairs, back through the alley where he'd come in. The two of them walked toward the street. Gideon peered around the corner to see if the cops were nearby. Their cars were still parked outside, but there didn't seem to be any officers there. They must have gone inside already.

"This way."

He led the Crusader to his car. It was a slow, agonizing walk. Gideon's face and arm were screaming at him, and he was still struggling to breathe through his nose. The blood had clotted and nearly blocked his nostrils. The Crusader pace slowed with every step.

"You shouldn't . . . be out here," the Crusader said. "This job . . . it's dangerous."

"Says the man with a bullet hole in his side." Gideon walked around the corner to his car and pulled the passenger door open. Carefully, he helped the Crusader inside. "I know what I'm doing as much as you do, I'd bet."

He shut the door and went around to the driver's side. He couldn't take the Crusader to a hospital. Dean was probably at work, meaning the apartment was empty, and they had a first aid kit there, plus some of Gideon's old medical tools. He'd be able to mend the Crusader's injury there.

As he drove, Gideon wondered if he should remove his mask completely. The Crusader had already seen his car and would soon see where he lived, anyway. His secret identity wouldn't be very secret at that point. *I really need a secret hideout.* He had nothing to lose; he jerked the ski mask off and threw it in the back seat.

"It's . . . you . . ." the Crusader said.

Gideon frowned. "You know me?"

The Crusader reached up, lowered his hood, and tugged at his mask. Now that Gideon could see it clearly, he realized that the emblem on the mask's forehead, between and just above his eyes, was a cross. The Crusader pulled the mask off. His features were familiar and dark. Gideon's jaw dropped.

"Wyatt?"

"Hey, kid," the man said. "Heh . . . what are the odds?"

CHAPTER 9

Dean was concerned.

He had walked through the biology lab three times today, and not once had he seen Gideon at his desk. That was extremely unusual. Gideon was one of the most faithful and consistent people that Dean knew. He hadn't missed a day of work since he'd started. He was always on time. So where the heck was he?

Dean walked back upstairs to the research and development floor and entered his own lab. His coworkers, Maddox Odell and Arianna Serafin, were busy as usual. Dean walked over to Maddox and leaned against the table.

"Still no sign of him?" Maddox asked.

"Nope." Dean shrugged. "And I've tried calling and texting him, too. Nothing."

"Maybe he's sick," Arianna suggested.

"I don't think so. I mean, I didn't check in on him, but I think he was gone when I left this morning." He checked his phone. "Maybe I should call him again . . ."

"Don't smother him." Arianna walked across the room carrying a tablet and swiped at the screen. Blueprints for a sonic weapon appeared on the wall monitor in front of her. "When he's ready to get in touch with you, he will."

"I know, I know. But—" Dean's phone rang. "Speak of the devil. I guess you're right."

Maddox smirked. "She usually is."

Dean answered the phone. "Hello? Gid, where the heck are you?"

"Sorry, Dean." Gideon sounded congested, like his nose was plugged. "I'm not feeling so great today. It hit me on the way to work from the church and I just came home. Sorry; I meant to call you about it."

"Oh." Dean looked at Arianna, who raised an eyebrow. *You told me so,* Dean mouthed. "Well, get better, bud. I'll see you tonight."

"All right. Bye."

"Bye."

"She told you so," Maddox said.

"I told you so."

Dean rolled his eyes. "I already said that, didn't I? Okay, come on, geniuses. Get back to work."

* * *

Gideon helped Wyatt lie down on the couch and ran for the cabinet where he kept the medical supplies. The bleeding from Wyatt's wound had been stanched somewhat; the vigilante had shoved his wadded-up mask into the hole to slow it. But it was still critical for Gideon to get him sewn up as quickly as possible.

He took what he'd need back to the living room and set to work. He sterilized the wound and checked for an exit wound. He didn't find one.

"The bullet's still in you," he said. "This is going to hurt. You might want to bite down on your belt."

He gave Wyatt a shot of painkiller, gave it time to set in while Wyatt removed his belt and placed it in his mouth, and then set to work removing the bullet. Wyatt screamed and bit into the leather. Gideon found the bullet quickly and pulled it free. Then he sewed up the wound and cleaned it up.

"Normally, we'd do this in a hospital." Gideon chuckled. "But I don't suppose you'd want to be found in one of those."

Wyatt shook his head. "Can't . . . have anyone telling my secret."

"Doctor-patient confidentiality should prevent that, ideally. But I understand."

"Boy, you . . . you are crazy." Wyatt laughed. "I think I might've misjudged you."

"Me too. You know, I never got your last name."

"It's Jonson. Wyatt Jonson."

Gideon picked up the Crusader's blood-soaked mask. "Well, Wyatt Jonson, I'm intrigued. This is a cross."

Wyatt nodded. "Symbolic . . . the crusaders of old wore them on their righteous missions."

"How long have you been the Crusader?"

"Oh . . . almost a year, I guess. Started doing it when I realized the Brooks were too dangerous for my family, but we couldn't afford to go anywhere else. Years ago, I served in the Marines, so I had the skills. I just got back into the practice of using them and . . . set out to clean up the streets."

"I can respect that." Gideon patted his shoulder. "You should get some rest. I do have to get you out of here before my roommate comes home."

"Oh, he doesn't know you're playing Crusader 2.0, I take it?"

"No." Gideon smiled. "No, he doesn't."

"So, what about you, kid? What inspired you to take this on? You live right here, and I expect you hardly ever see crime personally. So why did you get in the game?"

"Well . . . you, partially." Gideon began packing up his medical kit. "I watched you fight some thugs in an alley the other night. And after what happened to the church . . . the first time, I mean . . . I had already started thinking about doing something. After what happened today, I knew I had to."

"And what about the glowy hands? What's that all about?"

"Well . . . I'm not sure, honestly. Long story, and even I don't know all the details. I can't explain it, other than maybe you're right. This could be a gift."

"I noticed you didn't use it in the fight."

"No." *I don't really know how yet, or if I even can.* "Now, that's enough talking. Rest."

Gideon put his kit back in the cabinet and pulled out his phone. In all the chaos, he hadn't even checked in to see how Wes was doing yet. He dialed his mom.

"Gideon?" she answered.

"Hey, Mom. How's Wes doing?"

"Better. He's at the hospital and Dr. Edwin has just seen him. The cut wasn't bad and everything else is just bumps and bruises."

"Good."

"But where did you go, honey? You ran out the door so fast I would've thought you were going to track down those criminals yourself."

Oops. He couldn't tell her. She'd only worry, and she also couldn't lie if the police questioned her. It was better if she didn't know the truth for now.

"Well, I did drive around a bit to see if I could spot their van. I wanted to get a license plate number for the cops. It was . . . stupid. I didn't get anything." *Lord, please forgive me for lying.* "I can come see Wes, if he's up to it."

"I'm sure he'd like that. He's resting now, but whenever you get here would be fine, I'm sure."

But he still had the Crusader lounging on his couch. He needed to get Wyatt out of here before Dean got home.

"All right. I've got something I have to take care of and then I'll be straight over."

"Okay. See you soon, sweetie."

"See you. Love you, Mom. Bye."

"Love you, too. Bye-bye."

Gideon hung up the phone and stuffed it back in his pocket. First, he needed to change clothes. These were still dirty and sweat-soaked. He went upstairs, changed into a cream button-up shirt, dark blue jeans, and a pair of brown shoes. He pulled a brown jacket on and went back downstairs.

"Wyatt?" he said. "You asleep, old man?"

"Mm." The Crusader rolled over. "Not that old."

"Sorry." Gideon smiled. "Come on. I've got to go see my brother and you can't be here when my roommate gets home. I'll take you back to your house."

"My house?" Wyatt grimaced. "Well, okay."

"What? Don't tell me your wife and kids don't know about . . . "

"They do. Although my wife is not a fan of my extralegal activities, and my oldest son wants too much to be like me. I'm afraid of how my wife will react when she sees me like this, and I'm afraid he'll just go out and try to murder the guy who did it."

"I'm sure the cops have them already," Gideon replied. "But point taken. You still have to go home, though, you know."

"I know." Wyatt pushed himself up. "All right. Help me . . . down to the car."

* * *

A little over an hour later, Gideon walked into the hospital. He'd worked here long enough that all the employees recognized him. A few greeted him as he passed by, but he didn't stop. He weaved his way through the hospital to the room number his mother had texted him.

He rounded the corner into the room and found his parents there with Wes . . . along with Jolie. He glanced at her just long enough to see that she was glaring daggers at him, and then he looked away to Wes.

"Hey, bud. You okay?"

"Doing just fine." Wes grinned. "And anyway, it'll just be an interesting story to tell the ladies, you know?"

The joke was macabre, considering Pastor Jeff was still in a coma down the hall. But he knew Wes needed the humor as a coping mechanism. He could've died; if the gangster had been so inclined, he could've driven the knife into Wes' chest instead of his shoulder.

Gideon laughed. "Leave it to you to find some way to use this to your advantage."

"Anyway, they're actually getting ready to release me. Already stitched me up and everything."

"That's great."

"Yep. So, you wanna help me track these guys down and give them a little Turner talking to together?"

"That . . . doesn't sound like the best idea. I'm sorry I ran off. It was stupid."

Out of the corner of his eye, Gideon saw Jolie shake her head. He pretended not to notice and instead patted Wes lightly on the shoulder.

"I'm glad you're okay."

"Thanks, bro."

"Detective Walters is looking into the attack," Jolie said. "Between the witnesses at this attack and the video footage we managed to pull from the first one, he should be able to identify the vandals, or at least who they work for. Get better, Wes."

"Thanks, Jolie."

"Yes, thank you," Dad said.

Jolie stepped toward the door. "Hey, Gid, can I talk to you for a second?"

"Yeah." *Here we go.* "I'll see you all later. Love you."

His parents and Wes told him goodbye, and then he slipped out into the hallway with Jolie. She put her hands on her hips.

"So, reports are coming in that there was a second vigilante out there with the Crusader today. You know anything about that?"

Gideon studied the floor. "Look, I told my mom. I was just trying to see if I could get a plate number."

"And I told you not to get involved!" She shoved his shoulder. "You are going to get yourself killed, Gideon Turner."

"Jolie . . ."

"Maybe think about someone's feelings other than your own, okay?" She turned and walked off. "I've got a case to work. See you later."

"Okay . . ." He rubbed his shoulder and sighed. That hadn't gone well. "I love you."

She was already too far away to hear him. He closed his eyes and tilted his head upward in a *why me* posture.

He couldn't stop, though. If Walters wasn't corrupt, he was at least inept. And with the Crusader out of commission for the near future, someone had to take up his mantle and protect the Brooks. If the police couldn't do it—which they clearly couldn't—he'd do it himself.

CHAPTER 10

It was almost Christmas.

For the past month, Gideon had been going out into the Brooks and catching criminals. He got better at it each time, and he always made sure to disappear before the cops ever showed up. His clothes were similar enough to the Crusader's that at a distance, they probably wouldn't realize he was someone else, but up close, they'd know.

Tonight, he stood on a rooftop and watched as a pair of thugs chased a woman into an alley. He braced himself for a jump. As soon as they entered the alley, he dropped from the roof and landed on a dumpster.

"Get away from her." He'd taken to using a voice modulator to make his voice deeper and more menacing. "Run!"

The woman sprinted from the alley as the two men turned to face him. They wore the same leather-jacket-and-tie combo as the guys from the church. One of them reached for a gun. The other already had a knife in hand. Gideon leapt forward and swept his batons out. He knocked the gun out of the first thug's grip and smacked the second across the face. He followed up with a kick to the gun-wielder's solar plexus.

The knife-wielding thug, holding his face with his free hand, came at Gideon. He stabbed with the knife. Gideon stepped aside and elbowed him in the face—well, the hand holding his face. The man toppled to the ground. The first thug, who had been doubled over, straightened and swung a wild punch. Gideon smacked his wrist with one baton and then punched him in the ribs. He grabbed a fistful of tie and jerked him toward the ground. With his other arm, he brought his elbow down on the back of the thug's head. He, too, hit the ground.

Before either could recover, Gideon climbed the ladder back to the rooftop. He heard sirens. *Perfect timing.* That woman must've called them. He squatted behind a transformer and waited until the cops left, and then he moved on to find the next criminal he could beat down.

* * *

For over a month, Jolie had been trying to find any sign of Regina. But whoever the woman was, she was a master of vanishing, it seemed. Nobody had ever heard of her, or at least didn't want to give out information. She was beginning to suspect that whoever she was, she was much more than just a gambler.

Jolie was nearing her breaking point. Not only because she couldn't find this woman, but because she suspected that this vigilante who was prowling the streets right now was Gideon. She hadn't gotten a good look at him, but she could tell he was wirier than the Crusader from the few times she'd seen him at a distance. And he used some kind of fighting batons, while the Crusader had usually fought bare-handed. Gideon was a master with batons.

But he wouldn't admit to it. How could she trust her boyfriend, the man she believed to be the love of her life, if he consistently lied to her? Maybe she was wrong. Maybe he really wasn't this new vigilante. But if he was, he was lying to her on almost a daily basis, and she didn't know what to do with that.

It reminded her of the dream she'd had months ago—a demented Gideon, wielding a pair of guns, mowing down criminals and civilians alike. Would he actually go that far? No, she didn't believe he had that in him. So far, no criminals had turned up with anything worse than a concussion. But he was still breaking the law.

"Hey, Anderson!" Detective Pulaski—a recipient of a recent promotion—said. "I've got a lead on that lady you're looking for. A CI of mine ID'ed her."

Pulaski's promotion had been a boon for Jolie. He was a friend, and he wasn't on the take like Walters, so Jolie had slipped him everything she'd learned on Langston. He didn't know she was investigating Walters; she'd tell him that if anything turned up.

"Really?" Jolie picked up her badge and gun. "Where is she?"

"The Broken Glass, that old bar down on Third." Pulaski shrugged. "Don't know why she'd be there, but that's what he told me."

"Thanks, Pulaski. I'll check it out."

Maybe she would finally get to the bottom of this mystery. And if not, at least it would get her mind off Gideon for a while.

* * *

Luca Serban was a senior enforcer in the Romanian crime families. A modest position, but not one to be sniffed at. But here in Sojourn City, he was top dog. And he intended to stay that way. This so-called Crusader had been making that hard for months now, and he was ready to have it over. Last month, four of his boys had been beaten by the vigilante and arrested by the cops. And rumor had it there was another guy with the Crusader.

Serban had issued a bounty on the vigilante's head for a hundred thousand dollars, and he would deliver an extra fifty thousand if the hooded brute was brought to him alive, so he could finish the job himself. The problem was, the contract had been out since before the

Crusader's attack last month, and he only had one responder. And so far, she was taking her sweet time in doing anything about it.

So he was raising the bounty to a hundred fifty thousand, with an extra hundred if the Crusader was brought in alive. Now, thugs were coming from miles around looking to take out the hit, but he wasn't giving it out until he saw what this contractor could do.

In their usual meeting place, the back room of The Broken Glass, Serban paced around Katrina Monahan, assassin-for-hire. He kept his hand near his gun, which was displayed prominently at his hip. Monahan was a skilled killer, yes, but Serban was confident that he could take her, and he wanted her to know it.

"So, you get the extra money," he said, "but the vigilante must be dead by the year's end or the deal's exclusivity is off . . . and you have competition."

"Understood," Monahan said. "But these things, they take time. It would be easier to find him if I knew his identity."

"Don't you think I know that?" Serban rolled his eyes. Monahan was blonde, but he didn't think she was stupid. "If I knew his name, I would go find him and kill him myself."

"It will be done, Luca. Patience."

"I'm running out of patience. And—" Someone knocked on the door. Serban hissed. "Come!"

One of Serban's lieutenants, a man named Costin, stuck his head in the door. "Cop's here. She's looking for a lady by the name of Regina."

Serban glowered at Monahan. "You?"

"Me." Monahan sighed. "An unfortunate oversight. I will take care of it."

Serban pulled out his gun and cocked it. "You'd better. Or I will."

Monahan turned to Costin. "Tell her that I just left and that I am returning to my home."

"Understood." Costin left.

Serban went to the door and looked out. The cop was a young woman with dark hair. She wore an officer's uniform; she was not a detective. Good. Street cops died due to gang violence all the time. Detectives were harder to hide.

"See it done," he said.

"I will." Monahan slid a knife from her sleeve. "They don't call me Lancet for nothing."

* * *

Jolie growled and stormed out of the bar. Why was this case just one dead end after another? Maybe this was why she hadn't made detective yet; she would be lousy at it. She shoved her hands in her coat pockets and marched down the street toward her car. She wondered if Regina had gone back to the house Jolie had first met her at. But she supposed that would be too obvious. Still, it didn't hurt to try. Maybe she'd head over there. Technically, she was supposed to be on patrol with Paul, but he'd given her a wink and a nod and told her he'd be fine until she figured this out.

Did that make her any better than a vigilante? Technically, she was doing this against orders, which meant it wasn't legal. But she felt in her gut that this thread would lead to something bigger. She just had to find the end that would unravel it.

Jolie reached her car and was about to open the door when something scuffled behind her. She glanced down into the car window's reflection. There was a hint of movement . . .

She rotated and whipped up her pistol. A sharp pain jolted through her hand and she nearly dropped the weapon. She saw the blurred movement of another strike coming and threw herself awkwardly to the side. When she hit the ground, she managed to roll into a crouch and get her gun up.

She finally got a good look at her attacker. Regina! The woman was clad in black leather and held a long knife.

"You should've known when to quit," the woman said.

"Sorry. Not my style."

Jolie fired, but Regina had already moved. She jumped on the hood of Jolie's car and then jumped again, propelling herself at Jolie. Jolie raised her gun to fire at the other woman, but she was too close, too fast. The knife descended—and suddenly, another body slammed into Regina's.

The masked man backed away from the woman and raised his fighting sticks. Jolie started to raise her gun again.

"Kill them!" someone shouted.

Jolie turned. Three men, armed with knives and chains, rushed at her and the vigilante. They all wore matching outfits—black ties and leather jackets. Jolie fired, dropping the lead man, who was carrying a knife. One man with a chain closed in on her and whipped out his weapon, while the third thug rushed the vigilante. The chain smacked Jolie's hands and she gasped at the sensation of the harsh metal rings digging into her skin.

She fumbled her gun and it clattered to the ground. The chain-wielding thug advanced on her as she stepped back, removing her nightstick from her belt. She was no expert at hand-to-hand, but she could manage. He whipped the chain at her, and she ducked under it and rolled closer to him. She cracked the nightstick into his kneecap, and he howled and fell. As he came down, she brought her elbow up to intercept his face.

Then she quickly picked up her gun and turned to face the melee between the third thug, the vigilante, and Regina. The vigilante performed a wild spinning kick that knocked the thug flat. He returned his attention to Regina. The two of them battled in a flurry of blows and jabs with their weapons. Whoever this woman was, she was good. She was fighting like no one Jolie had ever seen.

Regina slashed her knife across the vigilante's belly. He cried out. As Regina raised her blade for a killing blow, Jolie fired. Her shot missed, but it got Regina's attention. The woman fled without a second look. Jolie started to pursue but stopped cold when she realized she would be leaving these thugs—and the vigilante—to get away.

Reluctantly, she tucked her gun in its holster and pulled out a pair of handcuffs. With her other hand, she clicked on her walkie-talkie.

"This is Officer Anderson, requesting backup at Third Street by The Broken Glass. I've got four suspects, including the vigilante. Send medical assistance; he's wounded."

She cuffed the nearest thug first and then went to get more cuffs from her car. As she did, someone groaned. She looked back. The vigilante was limping toward an alley.

"Hey!" She decided to take a risk. "Gideon!"

The vigilante paused—or maybe he just caught himself as he stumbled from his injury. Either way, it didn't last long. He took off into the alley and disappeared. She sighed and turned to cuff the remaining thugs. So much for that.

* * *

Gideon panted and stumbled into the elevator. He clicked the button for his floor and sagged back against the wall. That woman, whoever she was, had gotten him good. The cut was deep, but not enough to be instantly fatal. Still, if he didn't get help soon, he'd pass out. He only hoped Dean was home already. This was an unfortunate way to reveal his secret to his best friend, but he didn't really have a choice at this point.

The elevator chimed, and the door slid open. Gideon pushed himself down the hall to his apartment. He shoved the door open and staggered to the couch.

"Dean!"

"What?" Dean was up on the balcony. He peered over. "Oh, my—what happened to you?"

Gideon groaned and rolled onto his back. "Medical kit. Go get it."

Dean flew down the stairs and ran across the apartment to the cabinet. He yanked out the kit and returned to Gideon's side.

"What do I need to do?"

"Open . . . my shirt. I need you to . . . clean the wound and . . . sew it up."

Dean nodded. He pulled Gideon's jacket off and then rolled up his shirt. Gideon grimaced as the fabric tore away from the partially-clotted blood around the cut. Dean pressed his lips together.

"Hurry, Dean." Gideon tried to stay calm even as his pulse hammered, his heart threatening to jump straight out of his chest. "It's kinda important."

"Right . . ."

Dean opened the kit. Gideon pointed to each tool he'd need. His hands shaking, Dean followed Gideon's instructions. It was a painful process, and Gideon fought to stay awake as the edges of the wound slowly came back together. But finally, Dean snipped the thread and put the needle away.

"Good . . . job." Gideon leaned his head back on a pillow. "And ow . . ."

"Dude, what the heck?" Dean stood. "You're the vigilante? You're not the Crusader, right? You can't be. I'm pretty sure he was around while you were still in Venezuela."

"No, I'm . . . not him. I'm sort of . . . filling in for him right now, I guess? He got hurt."

"So did you, obviously! Are you insane?"

Gideon laughed. "Guess . . . so. Got into a fight right in front of Jolie—"

"Oh, man."

"I had to! Some crazy lady was about to kill her. I mean, this girl had moves like I've never seen. I . . . " Gideon moved a little too much, and pain shot through his body. He grunted. "Jolie would've died."

"Oh. That's understandable, I guess." Dean shook his head. "Okay, let's go back. How long have you been doing this?"

"About a month, I guess."

"So when you didn't show up for work that one day . . . "

"Yeah. That was my first day . . . doing this." Gideon sighed. "I'm sorry, man, I should've told you—"

"Yeah, you should've! I could've been helping you all along!"

"Helping me?"

"Well, it's clear that you're too stupid to be talked out of this. So yeah, I could've helped you. For one thing, you need a suit. You're literally wearing a shirt and a jacket. And a ski mask. Come on, man. You need something a little more protective than that."

Gideon had considered that before, but this was basically the same thing the Crusader had worn, and he'd done all right. Up until he'd been shot, anyway.

"We've got some stuff at the labs that we might be able to use. Of course, we can't talk about this at the labs." Dean sighed. "I guess we'll have to bring some stuff here. We do have that spare bedroom; we could convert it into your lair."

He had considered a hideout, but that was before he'd revealed his vigilante activities to Dean. Now, it was pointless. "I don't need a lair."

"Every superhero needs a lair."

"I'm not a superhero." *Although, technically . . .*

"Close enough. Anyway, I'll get what we need tomorrow and bring it back here." He started to walk away.

Oh, might as well. "Hey, Dean?"

"Yeah?"

"Um . . . about the superhero thing?" Gideon held up his left hand, focused, and let the light shine out.

"Oh, man . . . " Dean shook his head. "We're discussing this later. At length. For now, I think you need to rest. You idiot."

Gideon leaned his head back on the pillow. His vision began to fade even before he closed his eyes.

CHAPTER 11

Last year

Gideon reached between the bars of the cage for a rock. The metal bars dug into his shoulder and side, but he ignored the pain and kept stretching. His fingertips brushed the rock. If he could just get a hold of it, he could smash the lock and get free. *Almost . . . there . . .*

"You may as well give up," his cellmate said. "It won't do you any good."

Gideon gave one last effort, felt his fingers touch the rock, and sighed. It was too far to get a grip on, and it was too heavy to roll with just his fingertips. He drew his arm back into the cell and turned around to face the other man. Somehow, his bearded features seemed happy and carefree despite their situation.

"I don't understand. Have you just given up?"

"Of course not." The man shrugged. "I hope every day that rescue is just around the corner. I keep my spirits high and I do what I can to keep my body fit so I don't go crazy. But other than that? There's no way to escape." He pointed at the rock. "They put that there on purpose. They make you think there's a chance to escape so you'll do everything you can to reach it, knowing the prospect of getting free and not being able to attain it will drive you crazy."

"Are you serious?" Gideon shook his head. "How do you even know that?"

"I don't."

Gideon rolled his eyes.

"But that rock's been there since I got thrown in here. And it's the only one around. I mean, look around. I don't see any other rocks of that size within twenty feet or so."

Gideon scanned the jungle for other large rocks. The man was right; there were none anywhere else near the cage.

"Great. So it's about mind games." Gideon leaned his head back against the cage. "This is crazy. What do they want with us?"

"I don't know. Every once in a while, there's another prisoner in here. They usually stay for a few days. The guerrillas come back and drag them away. They don't come back."

"And you? Why don't they ever drag you away? You say you've been here for a year; what makes you so special?"

"Beats me." He ran a hand over his bald head. "They did drag me away the first week I was here. Took me to a lab of some kind. They ran some tests or something; I'm not sure what. But then they threw me back in and . . . well, I've been here ever since."

"They never took you back to the lab?"

"Not once. They kept me in there for a couple days, I think. And then it was back to the cage."

"Weird." Gideon frowned. "You know, I never asked your name. Sorry."

He smiled. "It's okay. I guess I didn't ask yours, either. I'm Joshua."

"Nice to meet you, Joshua. I'm Gideon."

Joshua chuckled. "Look at us. A couple of biblical heroes."

Gideon grinned and shook his head. He suspected Joshua was a little crazy from spending a year in this cage, but he didn't really care.

Having someone here with him, no matter how crazy, would help to keep him from going crazy.

The next few days helped Gideon get into a routine. Like Joshua, he spent a lot of time exercising. He did pushups, crunches, chin-ups on the cell's upper bars, and a series of other exercises to keep him fit. Every day around noon and then again in the evening a guerrilla would bring them food and water. That was the only sign of outside human life they ever saw. A large, metal building, stained green by the jungle, was visible just through the trees—Gideon suspected it was the lab Joshua had been taken to—but there were never any people around it, except when the guard came out of it and brought them food.

But every day, Gideon watched. He examined everything around him, and he waited for the day when he'd have an opportunity to escape.

* * *

"You don't remember anything they did to you in that lab?" Gideon asked one day.

Joshua pulled himself up on one of the upper crossbars and held himself there. "They put a bunch of needles and tubes in me. And they put something on my head. I figured it was to scan my brainwaves or something. I don't know, exactly. I'm not a doctor."

"Okay, but needles and tubes." Gideon began a series of pushups. "They must have injected you with something, then. Did you feel anything unusual afterwards?"

"Not that I can remember."

"Strange." Guerrillas weren't typically doctors or scientists. Maybe they'd hired one for some reason. "I'd like to see that lab."

"Oh, you will, I'm sure of it. You just probably won't like how."

Gideon sighed. "You're probably right. Hey, how many guards come to escort the prisoners to the lab?"

"Usually two."

"Do you think we could take them? If we fought the guards before they could get me to the lab, we might have a chance to escape."

Of course, Gideon wouldn't kill them. But being cooped up in a cage for over a week had begun to bring back his fighting spirit. He'd be willing to injure or knock out the guards if it meant he and Joshua could escape.

"I doubt it," Joshua said. "One of them stands at a distance with his rifle trained on me while the other unlocks the cage and drags the other prisoner out."

"Great." Gideon stood up. "What about once I'm out? That guard might be focused on me while the other one locks the door back. You could rush the door while he's locking it and knock it open. That would give me a chance to take out the other guard."

"It could work." Joshua dropped to the ground. "But honestly, Gideon, I've survived here for a year by keeping my head down. And no offense, but I've known you for only a few days. It's not that I don't want to get free, or that I don't want you to get free, but I really just don't want to die trying to escape when we don't even know where in the jungle we are and how to get back to civilization."

Unfortunately, Joshua had a fair point. Even if they did knock out both guards, they had no way to know which way to run to get away. And in the middle of a rainforest, it would be a very bad idea to run in a random direction.

"Okay," Gideon said. "So we wait."

However long it took, he'd wait. But one day, he would get out of here. He'd get back to his life. To his family. To Jolie.

Now

Dean walked out of the kitchen with a glass of orange juice in his hand. Gideon was still fast asleep on the couch and had been ever since he'd collapsed last night. As soon as Dean woke up, he'd checked on him to make sure he was still alive. He was, and he seemed to be doing all right. But he probably needed his rest, so Dean didn't want to wake him.

He checked his watch. He would need to head to the labs soon, but he wasn't sure it was a good idea to leave Gideon here alone. Maybe he should just call Maddox and Arianna and let them know he couldn't come in today.

Dean reentered the kitchen. He finished his juice, set his glass in the sink, and was about to go upstairs to get his phone when the doorbell rang. He frowned and turned around. He hoped it wasn't someone they knew; the couch was well within view of the front door so whoever it was would see Gideon lying there. He went over to Gideon's side and threw a blanket over him to cover his wound. The doorbell rang again. Dean went to answer it and looked through the peephole.

It was Jolie. *Oh no.* He cracked the door just enough to see her and poked his head out, smiling.

"Hey, Jolie! What's up, girl?"

"Is Gideon home?"

"Um, yeah."

"Can I come in and see him, please?"

"He's asleep now, actually." Dean scrambled for an excuse. "I think he's under the weather. He's been out cold ever since last night."

"Oh, really?" Jolie crossed her arms. "Are you lying to me, Timothy Dean Sterling?"

Ouch. "Gideon is not feeling well. He's asleep right now. I promise."

"Okay." Jolie sighed. "Well, tell him I want to talk to him . . . and that I hope he feels better."

"I will! See you around, Jolie."

"See you."

Dean closed the door and sat down on the floor. That was close. And she'd used his full name. That was never good. She was mad, and that probably meant she knew, or very strongly suspected at the very least, that Gideon was a vigilante. He hoped Gideon knew what he was doing. If he kept lying to Jolie, it could seriously hurt their relationship. Dean didn't want that; he and everyone else knew that Jolie and Gideon were perfect for each other. Dean also knew that Gideon planned to marry her sooner than later.

Was this vigilante thing really worth it to him? He was risking losing the love of his life and probably several other people close to him, not to mention his freedom if the police ever caught him or his life if he wasn't good enough to take on some bad guy. He was playing a very dangerous game.

Well, if he wasn't going to back down, that just meant that Dean had to help keep him alive. He stood and jogged up the stairs. He was going to call Maddox and Arianna—to tell them to get some things ready for him. He grabbed his phone and tucked it in his pocket. First, he needed to do some rearranging.

He went into their spare bedroom and set to work.

* * *

The first thing Gideon saw when he woke up was the Christmas tree.

He and Dean had set it up the day after Thanksgiving. Seeing it as soon as he opened his eyes somehow brought a unique comfort, like a blanket of childhood memories.

Or maybe that was the actual blanket draped over him. It hadn't been there when he went to sleep.

He tried to sit up and gasped. It felt like someone tearing his insides open. So, he wasn't ready for that yet. Gingerly, he lowered himself back to the couch. He moved the blanket and looked at his abdomen. Dean had done a surprisingly good job of stitching up the wound. Gideon should be able to work himself back to health now. But he was thirsty. He had lost a lot of fluids, and he hadn't even thought to replenish them before he'd passed out.

"Dean?" he called. "Hey! Dean?"

No response. He sighed and reached into his pants pocket for his phone. The screen blinked on and displayed five notifications. He had three missed calls and two texts from Jolie since last night. That was bad. He texted her back, *Just woke up. Sorry. Not feeling well.* Then he dialed Dean and brought the phone to his ear.

"Hello?"

"Dean. Where are you?"

"I'm at the lab. I need to get some things. For, you know . . . you."

"Oh." Gideon took a deep, shaky breath. "Okay. Well, get back as quickly as you can. I don't think I'm up for moving yet, but I need some fluids in me ASAP."

"Okay. I'll be back soon! Oh, and I guess I should mention that Jolie stopped by the apartment. I didn't let her in, and I told her you were sick."

"Thanks."

"Man, you can't keep lying to her."

"I know. I know, okay? We'll talk about that when you get back. And a ton of other things that we still need to talk about."

"Yes, we will. I gotta go. See you soon."

Gideon lowered his phone. Maybe he should call Jolie. But what would he say? Dean was right, he couldn't keep lying. It was wrong in the first place, but to lie to her specifically was even worse. But he knew what she'd say: stay out of it, you're getting in the way, you're going to get hurt, you'll get arrested.

And she was right. He'd gotten hurt, and he'd very nearly been arrested. By her. But he'd saved her life. That woman had been seconds away from killing her. If Gideon hadn't stepped in, she'd be dead now. She had to understand that, right? Surely, she would. And he was willing to keep risking his life if it meant keeping her and the other innocents in the Brooks safe.

It would cost him, though. He knew that. He hadn't considered it going in, but he was considering it now. Jolie would probably distance herself from him for a long time. Hopefully she'd come around eventually, but he wasn't betting on it being fast. And it would be even worse if she found out without him telling her. *What do I do?*

He looked at the Christmas tree again. Oh, for the simpler times of childhood. When he hadn't had to worry about saving the city. When he hadn't had to juggle a million responsibilities. When life had been easy. He sighed and rubbed his forehead. Would things ever be simple again? Probably not.

Well. He knew what he had to do. Simple or not, that decision was made. He couldn't leave the city unprotected. So, *Gideon Turner: the doctor, the scientist, the vigilante* had to be a reality. That was just the way it was.

* * *

Jolie sat down on her bed and shook her head. She had never felt so powerless in her whole life. She'd always been a proud girl—not prideful, or at least she didn't think so—and always known the right thing to do. She'd always been sure of herself and confident that her decisions would work out for the best.

When she'd started dating Gideon, she'd known for a fact that he was the right guy for her. When she'd chosen a career in law enforcement, she'd known that she was doing the right thing and that she'd be able to help people.

Now, for the first time, she felt helpless. She didn't have any idea what was right and what was wrong, and she didn't know where to begin looking for the answer. She wished there was a verse in the Bible that said *Thou shalt not be a vigilante* or something, because then this would be easy. Because she knew the Crusader—or Gideon, or whoever this new vigilante was—was breaking the law. But he'd also saved her life last night. Regina would've killed her, and he'd saved her, even though he had to have known that she was a cop and that she'd arrest him in a heartbeat if given the chance.

And she was worried about him, too, because if he really was Gideon, then the "not feeling well" excuse he and Dean had to mean the injury he'd sustained in fighting Regina. An injury he'd sustained protecting her.

She also wanted to be mad at him—at both of them—for lying to her, but she even understood why. Because she would be obligated to turn Gideon in if she knew for sure he was the vigilante. But at the same time, the more he lied, the less she trusted him. And that hurt their relationship.

Jolie loved Gideon. If she knew nothing else, she knew that. She loved him, and she didn't want to lose him.

Feel better, she texted him. *I love you.*

She groaned in confusion and frustration and flopped backward to lie down. She just needed a vacation. A very long, very relaxing vacation far away from Sojourn City and the Brooks and crime and vigilantes.

But the odds of that happening were, unfortunately, very un-likely indeed.

* * *

Luca Serban's benefactor was unhappy.

"This is not what we agreed to when I invited you to this city," the man said.

Serban smirked as he listened to him rant over the phone. Typical one percenter—not willing to get his own hands dirty, but unhappy with how everyone else handled things when he delegated.

"Your plan is dangerous. Most of the city's police have withdrawn to Lakeside or even onto the Platform itself. Going there would incite a war that my men are not yet prepared to fight."

"Yes, I know." The words came out through gritted teeth. "But I wanted you here to unleash terror on the rich, not the poor."

"Oh, we will. It will just take time."

"Time in which the poor of this city are suffering by your hands! It's gone on long enough. It's the rich who must face wrath now."

"You are one of the rich, my friend. You'd suffer, too."

"I know." His benefactor sighed. "But I deserve it as much as the rest of them. We have neglected the people of the Brooks and we must be punished."

"I don't care about your idealism. You're paying me to revive this city in a crucible of fire, and so I will. But I do it my way."

Serban hung up without waiting for a response. Indeed, he would do exactly as the rich man wanted . . . but not before he'd sucked the Brooks and the rest of the city dry. Then he'd move on to Lakeside and the Platform. But not until he had his talons in every money-making opportunity in the city. Serban was a god here. This was his kingdom. And he wouldn't rest until he had control of every inch of it.

CHAPTER 12

Even though he'd been initially skeptical, the more Dean worked with Gideon, the more excited he became. He'd spent most of his childhood reading comic books and watching TV shows about super-heroes, so to have his best friend become one was one of the coolest things he'd ever experienced. It distracted him from the fact that he was helping Gideon risk his life.

The two of them managed to turn the spare bedroom into a lair of sorts. They installed a hidden keypad on the wall that would reveal the tech and equipment the room held; otherwise, it was hidden in wall panels, so the room looked completely ordinary. The bed rotated to reveal the newest smart table underneath. Overall, being in the room was just awesome.

The best part had to be the suit Dean had designed. It was made of a semi-translucent material that was completely opaque on the outside, so Gideon could use his powers even through the gloves. It was also a hard-fiber material that would block knife blades and even stop a bullet—or so Maddox assured him. The whole thing was made in a midnight blue, navy, and gold color scheme and had a blue cape with a hood, plus a domino mask.

He planned for it to be Gideon's Christmas present of sorts. He didn't need it yet, anyway; he hadn't gone out into the field since his in-jury. Gideon had gone to visit the Crusader—the actual Crusader—but he hadn't wanted Dean to come with him. All he said was that the Crusader was recovering and would probably be back out in the field before Gideon was.

Dean had also paid for a generic black motorcycle. Gideon couldn't be driving his own car around as a vigilante.

He spent about an hour each day sparring with Gideon to help get him back up to one hundred percent. Dean had never been a fighter, so this served dual purposes of physical therapy for Gideon and training for Dean. Not that Dean ever expected to go out with Gideon—but if someone ever attacked him, now he'd be able to fight back.

Dean jabbed a fist at Gideon. "So, how much longer do you think before you're ready to get back out there?"

Gideon blocked the jab and crosscut with his other hand. "Hopefully another week or so. My goal is to be back out there before New Year's."

"Bold." They grappled for a moment, ending with Gideon shoving Dean backward and sweeping his legs out from under him. Dean's back slapped onto the mat. "Oof. So . . . " Dean jumped back to his feet. "What about your powers? You said you haven't used them to fight yet. Why not?"

Gideon circled the mat, and Dean matched him step for step. "I'm not sure how."

"Well, intimidation, for one. Police shine their flashlights on criminals to scare them. You drop into an alley with two fists lit up like New York City on the Fourth of July and they'll be pretty intimidated."

"Good point." Gideon kicked at Dean. Dean pulled back. "Any other ideas?"

"Well, I've been thinking. You can project light. Can you do anything else?"

"I think I can sort of . . . read people's emotions? I can't read their minds thought for thought, but I can sort of, I don't know, get traces of their surface feelings."

"Interesting." Dean lunged. Gideon caught his elbow, spun him around, and shoved him away. "So, like, you're bringing their true thoughts to light, huh?"

"I . . . hadn't thought about that." Gideon straightened. "That's a good way to put it, though."

"All right, so you can project light and feel emotions." Dean ran a hand through his hair. "I wonder if you might be able to harness your light projection and actually shoot light rays."

"I've never done that before."

"Worth a try, though, right?" He jerked a finger toward the lair. "I've got a target in there you could practice on."

Gideon shrugged. "Worth a shot."

"Heh. No pun intended?"

"Right." Gideon rolled his eyes. "Let's go."

Dean led Gideon into the lair and raised the target from the floor. He stepped aside and gestured for Gideon to stand in front of it.

"So, what do you think, I just . . . try to push the light out of me?"

"Makes sense to me! Honestly, I'm just spit-balling. I just really want to see what happens."

Gideon looked down at his hands. They began to light up, softly at first, and then with a greater intensity. He held his right hand up, palm-forward, and aimed it at the target. He closed his eyes. Dean took an extra step back—just in case.

"Now just . . . let it go," he said.

A blinding ball of light flashed across the room and slammed into the target. Dean shielded his eyes and stumbled back at the force of the impact. He gasped.

"Whoa."

Gideon looked down at his hands. "Wow. Dean, you're a genius."

"You'll have to be careful with that." Dean pointed at the target, which had a sizable burn mark on it. "You don't want to kill anyone. But man, if that isn't cool!"

"That is . . . " Gideon nodded. "That's pretty cool, yeah."

"Dude, my best friend's a superhero!" Dean cackled. "That's awesome! Wait. We need to come up with a codename!"

"A codename?"

"Yeah. Every superhero has a codename, right? I mean, even the Crusader. He's not even a real superhero, just a vigilante, but he still has a name people call him. They don't just say 'the vigilante.' He's the Crusader. You need a name. Not just 'the vigilante' or 'the New Crusader' or 'Crusader 2.0.' Something unique. Something you."

Gideon scratched the stubble on his chin. "Yeah, I see your point."

"How about 'the Guardian Angel?' Nah, that's too long."

"No, but I like the idea." Gideon snapped his fingers. "I've got it. The Seraph."

"The Seraph." Dean grinned and hugged Gideon while laughing. "The Seraph! Dude, that's so cool."

"I like it." Gideon looked down at his hands again and let them shine a bit. "I'm the Seraph, the guardian angel of Sojourn City."

"Yeah, you are." Dean grinned. Then to himself, he whispered again, "My best friend's a superhero!"

* * *

Jolie pulled on a comfortable cream turtleneck sweater and brown leather jacket. Looking in the mirror, she fluffed her dark hair. Satisfied, she tucked her sidearm in her purse, slung it over her shoulder, and headed out for the door. It was Christmas Day. She had planned dinner with her parents, but she was spending the afternoon at Gideon's.

The past week had been tense. She was all but certain now that Gideon was the vigilante, because ever since he'd started "feeling bad," the vigilante hadn't shown up again. But of course, that could be because the vigilante had succumbed to the wounds Regina had inflicted and Gideon feeling bad could be totally unrelated. But Jolie doubted that. Her cop's intuition—coupled with her woman's intuition—told her that Gideon was feeling bad because of those same wounds. But she wasn't going to bring it up. Not today. Today was Christmas, and she wasn't going to ruin it with this.

The day had started with an unexpected blessing. Jolie had awakened to a text, sent out as a mass burst to members of Refuge Church, that Pastor Jeff had awakened from his coma last night. It would be some time before he could go home, but his family would be able to visit him on Christmas.

She picked up Dean's and Gideon's presents, tucked them under her arm, and walked out the door. The drive to the guys' apartment was pleasant; the roads were nearly empty because of the holiday and there had been a gentle snowfall the night before that left everything pure white. Jolie put Christmas music on the radio and took her time driving across town.

When she arrived at Lakeside Central Tower, she parked her car on the street and took the elevator up to the guys' floor. She rang the doorbell. Dean answered it and grinned at her.

"Jolie!" He opened the door wide and hugged her. "Good to see you, girl."

He was wearing a very festive sweater—bright reds and greens everywhere—and had a Santa Claus hat perched over his curly brown hair. He waved her inside and took the presents from her. While he walked them over to the tree, Jolie stepped into the living room. She heard footsteps on the balcony above and turned around. Gideon leaned on the balcony railing, looking down on her and smiling.

"Merry Christmas," he said.

"Merry Christmas." She smiled back.

He walked down the stairs. He wore gray jeans, dressy black boots, and a burgundy sweater. She walked to the foot of the staircase to meet him and hugged him when he reached her. Gideon stepped back and examined her outfit.

"You look good."

"So do you." She took a step back. "How are you feeling?"

"Better. Much better."

"Good!" She took his hand and they walked over to the couch together.

Dean—who was a surprisingly good cook—had prepared lunch, and the afternoon was spent eating, watching Christmas movies, and opening presents. Through it all, Jolie almost forgot about vigilantes, the Brooks, and her suspicions about Gideon. It was just like old times, and she loved it.

They had just finished watching *Home Alone* when Jolie checked her watch, wiping tears of laughter away so she could see it. It was getting to be early evening; she needed to leave now if she wanted to make it to her parents' when she told them she'd be there.

"I've got to get going." Jolie stood. "Thanks for the day, guys. It was great."

Dean hugged her first and then headed into the kitchen to do the dishes. Gideon smiled and stepped forward.

"Want me to walk you out?" he asked.

She nodded. "Sure."

He took her hand and the two headed down to her car. Jolie smiled. Again, it was just like old times. She fondly remembered the evenings spent watching movies with Gideon, and then him walking her to her car for goodbyes that sometimes lasted fifteen minutes or more. She had never wanted to be apart from him. Now, it seemed they spent far more time separate than they did together, even when they were in the same room. But not today. Today had been . . . well, it had been just what she'd needed. Gideon hadn't changed. He was still the same person she'd fallen in love with.

She opened her car door. "Thanks again. I had a great time."

"Me, too." Gideon leaned in and brushed his lips against hers. "I love you, Jolie. I'm sorry I haven't shown it too much lately."

"Well, I could say the same. And I love you, too." She kissed him back. "Have a good night, Gideon. And . . . be safe."

"You, too."

She climbed into her car and shut the door. Gideon walked back to the sidewalk, where he waited. She waved goodbye one last time and then pulled away. She looked in the rearview mirror and caught a last glimpse of him disappearing into the apartment building.

"Love you," she said softly.

* * *

Gideon stepped back into the apartment and smiled, even as he shivered. He removed his jacket, draped it over the chair, and flooded a bit of light energy through his body to warm him. Dean walked in from the kitchen, carrying a bag of Cheetos in one hand and popping the cheesy crisps into his mouth with the other.

"That went well!" he said. "So, is the romance restored?"

"Dean."

"Come on, you've got to admit things went really well today. As far as I could tell, she wasn't angry or suspicious at all."

Gideon had felt the same, too. But his powers had also shown him a little about how she had been feeling. Yes, it had seemed like old times, and yes, she had even felt like she was having a good time and wasn't thinking about it. But he'd also felt her conflict as they walked out to the car. When they'd said goodbye, she had once again seemed happy with him, but there had been a few moments where there had been just enough . . . something . . . that he'd been able to tell that she still suspected.

But maybe it didn't matter. If she was intentionally putting that aside in favor of being with him, that might be all that mattered.

"Time will tell."

"Wow, you know how to pour water on every single fire, don't you?"

"Sorry." Gideon tucked his hands in his pockets and shrugged. "I don't do it on purpose."

"I know." Dean set the Cheetos bag down on the counter and licked the dust from his fingers. "Come on, I've got another Christmas present for you before you go see your family."

"Oh, you mean the oh-so-subtle Batman DVD wasn't my real Christmas present, huh?"

Dean laughed. "No, but it was a pretty good joke, wasn't it?"

"Yes." Gideon kept his expression and tone deadpan. "Hilarious."

"Again. Water on every fire. Come on!"

Gideon followed Dean upstairs. Outside the "lair"—they really needed to come up with a better name for it—Dean held up a hand.

"Cover your eyes."

Gideon sighed and closed his eyes, then held his right hand over them. Dean opened the door, grabbed Gideon by the shoulder, and guided him in. He heard Dean typing on a keypad.

"And . . . open."

Gideon opened his eyes. Directly in front of him was a mannequin clothed in a suit. It looked like it was made out of some sort of armored material like Kevlar. It was midnight blue and navy with gold highlights, including a section of the abdomen that was shaped vaguely like wings. The suit was tied together with a blue hooded cape and a domino mask.

"Wow," he said. "This is . . . ?"

"This is the Seraph, man." Dean grinned and slapped the suit on the shoulder. "It's super impact-resistant, and it's partially translucent. That means your light can shine and even shoot out of the gloves, but nothing comes in."

"I know what translucent means."

"Don't kill the moment." Dean shook his head. "The armor should withstand stabs or gunshots. I know domino masks aren't super concealing, but I figure since you go out at night and you're also wearing the cowl, it might be enough. Plus, people will probably be paying more attention to your glowing hands than your face."

Gideon stepped toward the suit and ran his hand over it. Without a doubt, it was one of the coolest things he'd ever seen.

"Oh, and here." Dean picked up a pair of truncheons. "These are made of a unique carbon polymer. Super strong. They won't bend, and knives shouldn't cut them. Plus, the tips are electrified. You hit these buttons down here to activate it. They're basically like an epic baton-and-stun-gun combo."

Gideon took the truncheons and twirled them. They were well-balanced, too. He whistled.

"So what do Maddox and Arianna think these are for, exactly?"

"They think I'm working on new gear for the cops." Dean chuckled. "Of course, they don't know about the mask or the cape. And I added the color myself."

Gideon nodded and looked up at the costume again. "Thank you, Dean."

"You're welcome, Seraph." Dean grinned. "You're about to be the coolest superhero to ever exist."

CHAPTER 13

Serban tossed a hand of chips into the growing pile in the middle of the table. He'd long ago lost interest in the game and had decided to see how lazily he could play and still win. So far, he had yet to lose a hand.

Monahan sat across the table from him, twirling a knife casually between her fingers with one hand while examining her cards with the other. She was still trying to coerce Serban into paying her for getting rid of the vigilante, but he was not convinced. She claimed she had dealt him a fatal blow, but he countered that she had not stuck around to check his body and confirm his death. Until he saw the body himself, he was not paying her.

She insisted that he must be dead, because he hadn't shown up in the streets once since that night. Still, Serban remained unconvinced. If she had wounded him, he might just be taking his time in recovery to ensure that he was back up to full strength when he took to the streets again.

He turned his attention back to the game. One of his men groaned and folded his cards. The others soon followed, leaving only Monahan and Serban.

"I'm telling you, he's dead," Monahan said.

"And I'm telling you, even if that's true, I need proof. You failed to kill that cop, so why should I believe you were any more effective at taking out the vigilante? If you cannot bring me proof, you will not be paid."

Monahan huffed. "And how do I bring you proof if the police already have his body? We don't know who he is under the mask. If they've already performed an autopsy, I couldn't even find his body."

"Your failure. Not mine." He put his cards down. "Like this game."

She examined his cards, scoffed, and rose from the table. Serban scooped in his winnings. He was unconcerned with Monahan's opinions. She was a good fighter, maybe almost as good as him. But he'd risen close to the top of the mob back in Romania by fighting tooth and nail. No one was fiercer than he, no matter their skill.

"Fine." Monahan strutted across the room to the door. "I'll get your proof and—"

"Boss," Costin, one of Serban's lieutenants, said.

"What?"

Costin pointed at the TV in the corner of the room. There was live helicopter footage of the vigilante—the Crusader—fighting several men on a rooftop. Serban tossed a glance at Monahan and gave her a knowing smirk.

"That's the other one," she said.

"Is it?"

"Yes. Look. He fights with his fists and wears black. The other one used batons, and he wore a navy jacket."

"Because vigilantes never change clothes." Serban rolled his eyes. "Maybe there are two; my men have reported as much. That just means potentially double the payday for you. Kill this one and I pay you. Find proof of the other one's death and I pay you again."

She headed for the door again. "It will be done."

"Oh, and Monahan?"

"Yes?"

"By my count, you only have two days until the new year. And then our deal expires. You'd better hurry."

* * *

"Gideon!" Dean called. "You need to see this."

Gideon, who had been firing practice shots at the target, lowered his hand and let the light dissipate from his fingers. He ran from the lair and to the balcony. Downstairs, Dean stood in front of the TV, remote in his hand. Gideon sprinted down the stairs and stood next to Dean.

On the TV, a black-clad man was fighting someone on a rooftop. Three others lay unconscious around him. Suddenly, the rooftop access door smashed open and cops poured onto the roof. The Crusader—that had to be who it was—turned to look at them in surprise. He sprinted across the rooftop and jumped. Gideon's jaw dropped. The Crusader made the jump and landed on the next rooftop.

"Looks like your buddy's back in action," Dean said.

Gideon shook his head. "He's going to get himself killed."

He bounded back up the stairs, Dean hot on his heels. He went into the lair and typed in the access code to raise his suit from the floor.

"Looks like it's time to give this thing a test run," he said.

"Motorcycle's in the garage," Dean said. "Keys are in the utility belt."

Gideon pulled on the suit. *Hang on, Wyatt. I'm coming.*

* * *

The motorcycle that Dean had provided was fast. Gideon sped down the road toward the Brooks, weaving between cars and using the bike's maneuverability to his advantage. It was a miracle he hadn't been pulled over yet, but he suspected that most of the cops in the area were going after the Crusader. He tapped his earbud, connecting him to the tabletop computer in the lair. Dean should be able to guide him from there.

"Where am I going, buddy?" he asked.

"They're pursuing him down Sixth and Teller. Take the next right."

Gideon turned the bike in that direction and scanned the rooftops. This was Sixth, but Teller was two miles from here. Where was that helicopter, though?

"The Crusader just went into an alleyway," Dean said. "He's running down Teller away from Sixth."

"What about the cops?"

"The ones on the rooftop are trying to get down to street level. There are some cars on the ground already, though. You're probably about to see them."

Just ahead, Gideon did see police lights. Their cars sped down Pattinson, the road parallel to Teller. Gideon slowed down a bit until they had passed, then he revved his engine and sped toward Teller.

"They're going to try to cut him off," he said.

"Right. They'll take Pattinson down to Fifth and cut him off at the intersection of Fifth and Teller."

"And he won't be able to turn around because by then the cops on the roof will be on the ground behind him."

"Exactly."

"I can't fight cops, Dean. That's not what I do. So how am I supposed to help him?"

"I don't know; you're the hero!"

Gideon frowned. If he couldn't fight the cops directly, maybe he could draw them away from the Crusader instead. It would be risky, but if he could split their attention, Wyatt might have a chance to slip away.

He turned onto Teller. A handful of cops ran down the street ahead of him. Above, a helicopter's propellers thumped. It was a news station copter. *Well, looks like the world is about to be introduced to the Seraph.* He sped up until the police noticed him coming, and then skidded to a halt.

"Freeze!" The shout came from Detective Walters.

"Who's that?" a uniformed cop asked.

"Another vigilante?"

"I'm the Seraph!" Gideon shouted. "I'm the guardian of the Brooks and that includes the Crusader!"

"Then you're coming in with him," Walters said.

Seraph clenched his fists and let the light shine through them. His hands began to glow. It took a moment for the policemen to notice, but when the first one did, he gasped and took a step back. The others hesitated, too. Gideon raised his right hand, aimed for the streetlight above their heads, and fired a small blast of light. It connected with the lamp but didn't do anything more than create a shower of sparks.

"What kind of freak is he?"

Gideon spun his bike around, gunned the engine, and sped away. A bullet pinged off the back—fired by Walters, most likely. One of the cops radioed for backup. The Seraph hoped it was enough of a distraction.

* * *

Katrina Monahan drove cautiously as she monitored the police pursuit. She would be ready for the moment when the Crusader slipped away from the police—it was inevitable that he would; he hadn't been a player in the game this long if he was sloppy enough to get caught by the police. But she had not been expecting this new arrival, the blue-clad man on the motorcycle with the strange, glowing hands.

A new player? Or perhaps he was the same vigilante she'd fought days ago and injured. They both favored blue. But this man's uniform was far different, far more advanced, than the simple jacket and mask her previous adversary had worn. She twirled a lock of blonde hair around her finger and considered. Which one to go after?

The Crusader, she decided. This . . . enigma would have to wait. She needed to study him, to be sure of his abilities before she confronted him. It would be foolish to engage someone whom she did not have a good read on. The Crusader would be a simple enough kill.

She turned her car toward Fifth. It was almost time to engage.

* * *

"Dean, I'm starting to think this was a bad idea."

Gideon swerved through an intersection and glanced in the motorcycle's little rearview mirror. There were still two police cars and three police motorcycles on his tail. Most of the traffic in this part of the Brooks had been rerouted by the cops so they would have a clear shot at the Crusader. But that proved equally true for them being unhindered in their pursuit of Gideon.

"Okay, take a left on Washington."

Gideon banked left. "What good's that going to do?"

"Can you make a distraction? Like, maybe a really bright flash of light?"

"Sure, but why?"

"I'm going to take remote control of the bike. When you fire off your distraction, hop off the bike and go hide somewhere."

"Dean, they're not going to keep following a bike with no rider." He glanced up. "And anyway, that helicopter is still on me."

"Okay, so make that your distraction."

"What?"

"Shoot out the helicopter's spotlight."

"You've lost your mind, you know that?"

There was a railroad crossing ahead. Gideon realized what Dean had planned. He looked up again and started channeling light into his left fist.

"There's a train coming in about ten seconds," Dean said. "Ready?"

"Ready."

"Now!"

Gideon fired his pent-up burst of energy at the copter. It missed, but it was close enough to cause the pilot to bank away, taking the spotlight off Gideon. He leapt from his bike and rolled onto the sidewalk. The bike kept going and crossed the train tracks. Gideon rushed into an alley and crouched down. The police followed the bike—but then the gates lowered. The cars and bikes pulled to a stop.

I can't believe that worked. Gideon went further into the alley, found a ladder, and climbed to the rooftops. He was about half a mile west of the Crusader's last known position. He had to get over there fast.

He hopped from building to building until he reached an intersection he couldn't cross. He clambered down a ladder into the streets and ran east toward Teller.

"Any news on the Crusader?" he asked.

"Nothing," Dean replied. "He's still out there somewhere; they haven't reported catching him."

"Good." Gideon crossed the street and scanned the rooftops and alleyways as he ran. "And what about the bike?"

"I parked it in an abandoned warehouse on the other side of the tracks. The cops have lost your trail. Hopefully."

"Thanks, man. I don't know what I'd do without you."

"You'd be sitting in a jail cell, brother, that's what."

Gideon chuckled. "Probably true."

He turned his attention to the streets again. He was passing an alley when a hand shot out and grabbed him by the shoulder. He spun, surprised, and raised one of his batons. The Crusader stood in the alley, hunched and ready to fight.

"Who are you?" the Crusader demanded.

"What?" Gideon frowned. Wyatt knew about his powers and that he was a vigilante. Surely, he would've recognized him. "You know me."

The Crusader pulled him into the alley and peered back out. A police car drove by ten seconds later. Gideon blew out a breath and nodded.

"Thank you."

"You didn't answer my question. Who are you?"

Gideon shook his head. "I don't understand. You know me, Wyatt."

The Crusader grabbed his mask and pulled it off. Gideon recognized him, but he wasn't Wyatt. His features were similar, but he was much younger—even younger than Gideon.

"I'm not Wyatt," the young man said. "I'm his son, Carter. Now, who are you?"

* * *

Monahan crouched on a rooftop and looked down into the alley. The Crusader stood behind a dumpster, speaking tensely with this new interloper—the Seraph, as the police were calling him. The Crusader pulled his mask off, revealing the face of a dark young man—probably no older than eighteen. It took a lot to surprise Monahan, but she had been expecting the Crusader to be . . . well, older. He fought with the experience of a seasoned warrior.

No matter. He was still the target. She hadn't wanted to fight him and the Seraph at the same time, but time was running out for her to fulfill her contract and kill the Crusader.

She balled her hands into fists to check her gauntlet blades. The blades snapped into position almost silently. Monahan connected a rappelling line to the edge of the rooftop and jumped. Her feet touched the ground and she disconnected herself from the line. Neither man had seen her yet. She crept toward them. If she could kill the Seraph before he even saw her, then the fight would be even easier.

But though she was completely silent, even her footsteps not making a sound, the Seraph's hooded head whipped toward her and he dropped into a fighting crouch.

"You!" he growled.

So he was the man she'd injured. "Time to finish the job."

"Crusader, run!"

He drew a pair of truncheons and leapt at her. Blades extended, she rushed forward to engage him.

CHAPTER 14

It had been a crazy night.

Jolie had been part of the task force assigned to hunt down the Crusader. They'd been at it for at least an hour already when the Seraph had appeared. At first, she'd wondered if it was Gideon, but when he'd fired a burst of golden-white light from his hands, she decided that wasn't possible. Gideon was just a good fighter. This Seraph was . . . something else.

Her part of the task force had been ordered to keep on the Crusader while others pursued the Seraph, but the distraction had allowed the Crusader to slip away. They had spent the next ten minutes trying to pick up his trail, but he had gone to ground. There was no sign of him. And then Sergeant Andrews had informed them that the Seraph had escaped, too.

"I'm getting too old for this," Paul said. "I mean, an actual superhero? Really?"

"That light had to have come from his suit, right? Like some crazy Iron Man tech?" Jolie asked. "I mean, what else could it have been?"

"I don't know, kid. Either way, it's beyond me. Hey, check in, will you?"

Jolie picked up the radio. "This is Officer Anderson. There's no sign of any activity out here."

"Ten-four, Anderson." The dispatcher paused. "Proceed to Fifth Street. There's been reports of a disturbance in an alleyway."

"Ten-four."

The radio crackled again. "Officer Anderson, this is Detective Pulaski. Officer Bates and I will back you up there."

"Thanks, Detective. See you there."

Paul spun the cruiser around and headed toward Fifth while Jolie checked her sidearm.

"Here we go," she said.

* * *

The woman stabbed her right forearm blade toward Gideon's throat. He blocked with his left baton and swung the right at her head. She jerked her head back to avoid the swing, disengaging their weapon lock. Gideon stepped forward and punched low. She scissor-blocked with her blades, and Gideon had to arc his swing so that she caught his baton instead of his arm—although he suspected his gauntlet would have taken the blow without harm.

With both her arms now low, he swung at her head again. She disengaged and moved to the side, but his truncheon caught her across the shoulder. He clicked the buttons on each baton, activating the stunners at the ends.

The woman smirked. "Nice toys."

Gideon nodded at her wrist blades. "I could say the same."

Then the two of them joined in a flurry of blows—punches, kicks, stabs, elbow strikes. Gideon was as impressed with her skills as he had been the first time they'd fought. She had some serious training, whoever she was.

He jabbed one of his batons low, under her guard. She stepped aside, and the sparking end of the truncheon just missed her ribs. She spun around his arm, came around at his side, and elbowed him in the side of the head. Gideon's ears rang, and he dropped to his knees. He had the presence of mind to somersault away from her and spin around into a crouch.

He was dizzy now. She strode toward him, a forearm blade raised for the killing blow. Gideon tensed, tried to clear his head, and prepared to move—

The woman grunted as an arm wrapped around her throat and jerked her backward. Gideon pulled himself to his feet. The Crusader—his son, anyway—held the woman in a chokehold and refused to let go. He was strong; Gideon gave him that much. The woman jabbed one of her blades backward at his head and he moved it aside.

"Let her go, Crusader! I've got this."

He wasn't about to let Carter get hurt fighting this woman. He might be strong, but she was way out of his league.

"No, it's okay. I—"

The woman collapsed her blades back into her sleeves, grabbed the arm around her throat, and lifted herself in the air. She brought her whole body back to the ground and used the leverage and force of the movement to hurl Carter over her head. He flipped and landed flat on his back.

"I said, I've got this," Gideon said.

He staggered forward, still light-headed from her elbow strike, and brandished his truncheons. She stepped forward—

Police sirens blared close by. The woman hesitated. Gideon took two quick steps in, jabbed the end of one baton into her gut, sending a jolt of electricity through her body, and shoved her to the ground. Then he turned and helped Carter to his feet.

"Let's move. Up the ladder. Go!"

* * *

Monahan convulsed as the electric current from the Seraph's weapon coursed through her body. She curled into a ball and tried to stop twitching. Whoever designed that baton had intended for it to be able to take down some big opponents—like maybe grizzly bears.

Footsteps sounded behind her. The police, no doubt. *Maybe I'll get lucky and it'll be Detective Walters.* She steadied her breathing. She didn't have much time to make her move.

"Got someone down!" a voice said. Male. Young. "Call an ambulance!"

He knelt next to her. She kept her eyes closed and began to form her left hand into a fist. She could bring her blade straight up into his body before he knew what was happening.

"Is it one of the vigilantes?" another voice asked. Another male, about the same age.

"No, a woman." Monahan heard the frown in his voice. "She's got some kind of tech on her arms."

Monahan clenched her fist and turned. She brought the blade straight up into his sternum, pushed his body up to shield her own, and rose to her feet.

"Bates!" The second officer raised his pistol. "Drop your weapons now!"

Two other officers appeared in the alleyway. An aging man and an all-too-familiar woman. The same cop who'd been pursuing her for weeks.

"That's Regina!"

"I'm afraid I can't stick around," Monahan said. "I still have a contract to fulfill."

She shoved the dead cop's body at the second cop, hooked herself to her rappel line, and reeled it in. The officers opened fire—too slow. Their shots hit the wall below Monahan, blowing chunks of bricks everywhere. She reached the rooftop, unhooked herself, and rushed off into the dark. The vigilantes didn't have too much of a head start on her. If she could locate their trail, then she could catch up and finish what she'd started.

* * *

Jolie rushed to Bates' side. Pulaski held his hands to the wound and tried to stanch the bleeding. Jolie knelt beside him and put a hand on his shoulder. Paul was behind them, yelling for an ambulance to get there now.

But it would be too late. Regina had placed her blade perfectly for maximum effectiveness—and maximum damage. Even if an ambulance arrived at that very moment, Bates wouldn't make it.

"Who was she?" Pulaski asked.

"We do not know her real name. But I've been looking for her for weeks; she is the woman you helped me track down at The Broken Glass."

"She's dead." Pulaski shook his head. "I'm going to kill her."

Jolie looked down at Bates. His eyes were glassed over, unseeing. She reached down and closed them. She took Pulaski's blood-soaked hands and brought them away from the wound.

"I'm sorry."

Pulaski groaned, pulled his hands away from hers, and wiped away tears. In the process, he smeared Bates' blood all over his face. He stood and stormed out of the alley. Jolie stood, too, tears welling in her eyes. *We're out here searching for vigilantes and the real monster is that woman.*

She'd pay. Jolie would make sure of it.

CHAPTER 15

"Are you stupid?"

Gideon slammed Carter against the wall of the boy's bedroom. He'd brought Carter from the alley to where the bike was hidden. They'd circled the Brooks for half an hour to ensure they'd lost the assassin. Finally, he'd taken the boy to his house, and the two of them had climbed up the outside of the building and into his room.

Gideon kept one fist tight around Carter's collar and used the other to pull the mask from the boy's pocket. He held it in front of Carter's face.

"Your dad goes out and gets himself shot, so you think it's a good idea to put on his mask and do the same?"

"I–I'm sorry. But look, someone had to do something. There was another guy out there for a while who was fighting crime while my dad was hurt, but then he disappeared too!"

"That was me. And I 'disappeared' because I got hurt, too! I wasn't going to give up."

"No one knew that." Carter pushed himself out of Gideon's grasp and took the mask back. "Look, the people here are tired of living under the mob's thumb. My dad was doing something about it, and then you were . . . so I figured I'd do the same. And I know how to fight!"

"You know a few tricks. That's different."

"I'm a champion high school wrestler two years running. I'm good. You can't deny me the right to protect my home."

"You're just a kid, Carter!"

"I am eighteen! And you don't look that old under that hood, anyway."

Gideon rolled his eyes, jerked his hood back, and pulled his mask down around his neck.

Carter blinked. "You're the guy from the church."

"Yeah, I am. Forget that for a minute. I may not be that much older than you, but I've gone through a lot more, kid. More than you better hope you ever have to go through in your whole life."

Carter sat down on his bed and removed his jacket and gloves. "What's that supposed to mean?"

Gideon shook his head. "Nothing. I can see I'm not going to convince you that you don't need to be doing this. But what is your dad going to think? He's going to see you on the news, you know—if he hasn't already. And he'll know it's you."

"Well, I . . . "

"Hadn't thought of that? Exactly. Carter, your dad is trying to protect you when he goes out there. Don't mess that up." He stepped toward the window. "How is your dad, anyway?"

"Getting better. Mom doesn't want him going back out, though."

"Not surprised. And how do you think she'll feel knowing you are doing it?" Gideon ducked out the window. "Think about what I've said, Carter. You've got your whole life ahead of you. Don't waste it."

He dropped to the ground and shook his head. He'd need to come back soon and talk to Wyatt. If there was a Crusader out there, Gideon needed to know about it. If it was Wyatt, that would be great. He'd been doing this for a long time, and once he'd recovered, he would be a good ally to have. But if it was going to be Carter, then Gideon's job had just gotten a whole lot harder, because now he'd have to protect him, too.

But for now, he needed rest. He put his hand to his ear. "Dean, I'm on my way back."

"Roger that." Dean blew out a breath. "Boy, you really gave it to that kid, huh?"

"You heard that?"

"Every word."

"And you disagree?"

"No, I don't. Kid needed to hear that. You're right. He was going to get himself killed."

"He still might." Gideon mounted his bike. "I need to find out who that woman was, what she wants, and who she's working for."

"Already on it. I installed a micro-cam in the lining of your cape's clasp. It should've gotten at least a glimpse of her face. I'll start running it through facial rec and see what we turn up."

"Good." Gideon pulled into an alley, removed his cape and mask, put them in a bag on the side of the bike, and put on a motorcycle helmet. "I'd say that overall, the Seraph's first outing was at least a partial success."

"Agreed. You saved the Crusader and that is what you went out to do."

Gideon pulled out of the alley. "Now let's see if we can actually clean up the Brooks a bit. I'll see you soon."

"See you soon."

Last year

Gideon paced around the cage. He was going crazy in here with nothing to do and no chance of escape. Knowing that at some point, they'd come and drag him into that building for some unknown reason made it even worse. He felt like he was on death row, waiting for someone to take him to his execution.

"You know, that doesn't do any good. Pacing, I mean."

Gideon sighed. "I know, but I can't just sit."

"Why not?"

"I—" He didn't have a good answer to that. He both appreciated and hated how calm Joshua was all the time. It was reassuring and maddening.

"Sit." Joshua smiled. "We can always pass the time by getting to know each other."

"Do you really want to do that, knowing that I'll probably be gone for good soon?"

"Might as well. I'll be losing you anyway so at least I could be satisfied in knowing that I will remember you as a person, and not as a mystery."

Gideon frowned. That was a unique way to look at it. He sat down across from Joshua and crossed his legs.

"What do you want to know?"

"I'll start, give you some time to think." Joshua put his hands behind his head and leaned against the cage. "I was in Venezuela for a jungle excursion. I've always been an adventurer. I've been to almost a dozen countries for no reason other than to explore their wildernesses. My closest relatives are my grown son, Mike, and his wife, Rebecca, and their son, Patrick. He's an adult by now. At least, in my culture. And my wife passed away a few years ago."

"I'm sorry to hear that. You mentioned your culture. Where are you from?"

"Israel."

"Ah." That would put his grandson in his mid-to-late teenage years. Joshua didn't offer more than that, though. After a short silence, Gideon spoke. "My parents are still alive . . . Matthew and Tasha. I have a brother, Wes, and I'm not married, but I am going to propose to my girlfriend, Jolie, when I get back. I'm a doctor . . . I was here on a medical mission trip."

Joshua looked up. "Someone's coming."

Gideon turned. It took a moment before he heard footsteps crunching on the forest floor. Two guerrillas walked up to the cage, and one of them pointed at Gideon.

"Up."

Guess it's time. Gideon sighed and hoped that he made it back, like Joshua did, and didn't disappear like the others he'd mentioned. Whatever the case, he was about to get a lot more familiar with whatever was in that lab.

Now

Gideon walked into the lair and draped his cape and mask over the mannequin that held his suit. Dean was still at the computer, watching faces scroll across the screen as their system tried to identify the woman. He looked up at Gideon.

"Bad news."

"What's that?"

"She killed a cop after you left the alley."

"Oh, no." Gideon sighed. "We've got to stop her, Dean."

"You won't get any argument from me. But she doesn't seem like the type who'd be working alone, you know? More like a gun-for-hire. So like you said earlier, who is she working for?"

"That's the question."

Gideon began pulling off his suit and placing it on the mannequin. He wondered if he should try to call Jolie. No doubt she would be feeling the death of that cop. But would that be a good idea? She might be suspicious of how he'd heard about it. Maybe he should wait until tomorrow. The department would probably release a press statement by then.

He finished removing the suit. Clad in a pair of black sweats and a tank top, he walked over to Dean's side.

"Anything?"

"Not yet. She's not in any American criminal databases so far."

"Try widening the search to international." Gideon scratched his beard. "Signs are pointing to a foreign cartel moving into the Brooks, according to Jolie. This woman might be working for them, and if she is, she might be foreign, too."

"Good thinking. I'll get on it." Dean typed in a few commands and looked up at Gideon. "You should get some rest, dude. You look exhausted."

"Yeah." Gideon backed toward the door. "I think I'll do that. See you at work tomorrow."

"Night, buddy. Good work out there."

"Thanks. Good night."

Gideon walked down the hall to his room and flopped down on his bed. Foreign cartels, mysterious women with knives killing cops, teenagers dressing as vigilantes, his own superpowers . . . how was it possible that captivity in Venezuela had actually been simpler than this?

* * *

The next day was one of the worst Jolie could remember. Everyone at the precinct was despondent over Bates' death, and a sense of gloom and fear hung in the air. They had all felt inefficient and outnumbered. Now, one of their own was dead and they felt hopeless. That it was Bates who'd died made it worse; the absence of his jovial spirit was like a sucking wound. They were waiting for the last blow to fall.

Jolie ducked between officers talking in hushed tones and made her way toward Pulaski's desk. The detective was heartbroken. Bates had been his partner since he'd joined the force, and the two had been best friends. Jolie wouldn't have blamed him for taking the day off. Yet here he was, working as diligently as ever.

"Find anything?"

He looked up. "Actually, yeah. I took the dash cam footage of the alley from our cars and plugged the woman's face into our facial recognition system. It took a while, but I got a hit."

Finally. "Okay, who is she?"

"She's a foreigner, an assassin from Ireland named Katrina Monahan."

"Ireland?"

"Yeah. She's a freelancer, sells her services to the highest bidder—internationally."

"So she's working for someone here in Sojourn City."

"That's right."

"We need to find out who." Jolie tapped her foot on the floor, thinking. "If she's worked all around the world, maybe the head of the mob here is connected to her. We've suspected for a while that the mob's got overseas connections. Maybe if we find the connection between her and the mob, we find out who's running things, and we can finally make some headway in cleaning up the Brooks."

Pulaski looked back at his computer. "I'll dig into her past accomplices and see if any of them look good for the activity in the Brooks."

"Thanks." Jolie put a hand on his shoulder. "How are you holding up?"

He didn't even look at her. "Best I can, Jolie. Long as I keep my mind on the job, I can keep functioning."

"All right. Well, I'm going to get out on patrol. Let me know if you find anything, or if you need anything."

"Will do. Thanks."

* * *

Gideon had just started running a test on some blood samples he'd been assigned when Edgar Sterling entered the lab and approached Dr. Sung, Gideon's supervisor. Sung and Sterling exchanged a few whispers and then walked in Gideon's direction. Gideon gave the samples a last look before turning his attention to the two men.

"Dr. Sung, Mr. Sterling. Pleasure to see you both."

"And you, Gideon." Edgar extended a hand, and Gideon shook it. "I was just talking to Dr. Sung and he told me that you would be ideally suited to a project that I need handled."

"I'll be happy to help however I can, sir. I'm just running these tests now—"

"Of course. Those can be reassigned. This takes precedence." Sterling held out a folder to Gideon. "It's a serum that Sterling

Enterprises has been working on for some time, but now it has become top priority."

"What is it?"

"It would enhance the senses and abilities of the user. The near-crisis situation in the Brooks leads me to believe that this may be necessary sooner than later."

Gideon frowned and took the folder. "A super-soldier serum? Couldn't that be dangerous?"

"It could, but it seems to be the only option." Sterling shrugged. "Have you seen the news? Assassins, vigilantes, and superhumans running around, causing chaos. It seems like a movie, but it's real life. That means we have to adapt."

"Okay . . . " Gideon opened the folder. "I'll see what I can do."

"Thank you. As always, your contributions are most appreciated, Gideon."

Sung gave Gideon a stern nod. Then he and Sterling turned and walked away. Gideon sat at his desk, put the folder in front of him, and sighed. Well, this had just made both his jobs a *whole* lot more interesting.

CHAPTER 16

The streets of the Brooks had been relatively peaceful lately, compared to how they'd been for the last year. Ever since the local news had broadcast the footage of "the Seraph" shooting light out of his hands, leading the cops on a wild goose chase, and then disappearing, the citizens of the Brooks had started to feel safer.

Serban didn't like it. He had worked very hard to maintain an aura of fear and menace in this neighborhood, and now it was all coming down thanks to some guy in a blue cape.

He was about done with Monahan. It was the day before New Year's Eve, and she still hadn't killed either the Crusader or the Seraph. What kind of assassin couldn't even kill their target?

Serban strode down the street feeling the crisp, winter afternoon breeze. It reminded him of home, and he smiled a little. Back home, he wasn't the top dog, but people respected him. Here, only his men knew who he was. Some of the other gangs had made deals with Serban's mob, but they hadn't interacted with him face-to-face. Maybe it was time to change that.

After all, it was almost the new year. Resolutions had to be made.

It had taken entirely too long for him to attain his status in Romania. From the ground up, tooth and nail, he had struggled just to get the scraps from the bosses' table. Born a gypsy and thus considered less than nothing by most Romanians, he'd had to prove himself through countless tests to even get in the mob in the first place. He was proud that he'd attained such a high standing. But he'd never have made it to the very top, because the bosses, at least, still viewed him as just a gypsy.

No matter. Here in America, here in Sojourn City, he could be whoever he wanted to be. And he wanted to be in charge.

He turned the corner and bumped shoulders with a woman. She apologized under her breath and kept walking. Serban turned to watch her. There had been something familiar about her . . .

The cop. The lady who'd been searching for Monahan. He clenched his jaw and reached into the inner pocket of his overcoat for his gun.

No. It was still daylight and there were too many pedestrians around. Killing her now would expose him in a way that he wasn't ready for yet. He wanted the city to fear him but putting himself at the top of the cops' most wanted list by publicly killing one of their own—especially so soon after Monahan had killed one—would be the wrong move.

He removed his hand from his coat and walked on, forgetting the woman for now. He had a meeting to get to. It was time to consolidate the gangs of this city under one rule. His. Once that was done, they could branch out from the Brooks and take whatever they wanted—just like his benefactor wanted.

Well. Maybe not just like. Whatever the rich man had planned for the city, once the other one percenters had been put in their place didn't matter. He would play along with his benefactor as long as it suited Serban's purposes. When that moment came, one more rich boy would get his, and Serban would take over from there.

Then his name would be known, and the city of Sojourn would bow to Luca Serban. Then he would be somebody.

Monahan strode out of an alley as Serban passed it, and she fell into step beside him. She had pulled blonde hair tightly into a bun and hidden as much as possible in her red scarf and hat.

"You've got one day left," Serban said. "After that, the contract goes to everyone. First person to gut the vigilantes gets the payday."

"I know." She did not sound concerned. "I've seen the Crusader's face. I will find him, and I will kill him."

"You'd better." Serban stopped in his tracks and faced her. "Everything is riding on this. The vigilantes are the only real threat to my plan. They die, and we're set. Don't mess this up, Monahan."

She nodded. "It will be done."

Serban continued walking. Monahan disappeared back into the shadows. Serban whistled to himself. Soon, everything he deserved would be his at last.

* * *

Dean scrolled through all the information he'd just downloaded on Katrina Monahan. When he'd returned from the labs, the smart table had been waiting on him, proudly displaying her identity. He quickly dug up all he could on her so that it would be ready for Gideon when he arrived.

This woman was all kinds of scary. A skilled assassin and had worked for the worst of the worst all over the world—the Russian mob, IRA, the Chinese triads . . . her rap sheet just went on and on. The worst part was, she'd been identified, but never caught. She seemed to want people to know who she was, what she did, and that she could get away with it.

Well, not for much longer. The Seraph was about to rain some fire down on this woman's head.

Dean wished he had superpowers or wicked fighting skills. Sure, Gideon had been teaching him a few things, but mainly as a precaution, not with the intention that Dean would eventually join him in the field. Oh, well. The door to the lair slid open and Gideon walked in. Dean quickly compiled all the information on Monahan into a single file and highlighted it.

"Good news," he said.

"You've got our woman?"

"I do. Told you I would."

"Never doubted you for a second." Gideon dropped into a chair across the table from Dean. "So, who is she?"

"Her name's Katrina Monahan. They call her Lancet." Dean swiped the computer screen, and all her info came up. "This is all we have on her—all anybody has on her."

Dean watched as Gideon perused the file. Monahan's weapons of choice, her tactics . . . there wasn't much to it, but everything that any law enforcement agency across the globe had, Dean had put together.

"She's something, isn't she?" Gideon shook his head. "It's a miracle I'm not dead. Or Carter, for that matter. Even Jolie."

"Divine intervention, my friend. God wants you to get this girl."

"Well, the cops definitely aren't suited for it, and Carter or even Wyatt aren't skilled enough for it either." Gideon stood. "Looks like it's my job."

"Check her known associates. I didn't recognize any names, but I thought you might. You frequent the Brooks more than I do."

"Hmm . . ." Gideon looked over the list. "No. But we need to figure out who she is working for. Because once we do, we'll know the source of a lot of the trouble in the Brooks. She targeted the Crusader and I specifically; that means someone there wants us out of the way."

"I'll look over the list again and run facial rec with street footage from the Brooks. If anyone turns up, I'll let you know. Oh, and I've got a new toy for you."

"What's that?"

Dean handed Gideon a small bead. "It's a listening device with a GPS tracker in it. Once you find Monahan or someone involved with her, you can plant it on them, and we can follow them and hear their conversations."

"Thanks." Gideon took his jacket and outer shirt off and looked at the Seraph suit. "I guess it's time to get back out there."

* * *

The first time Gideon had encountered Monahan had been outside The Broken Glass, when she'd been attacking Jolie. He didn't know if that was one of her regular haunts or not, but it didn't hurt to check. If she wasn't here, maybe one of her contacts was. He knelt on the edge of a rooftop across the street and watched the door to the bar.

People came and went, but none of them looked any more suspicious than the others. Their manner of dress was like a lot of the criminals around here, which made things problematic for Gideon. Likely for the police, too.

"Thank you."

Gideon spun around and raised a light-encased fist.

"Easy." It was the Crusader—the real one. "I just wanted to say thank you for saving my son's life."

"You're welcome." Gideon lowered his hand, let the light dissipate. "You're back in the field. Your family know?"

Wyatt nodded. "They're not happy about it, especially my wife, but she'd rather have me out here than Carter. And we both know the only way I can stop him from doing this himself is if I'm doing it."

"I am sorry. You know, neither of you need to. I can do this job myself."

"Sure, but you're out here for the same reason I am: one man can't protect a whole city alone. And fancy superpowers or not, you're just one man."

"Fair enough." Gideon stepped toward Wyatt. "I've discovered the identity of the woman who attacked Carter and I last night. She's an assassin."

"Scary stuff." Wyatt pointed at the bar. "That her watering hole?"

"Hers or someone she works with." Gideon glanced back at The Broken Glass. "You know anything about that place?"

Wyatt chuckled. "I don't frequent it, no. But I've heard from folks on the street that foreigners hang out there."

"Foreigners? Interesting."

"You know, we get out of these suits and we could go down there and do a little recon."

Gideon chuckled. "I'm pretty sure they'd make me as soon as I walked in. I don't belong in the Brooks; I mean, you noticed pretty much as soon as we met, too."

"True. But what's it hurt to try?"

"Fair enough. I—"

Gideon paused as three men exited the Broken Glass. All three were dressed in leather jackets over button-up shirts and skinny ties, just like the four men who had attacked Wes at the church. They had to be part of the same organization.

"We may not have to go in at all. Look at them."

"Now that's interesting," Wyatt said. "I thought the attack on your church was just gang scare tactics. Why would the mob have been involved?"

"Let's find out."

The two vigilantes climbed down a fire escape and snuck out into the street. The three mobsters were headed toward a black SUV. Gideon held out his hand and fired a burst of light that hit the vehicle in the grill. The SUV rocked, and the criminals shouted and jumped back, reaching for their weapons.

Gideon crossed the street toward them, hand outstretched and glowing. This was risky; if they fired, he was exposed and would likely get hit. He'd just have to trust Dean's assessment of his suit's durability.

"Who are you working for?"

They opened fire. The first few shots went wide, but two came closer and grazed across Gideon's shoulder. They barely scratched the armor. Gideon kept moving forward. He clenched his fist, pulled his arm back, and shoved it forward. A ball of light shot from his hand and struck the center mobster in the chest. The man flew back, struck the building behind him, and sank to the ground.

The other two looked down at their companion for a moment. The distraction was enough for Gideon to rush in. The Crusader, who'd been circling around, came in behind one of them, got him in a choke-hold, and kicked his knee out. The off-balance criminal cried out and tried to free himself from Wyatt's grasp, but had no leverage to work with. Gideon closed in on the third and swung his still-glowing fist into the man's jaw, splaying him out on the sidewalk.

The Crusader tightened his grip on his captive's throat. "Now. You'll talk to us."

The man he was holding panted and shook his head. "I can't."

"You will!" Gideon pointed his glowing hand at the mobster. "You know what we can do."

"I–I know you don't kill." The man's words carried a thick accent. "And that's what the boss will do to me if I talk. Do what you want; I'm not saying nothing."

"We'll see." Gideon grabbed the man and jerked him from the Crusader's grip. "Who are you working for?"

Fear rushed through him. His life was over either way now. He'd either get thrown in jail or, if he talked, taken out. Gideon probed the man's emotions to see if he could get anything else. *All his pride deflated as he realized he wasn't going to get to take part in something big.*

"You're planning something." Gideon shoved the man back into a streetlight. "Your mob has big plans." Gideon brought his face close to the mobster's. "You know, light means heat. All I have to do is intensify the amount of light I'm producing right now, and you'll start to get very warm."

"Seraph, they're waking up." Wyatt punched out the other two mobsters again. "And someone will have heard the gunshots. We need to hurry."

"I ain't talking." The mobster was sweating now. "But it don't matter anyway. Lancet said she knows your identity—" He nodded at the Crusader, "—so you're as good as dead."

Gideon punched the man out and tossed him on the ground beside his comrades. He turned and looked at Wyatt.

"She knows your identity?"

"How could she? Tonight's the first night I've been out since—"

"Oh, no." When she'd fought Gideon and Carter in the alley . . . "Before Monahan engaged Carter and I, he had his mask off. He pulled it on when she dropped into the alley, but if she was watching us before that . . . "

"Carter." Wyatt looked around frantically. "I've got to get home now."

Gideon tapped his earbud. "Dean. Bike, now." Seconds later, the motorcycle had pulled up next to them. "Go. I'll catch up however I can."

"Thank you." The Crusader hopped on the bike and peeled off.

"Dean, alert the police, somehow, to get to Wyatt's house now." Gideon knelt next to the three mobsters and searched their pockets for the SUV's key. He found it and as he stood, he tucked the bug Dean had given him inside the man's jacket pocket. Then he ran to the driver's side door. "And activate the bug."

"On it."

Gideon swung the SUV around and followed Wyatt. He just hoped they weren't too late.

CHAPTER 17

The night had been relatively low on activity. Maybe it was because of all the chaos the night before, and every criminal was scared to step onto the streets now that the Seraph and the Crusader were back, or maybe it was because a cop had died, and they all knew that every other officer would be on mission. Jolie didn't know the exact reason, but there was a definite lull.

Not that she was complaining. She was exhausted, and she really wanted to go home and crawl into bed. But she still had an hour left on her shift. As Paul drove their cruiser down the streets, she kept her eyes peeled for activity.

The radio squawked. "Officer Anderson, 10-71 at 52 Templeton Street."

Jolie picked up the radio. "10-4. We are 10-49 to 52 Templeton."

Jolie put down the radio and flicked on the lights and sirens as Paul drove them toward Templeton. 10-71—a shooting. Just another night in the Brooks.

They arrived at 52 Templeton in less than ten minutes. It was a small, two-story house. Everything seemed quiet. All the interior lights were off—which made sense, at this hour. A chain-link fence surrounded the front yard—common in the Brooks—but the gate was open. Jolie exchanged glances with Paul, and then the two of them exited the cruiser together.

As they approached, several lights flashed inside. Not artificial lights—bright bursts of pure, golden light. Jolie reached for her sidearm and saw Paul doing the same.

The front window crashed open and a body came flying out, hit a pillar on the porch, and tumbled down the stairs into the front yard. A moment later, a blue-and-gold clad figure leapt out the window, his fists encased in spheres of pulsing light.

Jolie stormed forward, gun trained on the Seraph. "Freeze!"

The body on the ground rolled into a crouch. It was a woman—*Monahan*! Jolie swiveled her gun from the Seraph to Monahan.

"Don't move. Hands in the air. Now!"

Monahan had already leapt at the Seraph. The two tangled in a flurry of blows. The Seraph swung a glowing fist at Monahan's head, and she ducked and retaliated with a punch to the ribs. The Seraph flinched, but his gear seemed to be armored; he recovered quickly and attacked with a kick-punch-kick combo. Monahan blocked the first kick with a forearm, took the punch to the jaw, and rolled with the second kick.

The Seraph pressed in, not letting Monahan get her guard up again. They were too close together for Jolie to get a clean shot. She nodded at Paul and the two of them closed in on the combatants.

A third figure emerged from the house—the Crusader. Jolie thought there were several others moving around inside. The residents, no doubt. She kept her attention focused on Monahan, though. The woman ejected a small blade from her left gauntlet and jabbed it at the Seraph. It glanced off his armor, but Monahan followed it up by hooking her leg behind his left ankle and taking his leg out.

Now she was standing on her own, and Jolie took the opportunity to take control of the situation.

"Monahan, freeze! Drop the knife or I'll shoot!"

"You shouldn't have come here."

Jolie frowned and stepped toward her. Suddenly, Monahan spun and fired the knife from her gauntlet. Jolie stepped back and then a body slammed into her, jarring her aside. She hit the ground, rolled, and brought her gun back up. Monahan was running. Jolie opened fire as Monahan reached the chain-link fence, climbed it, and vaulted over. None of her shots found their mark.

She considered pursuing. This woman had escaped her too many times already; she couldn't get away again. But . . .

Jolie glanced down to see who had knocked her out of the knife's path. It was Paul, and the knife was sticking out of his shoulder.

"You all right?" she asked.

Paul grimaced, but nodded. "I've had worse."

Jolie looked up. Both vigilantes were gone. She turned to see if Monahan was still there and realized the Seraph had taken off after her. She could see his blue cape trailing him on the other side of the fence.

"I hate my job."

* * *

Gideon jumped and tackled Monahan. He landed on top of her in the middle of the street and wrapped his arms tightly around hers, pinning them to her side. He stood and dragged her to her feet. She struggled against his grip and jerked her head backward, trying to headbutt him. He kept his head back out of her reach.

"Stop struggling before I break a bone," he growled. "Tell me who you work for!"

She did stop struggling—but then a sharp pain jabbed into Gideon's ankle. He cried out and looked down. A blade had ejected from the heel of her boot, and she'd driven it into the joint gap in his armor. She took advantage of his surprise, pushed her arms out, spun, and punched him in the jaw. Gideon stumbled back and held up a hand. She advanced, ejecting her remaining forearm blade and swinging it at him.

He ducked under the blade and punched her in the ribs. As she stepped back, he spun inside her guard, grabbed her arm, and threw her over his shoulder to land flat on her back. He was angry now; the pain in his foot flooded his body with rage and he struggled to keep it down. Fighting angry was never good, and that went double for using his powers. He had to keep them under control, or he could easily kill her without meaning to.

She stabbed upward at his face and he tilted his head aside. The blade slashed a thin furrow in his hood. He punched down, his fist glowing, but she rolled aside, and his light-energized fist hit the pavement and left a crack in it.

I didn't know I could do that. A punch like that could've shattered her skull. He lessened the intensity of the energy swirling around his hands and reached for her, but she kept rolling and came up in a crouch a few feet away. Gideon pulled his truncheons from his belt, dropped into a fighting stance, and waited for her to move.

"You must die tonight," she said.

"That isn't going to happen. Just surrender. You know you can't beat me."

"Can't I?"

Monahan leapt at him and extended her forearm blade. It shot out from her gauntlet and hit Gideon's chest plate—it left a gash, but didn't puncture the suit, let alone break skin. The blade clattered to the ground. Gideon stormed toward her and swung his batons. Monahan spun inside his guard and jabbed her elbow at his jaw. Gideon brought his arm up to push the blow aside.

The frustration was evident on her face and in Gideon's perception of her emotions; she wasn't used to fighting someone who could match her. He could use that.

But before he had time to wear her down, she pulled a canister from her belt and threw it to the ground. Smoke exploded everywhere. Gideon held out his hands and cast as much light as he could, but he couldn't see her. The smoke was too dense for the light to penetrate. He lowered his hands, sheathed his truncheons, and shook his head. She was gone.

* * *

An hour later, dressed in plainclothes, Gideon returned to Wyatt's house. They had arrived just in time to stop Monahan from killing Carter; she'd been climbing in his window as they had shown up. Wyatt had jumped on her just in time to shift her aim, so her bullet had struck the wall instead of his son. After the fight had moved outside and the police had shown up, Wyatt had snuck back inside the house and changed out of the Crusader outfit.

Gideon, hands stuffed in his pockets, strode up the front steps, limping a bit with each one. The police had gone; no doubt they'd taken the Jonson family's report and headed back to the station. Gideon hoped Jolie's partner was okay. Of all the officers to show up . . . of course it had been her.

He knocked on the door. A moment later, Wyatt's wife, Joanna, opened it. She smiled and gestured for him to enter.

"If it isn't the boy from church." She hugged him. "Thank you for saving my son's life. And my husband's, too, if you're the man who mended his gunshot wound."

"You're welcome." It was the first time he could remember being thanked for what he was doing. "Are you all doing okay?"

"We are. We're just packing our things now. Considering our front window is busted out, I don't think staying here is the best idea anymore."

"I guess not." Gideon laughed politely. "Can I speak to Carter?"

"Yes. He's in his room now."

"Thank you."

"No, son. Thank you. We can never repay what you've done."

Gideon walked upstairs to Carter's room, passing the boy's two younger siblings on the way. The young man was packing clothes into his backpack. He looked up as Gideon entered, and he smiled a little.

"Thank you for saving my life." He zipped up his backpack. "You were right. It was dumb of me to try to be like my dad."

"No, it wasn't." Gideon sat down on Carter's bed. "It was brave. But now you know the risks he takes. I hope you'll leave the crimefighting to us now."

"I will. As long as you and my dad are out there, I know the streets will be safe."

"I hope so." Gideon reached into his pocket and pulled out Monahan's blade. "This is one of her weapons. She shot it at me during the fight. You should keep it."

"Really?" Carter took the blade. "Thank you."

"Let it be a reminder of what almost happened—what could still happen, if you're not careful. And you may want to keep is around as a precaution, too."

"I will. Thank you again."

Gideon stood and started to walk out. He grimaced as he put pressure on his left foot. Carter noticed and put a hand on his shoulder.

"You okay?"

"Yeah. She just . . . cut my ankle a bit. It'll heal."

"Okay. You be careful out there, too."

"I will."

Gideon walked back down the stairs, leaning on the rail for support. In the living room, Wyatt was sitting on the couch, waiting for him. He had changed out of his black leather and into dark blue jeans, a gray t-shirt, and a red and black flannel jacket.

"It's a good thing you were there, kid." Wyatt laughed and stood up. "I'm glad you're doing this."

Gideon shook Wyatt's hand. "Where will you go?"

"We'll stay in a hotel outside the Brooks. I've saved enough at my job to afford it now."

"Good. If you're outside the Brooks, there's less chance that she'll follow you."

"That's what I'm hoping." Wyatt sighed. "Guess I'm hanging the hood up again for a little bit. Too bad; I just got back out there."

"Don't worry. I'll keep a watch on the city in your place. And as soon as I need help, I know who to call."

"Yes, you do. Take care, Seraph."

"You, too, Crusader."

CHAPTER 18

The Turners' New Year's Eve party was a well-known and loved tradition among the staff of Refuge Church. Gideon could remember the annual celebration going back to when he had been a child. It was one of his favorite events of the year, and of course, he'd missed last year's since he had been in captivity. Even better, Pastor Jeff was going to be at the party. Busy as he'd been with Seraph business, it would be the first time Gideon had seen him since he'd awakened from his coma.

Tonight, everything melted away—concerns about the Brooks, Monahan, Wyatt, being the Seraph, everything—as he dressed for the party. Clad in black jeans and boots, a red button-up shirt, and a black denim jacket, he walked down to the living room where Dean and Jolie were waiting for him, very careful with each step to hide his limp.

"Ready to go?" he asked.

"Yep!" Jolie said.

Dean chopped his head in a nod. "Always."

Jolie wore a dark blue dress with her brown leather jacket over it. Gideon took her hand and walked toward the door. Dean followed and locked the door behind them.

Jolie squeezed his hand. "I'm so glad I get the night off. You have no idea how stressful this past week has been."

"Really?" The three friends entered the elevator. "Have things been that bad?"

"Do you watch the news? Well, my friend Pulaski lost his partner two nights ago, and then last night there was this crazy battle between the vigilantes and the same person who killed Pulaski's partner. And my partner, Paul, was stabbed in the arm."

"Wow. Sounds nuts."

Dean side-eyed Gideon. Was he picking up on the same thing? Jolie didn't seem to believe Gideon was one of the vigilantes anymore. Gideon wasn't complaining.

The elevator reached the ground floor and the three of them walked to the apartment's parking garage and climbed into Gideon's Mustang.

"This feels like old times," Dean said. "The three of us going to stuff together . . . me being the third wheel . . . "

"Yeah, when are you going to get a girl, Dean?" Jolie asked.

Gideon looked at his friend in the rearview mirror just as Dean rolled his eyes. "Your guess is as good as mine, Jolie."

He pulled up to his parents' house and parked on the curb. They were about half an hour early, but Gideon had wanted to be so that they could help with any setup that might not be done yet.

Dad greeted them at the door with a big smile and hug. The family Christmas tree was still up—Gideon's mom liked to keep it there until the first of the new year. There was a fire crackling in the fireplace, and mellow music played softly from the TV speakers.

"Anything we can do to help, Dad?" Gideon asked.

"Oh, I don't think so. Your mother's just finishing up the snack platters."

"Where's Wes?"

"Right here!" Wes appeared from the kitchen, balancing a tray of cookies on his fingertips. "Hey, guys."

"Don't you dare drop those cookies," Dean said. "They're the only reason I come to this party."

Gideon—and everyone else in the room—turned to look at him. He grinned sheepishly and scratched the back of his head.

"Kidding."

"Uh-huh." Dad chuckled. "Well, take a seat! All of you. Our guests should be arriving soon."

* * *

Inside the warehouse that had been repurposed as the mob's center of arms distribution, Serban paced between his men as they unloaded rifles and ammo from the crates they'd just received. It was almost the new year, and they were preparing for the big move. Their time had come.

He swiveled to face Monahan, who stood across the room, examining a crate of AK-47s. She looked up at him, made brief eye contact, and looked away again. Ashamed, as she should be. She'd had multiple chances to take out the vigilantes and had failed every time she'd engaged them.

Serban walked over to her. She stiffened as he approached, put the AK-47 back in the crate, and faced him. Serban eyed the weapons.

"Time's up. Contract is free for all."

"Not yet. I still have two hours."

"Don't bother. You failed. You had your chance. How you managed to fight these guys three times and not even kill one of them, I don't know. What I do know is that you're not cut out for the job. I need you here tonight."

"You know my reputation. I am cut out for it."

Serban shrugged. "If you aren't, somebody else will be. It doesn't matter anymore." He waved his arm, gesturing at the room around them. "With this kind of armament, even the Seraph can't stop all of us. It's time for us to rise."

"Just keep your focus on the city. I'll deal with the vigilantes."

"You've got to earn trust to receive it." Serban walked away from her. "You haven't. You're staying here."

* * *

Although confined to a wheelchair, Pastor Jeff's spirits were as high as Gideon had ever seen them. He had every right to be joyful—he should've died. Gideon, Jolie, and Dean gathered around their former youth pastor and caught him up on everything he'd missed since he'd been in a coma. Being there, with him, seeing him all right, melted away some of Gideon's anger.

"So, Matthew, what's your opinion on the vigilantes?"

Gideon perked up at the question. His father was behind him, speaking with a deacon.

"So was it difficult transitioning back to civilization, Gideon?" Pastor Jeff asked.

Gideon's attention snapped back to his friends. "Not too bad. It was . . . nice, honestly. After living in a cage in the jungle for a year, I saw all the amenities and luxuries we have here in a new light."

"I'd imagine. You know . . . "

Gideon's father said, "Personally, I prefer for the law to be enforced by the police. But I can't argue with the vigilantes' results."

"So you're saying you approve of them?"

Gideon shifted his attention back to the man in front of him as he finished, " . . . and we all take what we have for granted."

"Yes, I agree." Gideon smiled. "Please, excuse me."

He walked to the small table where refreshments were set up, grabbed a couple cookies and a cup of punch. This was a little closer to his father's conversation.

"Regardless of their intention, the vigilantes are breaking the law," Lou said.

"Sure, but what's more important? Law or morality?"

"Well, morality of course, but . . . "

Jolie reached out and looped her arm around Gideon. "Hey, babe. Something on your mind?"

"Oh." Gideon chuckled. "No, I was just . . . well, I was kind of eavesdropping on Dad's conversation."

"Typical pastor's kid." Dean shook his head.

Gideon followed them back to Pastor Jeff. "Says the deacon's kid."

"Whatever."

"Hey, where is your dad? I thought he was supposed to be here tonight."

"He is—ah, there he is."

Edgar walked out of the kitchen with two other church officers. As the three of them entered the living room, Dad turned to look at Edgar.

"Tell me, Edgar, what do you think of the vigilantes? Lou here thinks they should be locked up."

"I agree, they should." Edgar shrugged. "But at the same time, they shouldn't."

Now that he had an excuse to listen to the conversation, Gideon turned fully to face them. Dean and Jolie did, too, and Gideon noticed Jolie give him a look. *Whoops.* He'd just told her he was listening to his father's conversation, and now she knew he'd been talking about vigilantes.

"Care to elaborate?" Jolie asked.

"Oh, no offense, of course, Ms. Anderson. I know you and the other officers are doing the best they can, under the circumstances . . . "

"But not well enough."

Gideon cringed. Well, this was going to get ugly. He could see by the way his father pinched the bridge of his nose that the elder Turner felt the same way. He had tried to steer the conversation away from the subject, after all. But it was too late now.

"It's not your fault, my dear. The truth is, the higher-ups in the police force and in fact in the city government are too blind to the needs of the denizens of the Brooks. They only care for those with a great deal of money."

Jolie nodded. "I'm with you there."

"The Brooks have been abandoned, left to be patrolled by a handful of officers that cannot handle the level of crime they are facing. The police chief, the mayor . . . they should be sending reinforcements. But they have instead pulled back to protect us, when we live in the safest part of the city."

Dad pursed his lips. "So, then, you think the vigilantes are the answer to that?"

"I suppose so. If the government won't protect the people . . . well, then, the people must protect the people."

Jolie fidgeted, and Gideon patted her shoulder. He could tell she wasn't sure how to feel, even without his powers. But with them . . .

Confusion, her confidence that she was right wavering.

"Well said, Dad." Dean smiled.

Edgar's passionate opinion about the Brooks explained why he wanted a super-soldier serum. It could allow anyone to protect the Brooks. It also explained why he'd helped Wyatt and his family by giving them money and him a job.

Dean tapped Gideon on the shoulder. "Hey, come here a sec."

Gideon excused himself, leaving Jolie to talk with Pastor Jeff, and followed Dean to the upstairs balcony.

"The guy you bugged has found his home." Dean held up his phone, which displayed GPS coordinates. "It's a warehouse in the Brooks. And I've been listening to the conversation in my earbuds. Some of it's foreign; I'll have to figure out what language and what they're saying back in the lair. But what they're saying in English sounds like they're getting ready to make a move."

That was the impression Gideon had gotten from the man he'd interrogated and bugged, too—something big was looming.

"New year, new goals?"

"Maybe so." Dean shrugged. "Either way, we know their home base. The Seraph could hit them anytime he wanted."

Gideon nodded. "New year . . . new goals."

They went back downstairs and spent the rest of the evening enjoying their family and friends. At midnight, they prayed in the new year, spent a few minutes celebrating, and then one by one people began to trickle out.

"Good night, Mom, Dad." Gideon hugged each of them. "I had a great time. I missed this."

"We missed having you." Mom smiled. "Love you."

"Love you, too."

He, Jolie, and Dean headed back out and drove back to the apartment. Gideon was exhausted, but a part of him felt energized. They had a lead on where the center of the mob could be located. If it panned out, maybe he wouldn't have to be the Seraph forever. Maybe he could clean the Brooks up and be done.

Maybe he could have a normal life again.

CHAPTER 19

Gideon parked his bike in an alley two blocks down from the warehouse. It had been three days since they'd discovered the location, and they'd spent the time poring over the recordings from the bug. The gangsters were speaking Romanian. Using that knowledge and a list of Monahan's known associates, they were working under the presumption that the mob they were facing was the Romanian mafia. At least now they had an idea of who they were dealing with.

They still didn't have a name for the top man, though. They'd need facial recognition for that. That's why Gideon was here.

He snuck down the street to the warehouse and climbed the side of the building. On a small catwalk that circled the rooftop windows, Gideon crouched and looked inside.

"Hello there."

Gideon spun. Monahan stood right beside him. She fired three shots from a small handgun. He stumbled back as the bullets struck him square in the chest and lodged in his armor.

Monahan leapt at him, swinging her empty fist and the butt of the pistol. Gideon struggled to move aside and strike back. His heart rate already accelerated, light poured freely and uncontrollably from his hands. He clenched his fists and punched, using the added force of the light energy to knock her back.

Monahan dropped the pistol, reached into her belt, and withdrew two knives. "Tonight, you die."

Gideon stepped in and jabbed at her head. She brought up her right arm to block it and slashed her knife along the inside of his left gauntlet. The blade found the gap at his elbow and dug deep. He cried out and unintentionally fired off a burst of light into the air. Monahan followed up with an elbow to the jaw. She swiped her knife at his throat.

Gideon raised his arm in time to catch the blade, where it lodged in his gauntlet. He punched her, knocking her backward and leaving the blade in his arm. She twirled her remaining blade and advanced again. Gideon kicked, catching her in the gut. She doubled over, and he grabbed her and tossed her to the ground. He pressed in, bringing a fist down to knock her out.

Monahan moved her head aside. Gideon's hand struck the metal walkway. She kicked out twice, striking him in the legs and chest. He panted. It was like dragging sandpaper through his lungs. *She's too fast.* Monahan leapt to her feet and brought her knife down toward his head. He moved to the side, and the blade bit deep into his shoulder joint.

"Goodbye, Seraph."

Monahan pushed Gideon back into the catwalk's railing, spun, and roundhouse kicked his solar plexus. Gideon grunted and fell over the railing . . . and fell . . . and fell . . . and fell.

The force of slamming into the ground two stories below was nothing like Gideon had ever felt. Pain like a massive punch exploded in his back and traveled through his nerves to every inch of his body. He felt cold wetness—he'd landed in a snowbank, but it hadn't done much to cushion the fall. His vision grayed. Above, Monahan stood on the catwalk, looking down on him. A small light flickered, like a camera flash.

Stay awake, Gideon. Stay . . . awake . . .

He blinked. Everything was still fuzzy, but he thought Monahan was gone now. She must have thought he was dead. Maybe the flash had been a camera; maybe she needed proof of his death to receive payment.

Gideon's head began to swim. If he passed out here, he'd die. Even if his injuries weren't that severe—medically, it was possible to survive a fall like that—some other criminal would come across him and finish the job. He had to get up.

"Dean . . . ? D-D . . . "

He didn't know how long after that he lay there when a figure appeared above him. Gideon tried to sit up, but his head dropped back onto the concrete and he blacked out.

* * *

Dean grabbed his jacket and rushed for the door. The last he'd heard from Gideon was that he was moving in on the warehouse. There had been a long period of silence that had been broken by a woman's voice, followed by gunshots and a lot of scuffling. Dean hadn't been sure who had won the fight until he heard Gideon weakly call for help.

He took the stairs two at a time and flew through the living room to the front door, which he didn't even bother to lock behind him. Gideon could be dying—could already be dead, for all he knew.

"Gideon, you there?"

Gideon didn't respond. Dean took the stairs down to the parking garage and slid into his Camaro. He slammed his foot on the gas and careened down the streets to the Brooks. *Please, God, don't let me get pulled over.*

Should he call Jolie? She was probably near Gideon's position already, on patrol. Closer than Dean was, anyway. But that would blow Gideon's secret identity way out of the water, and he wasn't sure that was the best idea.

"Hang on, buddy. I'm coming." He tried the comms again. "Gideon, you there?"

Nothing.

"Gideon? If you can hear me, bud, I'm on my way. Just hang on."

* * *

Wyatt had meant it when he said he was hanging up the hood for a while. For the past few days, when he hadn't been working at Sterling Enterprises, he'd spent every possible second with his family. He hadn't thought about the Brooks, assassins, the Seraph . . . any of it.

But three nights after New Year's Eve, he stood on the second floor of the motel just outside their room and looked out into the night. In the distance, he could see the edge of the Brooks. There was not really any visual difference from the rest of the city, but Wyatt knew that place by heart.

Maybe it was time to stop all this. He'd almost been killed, and then his son had almost died trying to take up his mantle. Maybe it was crazy for a normal man to believe he could take on all the city's crime with his bare fists. The Seraph would be much better at it, considering he had superhuman abilities to call on. He didn't need the Crusader, and neither did the Brooks. Not anymore. They'd outgrown him.

Maybe it was just as well. Carter was a semester away from graduating high school, and Rhonda and Ellis were in high school, too. They were becoming adults, all of them, and they'd need a father's advice for the situations they'd be facing in their new stages of life.

As Wyatt pondered, a golden-white flare shot up over the Brooks. He straightened. That had to be the Seraph, no doubt. But what did it mean? Was it a signal, and if so, was it for Wyatt or someone else? Was it a stray shot from a battle? A cry for help?

He needs me. He didn't have powers, let alone premonition, but he just had a gut feeling that the Seraph was in trouble. He went back inside the hotel room and grabbed the duffel bag that held his mask and jacket.

"Where are you going?" Joanna asked.

"I think the Seraph's in trouble."

"You said—"

"I know. I'm so sorry. But I can feel it—he's in trouble, and if I don't go, he could die. I'll lay low and not engage unless I have to."

She shook her head. "You're crazy, old man."

"I know." He kissed her. "But I have to do what I have to do."

He ran down the stairs, pulling on his mask and jacket as he went, and clambered into the family car. He raced across town toward the general vicinity of where he'd seen the flare. It had been near the border of the Brooks, slightly northwest—probably in one of the old warehouse districts. He drove through the area and scanned the sidewalks and rooftops, looking for any sign of the Seraph. It didn't take long.

The Seraph lay in a snowbank at the foot of a warehouse. Wyatt parked his car and ran across the street. His feet slipped on the icy roads, and he threw out his arms to keep balance. Taking each step carefully, he made his way over to the fallen vigilante and finally knelt beside him. He was breathing, and his eyes were open, barely. When they fell on Wyatt, he tried to sit up, and then slumped back and passed out. He had a knife stuck in his shoulder and another in his forearm gauntlet. There were three bullets lodged in the breastplate of his armor.

Wyatt picked him up and carried him back to the car. He laid him in the back seat, got in the car, and started it. Where would he take him? A hospital, he supposed, but which one? He would be giving up the Seraph's identity to the doctors. He just hoped they'd practice discretion and not reveal it to the police. He wished he were a doctor, like Gideon. He could repay the young man for saving his life. But he wasn't, so a hospital would have to do. He drove. The nearest one outside the Brooks was eight miles away.

"Doctor . . ." the Seraph gasped.

"I'm taking you to one," Wyatt replied. "Hang on."

"Doctor . . . Edwin."

"Edwin? What hospital?"

"East . . . East Regional."

"That's almost twenty miles away!"

"I'll . . . make it. Edwin knows . . . knows me. He won't . . . tell."

Wyatt took the next turn to head in the direction of East Regional Hospital. He glanced back at the Seraph. He was breathing heavily and what little of his face Wyatt could see was pale and covered in sweat. *Hold on, kid.* He pressed harder on the gas. He had to walk a fine line; if he got pulled over, the Seraph was going to be in a lot of trouble, and so was he. But he had to go fast enough to get him to the hospital in time to save his life.

Lord, let us make it there.

* * *

The Brooks' warehouse district loomed ahead like a fortress. Dean always hated this part of town. If he had his way, he'd find new, better homes for everyone who lived nearby and just grind all this down to dust. But that wasn't the way things worked. He kept his eyes on the road and made for the Romanians' warehouse.

His comms went active again. Gideon muttered something, but Dean couldn't quite make it out.

"What's that, buddy? I'm coming!"

"Doctor . . . Edwin . . . "

"You need to go to Doctor Edwin? Okay, I'm almost there."

"What hospital?" someone asked.

Oh. Someone had already gotten to Gideon. Good. He spun his car around and headed for East Regional.

CHAPTER 20

Last year

Gideon didn't remember much of his time in the lab.

They brought him in through long, dark halls. The first room they entered was occupied by half a dozen guerrillas and furnished with several folding tables and chairs, as well as a pool table. Some kind of common area. There was a door on the other side of the room—a big, metal door. Gideon's two escorts led him to it.

Inside was the lab. Gideon looked around, taking in all the details he could. It was a dark, two-story room with no windows, lit only by a few dim fluorescent bulbs high above. There was a lot of equipment, some which Gideon recognized and some he'd never seen before. There was an operating table in the middle of the room, with straps to bind the subject's wrists and ankles. There was some sort of helmet at the top of the table, as well, which had leads trailing out of it. Gideon couldn't tell where they went.

The guerrillas strapped him to the table and left. For a long time, he was alone. As far as he could tell, the only door to the lab was the one they'd brought him through. That wouldn't be a good escape route; he supposed there were always a few of them back in that common area.

Gideon tugged at the straps, wiggling and jerking his wrists and legs. The leather seemed too sturdy to break. It dug into his wrists, so he stopped struggling. There was no reason to rub his skin raw. He closed his eyes and waited. The room was cold, which was odd for a building in the middle of Venezuela, and it made it hard to rest.

Finally, the door opened, and a man entered. He wore a white lab coat and had unkempt black hair and a beard.

He tilted his glasses down to inspect Gideon over the rims. "Perhaps you'll be less disappointing."

"What are you going to do to me?"

"Well . . . we'll see, won't we?"

Gideon shouted and struggled as the mad scientist hooked a catheter and IVs into him. He asked again and again what the man was doing to him, but he never responded. He put the helmet over Gideon's head. Gideon was sure he was going to die, just like everyone else they'd brought in here, except Joshua.

I love you, Jolie. I'm sorry.

After that, everything was a blur. He remembered pain—searing hot pain like his blood was boiling. He screamed. A lot of time passed, but he had no idea how much. And then, the next thing he knew, he was being dragged. His mind was murky, and he could barely keep his eyes open. Where were they taking him? Maybe he was dying. Whatever the mad scientist had done might be killing him slowly.

The two men dragging him pulled him back and then hurled him through the air. He landed on his chest. He decided not to move for a while.

"You're alive!" Joshua said.

Gideon moaned and rolled over onto his back. He was back in their cage. It was dark . . . nighttime. Had he been in there all day? He tried to sit up, but everything hurt. Joshua put a hand on his shoulder and eased him back to the ground.

"How . . . long . . . ?"

"Must've been two weeks," Joshua said. "I thought you were dead."

"Two . . . ?"

What had that madman done to him?

Now

It took entirely too long for Wyatt's liking to get to East Regional Hospital. As he parked the car, he pulled off his mask and jacket. Better to be an honest civilian who'd found the Seraph than for both vigilantes to show up in the hospital. He pulled Gideon from the back seat and rushed to the door. A man about Wyatt's age was waiting there, along with a nurse and a gurney. Gideon had managed to dial Dr. Edwin and hand the phone to Wyatt before passing out, and Wyatt had conveyed the information to the man. Edwin had agreed to meet them at a side entrance where they could bring Gideon in discreetly.

"He was in a fight with an assassin," Wyatt said. "I didn't witness it, but I found him lying in the snow near a warehouse. I think he fell off the roof."

The nurse ran her hands along Gideon's hips. "Spinal trauma. And he's got hypothermia."

"I don't know what other injuries he's sustained, other than from the knives and bullets."

"Do you know how long after the fall you got to him?" Edwin asked.

"Probably ten minutes. And it took twenty to get him here."

"Thank you. That should be all we need to know. Please go into the waiting room."

Wyatt stepped into the hospital and leaned back against the wall. Edwin and the nurse wheeled Gideon away. The adrenaline from the stress and panic that had driven him from the moment he'd found the Seraph until now began to ebb, and exhaustion flooded his body in its place. He breathed out a long sigh.

He just needed Gideon to recover. If he did, Wyatt could relax.

Even though he knew it was irrational, he thought that if he'd never quit, maybe Gideon wouldn't be hurt right now. If Wyatt had encouraged the boy to live his life and leave the crime fighting to the old dogs, maybe . . .

Or maybe it would be Wyatt in there on that operating table right now. He couldn't be sure. But he still felt guilty.

"Excuse me," someone said. "Miss, I'm looking for a friend of mine. He may have been checked in recently. Gideon Turner?"

Wyatt opened his eyes and looked toward the front desk. A young man with curly brown hair stood at the desk, looking frantic.

"We haven't received anyone by that name," the nurse said.

Wyatt stood. "Excuse me, son?"

The young man turned. "You . . . " He walked toward Wyatt. "You're him, aren't you? The . . . other one."

"I am." Wyatt gestured for the boy to sit with him. "He's in the operating room now."

"Oh, good." The young man sat. "I'm Dean. I help Gideon with his . . . activities."

"Ah. So, he has backup. That's good. I never did until I met him. But I should've."

"How is he?"

"He got banged up pretty badly. Fell off a building, got shot and cut up. But I'd say his armor saved his life. You have a hand in that?"

Dean nodded. "I did. I helped design it."

"You should be proud." Wyatt leaned back. "I believe he'll be all right. All we can do now is wait."

"Just wait." Dean crossed his arms. "Never been good at that . . ."

* * *

When a call came in reporting gunshots in the warehouse district in the Brooks, Jolie was unsurprised. Calls like that came in every night. The warehouse district was bad, even for the Brooks. She and Paul had been dispatched to investigate.

Paul parked the car and Jolie stepped out. She secured her bulletproof vest and sidearm while visually scanning the area. She didn't see anyone around. There were, however, several tire skid marks in the snow, indicating at least one vehicle had come through here in a hurry. She nodded to Paul, and they headed toward the nearest warehouse.

"Look here." Paul knelt in a snowbank near the building.

Jolie walked to his side. There was a deep indentation in the snowdrift, roughly the shape of a human body, and a few spots of the white powder had been stained red.

"That's not a lot of blood," Jolie said. "If it came from a gunshot wound, then it was just a grazing one."

"That's what I was thinking." Paul looked around. "You know what's odd?"

"What?"

"The footprints. Other than ours, there's only one set coming and going to this pile. One person. And they walked up to this snowbank and away from it."

Jolie nodded. "So maybe this person got shot nearby and then limped here. What about the tire tracks? Maybe that was a friend of the victim's and when the car pulled up, the victim got up out of the snowbank and walked to the car."

"Could be. But I don't see a lot of blood following the footprints, either. Most of it's here in the snow. I wonder if the footprints don't belong to the victim—or at least, the footprints leading to the snowbank are from before he got hurt."

"Maybe it was a hit and run. The victim had walked over here, and the shooter pulled up in their car, opened fire, and drove away without waiting to see the results."

"That might explain the minimal blood—if the shot was wild, it's more likely to have missed or grazed. The victim could have fallen out of surprise or fear and just stayed down until the car drove away, and then realized their wounds weren't so bad and just walked away."

"Maybe." Jolie looked at the snowbank. "But this impression is deep, and the snow is packed tight. Would a fall from a standing position really do that? And how long would they have had to stay there to pack it like that? What if the victim fell farther? Say, from the roof?"

"So, in that case, the footprints would be from a rescuer. Someone who came and picked up the victim?"

Jolie shook her head. "But what are the odds of someone surviving a fall like that, especially with so little blood?"

She looked around for any other evidence. Maybe they needed to get up on the roof and see if there were any other clues up there.

"Hey, isn't this warehouse supposed to be abandoned?" Paul asked.

"Yeah. Why?"

He nodded up toward the roof. Jolie looked up. A dim light shone from the windows above a catwalk.

"Somebody's home," Paul said.

"We need to get up there."

Jolie scanned the area. There was a ladder near the back of the wall, leading to the catwalk. She climbed it and scanned the catwalk. No one was up there, so she pulled herself up and drew her sidearm while she waited for Paul. When he reached the top, they stooped and snuck to the window.

Inside the warehouse, there were perhaps two dozen men and women, all wearing gang jackets, milling about stacks of crates. Some of them carried rifles. Paul whistled.

"I think we found a major center of the mob's operations," he said.

"Which means . . ."

As they watched, another man ran into the room and shouted something. Jolie figured it was probably something akin to *There's a cop car sitting across the street!*

"We need to move now," she said. "Back to the car."

Paul nodded and clambered back down the ladder. Jolie followed, her heart racing. Every step against the metal rungs of the ladder seemed to echo through the yard. Any second now, she expected armed mobsters to burst from the warehouse and open fire. She followed Paul back to the car, holding her gun close.

Crack. Jolie froze, standing in the middle of the street, whirled, and raised her gun. A man stood in a now-open doorway, rifle raised. Jolie pulled the trigger three times as she backed toward the car. Paul, who was already at the car, provided covering fire. Jolie turned and sprinted to the vehicle.

More gunfire joined the first shooter's. Jolie grabbed the driver's door and yanked it open. Paul, standing on the passenger's side, continued to fire on the three men. One of his shots hit home and the frontmost man stumbled back. The other two moved aside as he fell and then stepped around his body. Jolie fired twice more, hitting the man on the left, and then climbed into the car and slammed the door. Paul fired a few more shots and then jerked the passenger's door open and pulled himself in.

"Go!"

As bullets peppered the cruiser, Jolie slammed her foot on the gas and the car shot away from the warehouse.

"We need to call for reinforcements."

Paul was already on it. "Officer Jordan to dispatch. Shots fired. We've got confirmed mob activity at our location. Send all available backup."

Jolie looked in the rearview mirror. There was no sign of pursuit, so she spun the car around a corner, parked the car, and got out. Paul continued to talk with the dispatcher. Jolie walked to the trunk, popped it, and withdrew their heavier weapons—a Remington 870 shotgun and a Colt M4 carbine. Paul's door slammed. Jolie looked up at him as he circled the cruiser to stand next to her.

"Backup's on the way."

"It's about to be a warzone over here." Jolie checked the sights on the carbine. "We have to hit them fast and hard or they'll move those crates."

"Agreed."

Within ten minutes, five more police cruisers and one SWAT truck—the only one assigned to the Brooks—pulled up. Paul briefed them on the situation as they geared up. Detective Pulaski walked up to Jolie.

"Is she there?"

"I didn't see her," Jolie replied.

He shrugged. "Either way, this will lead us back to her."

Jolie and Paul led the task force back to the warehouse. There were now two men posted outside the door. As the police approached, Jolie and Paul raised their guns.

"Sojourn PD!" Jolie shouted. "On the ground now! Drop your weapons!"

The men shouldered their rifles. Jolie and Paul fired, and both men dropped. The SWAT team moved in with Pulaski and the other officers behind. Jolie stood to one side with Paul and Pulaski while a fourth officer stood on the other, a flashbang grenade in her hand.

The SWAT held up three fingers and counted down. When her hand formed a fist, Paul pulled the door open and the officer threw the flashbang inside. Paul closed the door again. The grenade detonated, he jerked it back open and the SWAT team flooded the warehouse. Jolie took a deep breath and rushed in after them.

Jolie kept her focus on the room in front of her. Several of the stunned and blinded mobsters tried to reach for their weapons. Jolie grabbed one and slammed him into the wall. Several others managed to get their weapons out, but the SWAT team took them down. Jolie pushed her guy harder against the wall and lowered her rifle to grab handcuffs.

"You have the right to remain silent," she said.

The raid was over in thirty seconds. Many of the mobsters continued to fight and were killed. In the process, two cops and one member of the SWAT team were shot. But in the end, the chaos ended with only three mobsters in handcuffs, including the one Jolie had grabbed, and the rest dead.

"These guys don't play around," Pulaski said.

"They really didn't want to be captured." Jolie pushed her guy toward two officers, who took him outside. "That probably means their boss isn't here."

"No, and they probably have a much bigger operation than what we're seeing here."

"Detective!" Paul called. "Over here."

Jolie followed Pulaski to Paul's side. He was standing by one of the crates. Pulaski peered inside and sucked in a sharp breath, followed by an angry curse. Jolie looked inside. The crate was empty.

"They moved it," Paul said. "Whatever was here . . . they've already moved it."

"Which means that whatever their operation is, they're probably in the final stages of planning it," Jolie agreed.

"We need to find them." Pulaski headed for the door. "Fast."

CHAPTER 21

Dean agonized over whether he should call the Turners. The question had weighed on him ever since he'd arrived at the hospital. On the one hand, they deserved to know their son could be dying. On the other, they would find out Gideon was the Seraph. Dean wasn't sure it was a decision he wanted to make without Gideon's approval.

He ultimately decided that he should wait and see. They couldn't see him while he was in surgery anyway; all they could do was wait here with him and Wyatt and worry.

"Excuse me," a nurse said.

Dean snapped his head up and nudged Wyatt.

"Dr. Edwin sent me to talk to you."

"How's Gideon?"

"The car accident patient?" The nurse sat down and leaned in. "Things look good. He has a broken rib and it nearly punctured his lung, but it missed. The biggest problem right now is that Gideon has a hairline fracture on his spine. He'll need a brace."

Oh, his days as a vigilante are so over.

"But he'll make it?" Dean asked.

"Things look promising." The nurse nodded to Wyatt. "It's a good thing you brought him when you did. Much longer and he might not have made it."

"Thank you," Wyatt said.

She handed Dean a bag. "These are his personal belongings. I'll let you know when he's out of surgery."

Dean peered into the bag. Gideon's Seraph suit lay folded inside. They must've removed it before taking him in for operating. Now, no one—save that nurse and Dr. Edwin—would know his secret. He was just another victim of a winter car accident. Dean slumped in his chair and reached for his phone as the nurse exited the waiting room. At this point, he supposed it was inevitable.

"I'm going to go home," Wyatt said. "It's not that I don't want to be here for him, but my wife is probably worried sick. And besides, I probably don't need any of Gideon's other friends or family wondering who I am."

Dean nodded. "I understand. Thank you so much for saving him."

"You're welcome." Wyatt grinned. "And hey, if I were still in the crime fighting business, I might even ask you to design me a fancy suit like that."

"I might even do it, too. Be safe, Wyatt."

"You, too, son."

The older man departed, and Dean looked down at his phone screen. *Do I really want to do this?* He stared at it for a moment. Finally, he dialed.

* * *

Swimming back to consciousness felt like trying to push his way through a pool of not-quite-dry concrete. It would be easier to just stop, to release himself to the warm, struggle-free rest of sleep. But some part of Gideon warned that it was essential for him to wake up *now*. If only his body understood that as well as his mind did.

The first physical sensation he felt was a sharp pain running all the way down his back. He didn't want to move. Ever again. If he had to choose how to live the rest of his life right now, he'd do it lying in his bed and trying not to feel the pain that surely awaited him when he fully awoke.

Opening his eyes took him almost a minute after he first realized he was awake. His vision was fuzzy, so he blinked slowly a few times to try and clear it. He was in a dim but not unwelcoming room, and he was . . . warm. He looked around.

Oh. It was a hospital room. He was in the hospital. He turned his head to the left and realized there was someone sitting in the chair next to his bed. *Dad.* He was asleep.

"D . . ." he grunted. "Dad?"

His dad jolted and looked at him. "Oh . . . you're awake! Hold on, I have to call a nurse."

He did, and a middle-aged woman rushed in and checked Gideon's vitals.

"His vitals are fine," the nurse said. "I'll come back to check on him in a few minutes."

She stepped out of the room. Gideon closed his eyes and opened them again a few times, still wrestling with the sleep that threatened to drag him back to its peaceful embrace.

"Dad."

"Hey, son." His father reached down to tousle Gideon's hair. "I'm so glad you're okay."

"How did you . . . ?"

"Dean called us. Last week, actually. You've been in a coma since then."

"A week?" Gideon gaped. He started to sit up and his back reminded him that wasn't a good idea. He settled back down. "I've been out for a week?"

"Yes. Your injuries were pretty bad. It's going to take you a long time to recover from the spinal fracture you suffered."

This could not be happening. He had to get back out there. He had to go take care of the city. He had to stop the mob and Monahan and . . .

"No. No, no, this can't . . . "

"I am sorry, son." Dad sat back down and pulled the chair closer. Gideon could see him better now. "The truth is, you probably should've died."

Gideon closed his eyes and sighed. "You know?"

"Yes. We know. Dean told us."

"Are you mad? I'm sorry, Dad . . . I was just trying to help. I just wanted to do the right thing."

"I know. I know. Don't worry about any of that now. It's all going to be okay. None of us will tell the police, even Doctor Edwin." His father smiled. "It's a good thing you worked here. I think it saved you a lot of trouble."

"Thank you." *Wait . . .* "Jolie?"

"We haven't told her, either. She knows you are hurt, and she's been to see you a few times, but she thinks the injury was a result of a car accident."

"You lied to her? Why?"

"Because we thought that for her, at least . . . this should come from you."

"Thank you." Gideon felt awful. It was a terrible thing to thank his parents for lying to his girlfriend. It was wrong on so many levels. "Thank you."

"You're welcome. But Gideon, it's over. You can't go out there, can't risk your life like this anymore. Even if you do recover and get back to a hundred percent, we can't let you."

"Can't let me? Dad, I—"

"Well, let me rephrase that. We strongly advise against it. We can't force you. But son, we don't want to watch you die."

He sighed. "Are you mad at me for not telling you?"

"I've had a . . . lot of emotions about all this." Dad chuckled. "But mad? No. Not right now, at least. We're just glad you're alive."

"Thanks. I am, too. But Dad, the city's in trouble. And if the police can't fix it, and the government can't fix it . . . someone has to."

He smiled, nodded, and patted Gideon on the shoulder. "That's what I've always admired about you most, son. You want to help everyone. It's why you became a doctor. But sometimes, we have to start by helping one person, not a whole city. I'm going to let the nurses do their thing. But I'll be back later. And I'll send your mother, Wes, and Dean in to see you when I can."

"Okay." Gideon sighed. "I love you, Dad."

"I love you, too, son."

Gideon slumped back against his pillow and closed his eyes. Hot tears began to roll down his face. *What have I become?*

* * *

Dean walked in circles in the waiting room, trying to prepare himself to see Gideon. He was terrified that Gideon would be furious at him for telling his parents. And he'd have every right to be. But surely, he'd understand that Dean had just been trying to do the right thing.

He sighed. The rest of the Turners were already unhappy with Dean. They knew that he'd supported Gideon's vigilantism and had even helped him, and they were furious that he would help put their son in danger. Out of all of them, Wes was the least angry. He hid it, but Dean could tell that he thought that his brother being a vigilante was cool—especially since he was the one who had superpowers.

"How did he get his powers?"

Wes phrased the question soberly, as if he were asking how Gideon had developed cancer. But really, Dean thought, he wanted to learn everything he could about his brother's double life.

Dean stopped pacing and looked at him. "Honestly, I don't know. I think he has an idea, but still doesn't know enough about it to want to tell me."

"Oh." Wes scratched his chin. "Do you think he'll ever get to use them again?"

"I'm sure he will. To fight crime?" Dean shrugged. "That, I can't say."

"If I know my brother, he will."

Matthew and Tasha walked back into the waiting room. Wes hopped up and immediately headed toward Gideon's room. Dean followed, giving the Turners one last look as he did. At least Matthew gave him a small nod, but Tasha didn't acknowledge him at all. He sighed and put it aside. All that mattered right now was Gideon.

Dean walked into his room behind Wes and waved meekly. Gideon smiled and gestured for the two of them to come closer.

"Hey, guys."

"Hey," Wes said. "I just want you to know that I respect what you're doing."

"Thank you."

"And I'm glad you're okay."

"Thanks."

Dean stepped up. "Gideon, I'm so sorry. I—"

"You have nothing to apologize for, Dean. You did the right thing. Thank you."

"Oh. You're welcome."

Dean let out a breath he hadn't even realized he'd been holding. Wes went and sat down next to Gideon and started asking him about all the criminals the Seraph had stopped. Dean took the seat on the other side of the bed and listened as the brothers talked. He hoped that one day, Gideon could get back out there and save lives again. From what Dean was hearing about the situation in the Brooks, a superhero would be welcome right now. But recovery was going to take him at least two months, probably.

Whatever happened, Dean resolved to be right by Gideon's side when it did. Even if Gideon was eventually found out and arrested, Dean would stand up for him.

"Gid?"

Dean, Gideon, and Wes looked up. Jolie stood in the doorway, and when she saw him sitting up in bed, she grinned and rushed in. Dean moved aside so she could hug Gideon. He hugged back as best he could. Dean saw the guilt on Gideon's face. He wanted to tell her.

"I'm so glad you're okay," she said. "When your dad told me about the accident . . ."

"Yeah, I'm okay." Gideon forced a smile. "I'm okay."

Dean motioned for Wes to come out of the room. The two of them needed some space. Dean doubted Gideon would tell her right now, but either way, they deserved to be alone for a bit. As they left, Dean clapped Wes on the shoulder.

"Your brother's a hero, man."

Wes smiled. "I know."

* * *

Serban looked out over the crowd of drug dealers, thieves, murderers, gang members, and various other criminals that were gathered in Serban's new headquarters—this one set up on the other side of the Brooks from the one the cops had raided last week. Serban's men had sent out an invite to all the gangs and known criminals in the Brooks to meet here tonight. The response was impressive. But then, Serban had known it would be.

The Tyrants and the Red Dogs—what was left of them after that massive gang war a few months ago—were even here, and they weren't at each other's throats . . . yet. Serban allowed himself a small smile. Soon, they'd be united under one command: his.

A few more guests trickled in, and then one of Serban's men slammed the door and locked it. The chaos of over a hundred people talking at once began to quiet down. Serban glanced quickly at Monahan. She stood off to the side, sharpening a short, curved knife. He had let her back into his good graces now that she'd provided proof of the Seraph's death. She'd be a useful tool, anyway. Next to her stood Detective Walters. Another useful tool.

Serban jumped up on a stack of crates that had been set up as a stage of sorts. Some of the riffraff closer to him noticed first and began to quiet even more. Serban cleared his throat, waited a few more seconds, and then began.

"Quiet!" His voice echoed through the warehouse, and instantly, all conversation stopped. "I'm going to go out on a limb and say that if you haven't seen my face, you know my name. In the past year, you've bought your weapons from either myself or my boys. I'm the one that's made all that you've been doing possible."

He looked at Costin out of the corner of his eye. The man nodded and moved off behind the stage to grab another crate.

"That means you owe me."

The room erupted into chaos as dozens of criminals protested.

"Owe you?" one Tyrant asked. "We've already paid you for your weapons!"

"True! However, if I wasn't here, you wouldn't have any weapons at all, free or otherwise. Oh, sure, you might get a few pea shooters from some local schmucks, but the real stuff? You know that comes from me."

"I don't see your point," a Red Dog said. "Like he said: we've paid you."

Fascinating. For once, a Tyrant and a Red Dog agreed on something.

"Well now it's time for you to give back something more." Serban gestured to Costin, and he dragged out the crate. "I've got a new shipment. More guns with more power than anything I've given you yet. But here's the thing: the money you've got won't cut it. I'm not interested in your petty cash."

"Petty cash?" the same Tyrant scoffed. "Is that what you call the millions we have funneled into your mob this past year?"

"I call that a down payment."

"You would snuff the life out of us to take the city for yourself, is that it? You want us bankrupt, under your thumb!"

Serban withdrew a Ruger pistol from his coat pocket and shot the Tyrant dead on the spot. The room went silent. If Serban had allowed any of them to bring weapons in, he was sure they would have drawn them. But they were unarmed and surrounded by his men, who were armed.

"What I want . . . is to be on top! And all of you are gonna get me there. I'm taking over this city one way or another. It'd be a lot easier with your help."

The Red Dog spokesman frowned. "You want us to join your mob?"

"Exactly." Serban tucked the pistol away. "You wouldn't have guns if it wasn't for me. And I've got way more right here than you do. So, you can either join me and put those weapons to use . . . or I'll kill you and take 'em back."

"What about the Seraph?" someone asked. "And the Crusader?"

"The Crusader's nothing! He's a guy with a few moves in a mask. He can't stand against all of us. And as for the Seraph . . . " Serban gestured to a screen set up on a pillar next to the stage. An image of the Seraph's broken body lying in the snow appeared. "The Seraph's dead! He won't be bothering us anymore."

There was a short, stunned silence, followed by applause and cheers.

"What . . . what exactly do you have planned for the city?" another Tyrant asked.

"So glad you asked." Serban jumped off the stage and grabbed the crate's lid. "I told you: I'm going to conquer it. I mean that. I don't mean I'm going to conquer its criminal underworld. I just did that, right here in this room. I mean, I'm going to conquer the whole city."

He ripped the lid from the crate, reached inside, and withdrew an M-16 rifle with a grenade launcher attachment.

"The rich of this city have oppressed the Brooks for too long—even before I came here, it was a problem! We're going to end that. We're going to take the whole city by force—from here to Lakeside and then on to that floating platform of theirs. We're going to execute the one percenters and take their wealth, and we're going to make Sojourn City our own little empire. And I'll be at the top."

Serban tossed the rifle to the Red Dog spokesman. He caught it and looked down at it in surprise. Monahan straightened and put her hand on her pistol. It was almost sweet of her to look out for Serban like that. But the Red Dog didn't fire. He looked down at the gun and back up at Serban.

"So," Serban said. "Who's in?"

Over a hundred voices shouted in agreement. Serban grinned, nodded to Monahan, and strode away from the stage.

This was going to take months of planning, down to the last detail, but it didn't matter. It was all coming together at last.

CHAPTER 22

The past week had been very confusing and stressful for Jolie, but it only made her more determined to press on. She wanted with every fiber of her being to just give up and take a vacation somewhere very far from Sojourn City and all her problems, but that only temporarily pushed things to the side. The only thing that would solve her problems was . . . well, solving them.

The biggest and most pressing issue was the crime ring in the Brooks. After the warehouse raid, Pulaski had discovered a bug of some sort on one of the bodies he'd dropped. It was high-tech and appeared to have a GPS in it, but it wasn't a police device, indicating that someone else was watching the mob. That led Jolie to believe that perhaps the Seraph or the Crusader had planted the device, and maybe even the mysterious body-imprint in the snowbank had belonged to one of them. The police department's tech guys were working on back-tracing the GPS. Or at least, they were supposed to be. Jolie had just received a call from the lab that the device had disappeared. Walters' doing, most likely. Jolie was all but certain the detective was in the mob's pocket. He hadn't taken part in the warehouse raid, and he'd been scarcer around the precinct lately.

But she had another issue: Gideon. She had begun to believe that she'd been wrong about him being a vigilante. After all, there was no way he was hiding superpowers from her, right? But then, the same night as they found the mysterious crime scene with no sign of a body, Gideon turned up in the hospital with severe injuries from a "car accident." Was that really a coincidence? Jolie wasn't a big believer in those.

So maybe Gideon was the Seraph. He couldn't be the Crusader, because that vigilante had been active before Gideon had been rescued from Venezuela. Any other theory was needlessly complicated. She'd even considered whether the Seraph might have been the first Crusader, and Gideon had taken over as the new Crusader in his place when the first one got superpowers somehow, but that required a stunning amount of mental gymnastics to believe.

But the thought of him lying to her about such a big part of his life wounded her. She loved him. She believed that he loved her, too, and that his heart held only good intentions. But was he capable of lying to her about something so big for so long?

In any case, if he was one of the vigilantes, he wouldn't be doing any crime fighting for the next few months, at least. Dr. Edwin said that Gideon needed to be in a wheelchair for about two weeks, and then make a follow-up visit to the doctor. If he was cleared, he could begin walking again, using crutches, and attending physical therapy. After roughly five to six weeks on the crutches, he might be able to walk normally again. But even then, it would take him time to get back up to full strength. Which meant his body might not be ready for fighting again for a very long time.

Well. If the Seraph suddenly disappeared from the Brooks now, as Jolie suspected he would, she'd know the truth. And she and Gideon would have a very long conversation about that.

She drove her car down the street to Gideon's apartment. She, with Dean in the passenger's seat, was following Gideon's family in their van. They were dropping him off, and they had more room for the wheelchair than Jolie's small car. She parked behind them and climbed out.

"Here we are, son," Matthew said.

He unfolded the wheelchair and helped Gideon climb into it. The roads were still icy, so Matthew took his time maneuvering the wheelchair up to the sidewalk. Jolie stood back as Tasha and Wes climbed out of the van to tell Gideon goodbye.

"I'll take him from here," Jolie said to Matthew.

"Okay." Gideon's dad leaned down and hugged his son. "I love you."

"Love you, too." Gideon hugged him back. "Thanks for . . . everything."

"You're welcome. Take it easy, son. And if you need anything at all, call us. We're happy to help."

"Thanks."

"You wheel him on up," Dean told Jolie. "I'll get his stuff."

She nodded and pushed Gideon inside the Tower's lobby and toward the elevator. She pressed the call button. Dean reappeared a moment later with Gideon's duffel bag. Jolie eyed it casually, wondering if the Seraph's suit would be found inside that bag. But she didn't want to worry about that right now. A consideration for another day.

Once they got upstairs, Jolie and Dean helped Gideon from his wheelchair to the couch. Gideon cringed a bit at the movement.

"Sorry," Jolie said.

"It's fine." He gritted his teeth. "Just . . . gonna take some getting used to."

They set him down as comfortably as they could, and Jolie draped a blanket over him while Dean gave him the TV remote. Jolie rolled the wheelchair next to the front door and folded it up. When she reentered the living room, Dean was gone. She sat down next to Gideon.

"How you feeling?"

"Been better." Gideon chuckled. "Been worse, too."

After that, they sat in silence for a while. Gideon flipped through channels. He stopped on a local news show.

"I'm just saying," one anchor, a blonde woman, said. "There's no proof that these vigilantes have had any kind of a positive effect on the number of criminals in the city."

"True," the other, a black man, replied. "But what you can measure is the activity of those criminals. And we've dropped in the number of murders and rapes considerably just in the last two months."

"Are you saying you think the vigilantes are a positive force?"

"I think I am." The man looked soberly at the camera. "This city was in desperate need of hope. And I think these vigilantes, perhaps the Seraph in particular, have provided that."

"But what is the Seraph? Is he some kind of mutated being or superhuman? Or does his light come from his suit somehow? I think the question on everyone's mind is, who is the Seraph, and what does he want?"

"Maybe he's just what he appears to be. Maybe he's Sojourn City's shining knight, and all he really wants is to help."

When it was put that way, it didn't sound so bad. Jolie sighed. When she really thought about it, even from a cop's perspective, had the Seraph really done anything wrong? Yes, the act of vigilantism was technically illegal. She had told Gideon months ago, back in Wally's Diner, that even criminals had rights, and vigilantes took those rights away. The Crusader had annoyed her by getting in her way with Walters, true, but even he hadn't killed anyone. Morally, what they were doing was sound. As the anchor had said, the Seraph had saved lives.

If Gideon was the Seraph . . . didn't that make him a hero?

* * *

Gideon tossed and turned on the couch, frustrated and unable to sleep. Since they couldn't very well wheel him up the stairs to his bedroom, he was stuck down here for a few weeks, at least. Which also meant that he couldn't go to the lair. Good thing there was a bathroom down here, or Gideon would've been in real trouble.

He sighed. The couch wasn't uncomfortable; he just wasn't used to sleeping on it. But even that wasn't why he was having difficulty falling asleep. It was Jolie.

She had to suspect. The vibes he'd gotten off her as they'd sat and watched TV had been more conflicted than ever. Maybe she wasn't sure whether or not she should bring it up. Maybe she didn't know how. Or maybe she didn't know how she felt about it anymore.

Either way, it killed him to not tell her. He loved her, and he wanted to include her in every part of his life. But telling her this? It would put her in a difficult position with her job, it would potentially endanger her life even more than it already had been . . .

All the same arguments he'd ever had with himself about the subject played on repeat in his head. Now that his parents and Wes knew,

Jolie was literally the only person in his life who was important to him who didn't know. That wasn't fair to her.

Finally, still conflicted and unsure of himself, he drifted off. When he awoke, Dean was in the kitchen, flipping pancakes.

"Morning!" Dean called.

Gideon grunted. "Morning."

"Figured if you're stuck on the couch, you might as well get a good breakfast out of it. By the way, I called my dad and he's shifted your workload over to the other biologists for the next few weeks, at least until you're ready to go back."

"Oh. Thanks." *That means someone else is working on that super-soldier serum.* "Do we have anything new on activity in the Brooks?"

"You seriously want to talk about that now? Especially when you can't do anything about it?" Dean scooped a pancake from the pan and placed it on a plate. Gideon didn't respond, so Dean continued. "Well, then. The same night you got hurt, the police hit that warehouse and killed a lot of mobsters. Including the one who had our bug on him."

Gideon sighed. "So we've got nothing."

"Yeah. I shut off the bug's GPS, so they can't trace it back here, at least. But yeah, we're back at square one as far as the mob stuff. Which isn't too bad, considering you can't even walk. It's not like you're going to be back on the streets anytime soon."

"I know, I know."

"Okay. Well, what we do know is, they're up to something big. The police have been tracing criminal activity—which I've been following through means that I'd prefer not to mention to you—and think that there might be someone new in charge of everything. The gangs, dealers, everything. They're all working together like a machine. What the police don't know is who's operating it."

"The Romanians," Gideon said.

"Seems pretty likely. Whoever's at the top of that lot is now running basically all of the city's organized crime."

"Then he's got something big planned." He shook his head. "If only I'd been able to figure out who he is. At least we could tip the police off about him."

"Yeah." Dean walked into the living room and handed Gideon the plate with the pancake. "Actually, I can run all the audio we got from the bug through a translator and see if we can dig a name out of it."

"That would be good. I may not be able to fight crime directly, but I'm not going to just sit here and do nothing, either."

"Of course not. You're going to eat that pancake."

"Dean . . ."

"Yeah, yeah. I'm on it." He headed upstairs. "But then I have to go to the lab. I'm not crippled, you know. Still have to work and all that. Pay the bills, blah-blah."

"You're a billionaire, Dean."

"I like to stay humble." Dean shrugged. "But if you need anything, just call me. I moved the wheelchair right there next to the couch so if you need to go to the bathroom you can go yourself, hopefully."

"Hopefully?"

Dean chuckled and disappeared upstairs. Gideon sighed, took a bite of the pancake, and pondered. *I've got to get back out there.* Maybe his powers would allow him to heal faster. Or maybe he could find some way to use the light to propel himself without physically moving his body.

Probably not. But he knew he'd go crazy sitting here for the next few weeks, let alone the rest of the two-plus months it would take to completely recover.

God, please help me get through this quickly.

* * *

Serban's empire was put together exceptionally quickly, all things considered.

With Monahan as his right-hand enforcer, Walters keeping an eye on the cops, Serban's benefactor funding him, and a slew of locals helping him set up a network of contacts, he had the makings of the biggest force of criminals he'd ever seen before. His superiors in Romania would've been proud.

He hired hackers to help consolidate the finances of the one per-centers when the time came. He hired enforcers and mercenaries to be his muscle. He hired pickpockets and thieves to be his eyes in the streets. He bought out local government types to pave the way for a smooth transition.

It was a beauty to behold, really.

Of course, there was resistance. More than once, Serban's men got in shootouts with the cops. But slowly, the number of officers in the Brooks was dwindling due to sheer attrition. Most of the cops outside the Brooks who hadn't been bought out by the rich to protect them had now been bought by Serban to keep out of the Brooks and look the other way when he made his move.

There was still a lot to accomplish, though. When they did move on Lakeside and then the Platform, the cops that had been paid off by the rich, and those who weren't bought by anyone, would fight back.

It would be tough. And then there was the matter of the bridge from the shore to the Platform. It would be heavily guarded. Serban's plans for the Platform hinged on being able to eject the floating goldmine onto the lake.

And Sojourn City was just big. Even with the numbers Serban had, it would be hard to consolidate the whole city all at once.

But that's what his contacts were for. That's why it paid to be friendly to the right people. And that's why, once he did have control, Monahan would be there to take out anyone who tried to protest.

When Serban was in control, when Sojourn City was finally in his grasp, that would show all those arrogant bigots back in Romania. If he, a gypsy, could rise to the top of an entire city . . . well, then they'd have to admit they'd been wrong about him. And he would enjoy that day very much.

CHAPTER 23

Last year

After he was thrown out of the lab, time seemed to stretch into a loop. Every day was the same. He and Joshua talked and exercised and tried to keep themselves busy, so they didn't go insane. They ate the same meals, looked out at the same trees . . .

Gideon had no concept of time anymore. Poor Joshua had been there so long, often by himself. Gideon couldn't imagine having to face the same thing.

"Have you been a believer your whole life?" Joshua asked.

"Pretty much," Gideon replied. He scratched at his beard, which was getting long and scraggly. "My dad's a pastor and was before I was born. I was saved when I was nine years old. What about you? You mentioned you're Jewish."

"Yes, I was an Orthodox Jew for almost my entire life. I didn't come to know Christ until a few years ago. That caused some problems with my son and his wife; they're still Orthodox." He sighed. "I pray for them every day."

"I'm sorry. I'll pray for them, too."

Now

Dean scrolled through the transcription of the conversations their bug had recorded, searching for any sign of a name. He just needed to know who was in charge of this stupid Romanian mob. Just a name, just one name. They were saying plenty of names, even Monahan's a few times, but none of them in the context of someone giving orders.

Finally, he hit the jackpot.

"I heard Serban's calling everyone together," the bugged guy said. "Not just our people; anyone who'll respond."

"He's ambitious, I'll give him that," someone responded.

Dean used his finger to highlight the name Serban on the screen. He set the smart table to search for that name in records of organized crime in Romania, and then he ran downstairs to see Gideon.

"We've got him."

"Good." Gideon looked up at Dean. "I need you to do something else."

"Whatcha got?"

"I need you to suit up as the Seraph and make an appearance in the Brooks."

. . . oh.

* * *

Dean tugged at the cape and hood and shook his head beneath the cowl. Maybe this hadn't been the best idea, design-wise. Sure, the cape was intimidating, but he could imagine how it got in the way while fighting. It was a heavy, and the whirling folds would probably interfere with fancy spins and kicks. Gideon had never complained about it, but Dean put it on the list of things to revise if he ever redesigned the Seraph suit.

Oh, who am I kidding? He was definitely going to redesign the Seraph suit. Designing it the first time had been just about the coolest thing he'd ever done. It would be a genuine pleasure to be able to do something like that again.

Wearing it was pretty cool, too.

As Dean walked across the rooftop, he considered Gideon's instructions. He was supposed to make himself seen for a few minutes, duck out, maybe show up again a few blocks away, and then disappear and go home. He wasn't supposed to engage any criminals.

"It's just so people know the Seraph is still out there," Gideon had explained. "Just make sure some people see you."

Dean wondered if it was more about Jolie knowing the Seraph was still out there. If he was spotted while Gideon was in the wheelchair, she wouldn't be suspicious of him anymore. It was a win-win for Gideon.

Either way, there was bound to be a confrontation between the two of them at some point, and Dean didn't expect it to be pretty.

After a few minutes of posturing and roaming the rooftops, he grabbed two high-power flashlights and waved them around. *Yes, these are my glowing fists of power. Very convincing.* A few people on the streets below saw him and pointed. *There, my job's done.* Dean climbed back down to the alley, mounted Gideon's motorcycle, and drove to another part of town to repeat the process. Oh, the glamor of being a superhero.

* * *

Gideon clenched his jaw and pushed himself out of the wheelchair and to his feet. His legs wobbled, and he grabbed a railing to steady himself. The pain in his back was now a dull ache. He closed his eyes, focused on staying on his feet, and released the railing. His physical therapist made a noise that Gideon hoped was satisfaction. Gideon allowed himself a short laugh. He was doing it!

"Well, I'm impressed," the physical therapist said. "You'll still need crutches, and you'll need to do the exercises I've prescribed every day. But if you keep improving at this rate, I'd say you'll be off your crutches in about a month."

Another month? Well, that wasn't so good. It had already been over two weeks since Gideon had come out of his coma. Dean had gone out to the Brooks dressed as the Seraph three times since then, but he'd never engaged any criminals and he'd only stayed long enough to be noticed. Sooner or later, someone was going to realize the vigilante wasn't fighting any crime.

Gideon sat patiently through the rest of the appointment and accepted the crutches the physical therapist gave him. When he hobbled out into the hallway, Dean was waiting for him.

"Well, look at you. Not quite back on your own two feet. But getting closer."

Gideon nodded. "Getting closer. Let's go home."

As Dean drove them home, Gideon revisited what they knew. Dean had tracked Serban's travel history and found that he had, in fact, come to the States around the same time crime had spiked in the Brooks.

One of Dean's nights out in the Brooks, he'd managed to place another of his listening devices, this one inside The Broken Glass. He'd also tipped off the police. It seemed Serban was a very difficult man to find, but he'd also been very busy.

"We need to figure out what Serban has planned," Gideon said.

"Oh, I agree. Problem is finding him." Dean shrugged. "I've managed to get some snippets of conversations he's had, but he's using some kind of spoof on his phone that's keeping me, and presumably the police, from tracking his location."

"Well, let's start small. What have you gotten from his conversations?"

"Whatever he's planned, it seems to be city-wide." Dean shook his head. "He talks about reaching the top and being the man in charge a lot."

"What else?"

"Some of his lieutenants have mentioned the Platform."

"There may be someone with a lot of wealth behind all this, then."

"Or he may be blackmailing someone into helping him. Either way, if there's someone from the Platform involved, that mean's at least one of the city's elite is probably on Serban's side."

"And if that's the case, who else could be in his pocket? Police? Government officials? We need to get a better idea." Gideon scratched his chin. "You're going out as the Seraph again tonight, but you're not going to the Brooks."

"I'm . . . what? Where am I going?"

"You're going to city hall. You're going to tap the phone lines, so if any officials get a call from Serban, we'll know about it."

"Brilliant. And if I get caught? Being the Seraph outside the Brooks will go a whole lot differently if the cops catch me."

Gideon sighed. He hadn't even thought about that. All this time, he'd really only been thinking about the mission, never about how Dean felt or what he wanted. *You idiot.* He had empathic powers and yet he'd been so focused on his own feelings, his frustration about being injured and his fears about Jolie, that Dean's feelings had stopped mattering to him.

"Look, I don't want you to put yourself in danger if you don't want to. I can probably reach out to Wyatt and see if the Crusader can do one last job."

"No, no. I'll do it."

"Thanks." Gideon looked at Dean. "And I am sorry. Look, man, I don't know if I have said it enough, but thank you. Seriously. You didn't have to do any of this and I know I've sort of forced it on you. Even joining my fight in the first place. But I couldn't have done any of this without you and I hope you know how much I appreciate that."

"Yeah." After a moment, Dean smiled. "You're welcome, buddy."

Dean and Jolie. Gideon's best friends and biggest support in the world. And he'd been lying to them and using them. *What's wrong with me?* Okay. It was time to make this right. He pulled out his phone.

"What are you doing?" Dean asked.

"I'm going to call Jolie and ask her if she'll come over tonight after she gets off her shift. The lies end now."

"Proud of you, buddy. You're doing the right thing."

Gideon knew he was, but he feared for his future with Jolie after this. Would she ever forgive him?

One way to find out. He dialed.

* * *

"You owe me," Serban growled.

Monahan looked up from her card game and frowned. Serban almost decked her right there; he had no reservations about it. She had messed up one too many times and this time she was going to pay for it.

"What do you mean?"

"The Seraph. He's showed up a few times the past few weeks. He's still alive."

"You mean the bumbler in a cape and hood standing on rooftops and waving around lights? That's not the Seraph."

"Oh, no? Looks a lot like him. And he showed up here, in fact." Serban held up the small listening device Costin had found in the stock room. "Seems like him, too."

"Hm." Monahan studied the device. "Not dissimilar to the one Walters brought me. That, I expect, is how the Seraph found the warehouse. But this new guy isn't him. He hasn't engaged any criminals and he has only shown up long enough to be seen. He's an impostor, out to make people think the Seraph is still alive."

"That may be." Serban leaned down so his face was right in hers. "But if that's so, who's he doing it for? Maybe the Seraph's still alive and calling the shots."

"Doubtful." Monahan shrugged. "But if you're so concerned, I'll track down this impostor and kill him, too. I won't even charge you for it."

Serban shook his head, turned, and stormed off. "Your mess, Monahan! Fix it."

It was too close now. Too close to time for Serban's rise for it to be interrupted by an upstart vigilante. He crushed the bug between his fingers, dropped the fragments on the floor, and stomped them to dust. Nothing was getting in his way this time. Nothing.

CHAPTER 24

Dean studied the schematics for city hall, committing the layout to memory. Around midnight, when he'd be going in, there would be three security guards on duty—one on each floor. Dean would have to place a bug on each floor for his wireless signal to be able to reach every phone in the building. That meant sneaking through each floor and avoiding each guard, and then getting back out again without being noticed.

There was also the issue of security cameras. Normally, Gideon could go in and Dean could hack the cameras from here, but that obviously wasn't an option right now. But another of Maddox and Arianna's timely inventions was a baffler that created a second of static on the video feed as the user passed the camera. That would allow Dean to sneak past them, but he'd have to be careful. If one of the guards watching the cameras noticed a pattern in the static, he might get suspicious.

"I can do this," he said. "I can do this. I can do this."

"Relax, Dean." Gideon sat in a chair near his training area on the second-floor balcony. "You'll be fine. These are two-bit security guards who have probably never had to deal with anyone breaking in . . . well, ever. And if one of them does notice you, you remember what I taught you about how to use the baton."

"Yes, but I don't want to hurt them. Odds are, they aren't corrupt."

"A quick hit to the back of the head won't seriously hurt them, just knock them out. They'll be fine."

"But if they notice me, I won't be behind them."

Gideon frowned. "Excellent point. Well, just do the best you can not to be noticed and if you do have to fight, go for a quick knockout. Just get in, place the bugs, and get out. No muss, no fuss."

"Okay. Yeah. Right. No muss, no fuss."

"I'll be in the lair monitoring your progress. If you need anything, just let me know."

"Will do."

Dean slipped the domino mask over his eyes and clasped the cape and hood around his neck. It really was a great feeling to wear the suit. It made him feel powerful.

"Provided everything goes without a hitch, I'll be back in about an hour." Dean headed for the stairs. "Here we go."

* * *

Gideon didn't know how Dean sat in the chair every night and just waited while he was out there fighting crime. He was doing it right now, and it was stressing him out. Even watching through the small button-cam Dean had installed, and even able to talk to him at any moment, he still felt completely separated from his friend. He drummed his fingers on the computer table, watching through Dean's feed as he weaved through traffic in the government district. It was a lot different than driving through the Brooks.

As he waited, he tried to think of what he'd say to Jolie. *Oh, hey, I'm the Seraph. Yeah, I've got superpowers and I've had them ever since I got back from Venezuela; I think I got them there from a mad scientist. And yeah,*

I've been using them to fight crime even though it's illegal. And I've kept it from you for months.

Yeah. That'd go over well.

* * *

Dean parked his bike several blocks from city hall, in front of a small coffee shop. He made his way down the street, trying to stay hidden behind parked cars, mailboxes, and anything else big enough to conceal him. He was thankful that the sidewalks were mostly abandoned at this time of night.

The three-story façade of city hall was directly across the street. Dean crossed and wound his way around to the back of the building. They had identified an old, unsecured window in the city planning department as the easiest access point. Dean removed a small knife from his belt and used it to pop the locks on the window. He inched it open and crawled into the dark office.

"Gideon, how am I doing?"

"Looking good. The first-floor guard is two halls down so you're good to go. Turn on that baffler before you leave the office."

"Right."

Dean flipped on the baffler and opened the door to the hallway. He crept down the hallway toward a central location where he could plant his bug. He'd never had to walk this slowly in his life; it was agonizing. But at least there was no sign of the guard.

As much as possible, he tried to time his movements so that he was never even within range of the security cameras, so that a static jump would never show up on them. He made it to his first destination with no interference. He removed the first bug from his belt and placed it on the underside of a bench. The signal should spread to the whole first floor from here.

The stairway to the second floor was one hall back. He turned and made his way in that direction.

"Hold up," Gideon said. "Guard's coming. Hide."

Dean slipped into an empty office to his left and hid in a corner, keeping his eye on the shadows in the hall. When the guard passed, he waited a few more moments and then slipped out into the hallway and headed for the stairs.

"Nice work," Gideon said. "You're a natural at this."

"Thanks. Second floor guard?"

"Nowhere near you."

Dean breathed out a long, slow sigh. So far . . . so good. He tried to keep his heart rate down as he moved, but this was stressful. It was like playing a stealth video game, and those had always made him the most nervous. First person shooters, RPGs, hack-and-slash, they were all fun, and he was great at them, but anything that required sneaking . . .

Focus, Dean. Not the time to be thinking about video games. He reached the landing for the second floor and slipped the door open. As Gideon had said, there was no sign of the guard. He walked out into the hallway and toward the second destination.

That, too, went off without a hitch. He placed the bug on a ledge above a painting. One more to go.

"Third floor guard is standing right where you need to go," Gideon said, "so take your time getting up there."

Dean snuck back to the stairwell and climbed slowly, feeling the agonizing seconds tick by. Maybe he should've started at the third floor and worked his way down. When he reached the top, he inched the door open and peered out.

"Guard's moving, but he's coming in your direction," Gideon said. "Drop back behind the door."

Dean did. His heart thumped as the guard's footsteps clacked on the marble floors outside. Soon, they began to fade off in the distance. Dean waited another ten seconds, and then peered back into the hall. No guard.

All right. He slipped through the door and down the hall. He placed the last bug high up on a display case containing city memorabilia.

"That's it," Gideon said. "Now just get out of there and you're home free."

He breathed a sigh of relief and, as quickly and quietly as possible, headed for the stairs. When he reached them, he rushed down them to the first floor. He swung open the door and stepped out—

"Dean, wait!"

—right into the path of the security guard. The guard's eyes widened, and he reached for his nightstick. Dean whipped out his own baton and swung it at the guard's other hand as he reached for his radio. The truncheon smacked the guard's hand and he recoiled. Dean swung again, this time at the guard's head.

The guard got his nightstick up and blocked the blow. Dean spun and angled his baton to the other side of the man's head. The guard ducked and struck Dean's knee with his nightstick. The Seraph armor was too thick for the blow to do any serious damage, but it stung. Dean gritted his teeth and kicked out at the still-crouching guard. It caught the man in the chin and knocked him back. Dean grabbed his collar and jerked him forward, punching him in the face. The guard slumped.

"Nice job," Gideon said. "You'd better get out of there."

Dean laid the unconscious guard on a bench and ran outside. Stupid! He'd been in such a hurry to get out. If he'd taken it a little slower, he could've avoided that fight altogether. Now there was a guard who'd remember seeing the Seraph in city hall, and he'd been standing in one place fighting the guard for long enough that it was possible he'd been in range of a camera for more than the few seconds the baffler could work. He'd have to get back to the lair, hack into the security system, and erase all the footage.

At least the bugs had been planted. It wasn't a total loss. He returned to the bike, mounted it, and headed back home. It was after one a.m. now.

"I hope this works," Dean said. "Otherwise all that stress was for nothing."

"It will. Thanks for doing this, Dean. It meant a lot."

"No problem." He sighed. "I don't know how you do it."

"Sheer force of will, man."

"Stubbornness, you mean."

Gideon laughed. "Yeah. Maybe that, too."

* * *

Monahan peered through her binoculars at "the Seraph" as he snuck out of city hall. Serban wouldn't be happy about this. If the Seraph had discovered the mob's government contacts, it could compromise the plan. Of course, that wouldn't matter if Monahan killed him tonight. For good this time.

This was not the Seraph. He moved differently, not like someone who had a lot of combat training. He ran awkwardly, as though he still wasn't used to the suit and cape. She'd even watched him fight the security guard from across the street, and he had handled himself adequately, but not with the professional precision of the man Monahan had combated on several occasions.

No, this was someone else. But she supposed it was possible that the real Seraph had survived and was mentoring this new one. Either way, this wannabe was going to be dead tonight. And if the real Seraph was still alive . . . well, he wouldn't be for much longer.

Monahan checked her pistol and knives. She turned on her car and followed the motorcycle-mounted impostor.

CHAPTER 25

Last year

Months had passed, Gideon was sure of it. He didn't know how many, but he knew he'd been here a long time. And still, nothing had changed. It was like, in the mind of that mad scientist and even the guerrillas, he had ceased to exist after he'd been brought back from the lab. They still brought food and water, but that was all.

"What do you think he's studying?" Gideon asked one day.

"I don't know." Joshua leaned against the cage bars, looking out at the jungle. "I have a theory, though."

"Yeah?"

"I think he's monitoring us right now. There must be some hidden cameras somewhere. Whatever he did to us in that lab, I think he's observing us to see what kind of effect it had."

"I haven't noticed any effects."

Joshua shrugged. "Maybe it didn't work. Maybe that's why he threw us back in here; maybe it worked on all the others but not us."

"Then why not kill us? What if it did work on us, and not anyone else?"

"But like you said, if it worked on us, why haven't we noticed any effects?"

"It could be a psychological experiment." Gideon tried to see if he could spot any hidden cameras. "Maybe he didn't do anything at all, and he just wants us to sit here so he can watch us go insane doing exactly what we're doing right now, trying to get into his brain."

"Could be . . . but to what end?"

"I don't know. He didn't seem all there to me, you know? A little unhinged."

"So, in theory, we're nothing but puppets for a madman. That's a lovely thought."

A few days after that conversation, two guerrillas appeared. Gideon frowned and moved over to the cage door.

"Move aside," one said in thickly-accented English.

"What do you want?"

"Him." The man pointed his rifle at Joshua. "Move aside."

"I'm not letting you take him."

Sudden pain stabbed into Gideon's left foot. He screamed and fell to the ground, clutching at the wound that had appeared just above his toes. They'd shot him!

"I didn't ask." He opened the cage and the other guerrilla came in and grabbed Joshua.

The older man complied without a word. Gideon watched him go, shaking his head. He wanted to protest, to shout at Joshua to fight back, but he knew he'd probably just get shot again. He watched them drag Joshua away.

But as they did, Joshua's foot bumped the rock that had been sitting just out of reach all those months. It rolled backward, just a little bit, toward Gideon. Joshua spared a quick glance back at him, smiled as he always did, and then let the guards take him.

Gideon grabbed one of the cage bars and pulled himself into a sitting position. He removed his shoe and sock and wrapped the latter around the bullet hole. He found the bullet itself lodged in the sole of his shoe, so he removed it before pulling the shoe back on.

He'd have to wait a while to walk again, but he had his way out now. He reached out, grabbed the rock, and pulled it into the cage, where he covered it with as much grass and dirt as he could. Hopefully, no one would see it. Unless, of course, Joshua was right about them watching on hidden cameras.

Gideon had to risk it anyway. He had to get Joshua back and then get out of here. He had rotted in a cage long enough.

Now

Gideon limped out to the balcony and looked down on the living room. Outside the massive floor-to-ceiling window that was their south wall, the city sparkled and gleamed, oblivious to the suffering just miles away on the other side of town. Sometimes living here made Gideon feel sick. He shook his head. Really, he just wished that someone—preferably him—could grab every wealthy person in Sojourn City by the collar and shake them until they realized how much they could be doing to help if only they'd get their heads out of the clouds and do something with their money other than spoil themselves. Did he have any room to talk, living in an apartment like this? Maybe not, but Dean was footing the bill, not him, and Dean and his family already did a lot of philanthropic work in the Brooks. Gideon was sure enough that he wasn't a hypocrite. At least, he hoped.

He walked over to the stairs. He'd have to be careful about this; taking the stairs with crutches was not an easy feat. But Jolie should be here any time now, and he didn't want to make her wait at the door for him to limp down the stairs to her. Better to be waiting down there when she arrived.

After a few long, painful moments, he made it to the living room and sat down on the couch. *I really hate this.* He was so ready to be off these crutches and back out on the streets. He was glad Dean was able to do some of this for him, but it wasn't the same. No one was actually fighting crime.

Gideon looked down at his fingers and coaxed a little bit of light into them. It really was an amazing gift he had. He wondered if he could go back a few months and tell himself that then what he would've thought. He would've called himself crazy, probably. As crazy as the man who had done this to him.

Or had probably done this to him. That was the only explanation Gideon had been able to come up with. That mad scientist—whose name he'd never learned—had to have been the one who had given him these powers. How and why, he didn't know. He didn't suppose he ever would, because there was no way to track him down. Maybe Joshua had developed the same powers and never even realized it. There had been the time when Joshua had known that the guerrillas were approaching long before Gideon had seen or heard them. He'd thought Joshua was just more familiar with the ambient sounds of that area, since he'd been there longer, but maybe he'd had the same empathic abilities Gideon did, and he'd sensed some of their trace emotions as they approached. Maybe the guerrillas had thrown Joshua and Gideon back in the cage because they were the only two subjects who had developed powers after the procedure—or they were the only two who had survived it.

The front door opened, snapping Gideon out of his reverie. Dean walked in, carrying the Seraph suit in a duffel bag.

"Welcome home."

"Thanks." Dean headed through the living room toward the stairs. "I'm going to go erase all the camera footage from city hall."

"Okay . . ."

"Just in case."

"Won't that make them more suspicious? All their footage being gone?"

"Better than me accidentally leaving a few seconds of footage that the baffler couldn't blur."

"Fair enough. Okay, well, I'll just be down here waiting for Jolie."

"Right. Good luck with that!"

"Thanks."

As Dean disappeared up the stairs, Gideon interlaced his fingers and began thinking, again, about what he'd tell Jolie. She'd be mad, he'd already resigned himself to that. But if he didn't try to make excuses, if he was honest and took the blame and apologized, maybe she would forgive him in time.

The door crashed in. Katrina Monahan stood at the entrance, pistol in one hand and knife in the other. Gideon jumped to his feet, feeling the pain of exertion in his back, and stumbled. Monahan smirked, pointed her gun at him, and pulled the trigger.

Gideon held up his hands in front of him and closed his eyes, waiting for the bullet to strike. But he felt nothing. Monahan's gun fired three more times. Still, Gideon felt nothing. He looked up—into blinding, white light.

"Impossible," Monahan said.

Gideon shook his head. His arms were glowing with a light as bright as it had been on the night he'd discovered his powers, back in Venezuela. Monahan fired again. The bullets disintegrated in the aura of light.

"What the heck?" Footsteps pounded above and Dean appeared on the balcony. "What's going—whoa!"

Dean ducked as Monahan swiveled her gun and fired on him. Gideon held out his hand and discharged some of the light built up in his hands. Monahan flew backward and dropped her gun. Gideon would've moved forward to finish her off, but his back was screaming, and he doubted he could even take one step without falling over. Monahan slowly got back to her feet, brandished her knife, and stormed toward Gideon.

* * *

Jolie was nervous about why Gideon wanted to meet. Maybe he just wanted to spend some time with her. She hoped that's what it was. But that didn't seem very likely. Otherwise, why ask her over as soon as her shift ended? He could've asked to see her the next day, after she'd rested, not when she'd be dead tired from a night of work.

He was going to admit that he was a vigilante. She had doubted it these past few weeks, because the Seraph had shown up a few times in the Brooks. But then she realized he'd never done more than appear for a few minutes before vanishing again. She didn't think it was the real Seraph; it was a body double, going out just to scare criminals. Jolie was almost positive.

Which only reinforced her belief that Gideon was the real Seraph, despite the impossibility of him having superpowers. He must have gotten them while he was in captivity, somehow, or maybe he'd somehow given them to himself while working at Sterling Labs. She didn't know for sure. It all sounded crazy.

And it only reminded her of the dream she'd had months ago, when Gideon had gone into the Brooks, guns blazing, mowing down criminals and innocents alike. It was extreme; it would never happen like that. But still, that dream haunted her.

She tapped her foot as the elevator rose to the apartment. She hadn't even changed out of her uniform yet; she had come straight here, just as he asked.

The elevator door opened, and multiple gunshots echoed through the hall. Jolie grabbed her handgun and ran down the hall toward Gideon's apartment. The door was wide open. She rushed inside.

Gideon stood in the middle of the living room, light radiating from his arms and torso. A woman was rushing at him, holding a knife. Monahan! Jolie's snapped her pistol up and trained it on Monahan.

"Freeze!"

The cry was enough to startle Monahan. She stopped her charge and whirled to face Jolie. When she saw her, her face contorted in anger and frustration.

"You! Always you!"

"Drop the knife!"

"I don't think so."

Monahan hurled the knife at Jolie and rushed toward her. Jolie dove aside, and at the same time a burst of light shot through the air and knocked the knife off course. It embedded itself in the wall. Monahan bounded past Jolie and into the hallway. Jolie clambered to her feet, turned, and fired at Monahan. One of the bullets struck Monahan's shoulder and the woman stumbled, but she was already at the elevator. The door slid open and Jolie fired again, tagging Monahan in the leg. But then the elevator doors closed.

"Not again," Jolie growled. "I hate that woman." She grabbed her radio. "This is Officer Anderson. I had eyes on Katrina Monahan at Lakeside Central Tower. She got away."

"We'll put out a BOLO to Lakeside's precinct," dispatch responded.

Jolie lowered her radio and slumped to the floor. She knew she couldn't catch Monahan; this building was fifty stories tall, so even if she took the stairs, the elevator would reach the ground long before she did. Monahan was gone.

"Everyone okay?" Dean shouted.

"Fine," Gideon responded.

Jolie looked into the living room. Gideon still stood in the middle of the floor, but he was no longer glowing. His eyes were on Jolie, and he looked pitiful, sad, weak . . . a million other things. He grabbed his crutches and limped over to her side. His face contorted in pain with every move he made.

"You're the Seraph," she said.

"Yeah." Gideon sat down on the floor beside her. "Yeah, I am."

Jolie leaned on his shoulder and cried. She cried out her anger. Her anger at Monahan, for evading her for months. Her anger at Gideon, for lying to her for so long. Her anger at humanity in general, for being so terrible and crummy and hurting all the people in the Brooks that she was supposed to be protecting. She was angry at just about everyone and everything. *God, why? Why is this my life?*

"I'm sorry," Gideon said.

She didn't answer. She just cried, and he wrapped an arm around her shoulders and let her. She heard footsteps inside the apartment and supposed that it was Dean approaching to make sure they were all right. He must've known, too. He must've been lying to her all this time just like Gideon. It wasn't fair. Her two best friends had kept the biggest secret she could think of, and they'd lied to do it. How could they?

"Come on, Jolie," Gideon said. "Let's move to the couch."

She nodded and stood first, and she and Dean helped Gideon to his feet. He limped over to the couch with her, while Dean closed the front door.

"I was going to tell you," Gideon said. "Tonight. That's why I called you here."

Jolie sniffled. "I know."

"I understand if you hate me. If you never want to speak to me again, even if you have to report me to the police. I . . . I understand. I'm sorry."

"Me too," Dean said. "Why don't I go put on some coffee? I feel like we'll be up for a while."

He walked away, and Jolie sat and stared into Gideon's face. She saw even more clearly up close how sorry he was. The pain—physical and emotional—he was in right now. She had every right to hate him, he was right about that. But . . . how could she? She dried her tears and looked him hard in the eyes.

"Start from the beginning," she said. "I want to know everything."

CHAPTER 26

Serban's eyes snapped open. What had awakened him? Someone pounded on the door. Oh, yeah. That. He threw his covers off, grabbed the gun on his bedside table, and stormed toward the door. Whoever this was better have a good reason for waking him up at—he glanced the clock—2:30 . . .

He looked out the peephole. It was Monahan, and she looked bad. He opened the door and let her in but didn't put down his gun. He had a feeling he was about to be very angry with what she had to say. She limped over to a chair and sat down. Serban saw blood on her thigh and shoulder, and some of her hair looked like it was matted with dry blood, too.

"It was the Seraph," she said.

"I knew it!" Serban tightened his grip on his gun. "You failed again, you useless . . ."

"I know who he is now. I've seen his face. His and his friends. I didn't recognize him, but one of your contacts can track down a name."

"Tell me. You're not on that job anymore; consider yourself fired. I'll send my own people to clean that mess up."

"It's not a total loss," Monahan said. "He still has severe injuries from when he fell off the warehouse. He could hardly move."

"He could hardly move . . . and yet you look like this."

"He still has his powers. But in another second, I would've had him. His cop friend, the woman Anderson, interrupted. She's the one who shot me. And I saw his other friend, too. I suspect he's the one who has been posing as the Seraph the past few weeks."

"Good. Give me faces so I can track down names." Serban turned away. "I already paid you for killing him, so that means you owe me. And since you're fired from the Seraph job, that means you're my enforcer now. Full-time, no further pay."

There was a long silence. Serban could feel in the tension that punctuated the silence that she was weighing her options, debating on whether she should just kill him and cut her losses. He'd like to see her try.

"Very well." Monahan walked around him, so she was in front of him again. "Here. I had this pin on my tunic. It has a tiny camera in it; it will have recorded their faces. I even made sure to turn and get a look at his friend."

"Good." Serban took the mini-cam. "Now get out of here. We can discuss your future duties tomorrow."

* * *

The more Gideon told Jolie, the less he could tell what she was thinking. Even trying to reach out to her with his empathic abilities, she was so introspective and closed off that it was hard to get a read on her. A few minutes into the story, Dean came in with three cups of coffee and put them down on the table. He sat down in a recliner on Jolie's side of the couch.

As Gideon recounted everything, from when he'd escaped the guerrillas and discovered his powers to when he decided to become a vigilante and finally when he embraced his powers and chose to use them to fight crime, he didn't leave out any details. He told her several times how sorry he was he hadn't told her before, too.

"Wow," Jolie said when he finished. "I . . . wow."

"I know, it's a lot to take in."

"You could say that." She stood. "Gideon, I . . . you've got to admit, it looks pretty bad that you kept this from me for how many months? How many lies have you had to tell to keep me from finding out the truth? I love you—and I know you love me. But if you loved me the way you're supposed to, you would have told me a long time ago."

"I—"

"I know you've probably told yourself any number of excuses to keep lying to me. I know it must've been killing you, because you're such a good, moral person. But no matter the excuse, no matter how badly you felt . . . you did lie. You did keep this from me."

Gideon lowered his head. "I know. I'm sorry."

"Me, too." Jolie set her coffee cup down. "I'll call you tomorrow. For now, I need to go home and think about this."

"Okay."

Gideon watched her walk toward the door. Every instinct he had urged him to go after her, to plead with her to come back and listen. But he knew she was right. He'd been afraid of this, but it had still been the right thing to do. Of course, Jolie had every right to be upset about this. He would've been, in her position. She opened the door, glanced back at him once, and then stepped out and closed the door behind her. For a long moment, the room was silent.

"You okay?" Dean asked.

Gideon nodded. "I will be."

Whether Jolie would be or not was another thing—but he prayed she would be. He had no right to ask for forgiveness, but he hoped for it anyway. *God, I'm sorry for hurting her. Please forgive me—and please let Jolie forgive me, too.*

CHAPTER 27

As Jolie approached Gideon's apartment the next afternoon, she still didn't have any idea what she was going to say to Gideon. Her instinct was to chew him out, to break up with him and tell him she could never forgive him for all the lies he'd told. It would've felt good—for a little while, at least. But she knew that it wouldn't have been long before she regretted it. It wasn't the way God would want her to react. And she wasn't willing to lose the love of her life over this, either.

She stood outside the apartment door for a long time, staring at the knob and trying to decide what to do. She backed away and nearly fled back down to her car, but a surge of resolve built inside her. Taking a deep breath, Jolie stepped forward and knocked on the door. Seconds later, the door opened. Gideon, still supporting himself on crutches, stepped aside and gestured for her to come in.

"Hi."

"Hi." Jolie stepped inside. "How are you feeling."

"Not bad, all things considered. Do you want to sit down?"

Jolie nodded. She followed Gideon over to the couch and sat down. She looked into his eyes. In their blue shine, Jolie saw hope and nervousness mixed together and wondered if he saw the same thing in hers.

"Gideon, I want you to know, first of all, that I'm very angry that you've kept this from me for so long." She took a deep breath, but then continued before he could respond. "And secondly . . . I forgive you."

Gideon blinked. "Just like that?"

"Yes. I mean, it'll probably take me a while to fully process all this, but I know that I'll only be more miserable if I hold a grudge. It's better for me to forgive you now."

The words tumbled from her mouth almost of their own volition, but with each one, she felt a weight being lifted from her. She had been suspicious of him for months now, and finally, she didn't have to be anymore. And if she was honest with herself, she knew that he was only doing what he thought was right. If she was going to start confessing, she might as well go all the way.

"And I have something to tell you, too. Months ago, I had a dream about you. You were decked out in leather and strapped up like you were going to war. I tried to stop you, but you gave me this . . . this wicked look. You charged at a bunch of people in the Brooks, criminals and innocents alike. And you slaughtered them all."

"Oh. I . . . Jolie, you've got to believe I'm not like that, and I'd never do something like that. You know me; I'm no killer."

"I know. And . . . maybe that's another reason I'm forgiving you so readily. I sat here last night and listened to you tell me everything you've been doing, and there was no malice in you. Your heart is set on justice, but not on hurting anyone. So yes, Gideon, I forgive you."

Tears filled his eyes. "Thank you."

"But that brings me to my last point. Good intentions or not, super-powers or not, I really think you should stop being the Seraph. Both you and Dean. Sooner or later, one of you isn't going to walk away. You almost died last night."

"I know. But who else is going to do this? You know as well as I do that at the rate the crime wave is expanding, the police in the Brooks can't handle it alone. And the Crusader is retired, so he can't do it."

"It's not your job, Gideon."

"No, but maybe it's my responsibility." He held up a hand and let a little light trickle out. "I can do amazing things. It would be selfish of me to not use those powers to help others."

"I see your point, but . . . Gideon, you're just one man, regardless of how powerful you are."

"But I've been making a difference, and you know it."

"At what cost?"

"A cost I'm willing to pay."

"Are you? Don't just think about yourself, Gideon. If you die, what happens to your family? Or me, or Dean?"

"You think I haven't considered that? Every time I go out there, I know I might not come back. But it's the same for you, because you're in as much danger as I am every time you put on your uniform."

"Maybe. Look, Gideon, just think about it. I know you're not going to get back out there right away anyway, considering you can hardly move. But when you do get better . . . just think about what I've said, okay?"

"Okay. So, you're not going to turn me over to the police, then?"

"Of course not." Jolie sighed. "I can't argue with what that news anchor said a few weeks ago. I haven't been able to get it off my mind. You just want to help. You may not be going about it the way most would, but . . . you're trying to do the right thing."

"I am. And because I am, I'm going to give you some information that maybe the police can use."

"Okay. What's that?"

"We think we know who the leader of this whole thing is. Luca Serban, a Romanian crime lord. We also think he may have contacts in city hall. Even the police department; we've already sent in a tip, but I think they ignored it. Serban's planning something big."

"Luca Serban. I'll look into it." Jolie hugged him and stood. "This is going to take us some time to work through, but I do forgive you. And I still love you."

"I love you, too."

"Make sure Dean takes care of you. And . . . you take care of him, too."

"I will."

Jolie checked her watch. "I've got to get going. Feel better."

"I will. Love you."

"Love you, too."

* * *

Gideon slumped back into the couch as Jolie stepped outside. He allowed all the pain and fear and confusion he'd bottled up flood through him. Tears welled in his eyes. He sensed sympathy radiating from nearby and looked up. Dean stood on the balcony, leaning against the banister, and looked down on Gideon.

"Maybe she's right," Gideon said. "Maybe I shouldn't be doing this."

"I don't believe that."

"Why not?"

"Think about all the people who'd be dead now if the Seraph hadn't been in business for the past few months. You're a hero, Gideon. This city needs you."

Gideon blinked, and a few tears rolled down his cheeks. "Thanks, man."

"But she's right about one thing—it's still going to be a while before you're ready to get back out there. Speaking of which, we should probably get you to your physical therapy appointment."

"Right." Gideon grabbed his crutches and hoisted himself to his feet. "Let's do it."

* * *

Over the next few weeks, Gideon pushed himself as much as he could in physical therapy. He intended to get better as soon as possible, and if that meant wearing himself out a day at a time and then going straight home to sleep, that's what he'd do.

During that time, Dean kept an eye on the phone records from city hall. So far, nothing looked terribly suspicious, but anything that had the potential to be sketchy, he bookmarked for review. Their bug in The Broken Glass had gone quiet long before—likely discovered by Serban.

On his third week on crutches, Gideon returned to work. He entered the lab and looked around. It was the same as he'd left it: scientists milling about but mostly keeping to themselves, not interrupting another's work unless absolutely necessary. Had it always been this boring? Probably.

He hobbled over to his desk, leaned his crutches against the wall, and sat down. Doctor Sung approached him.

"Welcome back, Mr. Turner."

"Thank you, Dr. Sung." Gideon smiled. "I'm ready to get back to work."

"Good. The super-soldier project is being transferred back to you. I'll have all my notes sent to you for your perusal, so you are up to speed."

"You've been working on the project directly?"

"Yes, I have. It's getting close to completion, but there are still a few sequences that need to be perfected."

Gideon nodded. "I'll see what I can do."

He'd almost forgotten about the super-soldier serum, what with everything else that was going on. But now that it was in front of him again, he felt the same concern he had the first time he'd been told about it. This was an idea with a lot of potential to go wrong. All it would take was one bad person getting their hands on it and the city would have a monster on its hands.

But he wasn't paid to make that kind of decision. He'd do the work, give the results to Mr. Sterling, and if things went bad, he'd take on whoever abused the serum as the Seraph.

* * *

Serban's list of contacts grew every day. He now had access to almost every part of the city's infrastructure, and he was slowly using that to the advantage of his criminal empire. It felt good. This must be what it was like to be a king.

But sometimes, the most useful contacts were the ones who had been around longest.

Serban let few people into his apartment, and fewer live after they had seen it. Monahan, his lieutenants such as Costin . . . and now, Detective Walters. The corrupt cop had proven himself to Serban. Between covering up the shooting of the pastor at the church, scrubbing the van used on the second church attack, and consistently throwing the cops off Serban's trail, Walters had been quite the useful little asset. Serban didn't trust the man, by any means—if he would betray his oath to the police department for money, then there was always a chance that he would betray Serban, too—but he could rely on Walters' greed to keep him in line for the next few days, at least. After that, it wouldn't matter. Serban wouldn't need this apartment once he'd conquered the city. He'd have his pick.

Maybe he'd take the Seraph's fancy high-rise.

Walters sat at the small, circular four-person table on one side of the apartment. Serban picked up the file he'd put together on the Seraph, complete with the picture Monahan had gotten of the boy. If necessary, he would go to every hospital in the city to discover the Seraph's identity. After being thrown off the roof by Monahan, he had to have been treated somewhere. Someone knew who he was. But Serban didn't want to do that kind of legwork until he had exhausted his options within his own organization. Crossing the room to stand behind Walters, Serban dropped the file on the table in front of the detective.

"What's this?" Walters asked.

"Everything we have on the Seraph. Including a picture of him unmasked. We need a name to go with the face. Can you run the file?"

Walters nodded and opened the folder. The image of the towheaded boy stared out at Serban, taunting him with his youth. Serban estimated he was around twenty-five years old, nearly half Serban's age. And operating with relatively few assets, this child had been able to harm Serban's organization in ways that veteran police officers hadn't. It was infuriating.

"No need to run it; I know this kid," Walters said. "You're sure it's him?"

"No question," Serban said. "Monahan fought him unmasked, said he used his light powers and everything. It's him."

"Well, boss, this boy is Gideon Turner—he's the son of the pastor of Refuge Church. Not to mention, he's dating Jolie Anderson, the beat cop who's been giving Monahan fits."

Serban growled deep in his throat. "I should've known. That church has caused me nothing but grief since I got to this city, and that relentless cop would be connected somehow. It's time to deal with this, once and for all. Turner thinks he can fight me as a vigilante? We'll see if he feels the same way once I've got his family's necks between my fingers."

Walters closed the file. "You want me to round up the Turners?"

"Not yet." Serban crossed the room and opened the door, indicating that it was time for Walters to leave. "Just get me their address. I'll have a team ready to act—but this is an advantage we can't waste. Thank you for your help, Detective. I can guarantee you'll be generously compensated when all this mess is over."

"Thank you, sir."

Walters ducked out the door, and Serban closed it behind him. He drove his fist down into the cheap wooden table. The edge of the table cracked under the force of the blow. *Enjoy your little crusade while you can, Turner. Your days are numbered.*

* * *

Luca Serban was like a ghost.

Jolie had been searching for him ever since Gideon gave her his name, and so far, she had come up with a fat wad of nothing. She could confirm he was in the city; Pulaski had managed to nail down that much. But what he'd done since he'd gotten here and where he was currently living was a mystery. It was as if this guy didn't exist.

His supposed city hall contacts were equally nebulous. Although that was far from Jolie's district, she'd at least put feelers out in other precincts and received a few responses from officers who were willing to investigate. But so far, they couldn't find anything, either. Any illegitimate phone calls or meetings were being very cleverly disguised.

Finally, she decided to start where she'd already been. Her first hint about Monahan had led her to The Broken Glass. She knew Monahan was working for Serban, so maybe The Broken Glass was one of Serban's haunts.

"You're not a detective, you know," Paul said as they drove there.

"I know, but we're kind of short on those right now." Jolie shrugged. "Someone has to solve this thing before the whole city comes unglued."

"Where exactly did you get this information?" Paul asked. "You never told me."

"I'd prefer not to say."

"Uh-huh."

Jolie sighed and parked their cruiser across the street from The Broken Glass. Paul was right, she knew. This was more Pulaski's job than hers. But there was only so much that he could do, and the other detectives were busy with their own cases. She'd take things into her own hands if it meant protecting the city from something terrible.

She popped her door open and walked toward the bar, Paul trailing behind her. There weren't many people inside. Two men sat at a table in one corner, and two more in the other corner. It wasn't quite prime drinking time yet, apparently. The bartender looked at her as she entered. From the glint in his eye, he recognized her.

"Hello, officers. How can I help you?"

"We are looking for a man named Luca Serban. Happen to know him?"

"Can't say I do." The bartender shrugged. "Course, lots of people come in here that I don't know."

"Uh-huh." Jolie looked at the mirror behind him, watching the rest of the room. "He's a foreigner. Romanian, to be specific. Sure you don't know him?"

Behind them, the bar's few patrons were shifting. Jolie watched them all in the mirror, keeping track of their positions and trying to tell if they were armed. They were, but thankfully they all seemed to be carrying close-range weapons. She didn't spot any guns. Yet.

"Romanian? I have a few foreigners time to time, but I can't say I'd recognize a Romanian over any other nationality."

"No? Oh, well." Jolie glanced at Paul. Someone was moving behind him. "Guess we should go. But you will let us know if you hear his name?"

"Oh, sure. Sure. My pleasure."

Jolie whipped out her nightstick and lunged. Paul ducked, and she struck the man behind him as he raised a switchblade. Paul pulled his own nightstick and tangled with two men who wielded baseball bats. Jolie focused her attention on the attacker in front of her, plus the other one following him.

The switchblade wielder slashed at Jolie. She jumped back and then moved in as his arm cleared her, pressing it against him so he couldn't use the knife again. She hit him twice more with her nightstick and then shoved him into the bar as the second attacker came at her with a length of chain.

He tangled her nightstick in his chain and tugged. Jolie struggled to keep her grip on it, but he succeeded in throwing it to the ground. She swung her left hand in an uppercut that connected with his jaw. He whipped the chain low and she grimaced as the links dug into her ankles. She charged him and rammed him with her full weight—which wasn't substantial, but at least knocked him off balance. She kept pushing until he hit the ground and she was on top of him. She rained down punches, which he tried to block with his forearms. She snaked one arm between his, pushed them aside, and knocked him out with a sharp punch to the jaw.

She stood and turned. Paul had knocked out both his attackers and was holding his nightstick in one hand and one of their baseball bats in the other. The bartender reached under the bar—

Jolie whipped her gun out and trained it on him. "Don't!"

He pulled a shotgun out and aimed it. Jolie fired twice, and the bartender crashed to the floor.

"Well," Paul said, "I take it they know Serban."

CHAPTER 28

Gideon took a few short, careful steps. With each, he grew more confident and by his tenth step he was walking in a normal and balanced, albeit slow, stride. His physical therapist smiled and made a few notes on his computer.

"I am impressed, Gideon. I don't think you need your crutches anymore. A few weeks and you will be able to resume normal physical activity."

"Normal activity?"

The therapist nodded. "Like working out, running, and so on. Right now, that may still be a bit strenuous for you, although you should still do the exercises I've prescribed. But after our next appointment, I expect you'll have a clean bill of health."

"Thank you." Gideon sat down. "That's really good to hear."

After a few more minutes of conversation with the therapist, Gideon headed out. Dean looked up.

"Hey, no crutches!" he said.

"Nope." Gideon grinned as Dean fell in line next to him. "So, I can finally drive myself again, finally get places without those annoying crutches . . . "

"But not go beat the stuffing out of criminals just yet. Right?"

"Right." Gideon climbed into Dean's car. "Speaking of, anything in connection with city hall yet?"

"Actually, yes." Dean started the car and pulled away. "It was tricky to pick up on because they never used Serban's name, but using a vocal analyzer, I found a few calls that had a speaker with a Romanian accent on the other end of the line."

"Who did it go to?"

"Well, Deputy Mayor Hart, for one."

"You're kidding."

"No joke. This goes all the way to the top. Also seems like several city councilmen may be tied to him, too."

"I don't get it. What's Serban planning?"

"All their conversations with him have sounded very businesslike, but my guess is that they're paving the way for him to completely take over."

"What? The whole city?"

"Yeah. The deputy mayor talked about getting in contact with some people to make sure the interstate was blocked off, so no one could leave town. And one of the councilmen is buddies with one of the operators of the bridge that connects Lakeside to the Platform."

"Unbelievable." Gideon rubbed his forehead. "Hopefully, the police have this already, but if not, send it on to them, okay? The transcripts, recordings, whatever."

"How do we even know which police are or aren't corrupt?"

"Jolie's not. We know that. Send it to her, and hopefully she'll have a good idea of who to give it to."

"Right. Will do!" Dean glanced over at him. "You know, when Serban makes his move, we may not be able to handle this alone. Especially if it happens before your back to one hundred percent."

"I know. What are you proposing?"

"Maybe it's time to reach out to the Crusader, see if he'd be willing to be on standby in case everything goes south."

"I don't want to put him in danger, but . . . yeah, we may need him. I definitely can't take on the entire criminal empire of the Brooks alone."

"No, you cannot."

Gideon wondered if the super-soldier serum would be ready before then. He still had his reservations about it. He thought it was insane, in fact. But it might be a necessary insanity at this point. A few more super-powered individuals on the side of good might be a big help when Serban made his move. He decided to make that project his focus for the next few days. Maybe he could finish it before it was too late. And he should work on retraining his body, too.

"I'm going out tonight."

"What, as the Seraph?"

"Yeah. I won't get into any major scuffles; I'll find a few lowlife drug dealers or stop a petty theft or something. But I need to get back into the groove now, or I may not be ready when I really need to."

"Okay." Dean shook his head. "But you're insane, you know that, right? You're actually going to die."

"I'm not going to die. I told you, I'll be careful. Besides, I've got your armor. I'll be fine."

And truthfully, Gideon was ready to be back out there. Whatever everyone else said—his parents, Jolie, even Dean—he knew that being the Seraph was what he was meant to do. He had to keep doing it no matter what.

* * *

Jolie looked through the one-way glass at the suspect waiting in the interrogation room. Pulaski looked at him, at her, and then back at him again.

"Nice work, Anderson," he said. "You really did a number on his face."

"He tried to kill me with a switchblade." Jolie shrugged. "So I hit his face with my nightstick. And a countertop."

"Nice." Pulaski opened the interrogation room door. "If he tells me anything, I'll let you know."

"Thanks."

Jolie wanted to watch the interrogation, but she knew she needed to get back out on patrol. She cast one last glance back at Pulaski and the criminal and then walked down the hall. Good thing he'd been available to do the interrogation, rather than Walters. Paul sat in the break room, sipping a cup of coffee.

"You ready?" she asked.

He nodded. "Always."

The two walked together back to their cruiser. They were just exiting the precinct when a dispatcher shouted for them. Jolie turned.

"Officer Anderson, just got a call for you. Someone says they've got information you may be looking for."

"What? Who?"

"They said to meet them at 52 Templeton."

52 Templeton? Why did that address sound familiar? Then it clicked— the house where she'd seen Gideon and the Crusader fighting Monahan. Was this a message from Gideon?

"We'll check it out. Thank you."

As Paul drove to the address, Jolie wondered why Gideon wouldn't have just told her in person or called her cell phone. Maybe he wanted to make things look legit by going through the proper channels.

Paul parked the car on the street in front of 52 Templeton. The house was completely dark, the window still shattered from the fight. Clearly, the residents had moved out. Jolie didn't blame them. She got out of the car and looked around.

"Stay here," she told Paul.

He nodded. "Holler if you need me."

Jolie walked toward the house and kept her hand near her sidearm. It occurred to her suddenly that Monahan had also seen her here, and this could be a trap. Jolie placed her hand directly on the butt of her gun, ready to draw at a moment's notice.

As she approached the house, the porch lights flickered on. A figure walked out of the shadows and stood directly in the light. He was a black man, probably in his late forties or early fifties. She realized that he had been one of the residents of this house. He smiled at her and walked down the steps.

"Hello, Officer."

"Hello." Jolie didn't remove her hand from her gun. "You have information for me?"

"I do. I'm going to reach into my pocket now, but it's only to get a flash drive." When Jolie nodded, he reached slowly into his pocket. "A mutual friend of ours gave me this to give to you."

A mutual friend . . . "The Seraph?"

"Yes." He extended his hand, which held a white flash drive. "He says it has records of incriminating phone calls you might be interested in."

"How? We've been monitoring all of city hall's phone calls."

"He says they'll sound totally legit at first." The man handed it to her. "But the man on the other end of the line is either Serban or one of his associates. He has a Romanian accent. That's what the Seraph told me to tell you."

"Thank you." Jolie studied the man. "You're him, aren't you?"

"What's that?"

"The Crusader. You're him. That's why you both were here fighting Monahan. That's why you didn't chase her, even though the Seraph did. Because you stayed here. It was your house."

The man smiled. "Well. You'd make quite the detective, Officer."

"Thank you." Jolie tilted her head. "Why did you attack Detective Walters?"

"I discovered Pastor Jeff in the church the night he was attacked. When I got there, Walters was on the scene, but he was there to erase video footage of the attack. I let him go and called the ambulance. But I knew Walters was corrupt, so I went after him to get a confession about who attacked the pastor."

"And I showed up before you could interrogate him."

He chuckled. "Right."

Vindication. Jolie had been right to investigate Walters all this time. His connection with Monahan, the disappearance of crucial evidence . . . it had been him.

"But you don't do it anymore. The Crusader hasn't been seen in . . . months."

"No. My family needs Wyatt Jonson more than the city needs the Crusader." He shrugged. "But with what's coming? If the Seraph needs me, I'll be right by his side."

"You know, I could technically arrest you. You just incriminated yourself for vigilantism."

"You could." Jonson shrugged. "But I figure the Seraph wouldn't have sent me to you if he didn't trust you."

"True. Okay, I'll take this flash drive back to the department. Go back to your family. And take my advice: don't get involved again. Leave it to us."

"If I believed the police could handle it alone, maybe I would." Jonson turned and walked away. "But this is my city, too. Good night, Officer."

Jolie stood there for a long time, staring down at the flash drive in her hands. Maybe he was right. Maybe the police were out of their depth. She returned to the car. If they were, at least they'd do their best, and they'd go out fighting. This city would fall to Serban over her dead body.

* * *

Gideon dropped down onto a fire escape and fired a burst of light down into the alley below. The beam hurled a would-be mugger back against the alley wall. His victim looked up at Gideon, made a noise of gratitude—or fear, Gideon wasn't sure which—and ran from the alley. The Seraph jumped off the fire escape and to the ground below. Hitting the ground sent a small shockwave of discomfort from his knees up his back, but it wasn't debilitating. Gideon gritted his teeth and walked toward the mugger, who climbed to his feet and leaned on the wall for support, rubbing his head.

"Luca Serban," Gideon growled. "Do you know him?"

The mugger shook his head. "No. No, I don't."

Gideon fired another blast of light, this one at the wall just to the mugger's right, creating a cascade of dust and shattered brick. The mugger whimpered. The Seraph felt fear roll off him in waves.

"I don't! I don't! B-but I've heard of him."

"Do you know where he lives? What he's planning?"

"No! One of his people, the Romanians, they offered me a job to gather intel off the streets and bring it back to them, but I do it through an intermediary!"

"Who is the intermediary?"

"He's a regular at The Broken Glass; name's Costin! But he got collared by the cops the other day. I don't have any other way to get in contact with them."

Gideon sensed the desperation—and truthfulness—the man was emanating. He shook his head. This hadn't been as fruitful as he'd hoped. He'd taken down three other small-time thugs tonight, and none of them had known anything about Serban. This was the first guy who had, and his contact was already in police custody. Great.

"I believe you."

"Th-thank you. So . . . will you let me go?"

Gideon snorted. "No. But I won't break any bones."

He punched the thug across the jaw, knocking him unconscious. He took a length of cord from his utility belt, bound the man's wrists, and threw him out of the alley onto the street corner. He wouldn't get anything useful tonight, he could see. He climbed the fire escape and headed for home.

It had felt good to get back on the streets again, though—albeit exhausting. But it was a start.

CHAPTER 29

Last year

Gideon took a little longer than was probably necessary to make sure his foot was okay, but without medication or disinfectant, it was better to be safe than sorry. He moved around the cage for weeks, putting pressure on it and ignoring the pain, knowing that every moment he waited they could be torturing or even killing Joshua. The first day, he hadn't even been able to walk without the pain blurring his vision and causing him to stumble. After a few days, it was still a terrible stabbing sensation and he had to limp. Even by the end of the first week, he still hobbled with every step. It killed him to not run in there and rescue the man who had become his only friend in this place. But it wouldn't do him any good to get out of the cage if he was stumbling around and got himself shot.

Eventually, he felt that he had waited as long as he possibly could. His foot still wasn't healed, but the thought that Joshua could die if Gideon didn't do something was too much for him to bear. He grabbed the rock from its hiding place and, with three heavy blows, smashed the padlock from the cage. He threw the door open and rushed toward the building at a half-sneaking, half-running pace.

He came to the door and realized he had no idea what to do now. He'd sworn not to kill, but if it meant saving Joshua's life, would it be worth it? Maybe it wouldn't come to that. But considering his only weapon was a rock, and the guerrillas were armed with AK-47s, he didn't think much of his chances anyway.

The door was locked. Gideon shook his head and brought the rock down on the handle as hard as he could. It bent but didn't break. He hit it again. And again. And again. Finally, it snapped off. Metal pieces flew everywhere, including part of the locking mechanism. Gideon kicked the door and it flew open.

"Hey!" someone shouted.

A guerrilla, seated at a small table just inside the door, stood and reached for his rifle. Gideon hurled the rock as hard as he could—good thing he'd played baseball in high school—and struck the man square in the head. He collapsed.

Gideon went over to his side and found a keyring on his belt. He removed it and took the guard's rifle. He was committed now. *If I kill, I kill.* He knew it would tear him up inside, that he would be haunted by the faces of the men he killed, but he had no choice. He flicked off the rifle's safety and moved down the hall.

He had no idea where he was going. They could be keeping Joshua anywhere, and this was not a small building. He kept close to the walls, rifle raised, and decided to just take it one hallway at a time. He'd find Joshua eventually.

Now

Sterling Lab's tech was state-of-the-art. Inputting the exact formula for the super-soldier serum into a computer program, Gideon could run a simulation of what would theoretically happen if the serum, in its current state, was injected into a human being. Then, if it wasn't projected to work, he could fiddle with it and try again.

So far, there hadn't been a successful simulation. The first few tests had projected instant death for the user. That wouldn't do. After Dr. Sung had worked on it, the program predicted that the user of the serum would face serious mutations, including tumors and cancers, but would survive initial injection. Still, hardly an ideal solution.

Now, Gideon thought he was onto something. The current simulation told him that if a person were injected with this iteration of the serum, they would gain the expected attributes, but their metabolism and bloodstream would be thrown incredibly out of balance. It wouldn't be immediately fatal, but it could cause problems later in life. Still, it was better than what he'd started with. A few more days, and he'd probably have a solution.

His ideal final product would give temporary enhanced abilities, more like a steroid but without the negative effects. That would allow the user to have the abilities they needed in the moment, but once it wore off, they'd go back to normal. That would be better than providing an entire group of police officers permanent superpowers.

Gideon checked the clock. It was 5:00. He shut off the simulations, locked the serum and other ingredients away, and hung his lab coat on the peg next to his desk. Hands tucked in his jacket pockets, he walked out the door.

"Mr. Turner!"

Gideon turned. Dr. Sung approached at a brisk pace, his brow furrowed.

"Yes?"

"Mr. Sterling would like to see you."

"Of course. Is he here?"

"Yes. Upstairs."

"All right. I'll see him right away. Thank you, Dr. Sung."

Sung nodded and walked away. Gideon frowned. What was all that about? The man looked incredibly stressed. He had always been tightly-wound, but this seemed like something else.

Gideon took the elevator up to Sterling's office. Edgar Sterling spent most days at his high-rise office at Sterling Enterprises, the headquarters of his business. But on the days when he worked in the lab, he had a smaller office there, so he wouldn't have to commute back and forth. It was nothing if not efficient.

Gideon stepped out of the elevator and stopped outside the door to Sterling's office. He reached out to knock—

Fear, anger, stress. This isn't how I wanted it to go.

Sterling's emotions were rushing out at him like a tidal wave. Whatever Dean's father was dealing with, it was causing him a great deal of distress. Gideon strained to hear what was going on, but the doors were too thick. All he heard was indistinct muttering.

He knocked. The talking stopped, and the door's lock chirped, and it slid open. Gideon stepped inside. Sterling stood at the window, looking out over the courtyard below. He tucked his cell phone in his pocket and turned to face Gideon.

"Welcome, Mr. Turner!" He smiled. "Thank you for coming. I know your shift is over, but I wanted to inquire about the status of the serum." He gestured to a chair. "Please, sit."

"Of course." As Gideon eased into the plush chair, Sterling sat at his desk. "Well, I have narrowed down and eliminated the ingredients that were causing most of the negative results. There are still a few that need to be whittled down or replaced, and I'm working on that. But I expect to have a successful simulation within a few weeks."

Edgar smiled. "Excellent! However, I would encourage you to speed it up, if possible. The crime in this city is growing at an exponential rate, and I would like to have this serum to the police as soon as possible, especially since the Brooks' vigilantes have all but disappeared."

"I understand. I'll do my best."

"Thank you, Gideon. I cannot emphasize enough that I believe the sooner the serum is ready, the better."

Gideon kept a straight face, but something about that bothered him. Why exactly was this suddenly so important to Sterling? Did he know something? Had he heard rumors about the corruption in city hall? Maybe that's why he had been so stressed. If he knew how deep Serban's influence went, maybe he feared that a city-wide disaster was imminent. But as soon as next week?

"I'll see it done, sir."

"Thank you. That's all I needed, Gideon. It was good to see you."

"And you, Mr. Sterling. Good night."

"Good night."

On a whim, Gideon reached into his pocket as he walked toward the door. He had kept one of Dean's bugs on him, just in case he needed it on the spot. As he opened the door, he tucked the bug neatly on the doorframe, where it wouldn't be immediately noticeable. He hoped he was just being overly cautious, but if Sterling had an inside source, it might be good to know just what he was being told. Of course, there was still his office at Sterling Enterprises . . . maybe the Seraph should pay that office a building and bug it, too.

How's Dean going to feel when he finds out I bugged his dad? Hopefully, he wouldn't be too mad. It wasn't like he thought Sterling was working for Serban, or anything; he'd done too much good for the city for

Gideon to imagine that. But he might have a good source of information that was keeping him looped in on criminal activity that Gideon didn't know about.

Anyway, time would tell. He started to walk to the elevator but changed direction for the stairs. If something really was about to go down, he'd be suiting up again soon—for something much bigger than taking down a few muggers and drug dealers. And that meant he needed to kick his body back into fighting condition as much as possible. No matter what, the Seraph would be there when Serban made his move.

He walked outside into the brisk, late-February air. As he stepped out into the courtyard, he looked up at the top floor of Sterling Labs. He wondered if Mr. Sterling had gone back to looking out introspectively over the courtyard. His ponderings were broken as his phone rang. He pulled it from his pocket, checked the caller—Jolie—and answered it.

"Hello."

"Thanks for the information, 'Seraph.'"

He smiled and stepped out into the parking lot. "So, Wyatt got the file to you. Good."

"He did. Gave it to me last night. I've got our geek squad poring over it now. If it is what your friend says it is, then we may be able to get a jump on whatever it is Serban's planning."

"Good. I hope so. Are you doing okay?"

"I am. A little shaken up; I got in a pretty nasty fight at The Broken Glass."

Oh. He remembered what the mugger had told him about his contact being arrested there.

"Are you all right?"

"Yes; the other guys fared worse than me."

"That's my girl." Gideon unlocked his car and got in. "Look, I know you want me to be safe, but . . . "

"Wyatt told me already," she said. "He doesn't think we can handle it. And I know you don't either. I get that. But Gideon, do you really think you're ready to get back out there?"

"Not completely. But I am doing a lot better. I can hold my own again." He hesitated, but he had vowed to be honest with her from now on. "And I went out last night. Just took out a few small-time crooks."

"I know. I heard about it. But I'm honestly more worried about what the other cops will do to you than Serban's people. Gideon, a security guard at city hall reported that the Seraph broke in and attacked him."

He sighed. "I was afraid of that."

"It's only reinforced the idea that you're a criminal. It doesn't matter if it was you or Dean in the suit; they don't know the difference. And they don't know what he was doing in there, only that he was breaking and entering—and assaulting."

"I get it. And I'm sure that when the time's right, Serban's cronies will use that as ammunition against me, but that doesn't mean I can stop."

"Oh, they will. Be careful, Gideon."

"I will. But this isn't over until Serban is behind bars."

"I know. I should've known from the start, because I know you, Gideon."

"And I know you, Jolie. You won't give up either. The two of us, with a lot of help, are going to save this city."

"You got it."

"Good." Gideon looked at the intersection ahead. To the left was the route home; to the right, the road to Sterling Enterprises. "I've got to go. I'll talk to you later."

"Okay. I love you."

"Love you, too."

Gideon hung up and turned right.

* * *

Sterling Enterprises was one of the tallest buildings in the city. The sixty-five-story high-rise sat almost in the exact center of the business district on the Platform, just a few blocks from the lake. Its security was state-of-the-art, and it boasted over a thousand employees.

Gideon's Sterling Labs ID badge wouldn't get him all the way to the top floor, where Edgar Sterling's office was located, but it would get him high enough that he could work his way up from there with less trouble than trying to sneak all the way up without any kind of access at all.

"Name?" the guard at the front desk asked.

Unfortunately, the guard on duty wasn't Wyatt. If it had been, Gideon was sure he would've let him by without question. But maybe Wyatt was here, just at another post. Either way, it didn't help him now.

"Turner," he said. "Gideon Turner. I'm a bio-analyst at Sterling Labs."

"Reason for your visit?"

"I'm here to deliver a report from Mr. Sterling to the financial office."

"Where is it?"

"What?"

"The report." The guard frowned. "You don't have a briefcase or anything. Where's the report?"

"Oh, right." Gideon patted the pocket of the suit jacket he'd changed into. "Flash drive. You know, technology these days, almost makes carrying briefcases a thing of the past."

"Right . . . " The guard took Gideon's ID an examined it. "All right. Everything looks good. The financial office is on the tenth floor."

"Thank you."

Gideon took his badge back and went to one of the five elevators at the end of the lobby. He swiped his badge to open one, went in, and swiped it again. The floor numbers that he had access to lit up: one through sixty. Well, that was close to where he needed to go. He hit the '10' first, in case the guard was monitoring him somehow. Once the elevator was rising, he tapped the '60.'

He clasped his hands in front of him and whistled. If Dean knew what he was doing, he'd probably be extremely angry. But Gideon would explain, and he'd understand. He had to.

The door finally opened, and Gideon stepped out into the sixtieth floor's suite. To the left was a stairway that went up to the remaining five floors; to the right, this floor's main office. He looked around and didn't see anyone nearby except the receptionist at the desk in the center of the suite.

"May I help you?" she asked.

What floor is this? He looked around again, trying to get his bearings and come up with a valid reason for being there. *Stupid, stupid.*

"My badge doesn't seem to be giving me the access I need," he said. "I was supposed to be seeing Mr. Sterling today, but the elevator wouldn't let me access the upper floors."

"That's strange." The receptionist frowned. "Well, I'm not even sure Mr. Sterling is in today; I'm not his receptionist, I'm the CFO's, but I can call upstairs to his receptionist and see if he has your appointment recorded."

Gideon walked over to her. "No, that's okay." *Come on, man, on the fly.* "It was actually about his son's surprise birthday party, so it's not that important; probably wouldn't be on the record."

"I see. Do you want me to call up? If he is there, after all, I can use my card to get you up there."

"No, that's all right. I'll give him a call." He backed away. "Thank you."

I am absolutely the biggest idiot of all time. He stepped into the elevator and waited for the doors to close. He had to think of something. He looked down at the card reader. It operated by reading the magnetic strip on the card, so his light powers wouldn't affect it. If only he had magnetic powers . . .

He looked up. Maybe he could climb on top of the elevator car and then climb the shaft the rest of the way to the top. Too bad the receptionist was still in the suite. He could've just shorted out the cameras with a quick flash of light, kicked down the stairway door, and gone up that way. *Well, it's almost 6:00; how much longer can she be here?*

Gideon jumped up, grabbed the hatch to the car's roof, and climbed out. There was a support beam that crossed between two pillars directly behind him. He climbed onto that, closed the elevator car's hatch, and waited. He told himself not to look down. He wasn't terrified of heights, but his nearly-fatal fall had given him a new respect for them, at least. And that had been two stories, whereas this was sixty.

He balanced himself on the beam, holding onto one of the pillars to ensure his stability. It seemed like hours before he heard, faintly, the elevator door open. A few seconds after that, the car descended. Gideon steadied himself, knowing what he'd have to do next would be extremely dangerous. There was about a seven-foot gap between him and the door to the sixtieth floor. He closed his fist, aimed it at the door, and fired a burst of light. The elevator doors bent inward, providing his way in. He took a shaky breath, counted to three—

And jumped.

His feet scraped the edge of the floor and he nearly fell back, but he leaned forward and flopped down on his face in the middle of the sixtieth-floor suite. *Ow.* His heart was pounding so hard that it felt like it was slamming through his chest into the carpeted floor. He decided to rest there for a moment.

He rose and looked around. There was one security camera in the left corner of the room, nearest the stairwell entrance. He pointed his hand in that direction, not tilting his head enough to give the camera a good look at his face and fired a burst of light. The camera sizzled and its recording light blinked out.

Gideon walked over to the stairwell door and kicked. Hard. The door swung inward, and Gideon bounded up the stairs to the sixty-fifth floor. By sixty-three, he was exhausted. His back was screaming at him. He'd thought this would be a simple, low-risk mission. Apparently not. He huffed his way up to the top floor and kicked that door in, too.

Sterling's suite was nice, with a long glass wall separating the outer suite with its receptionist's desk from the actual office. Gideon blasted the camera in the corner and walked to the glass door. It was, of course, locked. This would take a lighter touch, since kicking the glass door in would shatter it completely and likely set off a whole slew of alarms.

He put his hand on the seam where the door met the wall. He could melt it, but it would likely leave an ugly mess. Still, he didn't see another way in . . .

A hand clapped down on his shoulder. Gideon spun and swung a punch, but whoever was behind him grabbed his arm, pushed it aside, and yanked him around into an arm lock. Gideon began to energize his arms to burn his assailant's hand—

"Whoa, easy there!" The attacker chuckled. "It's me."

"Wyatt." Gideon pulled the energy back and turned around as Wyatt released him.

"You're lucky it's me. What are you doing here, boy?"

"I had a conversation with Mr. Sterling earlier this evening that led me to believe he may know something about what's going on in the Brooks. I was going to bug his office."

"Risky. And you were just going to, what, melt his glass door down?"

Gideon scratched the back of his head. "It was the only option I could think of."

"Not anymore." Wyatt swiped his badge in front of Sterling's door, and it unlocked. "Get it done and get out of here. You're going to get me fired!"

Pulling another bug from his pocket, Gideon placed it on the underside of Sterling's desk. Then he returned to the door. Wyatt tipped his cap to Gideon, turned, and walked back to the elevator.

"Have a good night, Gideon."

"You, too. Thanks, Wyatt."

I am without a doubt the worst sleuth ever. Whatever. He'd done what he'd come to do, and it was doubtful anyone would suspect what that was. They'd probably check for stolen items and, finding none, would hopefully give up. The bug was tiny and inconspicuous. It would, at a glance, look like a knot in the wood desk. He hoped.

Gideon took the stairs again. Sixty-five floors to go. At least it was sixty-five floors down.

CHAPTER 30

In all his time in organized crime, Serban had never feared law enforcement. They were inefficient and could be bought or blackmailed, like Walters, and the ones who were too moral to be bought and too stubborn to be blackmailed could just be killed. Coming to America had only reinforced that opinion. But this small, stubborn remnant of "good cops" in the Brooks was about to drive him mad.

Just days ago, four of his men had been arrested at The Broken Glass, including Costin, and another—the bartender—had been killed. He had no idea what his men might've revealed. He vetted all his closest men to ensure they weren't the type to snitch, but even the toughest men could be broken. Still, the minimal information they knew about his plot shouldn't be enough to bring it crashing down. And if necessary, Walters could intervene. It was just annoying.

It wouldn't matter for much longer, anyway. Step one of his plan involved storming the Brooks precinct and killing any cops who refused to turn. He wouldn't deal with that personally; he had bigger plans. He would take city hall himself, while Monahan moved on the bridge controls and kept the Platform docked with the mainland. Hopefully, she could at least handle that much. If not . . . well, then Serban doubted he'd need her services much longer, anyway.

* * *

A day after Gideon had bugged both of Sterling's offices, he returned home from work on his lunch break to make sure he'd get to the lair before Dean did. He'd made a breakthrough on the super-soldier serum that morning, and he hoped to have a viable formula to present to Dr. Sung that afternoon. But for now, he wanted to check in on Sterling's conversations from that day.

He jogged up the stairs to the apartment's second floor. Any excuse to exert himself, he took. He needed to be ready to fight at a moment's notice. He went into the lair and turned on the computer table. They'd stopped converting it back into its bedroom disguise, since the only person who came over regularly and hadn't known their secret was Jolie.

Gideon pulled up the feed from the bugs in Sterling's offices. The lab office didn't show anything that day other than ambient noise from outside the office. But there were several spikes in noise on the Sterling Enterprises bug, so Gideon accessed that one and started playing the conversations through.

The first few were standard business meetings or phone calls. He'd expected as much, but any little detail could be important, so he listened to them all, anyway. None of them seemed to be particularly informative. Gideon started to rise. Maybe this was a waste of time.

"This is taking too long," Sterling said.

The authority and barely-contained rage in Sterling's tone caused Gideon to drop back into the chair.

"You have two weeks to begin enacting your plan," Sterling continued, "or I will turn over everything to the police. And trust me, no matter how many you have in your pocket, there will be enough that answer to me that you won't escape."

"I don't like threats." The voice was deep, menacing . . . and contained a trace of a Romanian accent. "This is my plan now. It's about to be my city. I don't need you anymore."

"You're a fool. You wouldn't have gotten anywhere without my funding. Two weeks. Don't test me."

That was it. Gideon stared at the screen, praying he'd somehow misheard, that this was all a mistake. He played the conversation back again, and with every word his doubt and sorrow turned to certainty and resolve. Edgar Sterling had brought Luca Serban to Sojourn City, and he had been backing him from the start.

Why, though? Sterling was a good man, a philanthropist, a faithful leader in the church. What could cause him to do something like this?

One thing was for sure; Gideon couldn't give Sterling the supersoldier serum now, not knowing this. Whatever he wanted it for, it couldn't be good. Gideon's first instinct had been right; having the serum at all was a mistake. He needed to go back to the lab and destroy those simulations and formulas now. He shut down the computer and rushed out the door. Halfway down the stairs, he heard the front door open.

"Gideon?" Dean asked. "What's going on?"

* * *

Dean was excited to bring some of his new tech to the lair. He had upgraded Gideon's batons, adding a clasp that would allow them to link together to form a short staff. That would help Gideon fight larger groups of people, as well as have a bit more reach when he wasn't using his powers. Dean, along with Arianna and Maddox, had also been working on small, marble-sized beads that released a strong adhesive. They could be used to trap Gideon's opponents in one spot, or even bind their hands in lieu of handcuffs, if needed. And he also had a high-pressure grappling gun that would allow Gideon to get around rooftops more easily.

He unlocked the door and went inside the apartment. Gideon was pounding down the stairs like the devil was on his heels. Dean frowned and closed the door behind him.

"Gideon? What's going on?"

Gideon froze. "Dean."

"Yeah, hi. What's the hurry?"

Gideon resumed his walk down the stairs, at a much slower pace this time. Dean didn't need his friend's empathic abilities to read the nervousness and concern written all over his face. He tried to mask it, but something was wrong.

"I just need to get back to the lab."

Dean put his hand on Gideon's chest as he tried to walk by. "Uh-uh. We're not doing the whole secrets and lies thing anymore, remember? Spill. What's going on?"

Gideon blew out a short breath. "Okay. Truth is, I've got a lead on one of Serban's backers."

"Well, that's good. Why wouldn't you tell me that?"

"Because, Dean." Gideon put his hands on his hips and stared at the floor. "Because it's your father."

Dean set the bag of tech on the floor. "What?"

"I'm sorry, man. I just heard it with my own ears: your dad talking to a Romanian, probably Serban, on the phone. He threatened to alert the police if Serban didn't enact his plan within two weeks."

That was nonsense. Dean's father was a hero, and he'd done more to help this city than any of the other one percenters. He actually used his wealth for good; he was making a difference. Why would he be in bed with a bunch of criminals who only wanted to tear the city down and rebuild it in their image?

"You . . . you had to have misunderstood." Dean shook his head. "That's not my dad. Are you sure it was him?"

"I'm sure. I . . . I bugged his offices."

"You what?" Dean stepped forward and got in Gideon's face. "Why would you do something like that? Why wouldn't you tell me you were going to do something like that? Don't you think I had a right to know?"

"It was just last night, Dean. I wasn't sure, so I didn't want to worry you for nothing."

"But why?"

"Because your father called me into his office, and when I got there, I felt some of the strongest emotions off him that I've ever felt. He was . . . guilty, stressed, angry . . . it was intense. I just followed my instincts by bugging him."

Dean shook his head. "I can't believe you, Gideon."

"I'm sorry, Dean. The recordings are still on the computer in the lair. You can go listen to them, if you want."

Dean nodded. "Believe me, I will. Very thoroughly. But where are you really going right now?"

"I really was going back to the lab. I was going to destroy all the data I've compiled on the super-soldier serum. I figured if your dad really is working with the mob, there's a very real danger of that data falling into the wrong hands. I didn't want that to happen."

He wanted to tell Gideon that was insane, that he would be an idiot to destroy something that useful. But . . . even if Dean's father wasn't working with the mob—and Dean was sure there had to be some logical explanation for the phone call Gideon had heard, and that Edgar wasn't actually a criminal mastermind—that data could still fall into Serban's hands if he had someone else inside Sterling Labs.

"Go," Dean said. "But don't you dare confront my father. We'll discuss this more when you get back."

CHAPTER 31

Last year

Gideon fired a burst of shots around the corner at the three guerrillas guarding an intersection in the hallway. With each shot, guilt and fear coursed through his body. He was about to take a life again—not one but possibly three—and that went against everything he believed. But his friend was in trouble, and he had no other choice. At this point, it was kill or be killed, and if he died, Joshua probably would, too.

He ducked back into a doorway to hide from their return fire. He blinked rapidly and fumbled with his rifle. He wasn't a soldier; he was a doctor! This was insane. He took a deep breath, spun, and fired. One of the guerrillas dropped. Gideon ducked back into the doorway as bullets ricocheted off the walls around him.

After repeating the process twice more, Gideon shot another of the guerrillas. That left only one more here, but he was sure there were dozens more in the building, and they would have heard the gunfire. He needed to hurry.

Using every ounce of discipline his instructors had taught him he slowed his breathing, steadied his hands, and rushed out into the corridor. When the third guerrilla swiveled from cover to fire on him, Gideon raised his rifle and shot him down.

He closed his eyes for a moment, shook his head to clear it of the thoughts that threatened to overwhelm him, and rushed down the hallway.

Two more turns in, he found a room of cells. *Why didn't they keep us in here if these are available?* Just as a form of psychological torture, he assumed. Maybe this was where all the other captives Joshua had mentioned had been brought. Maybe they hadn't all died, after all. He looked through the cells, hoping to spot Joshua.

Somewhere behind him, someone shouted in Spanish. Gideon turned and slammed the door to the cell block.

"Great," he muttered. "I just trapped myself in here."

"Gideon!"

Gideon surveyed the room. Almost at the opposite end, in a cell on his right, Joshua stood, his head pressed against the bars.

"You shouldn't have come," Joshua said. "There's no way you can get me out of here. Only the guerrilla's leader has the keys."

"The doctor?"

"No; from what I can surmise, the doctor hired the guerrillas, but he's not their leader. Just their employer."

"Got it. Well, keys don't matter. Get back!"

There was another way to free Joshua. Gideon aimed his rifle at the cell's lock. Joshua backed away from the bars and pressed himself against the wall. Gideon squeezed the trigger and fired. The lock exploded.

"Let's move."

"All these other cells empty?"

"Looks like it." Gideon shrugged. "Maybe this place was originally a prison before the guerrillas took over it."

"Must've been."

Someone pounded on the cell block door. Gideon trained his rifle on the door and backed toward the other side of the block.

"There another way out of here?"

Joshua nodded. "There's another door back here. I'm not sure where it leads, though. It may not be any better than that way."

"We've got to try something."

"Fair enough. But give me the rifle. You're a doctor; you don't need to be killing all these people."

"Okay." Gideon handed over the rifle. "I'll follow you."

Joshua led the way to the other door. Gideon glanced back. The pounding on the door had stopped; the guy with the keys must've arrived. That meant that guerrillas would be pouring in after them soon.

"What have they been doing to you?"

Joshua went through the door and turned left. "The doctor ran a few tests on me. Brain scans, I think. Took some blood, too. But then they threw me in that cell and left me."

"What do you think he was testing?"

"I don't know." Joshua took another turn. "Maybe he wanted to see if whatever he did to me—to us—worked. Maybe it has to have a certain amount of time to set in before he can tell for sure."

"I wish we could get in the lab and find out for sure." Gideon looked behind them. No sign of pursuit yet. "But we really just need to get out of here."

"Agreed. Curiosity can wait until we get back to civilization and have a real doctor look us over."

"Right." Gideon chuckled. "Was that 'real doctor' thing a shot at me?"

Joshua glanced back and laughed. "No. Honestly, I forgot for a second. Slip of the tongue."

They turned another corner—and Joshua ran straight into a meaty fist. As he stumbled back, the attacker grabbed his rifle and jerked it away. Gideon's eyes widened, and he jumped in, swinging a wide roundhouse kick at the guerrilla's face. The big man's head snapped back. He dropped the rifle to the floor. Gideon kicked him again, this time a straight snap-kick in the chest. He swept the guerrilla's legs out from under him.

As the large assailant hit the floor, Gideon turned to help Joshua to his feet. But as he did, the clatter of footsteps filled the hall and half a dozen guerrillas surrounded them. A seventh man appeared, a keyring clinking on his belt.

"You are most brave," he said, looking at Gideon. "But foolish. Stand up and put your hands in the air, *amigo.*"

"What are you doing to us? Who is that doctor? What does he want?"

The guerrilla leader shrugged. "Cannot say. We get paid to bring him people, not to ask questions. Lucky for you, he still wants you two alive." He snapped his fingers, and two of his men moved forward and grabbed Gideon and Joshua. "Take them back to the cells."

"Let us go!" Gideon said.

"Sorry, *amigo.*" The leader walked away. "The money is too good for that."

Now

The twelfth precinct was an emotional time bomb just waiting to explode. Two more officers had been injured yesterday, and the crime wave wasn't slowing down. None of the other precincts would send backup; the others in the Brooks had their own problems and those outside were poised to protect the rest of the city, should crime spread. The mayor's hands seemed tied, either willfully or through the skillful handiwork of Serban's men in city hall. The same could be said for the police chief. It was chaos.

Jolie had learned from Pulaski, who had learned from their computer lab team, that the flash drive Wyatt had given them had been enough to raise some suspicions about some people, but not incriminate them completely. They could at least launch an investigation . . . but that would take time. And they still were no closer to learning what Serban's plans were, let alone when he was going to enact them. The flash drive hadn't given them that much. But at least they knew to keep an eye on the bridge to the Platform. Unfortunately, that was far from the Brooks and would have to be handed off to another precinct—a precinct which would likely have corrupt officers in it.

And the four men Jolie and Paul had arrested hadn't cracked. Pulaski was frustrated and ready to just go beat their faces in. Sergeant Andrews had ordered them to be put in separate cells, as far away from one another as they could be. Then, in their next interrogations, he wanted Pulaski to make them believe that one of the others had already given up information. If they could turn them against one another, maybe one of them would cave.

"This is nuts. We all know something's about to happen. You can practically feel it in the air. And all we can do is sit here and wait."

"Our patience will be rewarded." Paul sipped at his coffee. "I believe that we'll come out on top here. It's not going to be easy, but good usually wins out over evil, in my experience."

"I hope you're right." Jolie looked around. Everyone else seemed to be too busy to eavesdrop. "Paul, what do you think about the vigilantes?"

"I think they've been strangely scarce lately."

"No. I mean . . . do you consider them criminals? I've heard so much debate about it lately, and I just wanted your perspective."

"Well, Jolie, from what I can tell, they haven't killed anybody. They were doing a good work in cleaning up the streets. There's an argument to be made that they were removing due process from the equation, not letting the criminals they attacked be considered innocent until proven guilty. But given the situation we're in? I'll take any backup I can get."

Interesting. Jolie sat back in her seat, took a sip of her own coffee, and considered. Maybe she had another way they could break their suspects, if this whole isolation thing didn't work . . .

* * *

Gideon rushed into the lab and dropped down into his desk. He called up the records of his projections, formulas, and simulations and hovered over the delete button. But as he did, he paused. The "last accessed" display had changed—on all of them. They had just been opened ten minutes ago.

He looked around. There were only two people he could think of who'd do that without his permission: Dr. Sung, or Sterling himself. Gideon deleted the files anyway and jumped out of his seat. He needed to find Dr. Sung.

A quick search confirmed that the doctor wasn't anywhere in the lab. Gideon looked out the window to the courtyard. He didn't see him down there, either. That meant he had already left, probably with the data, or he was somewhere else in the building—which was unlikely. Sung was almost always in the lab.

Gideon tapped another scientist on the shoulder. "Have you seen Dr. Sung today?"

"Not in the last few minutes." The young blonde woman frowned. "It's been about half an hour, I'd say."

"Dr. Sung?" another nearby scientist said. "He told me he was going to head up to the tech lab and then out to Sterling Enterprises."

"Thanks."

Gideon walked briskly toward the doors. Hopefully, Sung hadn't left the tech lab yet. Instead of going up there, Gideon rode the elevator down to the first floor and went outside. He sat on a bench in the courtyard to wait and called Dean while he did.

"Dean?"

"Yeah." Dean sounded very unhappy. "What's up?"

"Can you get in contact with Maddox or Arianna? Find out if Dr. Sung is still in the tech lab, or if he's left already."

"Got it. Just a second." Gideon watched the door while he waited for Dean's answer. He could've just gone up to the lab himself, but he didn't want to risk going up as Sung was going down in another elevator, or something. "Okay, I'm back."

"And?"

"He left right before I called."

"Great, thanks. I'll be in touch."

That meant Sung couldn't have left Sterling Labs yet. Gideon settled in to wait. About two minutes later, Sung exited the building, holding a briefcase in one hand. Gideon rose and walked toward him.

"Dr. Sung!"

"Ah! Hello, Dr. Turner."

"Is that my research on the super-soldier serum?"

Sung's eyes narrowed. "It is. I am taking it to Mr. Sterling."

"How do you know it's ready?"

"I came to see you, but you weren't at your desk. I checked your files myself. It looks quite promising."

"But it's not done. You can't take it to Mr. Sterling yet."

"I'm afraid I can. Mr. Sterling told me he needed your results today. I'm sorry, Mr. Turner, but I am taking it."

As he walked past, Gideon grabbed his arm. "Dr. Sung, stop."

"Get your hands off me before I call security."

Gideon stared Sung down. He could've easily knocked the man out and destroyed the files right there. He was tempted to. But there were dozens of people around—not just security, but scientists taking their break in the cool afternoon air, citizens coming to the lab on business, and even a group of children on a fieldtrip.

"Mr. Turner. Remove your hand."

He waited another moment, and then released Sung's arm and nodded. Sung stormed away. Gideon watched him go. Things were about to get a lot more difficult.

* * *

Dean listened to the recording of his father repeatedly. Each time, he tried to picture his father's face as he spoke the condemning words. Was he angry? Sad? Was this all an act, and he was secretly working with the police to lead Serban into a trap?

But each time, his father sounded totally genuine. The way he talked to Serban was the same way he talked to business competitors and investors who tried to manipulate him: firmly, but sincerely, as he would to a rebellious child—as he had to Dean more than once. But Serban spoke back with such disdain, such venom.

"Dean," Gideon said.

Dean tapped the comm switch. "What's up?"

"Dr. Sung already took the files on the super-soldier serum. He's taking them to your dad right now. Have you listened to the recording yet?"

"Multiple times." Dean sighed. "I just don't see how this can be real, Gideon."

"I don't want to believe it, either. But if he is working with Serban, then he just got his hands on all he needs to create and replicate the super-soldier serum. If we don't do something, we could be looking at an army of superpowered criminals. And I wouldn't be able to stop them."

Dean hung his head. Gideon was right. Even if this was all a misunderstanding, they couldn't risk it.

"You have to find out my dad's intentions for sure."

"How?"

"The Seraph needs to pay him a visit."

"Are you sure?"

"Absolutely. Confront him in his office. Whenever he's at the Enterprises building, he usually stays late. He'll be alone there tonight. And you can also take the opportunity to get the formula back. But Gideon . . . don't hurt him. Please."

"I won't." Dean heard a car door closing on Gideon's side of the line. "I'm on my way back."

"Okay. See you soon."

"See you soon."

Dean closed the line and pounded his fist on the table. He'd never imagined something like this was even possible. His dad at the center of a criminal conspiracy to bring down the city, or whatever Serban had planned? It was . . . madness.

He bowed his head began to pray that his father would see the truth of what was going on and change his ways before it was too late.

* * *

The city really was beautiful, but Gideon knew that beauty was deceptive. Everything was bright and shining, the kind of beauty that only an excess of wealth could buy. Here, on the Platform, and on Lakeside just across the bridge, Luca Serban's hand had not yet stretched its fingers to pollute the illusion that everything was good.

But it would soon. Gideon knew that. Everyone else—the many pedestrians walking by on the sidewalks and the drivers on the road around him—did not. They still believed they were perfectly safe, unaffected by the chaos unfolding in the Brooks. It was a belief that would be shattered all too soon. But maybe that was for the best. After all, that was what had gotten them all into this mess in the first place. Maybe when these people realized how much they had in common with the people in the Brooks, Sojourn City could finally become the utopia it had been meant to be.

He pulled his car around onto the bridge that connected the Platform to the mainland. His phone rang, and he reached into his pocket to pull it out.

"Hello?"

"Gideon," Jolie said.

"Hey! What's up?"

"Remember how I told you about those guys I fought the other day? Well, they're not breaking. So I've got an idea, if you're willing to help."

Gideon frowned. "Are you saying you want the Seraph to help on an active police investigation?"

"Yes, actually." She sighed. "I am probably going to get in serious trouble for this, but yes. We can't break these guys, and a polygraph only works if you can actually get them to talk. But . . . you . . . you're like a human polygraph, and you don't need words to get what you need."

"I can't read minds, Jolie. Just emotions."

"I know, but that's all I need. They've got to have some emotional response to the questions I ask. So I need you there to read them. When I ask the questions, you read them and see if you can tell how close I am to the mark based on their reactions."

"It's a long shot, you know that, right? It'll be very inexact."

"I know that, but it's all I've got. I'm going to talk to Sergeant Andrews. I won't give him the details, but I'll tell him that I can get them to talk if he'll let me."

"And if he says no?"

"If he says no . . . well, then we'll just smuggle you into the jail somehow and see what we can do from there."

"All right. I'll help you, but only if you're sure this is going to work. I'm not going to risk you getting fired or put in jail because you worked with a vigilante illegally."

"Yeah, well, you should've thought about that before you—my boyfriend—decided to become one. Too late for that now. We work with what we've got."

"Okay." Gideon pulled off the bridge and turned the corner to head toward his apartment. "I've got something else I need to take care of tonight. Can we say around midnight?"

"Sure. Meet me on the rooftop of the old theater in the Brooks."

"Will do. Love you."

"Love you. And thanks. Bye."

CHAPTER 32

The new gear Dean had provided was pretty sweet. The armor was still the same, though the bullet holes and slash marks in the chest plate, arms, and cape had been fixed. Dean had promised Gideon a whole new suit at some point, but that would take longer to develop. Right now, he'd have to settle for the grappling hook, adhesive beads, and *jo* staff attachment for his truncheons.

Gideon stood on a rooftop across the street from Sterling Enterprises. This building was just a few floors shorter than Sterling's, but with his grappling hook, he should be able to make it to the top floor. He planned to crash in through Sterling's office window and scare him a bit, and maybe see if he could spot the files for the serum—hopefully still in Sung's briefcase—while he did. He would ask Sterling about his involvement with Serban, steal or destroy the files, and get out.

The comms crackled. "Hey, Gideon."

"Yeah?"

"Please don't hurt Dad."

Gideon pitied Dean. He couldn't imagine how he'd feel if he found out his father was behind all this. He'd known Matthew Turner as a good man his whole life, so to see him fall this low would break Gideon's heart. Dean must've felt about the same.

"I won't." He aimed the grappling hook at the top floor. "I'll be in touch."

He fired. This was going to be interesting. He was still wary about heights, so grappling to the top of a sixty-five-story building with nothing underneath him to save him if he fell was a terrifying prospect. Theoretically, the lining of his cape should become rigid and act as a glider of sorts in an emergency, but he'd never tested it and didn't really want to rely on it. Adrenaline surged through his veins, and his hands began to glow a bit in reaction to his heightened emotion. The grappling hook bit into the wall, and the line went taut.

Okay . . . here we go. He jumped and squeezed the trigger again, and the line began to reel him in. It was a horrific feeling, like he was a helpless fish being pulled toward his doom. But as he ascended, he forced himself to steady his breathing. He became the Seraph again.

He closed on the building, and as he did, he raised his feet. As soon as he struck the window, he kicked out, shattering it inward. He released the grappling hook, letting it dangle just outside the window, and rolled inward to stand in the middle of Edgar Sterling's office.

Sterling, who had been sitting behind his desk, stood. The Seraph fired a bolt of light at the desk phone, knocking it to the floor. He raised a glowing fist and pointed it at Sterling.

"Edgar Sterling! Why are you providing funding for the Romanian mob?"

"What?" Sterling raised his hands and backed away from his desk. "I don't know what you mean, I—"

"Stop lying!" The Seraph took three steps forward, keeping his fist raised. "I know you did, because I intercepted your phone call to him this morning!"

As Gideon walked, he looked around for the briefcase. He didn't see it, but Sterling's computer screen was glowing faintly—it was possible Sterling had already downloaded the files onto his computer. The Seraph fired another blast of light, cracking the computer in half. Sterling jumped.

"Talk!"

"All right! All right. You don't understand! This isn't what it looks like; I never intended for any of this to happen."

Gideon shook his head. "You didn't intend for hardened criminals to commit crimes?"

"No, I—"

Footsteps pounded outside. The Seraph turned and, through the glass wall to the foyer, saw four security guards approaching. Wyatt was not among them. *Good, that means I can do this.* He built up energy in his hands and fired it in a wave of light that shattered the entire glass wall. The guards covered their faces to shield themselves from the light and flying glass. Luckily for them, they were too far across the room for most of the glass to reach them.

"Sterling! Start talking!"

"I only wanted to help the city!" Sterling said. "I thought this would be the best way to do it, and—"

"You're lying! Why would you bring criminals to help a city!"

"For justice!"

Gideon turned again as the guards began to advance again. He withdrew his batons and planted himself between Sterling and the guards. The guards, apparently taking the Seraph's blast as permission to attack, opened fire. Gideon closed his eyes and concentrated, creating a light aura from his hands, arms, and chest. The bullets disintegrated as they closed in on him.

"Take him hand-to-hand!" one officer said.

Gideon shook his head and clicked his batons together to form a *jo* staff. The guards ran at him and drew nightsticks. Gideon spun the short staff in tight circles, blocking the strikes they brought to bear. He struck one guard across the face, turned, jabbed another in the gut, and roundhouse kicked a third. The last guard hit the Seraph's shoulder with his nightstick, but it barely registered. Gideon punched him in the face.

With all four down, the Seraph reached into his belt, pulled out one of Dean's adhesive beads, and threw it on the floor between them. It popped as it struck the ground, and gel spread out to glue the four men to the floor. The Seraph turned back to Sterling. The man was on his cell phone, yelling at someone.

"Why do you need the super-soldier serum?" Gideon demanded.

"To keep things from getting out of hand!" Sterling put his phone away. "Please. You have to understand, we're on the same side."

"No, we're not. We're nothing alike."

"We are. We've both broken laws in order to protect the city we love. We've just gone about it in different ways."

The elevator behind Gideon chimed. He spun around. Five more people—Romanians, judging by their leather jackets and black skinny ties—stepped out. One, who stood in the center of the other four, wore a big black greatcoat instead of a leather jacket. Closest to Gideon was a woman, and he recognized her with a jolt of fear. *Monahan.*

"You must be the Seraph!" the man in the greatcoat said. "I've been wondering when I'd get to meet you. Allow me to introduce myself."

Gideon recognized his voice. "Luca Serban."

"So, you know me. Then you know that I am taking over this city, and there's nothing you can do to stop it." Serban held out his hands.

"Lay down your weapon, step away from Mr. Sterling, and I'll give you a quick death."

"Sorry. Not today."

Gideon leapt for the open window as Serban's men and Monahan opened fire. He grabbed his grappling gun and flicked the switch to extend the line. He began descending rapidly. When he was five floors below Sterling's office, he kicked the nearest window in and swung inside. He hit the ground smoothly, disconnected the line, and reattached the grappling gun to his belt.

He ran for the nearest stairwell. He had to get out of here fast. The Platform's police would be here soon, and they wouldn't be as merciful as the officers in the Brooks—which was saying something.

He made it to an emergency exit before Serban's men caught up to him. He ran outside and crossed the street, found his motorcycle, and drove off. He was afraid to call Dean, knowing his friend must be in agony over the conversation he'd just overheard. Better to leave him to his thoughts for a bit. He needed to get to the Brooks and help Jolie, anyway. Now that they knew that Serban had a direct line to the Platform, they needed to be ready at any moment. Gideon expected the criminal's move would be sooner than any of them expected.

* * *

"You fool!" Sterling growled. "What are you doing here?"

Serban smirked as he surveyed the damage the Seraph had caused. He had to admit, seeing him in action in person, he was impressive. But he wasn't the first one of his kind Serban had seen, and he doubted he'd be the last. Still, this tech was new. He knelt to examine the goo that bound the guards to the floor.

"You were the one yelling at me on the phone about us being found out." Serban shrugged. "Lucky for you I was already on my way up to your office."

"To which I again ask: what are you doing here? I didn't invite you."

"I know. I invited myself. I figured I'd do you the favor of telling you in person that the plan begins tomorrow. Just in case there was anyone you wanted to make sure was safe."

"Tomorrow." Sterling sighed. "It's about time."

"Yeah. My time. I'll see you tomorrow, Edgar." Serban stood and looked at Monahan. "Call all our boys. Tell 'em it's open season on vigilantes. If they see one of those masked lunatics tonight, put 'em in the ground. One hundred thousand reward for the man who kills the Crusader, and two hundred for the man who kills the Seraph."

* * *

Sergeant Andrews hadn't been thrilled with Jolie's vague explanation of her plan, but things were desperate, so he'd allowed her to try things her way, provided she took Paul with her as a character witness. Which was fine with her, given what Paul had just told her about how he felt about vigilantes.

Jolie adjusted the handcuffs on the subject she'd chosen to bring to Gideon. He was the one who'd attacked her with the switchblade—they'd at least discovered his name: Costin. He seemed the most nervous out of any of the four men, so she figured he might be easier for Gideon to read. Paul stood at a distance, hands on his belt, and watched. She nodded at him and pushed the suspect to the center of the rooftop.

"What are we doing here?" Costin demanded. "This . . . this doesn't seem legit."

"Oh, you're going to lecture me on legitimacy." Jolie laughed. "That's nice. Would you also like to help me with my paperwork?"

Costin huffed. A moment later, there was the sound of a metal *clink* against the brick rooftop. Jolie spotted its source, a small grappling hook, a moment before the Seraph was propelled into the air by the line. He did an impressive flip—Jolie rolled her eyes at Gideon's excess—and landed in a crouch in front of Jolie and her prisoner.

The Romanian backed away. "Hey! Hey, what is this?"

"This is your interrogation," Jolie replied. "You wouldn't talk to Detective Pulaski, so maybe you'll talk to someone a bit scarier."

And Jolie had to admit that up close, his face shrouded by his deep hood, Gideon did look intimidating. His frame, which had already been athletic, was bulked up a bit by his suit, and the deep blue and gold armor was equally imposing. His twin batons hung at his side along with a few other gadgets.

"What's your name?" Gideon growled.

He must've been using a voice changer; he spoke in a deep, rasping growl that startled Jolie. For a moment, it reminded her of the dark Gideon of her nightmare. Costin just about jumped out of his skin.

"C-Costin."

"You work for Luca Serban?" Jolie asked.

Costin trembled but said nothing. Jolie kicked him—just hard enough to get his attention—in the back of the knee. He stumbled forward.

"I asked you a question."

She spared a glance at Paul. If he was surprised by the Seraph's appearance, he didn't show it. He stayed exactly where he was, hands on his belt, and watched. Jolie smiled at him. His support helped her a lot; he was like an uncle to her. Seeing him so calm about this reaffirmed for her that it was the right decision.

"I won't say nothing." Costin shook his head. "Not a word."

"He does," the Seraph said.

"What? I didn't say that!" Costin looked at Jolie. "I didn't—"

"Don't look at me. Look at him. But answer me. What is Serban's plan? How is he planning to take over the city?"

"P-please, he'd kill me—"

The Seraph began to glow—hands, arms, and even chest. The light glowed straight through his armor. "You should be more worried about what I'll do."

"You . . . you don't kill! You ain't never killed any of us."

Gideon grabbed Costin's tie. "I can hurt you in other ways."

"Stop! Stop!"

"Then talk."

Jolie snapped her fingers. "Is Serban moving this week?"

"I definitely can't tell you that—"

"His nervousness spiked. That's a yes."

Jolie was impressed. Costin whimpered and dropped to his knees. She shook her head. How had this guy had the guts to come at her with a switchblade? He was a mess. But then, if he was one of Serban's Romanian cronies, he'd probably been around the crime lord long enough to know what he did to snitches.

"How many men?"

Now Costin snickered. "More than you can handle."

"What's his plan of attack? Where's he hitting first, and what's his goal?"

"I can answer the last one," the Seraph said. "He wants the city. The whole city. He said so himself."

Jolie looked down at Costin. "Where will he hit first?"

"First?" Costin laughed. "There is no 'first.' I told you: there's more of us than you can handle. He won't hit anywhere 'first.'"

The Seraph looked to Jolie. "Coordinated strikes. We need to shore up defenses anywhere that we think Serban may hit."

"Right." Jolie hauled Costin to his feet. "Paul! Take our friend back to jail now."

As Paul guided Costin away, Jolie turned to look at Gideon. The luminescence surrounding him had faded, and as Costin disappeared down the stairs, he slumped a little and finally removed his hood, though he kept his mask on.

"You saw Serban face-to-face?"

Gideon nodded. "I confronted Dean's father. It seems he's involved in Serban's operation—looks like he was the one who started it, in fact. Serban and some of his people, including Monahan, showed up. I had to run. But Serban told me himself that he wants to take over the city."

"Why?"

"I don't know. I'll see what else I can dig up on him."

"Poor Dean." Jolie sighed. "How's he holding up?"

"I haven't seen him yet. But one thing's for sure, this is all going down fast. If I were you, I'd suggest to your Sergeant Andrews that the police be ready to move at any moment. I'm going to go home and see Dean, and then see if our bug picked up any conversation between Serban and Sterling after I left."

"Okay. Keep me updated." On impulse, Jolie stepped forward and kissed Gideon. "I love you. And I'm sorry it took me so long to understand why you're doing this."

"It's okay. I would probably feel the same if the roles were reversed. I love you, too. I'll see you soon."

"Okay. See you soon."

Gideon pulled his hood back up, turned, and fired his grappling hook. As he swung away, and Jolie watched him, she wondered how they were going to stand a chance against Serban and Sterling, even if every police officer in the city united alongside the Seraph.

It was going to be a trick, that was for sure. She followed Paul down to street level and pushed thoughts of the future from her mind.

"So?" she asked.

"So, what?" Paul replied.

"What are you going to tell Andrews?"

"Exactly what happened. You questioned Costin and he responded. You didn't get too physical. He just seemed to fall apart."

Jolie smiled. "Thanks, Paul."

"Anytime, partner."

CHAPTER 33

Gideon rappelled back down to his motorcycle, reeled in the line, and mounted his bike. As he rode for home, he smiled. Jolie coming around to his side of things was more than he ever could have asked for. He'd only hoped that she would forgive him for lying and keeping secrets, but to think that she'd ask for his help as the Seraph . . . he hadn't dared to think it could happen.

It would've been all good if not for the looming dread of an impending attack. If Serban was bold enough to go to the Platform himself, it was because he was ready to move, to reveal himself. Costin's testimony had all but confirmed that.

He tapped his earbud. "Dean, you there?"

No response. Gideon wasn't surprised; Dean was probably processing his father's involvement in Serban's plot. He didn't try again. He'd give Dean time to think, and they could talk once he got home. He turned his bike toward the highway.

Bang! Gideon cried out as his bike flipped forward, the front tire blown out. He reached out wildly to try to catch himself, but he slammed into the pavement. He rolled over his shoulder and came up in a crouch, and then immediately threw himself to the left to avoid being flattened by his bike.

He scanned the area for whoever had blown out his tire. Several projectiles struck him on the back and shoulders, slowed by his armor.

Gideon grunted and projected a shield of light. Bullets turned to ash as they bore down on him. He stood, whipped out his truncheons, and clicked them together. Where were the shooters?

Thugs, armed with a variety of guns, rushed from a nearby alley. Gideon twirled his *jo* staff and bounded toward them. As he approached, they holstered their guns and charged him with knives, chains, and bats.

Gideon swung his staff, knocking the first one down with a blow to the head. A second and third lunged at him, stabbing with knives. Gideon kicked the one on his left in the gut and then swiveled to catch a knife strike from the second on his staff. He twirled the staff, slapped the man on the shoulder, and then spun it again to strike him on his left knee. As the first knife-wielder began to rise, Gideon back-kicked him in the chest, and then used that momentum to snap his leg forward into the one in front of him.

Four more thugs, three wielding bats and one a chain, surrounded him. Gideon thrust his staff toward the one with the chain. The man tangled the *jo* in his chain. As soon as the metal touched Gideon's weapon, he flicked the switch to activate the staff's electric ends. The jolts of electricity traveled through the staff, up the chain, and into the man's hands. He fell on his back, spasming.

Gideon flicked the chain aside into one of the bat wielders. The thug recoiled. Gideon used his staff to sweep the man's legs out from under him. The last two bat-wielders pushed in, swinging their improvised weapons. The Seraph side-stepped the leftmost attacker and elbowed him in the jaw. He grabbed him by the back of the head and shoved him to the ground. He stomped on his back for good measure.

The last man landed two blows on Gideon's back and then swung his bat at his head as Gideon turned to face him. Gideon jerked his head back and heard the *whoosh* of air as it sailed by. The man swung again. Gideon brought his forearm up, and the bat snapped in half against the armored gauntlet. He swung his staff and struck the man in the ribs. Then he activated the electric ends again and rammed them into the man's gut. He, too, jerked and spasmed as he fell to the ground.

Gideon heard a tearing sound from behind him and turned. One of the knife-wielders had gotten up and attempted to stab him in the back, only for the blade to get tangled in the folds of Gideon's cape. As he spun, the attacker stumbled forward, and the knife came free of his grasp, remaining in Gideon's cape. The man swung an uppercut at Gideon's jaw. Gideon dodged, but still took the punch on the side of his head. He grimaced as his ears rang. The man was in too close for Gideon to get a good angle with his staff. He punched with his left hand, knocking the man back a step. He kicked the man, once with his right leg and once with his left. The man fell to the ground, breathing heavily, and did not get up.

The Seraph surveyed the street around him. Seven men lay twitching, moaning, and trying to stand. He went to each of them, picked up their guns, and melted them to slag.

His bike lay in the middle of the street behind him. He walked over to it. The tire had been shredded beyond repair, and the body was banged up from the crash. That effectively stranded him, especially if Dean wasn't answering.

That was a hit. It hadn't been coincidental; it had been a coordinated strike. Serban must've put a price on his head. That meant that others were likely on the lookout for the Seraph, too. He needed to get out of here before he was overwhelmed. He pulled his phone from a pouch in his utility belt and dialed Jolie.

"Hey, I know I just left, but . . . I need a favor."

* * *

Jolie dropped Gideon off in front of the Tower. He thanked her and took the elevator up to his and Dean's apartment. As he walked in the door, he looked around for any sign of his friend.

"Dean?" he called. "You here?"

No response. Gideon bounded up the stairs to the lair. The door was open, but Dean wasn't inside. Gideon furrowed his brow. He checked the rest of the house—kitchen, bedrooms, restrooms. Dean wasn't anywhere. Gideon returned to the lair and looked down at the computer screen. There was a recording pulled up, and it had been paused.

Gideon clicked play, and Serban's voice growled from the speakers. "I figured I'd do you the favor of telling you in person that the plan begins tomorrow. Just in case there was anyone you wanted to make sure was safe."

Sterling spoke. "Tomorrow. It's about time."

"Yeah. My time. I'll see you tomorrow, Edgar."

Serban's next words were to put out a hit on Gideon and the Crusader—as Gideon had suspected. Which also meant that Wyatt could be in trouble.

The recording started again—Dean's voice, this time. "Gideon, I wanted to let you know I'm going to Sterling Labs to get some things. I'll be out of touch for a while, but don't worry; I'll be back. I'm not going to do something stupid like try to convert my dad back to the good or anything. I've seen enough superhero shows to know that only ends with me dying. Or him. I'm not going to let that happen. I'll be back tonight, though. Thanks for telling me the truth, Gideon. I hate it and I'm really mad at you, but I'm mad because you were right. You did the right thing."

The recording ended. Gideon sighed and slumped down in the chair, tears stinging his eyes. Poor Dean. He hadn't signed up for this. Gideon had basically forced him to help him in his crusade, and he'd never really stopped to consider the consequences. Then he'd tried to change and make sure Dean was doing what he wanted to do . . . and still, Dean got hurt because of what Gideon uncovered. It wasn't fair.

He stood and put the Seraph gear back on the mannequin that held it. He wondered what tech Dean was getting from the labs. Whatever it was, he hoped it would be useful in taking down a criminal army. Gideon picked up his cell phone. If this was really going down this way, he would need help. He dialed.

"Wyatt, it's Gideon. You may be in danger. We need to meet."

* * *

Gideon was going to need everything Dean had been working on, plus a lot more stuff that he hadn't been able to finish working on, just to survive, probably. He didn't have time to finish those projects, but the ones he had, he began packing in a case. He hoped there was enough tech here to get Gideon through the night.

"Uh . . . Dean?"

Dean looked up. Arianna stood in the doorway to the lab, eyes wide. *Aw, man.* It was past midnight, no one should be here. But Arianna had always been an odd one. When she got in the zone, she sometimes forgot things that other people would take for granted—like eating and sleeping, for example.

"Hey, Arianna . . . hey."

"What are you doing?"

Dean sighed. "Okay, look. I don't have time to think up a lie. This city is going to be in deep trouble tomorrow so I'm getting all the gear I can to help the Seraph, the Crusader, and whoever else is willing to fight. I know it's technically stealing, but it's also my dad's company so I figure it's not actually stealing if this stuff belongs to my family."

"Oh. Wow."

"Yeah. And here's the thing, you can't tell my dad, okay? You can't tell anyone. Because . . . because my dad's a criminal."

"You're kidding, right? Mr. Sterling?"

"I wish I was. But he's going to use some of our stuff to help the criminals take over the city, probably. So I figured we could use everything we had to fight back."

He prayed she wouldn't just decide to turn him in on the spot, and that their years of friendship meant more to her than company loyalty. He could almost see her brain working behind her eyes.

"Okay, I'm going to help."

"What?"

"This is my city, too, Dean. I've lived here since I was a little girl. Besides, you're my friend. I'm helping. And I'm sure Maddox will, too. I'm going to call him. Where should we meet you?"

"My apartment." Dean stuffed everything he could in the case and shouldered it. "And don't tell anyone else except Maddox, okay?"

"Okay. We'll be there in an hour."

"See you then."

* * *

Wyatt, clad in the costume of the Crusader, stood in the alley behind his hotel. On the balcony above, his wife looked down at him, and even at that distance he saw the concern on her face. He felt for her. Truth was, he would've rather stayed there with her. But with a hit out on the vigilantes, and at least one person able to recognize Carter's face and associate it with the Crusader, it wasn't safe.

"I love you!" he called.

"I love you, too," Joanna replied.

Wyatt looked over at Carter. He wore all black, too, and a bandana over his nose and mouth. He had a short blade—the remnants of the assassin's blade that Gideon had given him—tucked into his belt. Wyatt didn't like bringing the boy with him, but it would be safer than leaving him with Joanna and the other kids, who were packing to head for a shelter farther from the Brooks. If that assassin woman tracked Carter down, they'd be doomed. But if Carter came with him, she'd have to fight the two of them together.

"Where are we going?" Carter asked.

"To see the Seraph. He needs our help to save the city."

"Our help?"

"Like it or not, son, you're in this life now. I didn't want it for you, but it's how it happened. So yes, our help. That doesn't mean you'll be on the front lines, though, so don't get any ideas."

"Okay. I got it, Dad."

Wyatt circled around the hotel to where their car was parked—

"Dad, look out!"

Someone dropped from the balcony, a knife in hand. Wyatt rolled aside and came up in a fighting crouch. The attacker was a dark-haired man, young, but with the look of a killer in his eyes. He lunged at

Wyatt. The Crusader grabbed his knife arm, spun around it, and locked the man in an armbar. The attacker punched Wyatt in the back. Wyatt flipped the man over his shoulder.

The attacker landed flat on his back. Wyatt pressed the attack, punching down at the man's face. He rolled aside, and Wyatt pulled his punch to keep from hitting concrete. The man came to his feet. Wyatt charged him again, keeping his arms tight to block the knife.

The attacker stabbed. Wyatt pushed his hand aside and punched him three times in the chest. The man staggered back and waved the knife. The next time he swung, Wyatt grabbed his wrist and twisted it. Hard. The attacker dropped the knife. Wyatt kicked him square in the gut, spun him around, took him in a chokehold, and dropped him to his knees.

"Stay away from us," he growled.

He elbowed the man on the back of the head, knocking him unconscious. He picked up the knife and tucked it into his belt. Good thing Joanna and the kids were packing. It wouldn't be safe for them here anymore.

"Let's go," Wyatt said. "Before more of them come."

Speechless, Carter nodded. Wyatt climbed into his car, and Carter got in the other side. As Wyatt drove off, Carter shook his head.

"Dad, that was awesome."

"I don't think so. And I sincerely hope I never have to do it again . . . after all this is over, of course." He looked out the window. "Yes, I do believe that tomorrow will be my last crusade."

CHAPTER 34

Gideon and Joshua remained in their cells for a very long time.

It was even harder to tell how long from in here, because they couldn't see the sun, and the hours passed uneventfully. Their captors brought them meals twice a day, but Gideon soon lost track of whether they were the morning or evening meals.

He kept up his training, though. So did Joshua. They couldn't see each other, because they were in adjacent cells, but they could speak. They talked often and encouraged each other whenever one of them was feeling discouraged. Gideon had to guess he'd been gone for more than half a year, at this point. He just couldn't say how long.

Did his parents think he was dead? Did Jolie? Dean? Wes? It was hard to imagine that they still held out hope for survival, and yet painful to imagine them moving on as though he was gone. He imagined Jolie grieving, throwing herself into her job, and eventually finding a new guy and getting married. If he were dead, he would want that for her. But imagining a world where he was rescued and made it home only to find her married tore him apart. *But . . . she does deserve to be happy.*

"Gideon, I'm going to guess the doctor will have you brought to him sometime soon," Joshua said one day. "It's been a long time since he saw you the first time."

"I've been thinking that, too." Gideon went through a series of martial arts katas. "I think we should use that opportunity to escape."

"Because that worked so well the last time." There was no malice in Joshua's voice, only a hint of wry humor. "What exactly were you planning?"

"They come in here to get me. I rush the guy closest to me and use his body as a shield so the other one can't shoot me. After I take them both down, I use the rifle to blow your cell open. We both have rifles this time and we get out of here together. And I'm sure there's a garage in here somewhere, which means vehicles."

"That's possible." Gideon heard the shrug in Joshua's voice. "Well, I suppose we could give it a try. Haven't got anything to lose, right?"

"True." Gideon sighed. "Very true."

Now

"You told her what?" Gideon asked.

Dean shrugged. "What choice did I have? Besides, she can be a real help—they both can. If you don't want them to know your identity, just wear your hood and mask while they're here. Of course, given they know that Gideon Turner lives here, it's probably not a huge leap, but . . ."

Gideon shook his head. They didn't have time for this. Serban was going to launch his attack in less than twenty-four hours, and they only had that long to prepare. Right now, their assets were him, Dean, Wyatt, and Carter, plus Arianna and Maddox now—and then whatever help the police could provide. That was about six people and the police force against an army of criminals who had been preparing for this day for months.

"Okay, they can help. They know tech, so maybe they can use that to level the playing field somehow."

"Thanks. I trust them both. We've worked together for a long time."

Gideon slumped down on the couch. Right now, all they could do was wait for the others to arrive. They'd mapped out the city and highlighted the areas they needed to defend: the bridge to the Platform, shelters, city hall, and the police stations. But that was a lot of ground to cover with not a lot of people to work it.

What they really needed to do was take out Serban and Sterling. Once the leadership was gone, it would be chaos, because the criminals would fall apart without a guiding influence. If he and Wyatt could do that, then hopefully the others could handle crowd control from a distance while the police fought off the criminal army.

Knock-knock. Gideon straightened and tightened his fists. Dean picked up one of Gideon's truncheons and walked over to the door. They couldn't be too careful, since Monahan knew where they lived. He looked out the peephole, nodded to Gideon, and opened the door. Wyatt and Carter walked in, eyes sweeping the area.

Wyatt looked down at Dean's baton and then at his face. "Nice welcome."

Gideon walked over to the two newcomers. Carter was dressed all in black, and Wyatt wore the Crusader outfit sans the mask. Gideon gave each of them a handshake and a back-slapping hug.

"Come in," Gideon said. "We're waiting on a few others."

Carter whistled. "Nice place."

"Thanks," Dean said.

Gideon closed the door and, looking at Dean, nodded toward the kitchen. Dean went to get some coffee while Gideon joined Carter and Wyatt in the living room.

"Have any trouble on the way in?"

"One guy with a knife and too big an opinion of himself tried to kill us," Wyatt replied. "But I took his ego down a peg."

"Good. Your family's safe?"

"Yes. They drove to a shelter elsewhere in the city."

Dean returned with several cups of coffee. "Drink up. I doubt we'll be getting much sleep tonight—or tomorrow night."

"While we're waiting, can you teach me some moves?" Carter asked.

Gideon looked at Wyatt, who nodded. "Okay, but I want to make it clear that you're not going to be on the front lines with us, understand? I'll teach you so you can protect yourself if you run into any of Serban's men, but you won't be in the thick of it."

"I know." Carter stood. "Better safe than sorry."

Gideon led Carter to the upstairs balcony where he had his training mat set up. He pulled out a rattan *jo* staff and tossed it to Carter, and then picked up two shorter rods for himself. Dropping into a ready stance, left arm and leg leading, right arm back and higher up to be ready to strike, he motioned with his left stick to Carter.

"Ready stance," he said. "Spread your legs, bend your knees slightly, angle your body. Hold the staff at a forty-five-degree angle with the ground."

Carter tried to emulate Gideon's instructions as best he could. Everything looked good except his grip on the staff. Gideon walked over to him and adjusted that, and then returned to the other side of the mat and dropped into a ready stance again.

"The nice thing about a *jo* staff is that almost anything can be improvised as one," he said. "Broomstick, hockey stick, pipe . . . anything. If you're unarmed, you can use whatever's around you as a weapon."

Gideon spent the next half hour teaching Carter everything he could, mainly defensive techniques. He showed him how to spin the staff to knock an opponent's weapon aside and then quickly riposte. He showed him how to use his footwork, as well as his size, to his advantage.

"It's all about momentum and leverage. Use every movement of your body, and theirs, to your advantage."

"A lot of this is similar to what my coaches say." Carter laughed. "But a lot is different, too."

"You'll learn." Gideon lunged, and he and Carter went into a series of strikes and parries. "Not bad."

Gideon drilled him for close to half an hour. At the end of their session, his clothes were drenched with sweat. Carter was in a similar condition. Gideon lowered his rattan rod, took Carter's staff from him, and placed the training weapons back on the rack. Together, they returned to the living room.

Gideon made eye contact with Wyatt. "Kid's a natural."

The man's smile was equal parts pride and sadness. "Of course, he is. Takes after his old man."

Someone knocked at the door. Dean approached and looked out the peephole again, and then opened it. Arianna and Maddox entered, each carrying a backpack.

"Brought some other stuff we thought might help," Arianna said. "Hi, everybody."

Even if he'd had time to go change into it before they saw him, Gideon decided to forego wearing the Seraph suit for now. As Dean had said, they wouldn't have too hard a time figuring out who he was, anyway. He went over to them and shook each of their hands.

Maddox's almost-black eyes scanned the room. "Thank you for letting us help. I know it's dangerous for a lot of people to know your secret, but we're just glad to be a part of protecting our city."

"If Dean trusts you, I trust you." Gideon motioned for them to come in. "I think this is everyone, so let's head upstairs to the lair."

Someone knocked on the door again. Gideon glanced at Dean, who furrowed his brow and picked up the truncheon again. Gideon walked to the door and looked out. It was Jolie. He frowned and opened the door.

"What are you doing here?"

"We need to strategize." She came in and hugged him. "Paul's covering for me at the precinct. But I figured the police will need to know everything they can to launch an effective defense, and you're our best source of information right now."

Gideon nodded and stepped aside to let her in. She looked around at all the faces in the room, blinked, and waved.

"Hello, everybody." She looked at Dean. "I'm so sorry about your dad. I can't imagine what you must be feeling."

"Yeah, join the club." Dean half-smiled and hugged her. "Glad you're on our side, Jolie."

"Okay, head upstairs," Gideon said. He took his baton from Dean and picked the other one up off the kitchen island. "We've got a lot of planning to do."

The lair was a cramped with seven people in it, but they all managed to circle around the computer table as Dean pulled up schematics of the city.

"I've highlighted the places that are a high priority to defend." Dean tapped the screen, and several red dots appeared. "Primarily, we want to protect shelters and innocents, of course, but we also need to make sure the mob doesn't get control of the bridge to the Platform. If they do, they'll basically have the city in their grasp."

"The police will be busy keeping the streets clear," Gideon said, "so we need to see if we can locate Serban and take him out."

"I might be able to help with that." Dean typed on the screen. "I . . . may have hacked my dad's phone. I found which number he always calls to reach Serban, so if Serban makes any calls, we can triangulate his location using that."

Jolie studied the screen. "What are we likely to be up against?"

"Ideally?" Gideon replied. "Just a lot of criminals with guns. But Dean's father also has a super-soldier serum, and we're not sure what he plans to do with it. There may be some very strong, very quick criminals out there."

"Not to mention whatever else Mr. Sung may have taken from the tech lab when he took the serum to Dad."

Jolie shook her head. "Great."

"We have some things that can help with that," Arianna said. "Of course, we can't supply the entire police force, but we can make sure everyone in this room is prepared, at least."

"But we can supply the police with these." Maddox handed his backpack to Jolie. "They're adhesive beads. Throw them at the ground and they explode, leaving behind a strong residue that will trap anyone in range."

"Thank you." Jolie shouldered the backpack. "That should be a huge help."

Gideon stepped to the front of the room. "Wyatt, I want you defending the bridge. Arianna, Maddox, Carter: run crowd control. Dean . . ."

"I'm going to Sterling Enterprises." Dean held up a handful of adhesive beads. "I may not be able to talk sense to my dad, but I can stop him."

Gideon considered discouraging him, but someone had to stop Sterling and he would let his guard down for his son.

"Okay."

"And you, Gideon?" Wyatt asked.

"I'm going to find Serban. It's time he and I had a face-to-face chat. So." He looked at Arianna and Maddox. "Show us what you've brought."

Combined with the load of supplies Dean had brought with him earlier, they had a pretty sizable supply of tech. There were two pairs of what they called "concussion gloves."

Arianna moved the mannequin that held the Seraph suit to the middle of the room. "These deliver a sizable kinetic boost to your punches."

She put on one of the gloves, clenched her fist, and punched. The mannequin flew out the door and into the hallway.

Wyatt whistled. "I'd like one of those."

"Then we have what I like to call the Crybaby." Maddox held up a sphere roughly the size of a softball. "These babies emit a sonic blast at a pitch guaranteed to give you a headache. They'll put a group of grown men on the ground in seconds. And, of course, we have earbuds to go along with them, so you don't hurt yourself."

"How many of those do you have?" Jolie asked.

"About a dozen."

"I'd like to take those, too, if I can."

"Sure thing."

Jolie loaded the Crybabies into the backpack with the adhesive beads. Dean held up his duffel bag.

"Last item. Well, items. I have in here two suits made of the same armored material as the Seraph suit. I was planning on giving one to Wyatt."

"And the other one?" Gideon asked.

"I was going to wear it." Dean shrugged. "Never know what I might run into trying to get to Dad."

"Fair enough." Gideon looked around. "Anyone else?"

Carter raised a hand. "What about me? I know I'm not going to be in the middle of the fighting, but what if I do run into trouble?"

Gideon picked up his truncheons, clicked them together, and tossed the combined *jo* staff to Carter.

"Flick the switch there to activate the electrified tips, and twist and pull in the middle to break the staff back into truncheons, if you need."

Carter grinned at the weapon. "Thanks!"

"I should head back to the precinct," Jolie said. "These supplies will help a lot, and with what I know about your plans, hopefully I can help coordinate the police to maximize the spread of our defense."

"Before you go." Dean opened a file on the smart table. "I also managed to get Serban's phone records. They should reveal anyone on government payroll he's been talking to. Even on the police force."

"Forward it to me," Jolie said. "I'll go over it."

She hugged Gideon and kissed him on the cheek, and then she was gone. Gideon leaned against the computer table.

"Okay," he said. "Everyone get some rest. We'll need it."

* * *

Even in the Brooks, the city was quiet by 3:00 in the morning. It was a calming, peaceful quiet, at least to Serban's ears. He stood in front of the warehouse where dozens of his men gathered to prepare for the day. As they filed past him and into the warehouse, Serban studied each of them. Some were hardened, ready to fight and die if necessary; others were cowardly, but their fear of Serban would outweigh their fear of the police. He didn't much care why they fought, only that they did.

He drew his thin-barreled Luger pistol and turned it over in his hands. The weapon was an antique, given to Serban by the first mobster he'd worked for in Romania. It was an artifact of World War 2, the mobster had said, and had killed dozens of Americans. Tonight, it would kill more.

Monahan studied the weapon. "A nice gun, if . . . inefficient."

Serban cast a glance at the woman. She was one to talk about inefficiency. All these months, armed with the best weapons money could buy, and she had failed to kill the two men he had ordered her to target. It was not the weapon, but the hand that held it, that determined the efficiency of a kill. It would be so easy to raise the Luger and put a bullet in her head. That would show her how efficient it was.

Serban tucked the Luger back into his belt. "Call me nostalgic."

He more commonly carried a modern pistol, but the anticipation of the coming battle had reminded him of the thrill of killing. He had made his fist kill with the Luger. Tonight, he would conquer his first city with it.

"Walters called," Monahan said. "He's loading up Costin and the rest of your lieutenants that were arrested at The Broken Glass. Allegedly, he'll be taking them to another precinct where they'll be safe from the fighting. But in reality, he's bringing them back here to us."

"Good. Walters has proven himself well, don't you think?"

"He has." Monahan smirked. "Greed brought out the best in him."

"So it did. When they arrive, tell Costin to take a squad of our best men to West Brooks Refuge Church to await the Seraph. When he arrives, they are to take him out. I'd love to kill the blue-hooded freak myself, but there are more pressing matters to attend to today."

"Yes, sir. And Walters?"

"Have him sit on Turner's family. Just in case."

"Understood, sir. Anything else?"

Serban withdrew a folded piece of paper from the pocket of his greatcoat. "See this delivered to Turner. Don't engage—just slip it under his door and get back here. I've got more important plans for you."

Monahan bristled, no doubt offended that she had been delegated to messenger, but she took the paper and tucked it into her pocket. Then she turned and walked toward her car. Serban watched her go. Once she returned, he would put her in charge of the team that would hit the bridge to the Platform. The sooner they disconnected it from the mainland and set it adrift, the better. That would keep the Seraph from interfering.

Serban's fingers brushed his Luger again. It would be satisfying to shoot the vigilante himself, though. One more so-called American hero to add to the gun's tally. Who knew? Maybe fate would smile on him today.

* * *

Gideon woke to the sound of pounding on his bedroom door. He shot up into a sitting position, but before he could even call for the person to come in, the door swung open and Dean poked his head in.

"You need to see this. Now."

Gideon threw on a shirt and pair of sweats and ran downstairs. Everyone sat in front of the TV. Nervousness was pouring off them.

Gideon grimaced and dampened down his empathic powers as much as he could. He moved around behind the couch to see the TV.

"The man known as the Seraph is a menace." The speaker was Deputy Mayor Hart. "Just weeks ago, he broke into city hall and assaulted one of our security guards."

"What was the purpose of his attack?" a news anchor asked.

"We've been unable to ascertain that. He wiped the footage from our security cameras." The deputy mayor frowned deeply. "What we do know is that this man must be brought to justice. His accomplice, the Crusader, is no better. He assaulted a renowned detective months ago and has been on the run since. If you see either man, call the police immediately."

Renowned detective. Gideon snorted. He didn't know anyone who'd call Walters that.

Maddox muted the TV. "What are the odds Hart is on Serban's payroll?"

"No odds," Dean replied. "We already suspected that based on the calls we intercepted from city hall, and Jolie called this morning. The police went through Serban's phone records and Hart's on the list of people he's called."

"Are they going to make arrests?" Gideon asked.

"They can't. Several high-ups in the police department are on his payroll, too. They're protecting the deputy mayor and others."

"We need to expose them. Get those phone conversations to every news channel who will take them."

"Good idea."

"I'll do that." Arianna grabbed her phone and ran upstairs.

"There's . . . another problem." Dean put his hand on Gideon's shoulder. "This one's a big one."

Now Gideon felt a wave of worry, sorrow, and regret flowing from his friend.

"What is it?"

"We found this paper this morning. It had been slid under the front door."

Gideon took the sheet of paper from Dean. *We know who you are. We know who your family is. We know where they live. If you want to save them, meet me at West Refuge Church. Come alone.* Gideon stared at the paper for a moment, and then crumpled it and poured light from his hand until the paper burst into flames and finally incinerated.

"I have to go."

"Gid, that's just what he wants. If you're busy with him there, you can't be leading the fight."

"But if he's there, then I can take him out and end this before it starts."

"Do you really think he'll be there? It's gotta be a trap. It'll probably be Monahan, or an entire cadre of mobsters. Plus, every police officer between here and the Brooks is going to be on the lookout for you!"

"It's my family, Dean! I can risk it. I have to risk it." He marched for the stairway. "The rest of you gear up and follow the plan. I'll meet you as soon as I can."

CHAPTER 35

Dean clipped on the armor piece by piece; the process was now familiar after his weeks of posing as the Seraph. He wondered how different it would feel without the cape. Wyatt looked like he was having a little more trouble with his suit, but he was getting the hang of it. Both suits were a dull gunmetal gray; they had been backup prototypes that Dean had never decorated for use. But they were practical, and that's what they needed.

He also pulled on the second pair of concussion gloves. As he'd said, he didn't know what he would be facing on his was to find his father.

Dean sized up the older man. "Looking good."

"Not bad." Wyatt grinned.

"You know, if you want to keep the suit after this, I would be okay with that. You could make it your own, design it to fit your style . . ."

"Thanks, but no." Wyatt finished clasping the joints together and looked down at his ski mask, decorated with a gray cross on the forehead. "I've decided to give up this life after today. I have other things to worry about."

"Fair enough. I can respect that." Dean glanced at Carter, who was putting on Wyatt's old Crusader outfit, sans the mask. "He's pretty good, too. Could make a great hero, someday."

"He already is." Wyatt pulled the mask on. "To me. And that's all that matters."

Dean poured a handful of adhesive beads into the pouches on either side of his belt. If this went well, he could trap his father, hand him over to the police, and turn right back around and go help the others. He didn't intend to spend the whole battle dealing with family drama. After all, Gideon about had that part down.

His phone rang. He looked down at the screen and frowned. It was Jolie. He answered and held the phone to his ear.

"Hello?"

"Dean! It's started."

"What?" There was a loud series of pops. "Is that gunfire?"

"Yes! They're hitting the twelfth precinct right now. Serban's forces are on the move! Everyone needs to get in position now."

* * *

With his motorcycle destroyed, Gideon had to drive his Mustang to get to West Refuge. He wondered how it must've looked from the outside: a navy-blue Mustang driven by a man in a hood and cape. Probably insane.

He pulled onto the corner outside the church and hopped out. It was poetic, in a way. This church being vandalized had been the original cause of him wanting to do more to help the city. Everything that had happened since then, every fight and covert operation and hospital visit, had been a product of that night at this church. Now, it would be the beginning of the end of all this mess.

He wished he had his truncheons with him. Carter needed them more than he did, though. He surrounded his clenched fists with pulsing light. That added an extra wallop to his punches. And as mad as he was, it should be enough to make up for his lack of weaponry.

The inside of the church was even worse off than it had been the last time Gideon had been in it. Dust and cobwebs covered everything. Benches and wooden rafters had cracked and splintered. Some had been destroyed. There was more graffiti, too. It made Gideon sick. He stood in the center of the sanctuary.

"I'm here!"

His voice echoed through the empty auditorium. There was no response. He closed his eyes and concentrated, reaching out to search for any hint of emotion. He felt anticipation, tinged with nervousness, coming from multiple sources. One was closer than the others, though . . .

There.

Gideon fired a burst of light at the pulpit. The wooden lectern exploded into splinters, and a man wielding a high-powered rifle slammed into the wall. Gideon tapped his earbud.

"Dean, you were right; Serban's not here. Get someone over to my parents' house and get them to safety."

"On it! You might want to move it. Jolie just called; the attack has begun."

Pounding footsteps echoed through the auditorium as thugs swarmed in. Gideon counted at least ten before they were on him, and they were still pouring in, both from the front doors behind him and from the side doors leading to the offices. He shoved his hands downward and discharged a wave of light in a circle around him. Those closest to him stumbled back.

It didn't stop them long. They charged him, swinging bats, chains, wooden boards . . . anything they could get their hands on. Gideon held up his arms to protect himself from the blows. There were so many that he couldn't manage to strike anyone; he was on pure defense.

Something struck the back of his head. He fell forward onto his knees and the men around him began to kick him. Pain racked his body. If it weren't for his armor, he was sure he would've passed out already.

"No!" he shouted.

He thrust his hands out, shooting another encircling blast. He leapt up and went on the offensive before his attackers could recover. He kicked one square in the face, spun, and rapidly punched another three times in the chest and once more in the jaw. He swiveled just in time to see a baseball bat descending toward his head. He caught it with his left hand and used his right to lock the attacker's arm and bend it. The man yelped as his elbow crunched. Gideon released his arm, grabbed his head, and shoved it down into a bench.

About twelve still standing.

Several charged at him at once. He extended his hands and fired three bursts of light. Each one struck a gangster in the chest and knocked him flat. Two more men reached Gideon and grabbed his arms. The Seraph grabbed their arms in return and poured out a stream of light, burning their hands. They screamed and released him. As another attacker came at him, Gideon picked up a baseball bat and hurled it. It struck the man in the face.

Six more.

The Seraph grabbed one by his shirt and hurled him across the room. Another came behind him and tried to get him in a chokehold. Gideon grabbed his arm and lunged forward, throwing the man over him and onto his back. Gideon let the momentum carry him into a front flip, and he came down on top of the man, his elbow driving into the attacker's ribs.

He rolled back to his feet and looked around. Four more.

As two of them rushed him, a third grabbed his cape and jerked him back. Gideon released the clasp on the cape, sending the man holding it stumbling back and tangling him in its folds. The two in front of him attacked, swinging a pipe and a knife.

The Seraph blocked the pipe on his forearm and pushed the knife aside. He kicked the guy with the pipe back into a bench as the one with the knife swung again. The blade dragged along Gideon's forearm and left a furrow in the armor. The knife-wielder lunged again. Gideon tilted his head out of the way. The blade bit into his cheek, leaving behind a stinging cut. He gritted his teeth and batted the man's hand aside.

His attacker swung the knife from the opposite direction. Gideon caught his forearm and punched him in the gut. The last attacker jumped on Gideon's back, pushing him forward, and grabbed his head. Gideon fell on top of the knife-wielder. The blade lodged in his armor and snapped in half.

The attacker on the Seraph's back tried to shove Gideon's head forward into the floor. Gideon tried to roll to the side and throw his attacker off, but he was laying on top of two bodies, which made getting any momentum difficult. He reached up behind him, grabbed the man's wrists, and jerked him down. As he did, he threw his own head up and back, slamming it into the attacker's face.

As the attacker cried out and stumbled back, the Seraph pushed himself to his feet, faced the man, and fired a single blast of light that sent him hurtling through the air. There. That should be all—

Two gunshots sounded, echoing through the church. Gideon felt the impact on his back and tumbled forward. He spun as he fell and saw the man who had been behind the pulpit standing, several large splinters of wood embedded in his arms and face, with his rifle trained on Gideon. Gideon recognized him now—he was the man Gideon had interrogated on the rooftop with Jolie last night. Costin. He fired again, and the shot struck Gideon in the chest.

The air rushed out of Gideon's lungs with the force of the impact. He extended both hand and fired a blast of light. Costin tumbled through the air and dropped onto his chest. Gideon staggered toward the front and grabbed the gun. He poured light into it and squeezed, warping the weapon beyond use. He dropped it and walked toward the door, pulling his cape back over his shoulders.

Serban was next.

* * *

Jolie ducked behind a desk as gunfire rained through the door. She drew her sidearm, steadied it, and popped over the desk to fire. She didn't wait to see if she hit anyone; she pulled back as bullets peppered the desk.

Jolie looked around for the backpack from the Sterling Labs team. It was on the floor between her and Captain Cranston's office. Paul and Pulaski were hidden on the other side of the bullpen, in the doorway leading to the interrogation room. They took turns leaning out to fire.

"Paul!" she shouted. "Cover!"

Her partner popped out of the doorway and fired rapidly. Jolie crawled toward the bag. She was almost to it when a boot kicked the bag aside. She stopped in her tracks, raised her gun, and shot the man who'd done it. As he fell, she scrambled forward and grabbed the bag.

She reached in and pulled out a handful of adhesive beads. She would rather have used one of the Crybabies; it would've taken down the entire mob of attackers trying to pour into the precinct. But none of the cops around her were wearing the protective earplugs. They'd all drop as fast as the criminals.

She squeezed the handful of beads and hurled them across the room at the entrance. Some of them struck the floor and exploded, sticking the attackers' feet to the ground. A couple of the beads exploded on contact with a person instead, coating them completely in the goo. Those two cried out in surprise, flailed to try to free themselves, and succeeded only in falling to the ground and getting even more stuck.

Paul and Pulaski fired in unison, dropping the rest of the attackers pouring inside. Another officer ran to the door and slammed it shut. Sergeant Andrews came out of Cranston's office, smoking gun in hand, and nodded to Jolie. Cranston followed in his wake, scanning the room.

"Quick thinking, Anderson," Andrews said.

"Thanks, Sarge." She handed him the backpack. "These devices should be distributed to all our officers. And make sure they're wearing earbuds."

"Sir!" an officer shouted. "Look at the news!"

Andrews and Cranston looked up at the TV in the corner. A reporter was playing recordings that incriminated Deputy Mayor Hart and a whole slew of others in collaborating with Serban—including several police officers from other precincts. Finally, the reporter said, "Simon Walters." Andrews slammed his fist against the wall.

"Where is Detective Walters?" Cranston asked.

"I sent him to transfer the Romanian prisoners to another precinct for safekeeping," Andrews said. "No mystery what he did with them."

"No time to worry about that, Sergeant. We've got a city to protect." Cranston pulled on a bulletproof vest.

Andrews turned to address the precinct. "Everyone outside. Arm up and take as many of Anderson's toys with you as you can. Priority one is containing the chaos in the streets, but priority two is finding all the corrupt cops and taking care of them, too."

"Sarge, there's a list of collaborators in that backpack," Jolie said. "I was on my way to bring it to you when they attacked."

Andrews withdrew the sheet. "Someone make copies of this! I want everyone to have their eyes out for these people." As several officers scrambled to follow his orders, he looked at Jolie. "Where'd you get all this, Anderson?"

"A friend at Sterling Labs was generous enough to help us out."

"And the information?"

"Same friend."

"Well." Andrews pulled out a handful of beads and one Crybaby and put them in a pouch on his belt. "Must be some friend."

"I'm sorry, sir. I've been looking into Walters for some time now. If I'd told you about my suspicions sooner—"

"Like the captain said, Anderson. No time to worry about that now. Let's move. Pulaski, you're with me. This city won't fall on our watch, people."

CHAPTER 36

Last year

It was longer than Gideon expected before they came to bring him to the doctor. He wondered how long he'd been in captivity. He reached up and tugged at his hair. Judging by its length, and that of his beard, it had to have been a long time—almost a year, maybe. He couldn't believe it had been that long, but in some ways, it seemed longer. It seemed like he'd been here for an eternity.

But one day, at last, he heard the clanking sound of keys in the big door at the end of the cell block. He straightened and moved toward his cell door.

"It's time."

"Yes," Joshua agreed. "Gideon? I want you to promise me something."

"Sure." Gideon prepared himself to move. "Name it."

"If for some reason, you make it out of here and I don't, I want you to go to San Francisco. Find my grandson, Patrick Omer. My son and his wife, too, of course. But Patrick . . . tell him, tell all of them, that I love them. Tell them what happened to me, that I didn't run away from them."

"Don't talk like that, man. We're both getting out of here."

"Sure. But you already promised. Right?"

Gideon sighed. "Right. I promise."

The guerrillas walked into the block and made their way to Gideon's cell. Their captain, the big guy with the keys, led the way. He sneered at Gideon as he unlocked the cell. *Oh, great.* Gideon hadn't planned on him being the front guy. It would be a lot harder to pin him.

But Gideon lucked out. As the captain opened the door, one of the other guerrillas, who was significantly smaller, approached with his rifle raised and gestured for Gideon to exit the cell. Gideon raised his hands and slowly walked toward the guerilla.

God, please . . .

He lunged. He wrapped one hand around the rifle barrel, jerked it aside, and pressed his body close against the guerrilla's. The second soldier raised his rifle, and Gideon spun his captive's body around as the other guerrilla fired. The one Gideon was holding spasmed as the bullets struck him. Gideon shoved his body toward the second guerrilla, kept a hold of the rifle, and spun toward the captain. The big man swung a fist at Gideon. Gideon ducked under the blow and cracked the rifle stock over the captain's head. The big man sunk to the floor and Gideon shot the lock on Joshua's door.

"Let's go!"

The second guerrilla pushed his companion's body off him and raised his rifle. Gideon shot him, his heart aching at taking another life. He ran to the guerrilla's side and picked up his rifle to give it to Joshua. But as he turned, the captain stood back up and lunged. Joshua stepped in his path and punched the captain full in the face. Gideon thought there was a bright flash of light as Joshua's fist connected with the man's chin.

What in the . . . ?

He must've been imagining it. It didn't matter, anyway. He turned to run for the door. Joshua's footsteps did not follow. Gideon stopped and glanced back at his friend.

"Joshua. You coming?"

Joshua turned to face Gideon. A knife was embedded in his gut. The captain must've had it in his hand and been aiming for Gideon when Joshua stepped in the way. Tears welled in Gideon's eyes.

"We . . . we can patch you up when we get back to town."

"No, Gideon." Joshua smiled—that same kind, compassionate smile from when they first met, the smile of a man who knew a special kind of goodness. "No, I'd only slow you down. I'll stay here . . . hold them off." He pointed a finger at Gideon. "But you promised me."

Gideon blinked, and his tears streaked his cheeks. "Yeah, I . . . I did."

"Go. Go live your life, get your girl. But don't forget to find my family. Tell them I loved them. Tell them . . . tell them about Jesus."

"I will." Gideon wiped his eyes. "Thank you."

Joshua turned to face the captain, who was rising again. Gideon shook his head, turned, and ran. *Greater love has no man than this: that he lay down his life for a friend.* Gideon made it all the way to the front door before he heard a gunshot echo through the halls, and he knew that Joshua was gone. He threw down his own rifle in disgust.

He didn't have time to find a vehicle. He just ran, not knowing where to go. He just had to get away. He spent hours running. They pursued him, shot at him . . . and finally, when he thought he was going to die, rescue came. As impossible light flashed from his hands, blinding the shooters, FBI agents flooded the jungle and killed the guerrillas. They took Gideon back to town, and they put him on a plane. At last, he got to go home.

But he wouldn't forget Joshua's promise. He would find them—he would tell them about how great a man Joshua was, the love he'd shown—the love he'd found in Christ.

And he would never forget how Joshua had saved his life.

Now

Gideon's car roared down the street toward his parents' house. He would make sure they were safe, and then he'd find Serban.

He already knew where to look: city hall. He knew, somehow, that that's where Serban would be. The man was consumed with taking control of the city, and city hall would symbolize that domination. If he wasn't there already, he would be soon.

"Dean!" he called.

"Yeah. You okay?"

"Fine. You were right; there were a bunch of goons waiting for me."

"Take care of them?"

"They won't be bothering anyone today. Give me a status update."

"The fighting hasn't spread outside the Brooks yet, but it will soon. The police at the Brooks precinct have at least taken their office back, and they're setting up a command center there. No sign of Serban. We're all geared up and ready to move."

"Once the fight breaks out of the Brooks it'll spread quickly—very quickly. Get the Crusader to the bridge controls. Everyone else needs to start evacuating whoever they can."

"And you?"

"I'm going to make sure my parents are safe."

"What about Serban?"

"I'll take care of him. Right now, I need to make sure they're safe."

The streets were chaos. People were running around in a panic, some trying to find cover, some fighting, some rioting and looting. Gideon rolled his window down and fired bursts of light at several thugs who were assaulting a man.

"Gideon, I know they're your family. But don't you think it's more important to take Serban out as soon as we can?"

"I don't know where he is right now. But I know where he'll be."

Besides, if Gideon confronted Serban now, he would probably kill him in his rage. He needed to be sure his parents were safe; then he'd be calm enough to take on Serban.

"Gideon, I already sent Carter to rescue your parents. The fighting isn't at their house yet; he can get them out safely."

"I need to do it myself."

Dean sighed. "Okay. I understand. Be safe and be quick. I'm going to my father's office now. I'll let you know when he's . . . when I've got him."

"You be careful, too, Dean."

"I will."

Gideon was just pulling onto the interstate when a police car pulled up behind him and lit up its sirens. He rolled his eyes. Didn't they have more pressing matters to deal with? Gideon didn't have time to stop. He swerved through traffic, but the cruiser stayed on him doggedly, following him with every move, every lane change. Finally, he sighed.

"Sorry. I hate to do this."

He reached out the window, turned around—risky, but he was quick—and fired a burst of light at the cop's tire. The rubber exploded, and the car skidded to a stop. Gideon sped toward his parents' home.

* * *

"Wyatt, get to that bridge control center. Everyone else, on crowd control."

Carter had left minutes before, taking Maddox's car. Dean had given him instructions to protect the Turner family and get them to Refuge Church, which was being set up as a shelter.

Dean looked around his living room. At any other time, he probably would've been really impressed, and even geeked out at what he saw. He and the Crusader clad in body armor. Maddox and Arianna, each wearing a jumpsuit and carrying a stun gun and a handful of adhesive beads. It was awesome . . . but Dean's mind was on his father.

"Okay," Dean said. "Team Seraph, let's move. Godspeed, everyone."

He rode the elevator down to the garage, climbed in his car, and sped toward Sterling Enterprises. He had no idea what he'd say to his dad. No idea what he was going to happen when he went into that building. Given that he was dressed like a superhero, he wondered if he'd even be able to make it to his dad's office without a fight. At least he was geared up for it.

But then . . . what? "Hey, Dad, sorry I have to do this, but I know you're a supervillain," and throw a bunch of adhesive beads at him? He knew his dad would try to protest, would try to talk his way out of it. He'd have some logical explanation, as he always did, and Dean had to be ready for that. Maybe hearing a logical argument from his son would persuade him. After all, all those superhero movies where the son of the villain tried to change his mind only to get killed, they were only movies. Not real life.

But this was real life, and in real life, when someone like Edgar Sterling decided to do something, very few people would change his mind. Dean knew that. He might not be able to persuade his father to stand down. But he could stop him.

He rounded a corner and drove toward the Platform. Between him and the bridge, dozens of criminals and police officers exchanged fire. He wondered if he'd even make it through the skirmish.

An old-model car passed Dean, screeched into the middle of the chaos, and stopped. The Crusader stepped out, leapt at the criminals, and went to town on them. Dean grinned and swerved around Wyatt's car. A few stay bullets struck Dean's Camaro—*not my baby, not my baby*—but he pressed on. As he reached the bridge, he glanced in the rearview mirror.

"Good luck, Crusader," he said. "You'll need it."

* * *

When Dean reached Sterling Enterprises—not an easy feat, because traffic got heavier the father he got into the Platform—there were two guards standing at the front door. Dean stepped out of his car and approached them.

He looked them over as he neared. Although they wore the proper uniforms, they were not Sterling employees, he was sure of that. They were both armed, though, and their purpose was clearly to keep anyone from entering. And as they spotted Dean, geared up in gray armor, they raised their rifles and stepped toward him.

"Stop there."

"Turn around, buddy." The second man gestured to Dean's car with his rifle. "You don't have business here today."

"This is my father's company," Dean said. "I have business here whenever I want."

The men exchanged glances. Dean took a step closer. He was within reach now. All he needed was an opening . . .

"Not today, Junior." The guard had an accent—Romanian. "Building's on lockdown."

"And I would accept that, but there's one problem. I know every security specialist my father has ever hired . . . and I don't recognize either of you."

Before they could react, Dean grabbed both their rifles and squeezed. The rifle barrels cracked under the pressure applied by the concussion gauntlets. The men stepped back and reached for the sidearms in their belt holsters. Dean rushed in, grabbed the one on the left by the collar, and hurled him into a tree. The second man whipped up his pistol and fired. The bullet winded Dean but did not puncture his armor. He stormed toward the shooter, fists clenched. The man fired three more times, but none of the shots did more than slow Dean's pace.

Dean punched the guard across the jaw, pulling the blow so that the enhanced gauntlets didn't shatter his skull. The man slumped and dropped his pistol. Dean picked the gun up, and he snapped it in half. He then dropped an adhesive bead on the man and his companion.

"Next time you might consider being bad at your job," Dean said. "Might save you from being flattened."

He strode past the guards to the front door. It was locked. *Of course.* Dean sighed, pulled back his hand, and punched the glass surface with all his might. The door—and the one next to it—shattered. Dean stepped in through the hole and ran toward the stairway. He wouldn't have much time until his father realized he was here, and the elevators would be locked down. He punched the stairwell door open and bounded up the steps.

"Sixty-five floors," he muttered. "Here we go."

* * *

The streets of the Brooks looked like Armageddon. Jolie crouched behind a car, which had been crashed into a streetlight and abandoned, and held her gun in one hand and adhesive beads in the other. Paul was next to her, shouldering a shotgun and peppering gangsters with fire. The Red Dogs and the Tyrants had moved in on the police station only minutes after the cops had cleared it. Sergeant Andrews and Detective Pulaski had managed to squeeze out before the attack began. They were on their way to city hall now to arrest whatever complicit city employees they could find. Andrews had ordered Jolie to take control of the fighting here.

She was glad he trusted her, but she was beginning to think the situation was beyond saving. While many officers were escorting civilians to safety, the few who remained fighting were surrounded and cut off from reinforcements. It would take sheer brute force to punch a hole through the gangsters and fight their way to freedom. Jolie hoped they had it in them.

"Paul, left!" she shouted.

She jumped up and tossed her handful of beads at the cluster of Tyrants on the street corner to her left. As the beads exploded, cementing the Tyrants in place, Paul fired on them. That was their hole.

Jolie swept her hand at the opening. "That way! Move!"

Paul, along with three other officers who were backing him and Jolie, rushed in that direction. Jolie followed, firing at the Red Dogs who were swarming in behind them. The cops in front of her went around the corner toward the back of the precinct, where most of their vehicles were parked.

Jolie pulled her Crybaby from her belt. She didn't want to use it until she absolutely had to; she only had the one. But as quickly as these thugs were closing in, that would probably be sooner than she'd like.

They made it to the parking lot and clambered into their vehicles. As Paul started the engine, Jolie switched on the radio and filtered through the chatter.

" ... *half a dozen Romanians on Teller!*"

"*Sixth and Donovan is under control. Moving to assist at Teller.*"

" ... *backup at the bridge to the Platform! Need immediate backup!*"

Jolie stopped on the last frequency. "There! We need to get to the bridge."

Paul sped out onto the street. "Why? We need to clean up the Brooks before we worry about the rest of the town."

He was right, but the key to all of this would be the Platform. Serban and his goons didn't want the Brooks. They'd had it for months now, and they weren't satisfied. They wanted more. But then, there were all the people here who did need rescuing from the thugs who'd remained behind to consolidate their holding.

"Okay. But as soon as possible, get me to that bridge."

Gideon was going to be at the center of the fighting, and likely so would Serban—and Monahan. Jolie had been after that woman for months, and she was sick of seeing her slip away. As soon as she got her chance, she was taking her down.

But although Monahan was a threat, Jolie knew her own feelings well enough to recognize that her drive to find her was personal. For

now, the Brooks needed help, and its vigilantes were otherwise occupied. It was time for the police to do their job.

CHAPTER 37

Wes Turner watched the news in awe. He'd never thought that his own hometown would become a war zone. The latest reports had battles spilling out of the Brooks and even into Lakeside. There was a huge skirmish going on near the bridge to the Platform. It was insane. Wes looked at his father, who stood near the door and peered out the window.

"The news said the fighting's not near here, Dad. We're still safe for now."

"I know." His father walked away from the window and looked upstairs. "Still, we need to be prepared. Tasha! We need to go."

"Coming!"

Wes turned back to the TV. The news anchor spoke about corruption in city hall and on the police force. Apparently, even the deputy mayor was in on this plot. Wes shook his head. These were the people who were supposed to guard their city? No wonder Gideon had suited up and gone out to do it himself.

"Okay."

Wes turned. Mom appeared at the top of the stairs and rushed down them. Dad took her hand and led her toward the garage door. Wes turned off the TV and followed.

Knock, knock.

Wes' parents froze. Wes looked back at the door and cast about for something to use as a weapon. The fireplace was within reach; picked up the wood poker. Dad walked toward the door. Wes followed him, holding the poker in front of him and ready to attack.

Dad was halfway through the living room when the door exploded. Wes tackled his mother to the floor. Gunfire, punches, and grunts filled the small space. Wes pulled her behind the couch and then climbed to his feet, ready to fight.

But it wasn't necessary. Four men—two of them in police uniforms—lay unconscious in the doorway. Dad still stood in the middle of the living room, frozen. And over the four downed men stood another man, clad in black with a bandana over his nose and mouth. He held a short, metal staff that sparked at the ends. A vigilante?

"Get out of here!" the black-clad man said. "Hurry!"

Was that the Crusader? Wes wasn't sure, but whoever it was had just saved their lives. Dad snapped out of his frozen state and rushed over to Wes and Mom's side. Wes helped his mother stand.

"To the garage," Dad said. "Let's go."

Wes followed, but kept a hold of the poker. The Crusader might be there protecting them, but he couldn't be everywhere at once. If anyone tried to come for Wes' family, they'd have to go through him first.

* * *

Gideon parked his car on the curb. There was a police cruiser parked across the street, along with an old muscle car and a new-model economy car. That didn't look good. Gideon rushed through his parents' front lawn to the door and found it broken in. His heart pounded in his ears as he approached. What would he find inside? Was his family being held captive, or had they already been killed?

But just inside the doorway were four unconscious men. Two of them wore police uniforms; all four had guns lying near them. Carter must've gotten here first. Gideon walked into the house.

"Carter!" he called. "Dad! Mom! Wes!"

Carter entered the living room from the kitchen. He had a bandana over the lower half of his face and carried Gideon's staff.

"They're in the garage. I'm heading out to my car to follow them and make sure they get to safety."

"Thank you, Carter." Gideon put a hand on his shoulder. "If you hadn't been here, they—"

Several heavy projectiles struck him in the back. He grunted, stumbled forward, and leaned against Carter so he wouldn't fall on his face. He glanced over his shoulder. Two black SUVs had pulled up. Their doors opened, and six men climbed out and ran toward the house, all of them armed with guns.

Gideon clenched his fists. "Get to your car. I'll hold these guys off."

He reached back with one hand and fired a wild burst of light. The Seraph stormed out into the yard, fists glowing. Carter ran past him, sprinting to the economy car. Gideon's first blast had knocked out three men. He stepped over them and charged the remaining three who stood in the yard. They opened fire on him, and the Seraph's glowing aura disintegrated the bullets as he approached. He was on top of the first before the man knew what to do. He slammed his glowing fist into the thug's chest, and the man flew backward and slammed into one of the SUVs.

The other two attackers, a man in a Red Dogs jacket and a woman with distinctly Romanian features, continued to fire on Gideon, their bullets striking his armor. He grimaced with each hit. But at least while their focus was on him, they wouldn't see—

The garage door opened, and the Turner family's old but reliable van roared down the driveway. A moment later, the economy car peeled after them. The Romanian woman swiveled and trained her rifle on the van. Gideon blasted her, knocking her flat on her face in the grass. The last attacker rushed Gideon, throwing his rifle aside and drawing a machete the length of his forearm. He swept the blade at the Seraph's neck. Gideon ducked and punched the man twice in the gut. The man stepped back and swung wildly with his machete. The blade slashed Gideon's hood, tearing it at the collar. Gideon grabbed his wrist as he swung again. He twisted until the thug dropped the machete, and then he punched the man in the jaw.

The SUVs sped away. Gideon fired a burst of light at the rearmost vehicle, blowing out its back two tires. The first SUV swung around the corner and was gone. Gideon hoped his parents were far enough away that the SUV wouldn't be able to catch up. He walked back to his car. He put his hand on the door—

A burst of bullets pinged off the windshield. Gideon's head snapped up. The driver of the damaged SUV had climbed halfway out of the vehicle and was firing a submachine gun. Gideon raised his left hand and fired, knocking the man back into the vehicle and shattering his rifle.

He climbed into his car and drove away, leaving the Red Dogs and Romanians lying in the yard and the road. As the adrenaline began to wear off, Gideon began to feel the effects of the fight—his arms, chest, and back throbbed. The spot on his back where the first round of bullets had struck ached the worst—not good, given his recent spinal fracture. He was tired, too. Using his powers so much was draining him.

He only hoped his body would hold up long enough to get him through the night. Once he had taken down Serban and Monahan and stopped their incursion, then he could collapse—and recover . . . or die. At this point it hurt so bad he wasn't sure which anymore. But he had to stop them first. That wasn't a question.

He pursued the SUV, but the driver must've been booking it—it was out of sight now, and Gideon had no idea which route it had taken. He slammed his fist against the steering wheel.

He turned the car to city hall. He'd have to trust God to protect his parents now. They had gotten a pretty good head start. Hopefully the lone driver of that SUV wouldn't be a problem. And once they got to the church, they'd be safe. The police would have it cordoned off as a refuge—an apt name for the church, Gideon thought wryly—and would stop the attacker before he could hurt them. And even if they couldn't, Carter would.

Gideon turned his attention to Serban. Taking him down had to be the Seraph's main goal right now. The rest of Team Seraph was doing their part to protect the city. Now Gideon had to, too.

* * *

Dean stepped onto the sixty-fourth-floor landing and panted. He wished he could fly—or had superspeed, or something. Taking so many stairs all at once was just . . . too much. He put his hands on the back of his head, took three deep breaths, and nodded to himself. One more flight to go. He was almost there.

He grabbed the railing and walked up the steps toward the top floor. Above him, the door to his father's suite opened. Dean looked up but couldn't see who was coming. He was almost directly underneath the landing. He clenched his fists, readying himself for a fight, and continued his walk up.

On the landing halfway between the two floors, two "security officers" were waiting for him, brandishing nightsticks. Dean shook his head and walked toward them. The one on his left swung his nightstick at Dean's head. Dean ducked under the strike and punched the man in the knee. He heard a wet *pop* and the man cried out. The other faux-guard brought his stick down at Dean's head. Dean managed to twist aside so the blow only smacked his shoulder, but even through the armor, he felt it. The man swung rapidly again and again, striking Dean repeatedly.

Dean stood, taking each blow in stride as the armor absorbed it. The guard pulled back and swung at his head again. Dean brought his gauntlet up, blocking the nightstick, and shoved the guard. The man stumbled back and bumped the wall. Dean grabbed him, turned, and slammed him down on top of his friend. Leaving the two of them groaning in a tangle of limbs, he ascended the last set of steps to the top floor.

CHAPTER 38

The Crusader stood in the middle of an intersection, surrounded by cops—and for once, they were on his side. A few of them, who he suspected were on Serban's payroll, had shouted at him to put his hands up and one had even taken a shot at him. But several other officers, who seemed to have a better understanding of the situation, had managed to subdue the shooter and even cuff him. The Crusader made a mental note to watch the others who had protested his presence, but they appeared content to work with him for the time being. Probably nervous they'd be found out and cuffed like their overzealous comrade.

The advance of criminal forces had halted for the moment, so the Crusader and the police had set up a checkpoint in this intersection. Directly behind them was the bridge to the Platform. Behind them to the right was the bridge control station. Ahead was the road where most of the criminals would be coming from. On either side of that road were six-story apartment buildings, and the police had set up a sniper on the rooftop of each to create a choke point.

Once they began to pour through, Wyatt suspected they would break the choke point quickly. Some of them would go inside the apartments, climb to the rooftops, and kill or at least distract the snipers enough for their companions to slip through. Wyatt and the cops on the ground would have their hands full.

All Wyatt had to do was make sure no one reached the bridge controls. Simple enough.

It was mid-afternoon now; the sun was still above the edge of the buildings, but it was beginning to sink. Once it set, Wyatt suspected the battle would rage in earnest.

"Lord, protect this city," he said. "Provide its defenders strength and turn the wicked into our hands."

He wished he had a weapon. He'd always been best with his fists, but all the police around him were armed with M16s, Tasers, nightsticks, and riot gear, and it made him feel naked. Especially since the criminals were likely to be similarly armed. At least he had the armor and concussion gauntlets. That was more than Carter had, and that worried him.

"And Lord," he added, "protect my son."

Wyatt saw movement far down the street. He clenched his fists, knowing he wouldn't have to move for a while still but ready all the same.

Three huge black utility vans roared down the street toward them. No doubt each of them was loaded with Serban's forces. As the vans closed in, the snipers opened fire. One of the vans swerved, overcorrected, and flipped. It landed on its side. The other two roared on. Another shot from the snipers blew out a second van's tire—and another killed its driver. The third van continued its advance.

It was close enough now for the cops on the ground to fire on it. As bullets pelted the van, its driver spun the wheel and it crashed into the side of one of the apartments.

Wyatt turned his attention back to the streets. As the vans had trundled down the road, dozens of criminals pounded down the sidewalks on either side of the road. They were getting closer, and there was no way the snipers could take down all of them.

"On the left!" a cop shouted.

The Crusader spun to his left. Two more vans were rushing in from the avenue on the left. Then he looked right. Another van was coming from that direction, too.

Here we go.

As the thugs and gangsters poured into the apartments and past them to rush the blockade in the intersection, Wyatt squared himself, said one last prayer, and rushed to meet them.

* * *

Jolie snapped off a shot, dropping a Tyrant who had been spraying the streets with a machine gun. In the past hour, the police had managed to rally and push the criminals away from the precinct and back toward a central location: The Broken Glass. It helped that many of the criminals had trickled out of the Brooks and toward the Platform. Now there only a dozen or so left, holed up inside that bar.

Which made it the perfect time to use the Crybaby. That many people, trapped in such a confined space, would be quickly incapacitated by its sonic shriek.

"Cover me, Paul."

She rushed toward the bar, Paul's shotgun rounds echoing behind her. A Red Dog stuck his head out of the bar, only to be shot by one of the other cops. Jolie slid to a crouch next to the door and pulled out her Crybaby.

"Earplugs in!" she shouted.

She shoved her own in and activated the Crybaby. A small timer appeared on the screen.

:05

Jolie turned to the door, propped open by the body of the Red Dog, and hurled the Crybaby inside. Then she tore down the street back to Paul's side. She dropped to her haunches next to him and they waited.

The door flew open and thugs rushed out into the streets, holding their ears and screaming. Some of them—mostly locals, like the Red Dogs and Tyrants—dropped their weapons and fell to their knees, indicating surrender. But a handful of the foreigners fired wildly. It took only a few seconds to finish them off.

Jolie stormed out the door. "Now, get me to the bridge."

* * *

The parking lot of Refuge Church was filled to the brim with cars, buses, and pedestrians on foot. The police had set up a cordon at each entrance to the parking lot and were checking every vehicle as it entered—not only the IDs of the passengers and drivers, but also examining the vehicles to make sure that they weren't being used to smuggle in weapons, drugs, or bombs. It was a sad scene to see at the church, one Wes would've never expected in his lifetime.

He still couldn't believe all this was happening. It was insane. Criminals didn't just militarize and conquer a city; that's not how things worked. And yet, here they were. He hoped the police—and Gideon—were able to get things under control. If not, hiding at Refuge would be a temporary solution, at best.

The police officer checking vehicles at the north entrance waved the Turners forward. Dad pulled the car up and rolled down the window. He and Mom handed the officer their IDs.

"Son." Dad's voice snapped Wes back to the present. "Your ID?"

Wes reached into his wallet and removed his driver's license. Dad passed it to the officer. The cop walked around the car, peering in the windows and popping open the trunk. When he was satisfied, he returned to Wes' father, handed him back their IDs, and waved them through.

"About time," Wes muttered. "Not like it's your church or anything."

"They have to be thorough," Dad replied. "If even one shooter snuck in here, it would be a slaughter."

"I know." Wes sighed. "It's just so . . . crazy."

Dad parked the car far from the church, next to an empty school bus. Wes climbed out, keeping a tight grip on the fireplace poker. He knew his dad had taken this spot so that the remaining spots closer to the church could be used by others. It made him smile. He wondered if he would've done the same thing if he were the one driving.

A detective approached, dressed to the nines. Wes recognized him as Detective Walters, the man who'd been assigned to track down the church attackers. As far as Wes knew, Walters had never made any progress. Wes' father turned to look at him.

"Can I help you, Detective?"

Walters drew his gun and trained it on Dad's chest. Wes' eyes widened, and his mother screamed. Wes started to move forward, brandishing the poker but knowing he'd never reach the corrupt detective in time to stop him from shooting—

The Crusader dropped from the top of the school bus and landed on top of the Turners' car, spinning his staff. Walters' head and gun swiveled around to the new arrival. Before he could fire, the vigilante leapt, swinging his staff. The first strike knocked the gun from the detective's hand. The second took him across the chin, spinning him around. The Crusader kicked him in the back. Walters fell flat on his chest.

The vigilante's cheeks raised, indicating a smirk. "Sorry to ruin your suit."

"Thank you, whoever you are," Dad said. "It appears you're getting into the habit of saving us."

"I'm the Crusader," the dark-clad man said. "A friend of your son's."

From his voice and the little bit of his face Wes could see over his bandana, he seemed young—probably Wes' age or even younger. But he had the hard look of someone who had faced adversity.

"Why . . . why was that detective pointing his gun at us?" Mom asked.

"He works for Luca Serban, the criminal mastermind behind this uprising." The Crusader pulled out a small object that looked like a marble. He dropped it on the cop, and a blueish goop spread out across Walters' body. "He won't be going anywhere. Come on, let's get you inside the church before anymore of Serban's goons come after you."

Dad nodded and led the others inside. The Crusader hung behind, near Wes. As he ran, Wes looked over at the vigilante. He wasn't wearing fancy gear like Gideon's, just a leather jacket, jeans, and combat boots. But his staff and that weird sphere that had released that goo were pretty high-tech.

Wes' father opened the door to the church and Mom ran inside. Dad gestured for Wes to do the same. Wes glanced at the Crusader.

"What about you?"

"I'll stay out here," the boy replied. "Need to make sure no one gets inside."

"Good luck."

Wes ran into the church, following his mother through the foyer to the sanctuary. If this kid could be out there fighting crime like that, why couldn't he? Gideon was out there, too, and he was only three years older than Wes. He wished he had some tech like theirs. Then he could be out there with them, instead of hiding here in the church, clutching a poker.

But, as much as it pained him, he didn't look back. He ran into the sanctuary and dropped to a crisscross sitting position on the floor near the back of the room, next to his mother. His dad joined them a moment later and put his hand on Wes' shoulder.

"We're going to be okay."

"Yeah." Wes nodded. "I know."

He just wished he was a part of making sure everyone else was okay.

* * *

The police around city hall were putting up a valiant fight; Serban did have to give them that much. But there weren't enough of them. Their force was spread too thin, and as Serban had predicted, many of the wealthy denizens of the Platform had called whatever policemen they had in their pockets back to the bridge or even the Platform itself to defend them in case the fighting spread that far. Which meant that the officers here had almost no chance at reinforcement.

Serban's men had reported some officers and detectives swarming inside earlier that day, so Serban figured that most of the government officials in his pocket had been arrested by now. That was fine. He wouldn't need them once he conquered the city, anyway. They could rot.

He was tired of watching from across the street, though. Serban had risen through the ranks by getting his hands bloody. Now that he was in charge, he didn't have to—but that didn't mean he didn't enjoy it. He drew his Luger from within his greatcoat and strode out into the street.

One shot at a time, one officer at a time, he took down the police guarding city hall. His men ran interference, keeping themselves between him and the return fire from the cops. Serban smirked and strode toward the front steps. He felt invincible.

"Move in!" he shouted.

His Romanian comrades, along with the Red Dogs and Tyrants that had joined them, pushed past the last of the police resistance and up the front steps. One of Serban's lieutenants kicked down the front door—and then jerked and fell to the ground as he was met with a hail of gunfire.

The Red Dogs and Tyrants swarmed in. Serban followed in their wake and snapped off several shots, dropping an officer with every carefully-placed bullet. He reloaded the pistol as he entered the building.

City hall would be the symbol of his victory, but he didn't plan to stay here. For practical purposes, there was no place better to rule this city than from Sterling Enterprises. Mr. Sterling didn't know that yet, of course. But then, he didn't need to. He had played his part, and now he was irrelevant. That meant now he could be disposed of.

* * *

Detective Pulaski ducked inside the district attorney's office and shoved the last of their prisoners, the assistant DA, into the corner. He and Sergeant Andrews had rounded up all the government officials on Anderson's list, but then one of the officers stationed downstairs had called them to warn them that Serban and his men had broken the line and were inside.

Pulaski guided the mayor behind the DA's desk and motioned for him to get under it. He drew his gun and stood to one side of the door, Andrews on the other side.

"We're stuck," Pulaski said. "We're on the third floor and they're between us and our only way out."

"Not necessarily." Andrews peered out the door. "We might be able to make it to one of the side doors if we take the back stairway."

"That's risky. If we get trapped in the stairwell, we'll be bottled."

"Better than sitting here and waiting to die. We can lock these guys in here for now and just get the mayor out."

Pulaski sighed. "Guess we don't have much choice."

"I'll cover you. You go first with the mayor; I'll bring up the rear and make sure they don't get behind us."

"Right." Pulaski went back over to Mayor Crowe's side. "Come with me, sir. Keep your head down and do whatever I tell you, understood?"

The mayor nodded.

"Good. We're getting you out of here. Let's go."

Pulaski ran back to the door. Andrews held up three fingers and counted down. When he formed a fist, Pulaski sprinted out toward the stairs. He heard the mayor's footsteps behind him, and then Andrews' as the sergeant paced them.

Crack-crack. Pulaski jerked back before he rounded the corner to the next hall. Bullets smacked into the adjacent wall.

"Can't go that way. They're already there."

"Back to the DA's office," Andrews said.

They turned and had to duck back again as gunfire erupted from that direction.

Andrews fired back. "We're pinned!"

"We'll just have to push through." Pulaski checked his ammo. "You got one of those screamer grenade things Anderson handed out?"

The sergeant pulled the softball-sized sphere from his belt and nodded.

"But the mayor doesn't have earplugs."

Pulaski removed his. "Now he does. It is going to hurt like heck, but I can take it. Just throw the thing and take the mayor out of here."

"Pulaski—"

"I can't let you do that, detective," Mayor Crowe said. "I—"

"Yes, you can. It's my choice. Sergeant, Mr. Mayor . . . get out of here."

Crowe put in the earbuds. "Thank you, son."

Pulaski tightened his grip on his Glock and clenched his jaw. As soon as Andrews threw the sonic weapon, he'd turn the corner and give them covering fire until he passed out. At which point, he knew he'd probably be dead, because the thugs coming up behind them would find him and execute him. But at least Andrews and the mayor could make it out. He just wished that Monahan woman was here. He owed it to Bates to put a couple bullets in her.

Andrews handed him an extra magazine. "It's been an honor, Detective."

"Thank you, sir. Good luck."

Andrews spun around the corner and tossed the grenade. As soon as he did, Pulaski stuck his arm out and opened fire. He dropped two of the gangsters before they knew what was happening. Then the sonic weapon went off, and it was like someone had driven a spike through his brain. But he kept firing as Andrews and Crowe rushed down the hall. Pulaski's vision began to dim, but at least the criminals on that side of the hall were all passing out, too. He managed to shoot one more, and then he slumped to the ground.

He forced himself to stay awake through the pain. He wanted to at least be awake to see the face of his killer.

From his right, several men swarmed down the hall. The sonic screamer was fading now, and so was the pain in Pulaski's head. But that just meant all these guys standing directly over him weren't going to be incapacitated. While most of them kept running to chase the mayor, one of them stopped next to Pulaski and raised a gun. He wore a Red Dogs jacket.

Pulaski shook his head to try to clear it, but he knew he'd never get his pistol up before the Red Dog fired. He braced himself as the gangster began to squeeze the trigger—

Suddenly, the Red Dog was knocked from his feet by what looked like, to Pulaski, a wall of light. A blue-and-gold-clad man appeared from the same direction the Red Dog had come. Pulaski looked up at the man who had to be the Seraph. His face was shrouded under a cowl, and his features around his eyes covered by a domino mask. All Pulaski could see was a strong jaw, lined with a short, scruffy beard.

"Are you all right?" the vigilante asked.

Pulaski nodded. "I'll live. They went after the mayor."

"I'll get them." The Seraph reached down to help Pulaski stand. "Have you seen Luca Serban?"

"No. But he's here somewhere."

"Get to cover. I'll handle the rest of them."

"By yourself?"

"Trust me, I've already taken on way more than I thought I could. I'll get Serban. Go."

* * *

Edgar Sterling wasn't in his office. In fact, the entire sixty-fifth-floor suite was empty. Dean frowned and stepped inside. The glass wall dividing the office from the rest of the suite was in shambled—still ruined from Gideon's visit, Dean guessed. He stepped into the office. Maybe he could find some indication of where his father had gone.

From the blue-green light cast on the black leather chair at the desk, Edgar's computer appeared to be on. Dean walked around the desk. The screen was on, but it only showed the standard Sterling Enterprises login page. Dean typed in his own company username and password. As soon as he did, a video file popped up. He frowned. Edgar's face appeared, his brow furrowed in a deep scowl and his lips tight.

"Hello, son," Sterling said. "By the time you receive this video, the Uprising will be underway already. I wanted to leave this for you so that you understand what happened, and why."

Dean sat in the chair. He needed to see this.

"First of all, yes: I am behind it all. No doubt you'll find out only after I've turned myself into the police, and I'm sorry it happened that way. But know that I had my reasons. I did this to help our city, not destroy it."

"Yeah, right." Dean laughed scornfully.

"Sojourn City was meant to be an experiment; you know this. The poor, rich, and middle-class were supposed to live in unity, making decisions together and supporting one another. But it became clear to me that, as it is everywhere else, the rich soon became selfish and distanced ourselves from the destitute. I must include myself in that; I am equally guilty. The Platform, which was intended to cast us off if we ever became a hindrance to the city, instead became our bastion of solitude, separating us from those we swore to help."

Dean sighed. He'd seen the signs of that long ago; everyone had. The Brooks were a direct result of that separation.

"When I realized what had happened, and that I was part of the problem, I became angry. I formulated a plan to fix it. While I personally used my wealth to help what poor residents of the Brooks I could, I also hired high-class criminals, intending to use them to bring us down—the rich, the Platform dwellers. It was never my intention for them to move into the Brooks."

Oh, Dad. How could someone be so idealistic and naïve and so hardened at the same time? Edgar should've known better.

"I hired Luca Serban because I'd heard of his intelligence and fierceness. I thought he would make short work of the residents of the Platform—bleed us all dry and leave us just as destitute as the people in the Brooks. Then I would rally the police to Serban's location and have him arrested. We would have faced our justice, and then he would face his.

"But it didn't work that way. Serban, coward that he is, took over the Brooks first. When I saw that, I tried to pay off the police to go in after him, but many of my peers had already paid them off to stay here, to protect us. All the while, I tried to convince Serban to make his move on the Platform. But he wouldn't be content until he had complete control over the Brooks."

"And you're surprised?" Dean waved his hand at the screen. "He's a criminal."

The recording went on, undaunted by Dean's response. "So I had your friend, Gideon, work on the super-soldier serum. It's a last resort, an insurance policy in case Serban betrayed me. I think Gideon might suspect something; he tried to stop Dr. Sung from bringing the formula to me.

"I have it now, but I didn't have time to mass produce it. So I'm going to take it myself. When Serban has finished his invasion, when he has taken over the Platform, I will use its power to kill him. And then, I will turn myself into the police, content in knowing that I have rectified my mistake and will bear the weight of it myself. I'm sorry, Dean. I had the best of intentions, you must see that. I thought I could be God's tool of justice. But . . . I can see that what I have done has not been of God. And I am deeply sorry. But I cannot stop now. I must see this through. Goodbye, son. I love you."

The screen went black. Dean wiped tears from his eyes and stood. Well, then, Edgar had to be somewhere on the Platform still. He'd be waiting for Serban to arrive. Dean had to find him first, to stop him before he did something he'd regret forever.

"I'm coming, Dad. I'm coming."

CHAPTER 39

Gideon pounded down the stairs. He had to reach the mayor before Serban or any of his men did. Between the rails, he could see two figures moving. They were almost at the first floor now. He grabbed the railing and vaulted over to the next landing. The impact of the landing shot up through his knees and to his back. He shook off the pain and leapt down the next flight of stairs. Below, he heard the emergency exit door swing open, and then city hall's fire alarms began blaring.

They were outside now. Gideon turned to the stairwell window, blasted it open with a burst of light, and leapt out. He hit the ground and somersaulted into a crouch, absorbing the force of landing over his whole body. He jumped to his feet and looked to his left, where the emergency exit would be. The mayor and a police officer were running out toward the street. Gideon rushed toward them. The cop saw him and raised his gun.

"Freeze!"

Gideon held up his hands. "I'm here to help."

"Stay there, vigilante. We don't need your help."

Behind the officer, two thugs rounded the building and raised rifles. Without lowering his hands, Gideon fired a burst of light that knocked both to the ground. The officer spun, gun raised, and saw the two criminals.

The mayor gaped. "Maybe we could use his help."

"Okay, fine." The cop looked at the Seraph. "You can cover us. I'm getting the mayor to my car. Don't think this changes my opinions about your activities."

Gideon nodded. "Take him to Refuge Church. He'll be safe there."

The cop led the mayor toward the street. Gideon followed close behind, watching for Serban or any of his men. Most of them seemed to still be inside city hall. Gideon hoped that Serban would settle for having the mayor's office, and not actually worry about the man himself.

When the cop reached his car and pulled the door open for the mayor to get in, Gideon turned back to city hall. A gangster cried out and rushed at them. Gideon hit him with a blast of light. The shout got someone's attention, though, because gunfire began to pour down from city hall's second floor. Gideon created a shielding aura around himself and moved to the middle of the street. He looked over his shoulder at the cop, who had frozen as he climbed into the driver's seat.

"Go!"

The cop seemed awestruck by Gideon's aura. "Thank you."

He drove off as the bullets around the car turned to ash. Gideon looked up at the second floor, extended his hands, and blasted the windows where the shooters were stationed. When the gunfire stopped, Gideon dropped to his knees and let his aura fade. He was exhausted. He didn't remember the last time he'd had anything to eat or drink, and he hadn't exactly had a restful night's sleep before all this started. *Just finish it.* He struggled to his feet. His sole focus now had to be Serban.

He staggered toward city hall, calling in every bit of reserve energy he had in his body. Serban was in there somewhere, he . . .

Thump-thump-thump.

Gideon frowned and looked up. The air around city hall began to swirl. A moment later, a helicopter rose from city hall's roof. Serban sat in the back compartment, one leg dangling over the side. Gideon scowled and clenched his fists, building up a burst of light to bring down the chopper.

Serban opened fire. Gideon rolled aside to avoid the bullets, too tired to project another shield. Serban continued firing as the helicopter roared away from city hall.

"No!" Gideon cried.

The chopper was heading in the direction of the Platform. He rushed for his car. He had to get there fast. He had to end this.

* * *

The Crusader's fists were getting tired, even aided by the concussion gauntlets. Red Dogs and Tyrants lay in heaps around him. But still, they came. They had pushed through most of the police line minutes ago, and the last surviving officers had fallen back to the bridge control building for cover. As a last resort, the Crusader figured the officers would raise the bridge and destroy the controls to keep the criminals from getting across.

He continued to stand in the middle of the intersection and take down anyone who tried to cross his path. His armor was withstanding his opponents' attacks, but they were still taking a toll on his body. He knew his torso had to be covered in bruises where bullets, baseball bats, and nightsticks had struck him but not penetrated his armor.

But he would not be moved. He rooted himself in the intersection and took on all comers.

As two Red Dogs, a Tyrant, and a Romanian rushed him, he picked up a nightstick and hurled it. It struck the Tyrant square in the forehead and sent him tumbling to the ground. As the Red Dogs approached, the Crusader snatched one's gun from his hand and smashed it. The other fired several rounds. His armor absorbed each, and he punched the shooter full in the chest. The second Red Dog, he snap-kicked in the jaw.

The Romanian came at him with a jagged knife and swept it at his face. He pulled back, but the knife dragged across the fabric of his mask and tore it open. He felt a nick on the tip of his nose, and then the hot wetness of a trickle of blood running down his face. He grabbed the Romanian's knife hand, twisted his wrist, and punched him in the face.

Before the Romanian had even fallen, the Crusader felt something heavy hit his back. He fell forward but caught himself, flipped, and spun around. Monahan stood behind him, a smoking gun in one hand and a curved sword in the other.

"It has been entirely too hard to kill you vigilantes. That changes today."

The Crusader rushed her. She fired three–four–five times. Each shot struck the Crusader square in the chest, but he kept coming, even as the wind left his lungs with each impact. He swung a fist at her. Monahan stepped aside, avoiding the punch, and brought up her sword. Wyatt blocked it with his forearm and used his other hand to backhand her. She rolled with the blow and came up in a crouch.

Wyatt ran at her again. She stood and swept the sword at him. It slashed across his midriff and scarred the armor. She arced the blade around and came back the other direction. Her blade found the small gap in the armor's elbow joint and bit into his left arm. It wasn't a deep cut, but it hurt. The Crusader cried out and swung an angry punch.

Monahan stepped back and fired her gun again. This time, the bullet whizzed by Wyatt's ear. He surged forward, grabbed the gun, and jerked it away. She brought her sword up and slashed his wrist. Again, his armor protected him from the worst of it, but the blade still bit into the joint and drew blood.

"Stand still!" Wyatt growled.

He threw her gun aside and kicked her in the chest. She slashed his leg, but this time did not find a joint. The Crusader pressed in and punched her across the jaw with one hand, and then used the other to knock her sword aside. He punched again, and she dropped to her knees.

Wyatt grabbed a handful of her hair and jerked her up. "You're going to rot in jail for life."

Monahan smirked, showing teeth stained with blood from the Crusader's blows. "We'll see."

She clenched a fist, and a blade ejected from her gauntlet. Before Wyatt could react, she drove it through the joint gap at his armpit. She twisted the blade and pushed it in. Wyatt gasped and tumbled back, releasing his grip on her.

He coughed and felt blood in his throat, tasted it in his mouth. Her blade had gone deep. He blinked, trying to stay awake, and struggled to rise. But his body would not cooperate.

"No!" someone shouted.

And then there were gunshots, and after that, screaming.

* * *

The helicopter pilot's voice was tinny in Serban's earpiece. "The Platform is still connected, sir!"

Monahan. Could that woman succeed at nothing? Serban stared out of the helicopter at the city below. Fires burned randomly, stoked by Serban's forces. The majority of the damage was centered around the areas just outside the Brooks, but some of it had spread as far as Lakeside. Refuge Church was visible, though, and it appeared untouched by the chaos. How?

Serban leaned toward the pilot. "Take me to Sterling Enterprises. I don't care if the Platform's docked or not. The plan continues."

"Sir!" The copilot pointed out the front windshield. "Police choppers!"

Serban growled and reached under the seat. He'd had his men bring along an RPG for just such an occasion. He loaded the grenade into the rocket launcher and steadied the weapon on his shoulder.

"Give me an angle!"

The chopper pilot—an airport employee that Serban had blackmailed into working for him—angled the helicopter to the left, giving the open right flank of the chopper a clear view of the two police choppers converging on them. Serban took aim. *Should've just stayed out of my way.* He squeezed the trigger.

The rocket shot across the sky, slamming into the righthand chopper. The helicopter spun madly, slamming into its partner. Both aircraft plummeted toward the lake. Serban's pilot whistled, a sharp, tinny sound through the headset. Serban lowered the RPG and turned his gaze back toward Sterling Enterprises.

He was tired of playing games. Nothing would stand in his way anymore.

* * *

"No!" Jolie cried.

She snapped up her gun and pulled the trigger three times. Monahan, standing over the Crusader's body, jerked as each shot struck her, and collapsed to the ground. Paul rushed to the woman's side and Jolie ran to the Crusader.

"Stay with me," she said. "Please."

The Crusader reached up, tore at his mask. "H-help . . . me."

"We need an ambulance!" Jolie shouted. "I'm going to. I'll get you help."

"No . . . my mask."

Jolie pulled the mask off. Blood flecked Jonson's lips and trickled from the corner of his mouth down to his chin. He was in bad condition; she could see that much. Monahan's blade had to have pierced his heart. Which meant there was no way he'd survive until an ambulance got here. She shook her head and felt tears well in her eyes.

"I'm sorry. I should've gotten here sooner."

"N-no . . . " The Crusader patted her hand. "You . . . did good."

"So did you." Jolie forced a smile through her tears. "You did good. You fought for the city when even some of its police wouldn't. You're a hero."

The Crusader coughed, smiled. "Thanks. Tell . . . tell Gideon . . . to watch . . . over my family. Tell them . . . I love them. Tell Carter . . . "

He blinked rapidly, and Jolie grabbed his shoulders. "What? Tell Carter what?"

"He's . . . " The Crusader sighed. "He's my hero."

Tears ran down Jolie's face. The light went out of the Crusader's eyes.

"No. No, no, no, no."

Jolie pumped at his chest, pushing with all her might and hoping to hear him gasp for breath. But Wyatt remained unmoving, eyes staring past her to the sky. Jolie wiped her face and stood.

Paul looked up from Monahan's body. "She's still alive. She was wearing a vest."

Where was the justice in that? A hero like the Crusader dying in the streets, protecting his city to his last breath, while his killer survived? Jolie removed her handcuffs from her belt, went to Monahan's side, and snapped them on until they dug into the assassin's wrists.

"You'll pay for this," Jolie snarled. "You're going to rot."

Suddenly, a navy-blue car peeled around the corner. Jolie watched it pass. It was Gideon's car! He sped through the intersection and across the bridge. Several cops raised their guns and fired on it, but Jolie shouted them down.

"Let him go!"

She yanked Monahan to her feet, while Paul went to the Crusader's side and gently lifted his body.

"He's going to finish this." Jolie shoved Monahan in the car. "You lost. You'll be lucky if you get the death sentence. Because if you survive, I'll make sure your prison sentence is every second of torment you deserve."

* * *

Dean stepped onto the roof of Sterling Enterprises. As one of the highest points in the city, he suspected his father would come here to oversee all the chaos. He knew his dad; when he thought something was his fault—whether it was or not—he refused to look away until it was over.

Once, he had backed over Dean's dog in the driveway. They'd had to put the animal down. It wasn't Edgar's fault; it had been an honest mistake, and Dean had never blamed him for it. But as the vets had injected the dog, had put it down, Edgar had refused to leave its side, had refused to break eye contact with the animal until it was gone. Tears had streamed down his face and he had told the dog he was so sorry. And then he had apologized endlessly to Dean.

That had been a dog. This was a city. Edgar would take every life lost personally.

On the far end of the roof, standing so close to the edge that he had to be dizzied by the height, stood Dean's father. His hands were clasped behind his back. There was no external sign of the torment he must be feeling. Dean walked toward him quietly, not sneaking but not making his presence known, either.

He powered down the concussion gauntlets. He wouldn't need them; not for this. He had come here to stop his father, but it seemed Edgar was already there. The only thing Dean had to do now was keep him from killing Serban. That would destroy Edgar, Dean knew, even if he felt it was necessary at the time. He was too kind a soul. Intentionally taking a life, even the life of an evil man like Serban, would be too much for him to handle.

Something crunched under Dean's feet. He frowned and looked down. It was an empty vial. Dean's heart raced. His father had already taken the super-soldier serum, then. How long did its effects last? Gideon had said it was temporary, but . . . how temporary?

At the sound of the crunching glass, Sterling turned. "Ah. Hello, son."

"Dad." Dean stepped forward, hand extended. "Dad, come with me. Let's go talk to the police."

"No." Edgar smiled sadly. "No, I'm sorry. It's not time yet. I have to clean up this mess."

"Dad . . . it's not yours to clean."

"Yes, it is! I caused this! I brought them here and foolishly believed they would follow my instructions. This city is in pain because of me!"

"Yeah, and . . . and you'll have to pay for that. You'll go to jail, you'll . . . whatever. But you don't have to kill Serban. You don't."

"I must. I caused this, and now I must fix it."

"Killing him won't do that." Dean looked over Edgar's shoulder. A helicopter ascended toward the tower. "Dad, if you're going to do anything, at least just disable him. Let the police take him away. Don't kill him."

"I can't! He's too powerful; he can sway the courts and even if he goes to jail, he may have friends among the guards. And if he gets deported back to Romania . . . well, if that were to happen, it would be the same as letting him run free. No, the only solution is to kill him now."

"That's not true, Dad. Look, we know who Serban's government friends are. We gave their names to the police. It's all over, Dad; he can't win."

"I wish I could believe that." Edgar put a hand on Dean's shoulder. Dean tensed, ready to move. "Please, son. You should leave."

"I won't. If you face Serban, I'll do it with you—but I also won't let you kill him."

Dean knew this was risky—if Sterling was juiced up on the serum, his hormones might be raging. He might lose his temper and just throw Dean right off the roof. But Dean was betting he wouldn't do that. He might be emotional, but he still knew and loved his son.

The helicopter was directly overhead. It began to descend toward the roof. *Where are you, Gideon?*

"Dean, move," his father said. "Right now."

"Dad—"

"Now."

Edgar shoved him—not hard, but enough to send Dean stumbling backward. Luckily, he was facing away from the ledge. He landed flat on his back on the rooftop. Sterling started to walk past him toward the landing helicopter. Dean switched on the concussion gauntlets and stood. *I'm sorry, Dad.*

"You're not killing him! I won't let you."

Edgar turned. "Don't fight me, Dean."

"I'll do what I have to. I love you, Dad. I know you think what you're doing is right. But it's not. So I have to stop you."

"Very well." Edgar spread his hands. "Then come. Let's get this out of the way."

Dean rushed his father and prayed that they both survived the encounter.

CHAPTER 40

Gideon's car screeched to a halt outside Sterling Enterprises. The helicopter was overhead, descending onto the rooftop. He had to get up there fast. As he bounded out of his car and up the stairs, he wondered about the scene at the bridge control. He hadn't gotten a good look, because he was driving so fast, but it had appeared that the fighting was over. There had been bodies everywhere—he hadn't seen who was dead and who was alive. It made him sick to think about.

He made it to the top floor on adrenaline alone. A quick look in the suite confirmed that it was empty; everyone was probably on the rooftop. One flight of stairs to go. He rushed up them and burst through the door onto the roof.

Serban and two thugs stepped out of the chopper, weapons raised. Edgar stormed toward them. Dean was lying flat on his face; as Gideon watched, he rose, jumped up, and grabbed his father's jacket. He yanked the elder Sterling back and the two began to battle in a tangle of punches and kicks. Gideon considered going to help his friend, but—no, he had to stop Serban. He blasted both of Serban's lackeys and stepped toward the gangster.

"Well, well." Serban smirked. "So it comes down to this at last."

"I guess it does." Gideon clenched his fists and willed his body to continue functioning until this fight was over. "It is over, Serban! The police have arrested your government lackeys, you have lost the battle at the bridge, and your benefactor has even finally turned against you."

"It doesn't matter anymore." Serban shrugged. "Way I see it, all I've gotta do is kill you, kill Sterling, kill his brat over there . . . then no one can really stand in my way."

Gideon spread his hands. "Well, then, come on! Let's see what you've got."

Serban grinned. "Thought you'd never ask."

He charged. The Seraph, fists surrounded by a glowing aura, swung at Serban's face. The Romanian ducked and unleashed a flurry of brutal punches on his torso. Gideon grimaced and staggered back. The guy hit harder than anyone Gideon had ever faced. Shaking his head, the Seraph stepped forward, grabbed Serban by the shoulders, and brought his knee up in the crime lord's gut. Serban jabbed, and Gideon dodged it and punched back. Serban pushed Gideon's wrist aside. The two exchanged several more punches, all of which missed or were blocked or dodged.

The Seraph kicked at Serban's head. The gangster crouched under his spinning heel and came back up to grab Gideon and tackle him to the ground. Gideon spun through the tackle, using an *aikido* maneuver and grabbing Serban's arm, tucking it between his legs, and *yanking*. Serban cried out as his shoulder tore free from its socket. But the Romanian was tough; he rolled over and used his free hand to punch Gideon's knee.

The joint spasmed and the Seraph released Serban's arm. The man jumped to his feet, and Gideon pushed himself up, too. He extended a hand and tried to generate a blast of light, but in his body's weakness and fatigue, he was only able to create an aura of light, not fire it. He panted and lowered his hand.

Serban laughed. "Your powers don't scare me. I've seen your kind before."

What? Gideon straightened and, projecting all the light he could to use to amplify his punches, rushed in again, swinging. Serban dodged the first few, but then Gideon landed a blow on his jaw. The Romanian gangster reeled and tumbled back toward the open door to the stairwell. Gideon punched him again, from the other side.

"What do you mean?" Gideon punched again, this time the gut. "Who else have you seen like me?"

Serban growled and kicked Gideon in the chest. When the Seraph dropped to his haunches, Serban reached into his coat and pulled out a gun—an old-model Luger. He pointed it at Gideon's head.

"No one special."

Gideon summoned every reserve of energy in every cell of his body and *pushed*. The blast of light he emitted was small, but it was enough to knock Serban back—and down the stairs. Gideon followed him down to the landing. Serban pulled himself to his feet, but Gideon punched him in the face again.

"Who?"

"I . . . told you." Serban laughed. He slugged Gideon across the jaw. As Gideon staggered back, Serban grabbed him and then slammed him into the wall. Gideon grunted as his body crashed into the concrete. Serban pulled him back and slammed him forward again. Gideon felt his nose break, and he tasted the metallic warmth of blood. "No one . . . special. They had powers, yeah, but they were just lab rats."

Lab rats? Was it possible that Serban knew the doctor from Venezuela? Gideon pushed his hands against the wall as Serban tried to shove him into it again. He planted his feet against the wall and ran up it, backflipping over Serban. The Romanian swiveled, and Gideon punched him—again and again and again. Serban sagged to the floor.

"You know who did this to me?" Gideon demanded.

"You sure . . . seem like one of Ashcroft's abominations to me."

Ashcroft. Gideon lowered his fist and took a deep breath. Serban lay in a bloody heap. Gideon forced himself to calm down. Somehow, hearing the name—having some semblance of an answer—allowed him to finally expunge his anger. He felt it leave his system, replaced with a strange peace that washed over him like cool water. He wasn't going to kill Serban. He reached for one of his adhesive beads.

Serban reached for the Luger. Gideon kicked him in the jaw, and the crime lord slumped over. Gideon pulled out the adhesive bead, glued him to the landing, and stepped on the gun for good measure. The weapon shattered. He turned and headed for the rooftop. Dean still needed him.

* * *

Dean couldn't believe his father was fighting him. At first, they'd just thrown each other around a bit. But now it was a full-on skirmish, fists and feet flying as Sterling tried to push past Dean and Dean tried desperately to stop him. Several times, he tried to reach for his adhesive beads, but Edgar just grabbed his wrist and jerked it aside.

Some part of Dean recognized that Serban and his goons had not gotten involved—which meant Gideon must've shown up. But until Dean knew for sure that Gideon had taken down Serban and had him under control, he wouldn't stop fighting his father.

The helicopter pilot must've gotten the idea that all this was above his pay grade; he lifted off and ascended as quickly as he could manage. Dean ignored the hovering chopper and continued trying to accost his father.

"Son, just stop!"

Dean kicked Edgar in the chest. "I can't let you do this! You'll regret it forever."

Edgar advanced on Dean. "I'll never forgive myself if Serban gets away to continue his reign of terror elsewhere!"

"Dad, you have to trust that's not going to happen! You're not judge, jury, and executioner. You're not God!"

"No," Sterling agreed. "When I started this, I thought I could deliver God's judgment to those like me. I . . . was wrong."

Suddenly, a mass of navy blue and gold was on Sterling's back. Dean reached for his belt to grab his adhesive beads as Gideon struggled with Edgar. He pulled the beads out and raised them—

And Sterling hurled Gideon over his head, and off the edge of the building.

* * *

Gideon screamed as the momentum from Sterling's throw carried him through the air. The rooftop passed below him, and then he was looking down on the street far below. He waved his arms and reached for his grappling hook—

It was gone. It must've fallen from his belt at some point during the fighting. He closed his eyes, knowing he was doomed.

But it didn't feel like he was falling. There was no wind resistance, no gravitational pull. That wasn't right. Gideon opened his eyes . . . and found himself floating mid-air just two stories below the rooftop. He looked around. What had caught him? He didn't see anything. There was nothing holding him up.

There was, however, a subtle aura of golden light surrounding his body.

"No way," he said.

He was flying. Slowly, carefully, he moved his body . . . and it worked. He moved down, and then back up.

"I can fly." He laughed. "I can fly."

But he needed to get back to the rooftop before his body remembered that it was exhausted and broken. He exerted himself, and he flew upward and crested the roof. Dean stood on the edge and gaped.

"Bro. You're flying."

"I am!" Gideon laughed. "I don't even know how that's possible."

There was, apparently, a lot he didn't know about his powers. He flew down to the rooftop and settled between Dean and Edgar. The latter had his feet affixed to the ground with the gel from Dean's beads.

"Seraph," Edgar said. "I . . . I suppose it's fairly obvious now who you are. I don't know why I didn't see it before."

Gideon removed his hood and mask. "Hello, Mr. Sterling."

Sterling sank to his knees and hung his head. "All this time, you've been the one truly bringing justice to this city, not me. You've had to fix all the problems I caused. I'm so sorry."

"I forgive you. But I'm not the one you need to ask."

He stepped aside, and Dean stepped forward. Sterling looked up at his son, his sorrow evident in his eyes.

"You were right, Dean. This isn't my place. It never was, and I suppose I knew that all along. It's why I was so determined to fix it."

"Well, there's still a long way to go to do that, but with Serban taken down and his government cronies in police custody, I think the worst of it is over."

"But we can't just let you go, you know," Gideon added. "You'll have to go to prison."

"I know." Sterling nodded. "It's a price I'll willingly pay."

"I'll call the police." Dean reached for his utility belt. "Hey, speaking of. Have you checked comms lately? I've got no idea what's going on in the rest of the city."

Gideon nodded and flicked on his earbud. "This is the Seraph. Status report."

"Gideon . . . it's Jolie."

"Jolie." Hearing her voice lifted a weight he didn't know he'd been carrying. "I'm glad to hear your voice. Is everyone okay?"

"Not everyone. I . . . it's the Crusader."

Gideon's heart dropped. She didn't have to say it—he knew. He'd known something was wrong at the bridge control. He closed his eyes and lowered his head. There was no anger now. The only thing he could bring himself to feel was sorrow. Every victory came with a cost . . . but in his estimation, this one was entirely too high.

"How's Carter?"

"Taking it pretty hard. But he's a tough kid. He'll be okay."

Gideon swallowed a lump in his throat. "And the city?"

"Most of the fighting is finished; now it's just mop-up. I got Monahan, by the way, and Carter got Walters. So if you have Serban, I think . . . I think it's over."

"We have him. Sterling, too. Get the police to Sterling Enterprises as soon as possible to take them in."

"Will do. Good job, Gid."

"You, too."

Gideon removed his earbud, threw it to the ground, and let the tears come.

CHAPTER 41

Wyatt Jonson's funeral was nothing like the movies. There was no rain; in fact, the sun was shining brightly on the cemetery as the mourners gathered to say goodbye. Gideon put a hand on Carter's shoulder as the Jonson family approached the casket. Gideon had asked their permission to join them and Joanna had gratefully allowed it.

The casket had been emblazoned with the cross-like symbol that had decorated the Crusader's mask, and on the tombstone were etched the words "The City's Great Crusader" as an epitaph. Carter's jaw clenched and unclenched as the pallbearers lowered the casket into the ground. Gideon patted the boy's shoulder twice and lowered his hand. Farther back in the crowd, Jolie and Dean stood waiting for him.

"If any of you ever need anything," Gideon said to Joanna, "let me know. If it's in my power, it's yours."

"Thank you." Joanna shook Gideon's hand.

Before Gideon left, he glanced at Carter. "I'll see you later, kid."

As Gideon walked away from the family, Jolie approached. She made brief eye contact with Gideon but then kept walking and stopped next to Carter. Gideon stood next to Dean and waited.

"What do you think she's saying?" he asked.

"No idea," Dean replied. "Maybe Wyatt asked her to deliver a message to Carter."

"Maybe so."

Jolie returned a moment later and took Gideon's hand in hers. "Let's go home."

Gideon nodded. He, Jolie, and Dean returned to Gideon's car and climbed in. The drive to the apartment was sober and silent.

Ashcroft. Gideon rolled the name over in his mind. It was only one name, probably a last name, and it wasn't much to go off. It could even be an alias. But Serban had encountered him somewhere. If Gideon crosschecked Ashcroft's name with Venezuela and Romania, maybe he would find something.

That was a problem for another day. For now, they all needed rest.

One month later

Gideon adjusted his tie and frowned at his reflection. He was a super-hero who could fly and shoot light from his hands, but he was nervous about standing in front of a bunch of people and saying some words. Crazy.

He stepped back and looked at himself. Clad in a black suit and tie with a maroon shirt, he thought he looked about as presentable as he ever had. He'd had a haircut recently, though he had kept his scruffy, short-trimmed beard.

"You ready?" Dad asked.

Gideon turned and looked at his father, who was also dressed in a suit. He nodded and followed his father out of the office and into the church auditorium—which was packed to the brim with people. Even the balcony was full. Gideon swallowed. *It's just a speech, it's just a speech, it's just a speech . . .*

Pastor Jeff had parked his wheelchair next to the front row. Gideon sat down next to his old mentor as his father went up to the pulpit to say a few words. Gideon reached over and shook Pastor Jeff's hand,

and then glanced behind him. Dean and Jolie sat a few rows back, and both offered him a smile and a nod of encouragement.

"Two years ago," Dad said, "my son went missing. And for a long, terrible year, we had no idea where he was. All we could do was pray that the Lord would bring him home. And He did. In the midst of the chaos our city has faced, I thought it would be good to hear a story of hope straight from one who's experienced it. So today, I've asked my son to say a few words of encouragement. Welcome him."

Gideon rose and walked toward the platform as the church's congregation thundered with applause. His cheeks warmed, and he forced himself to calm down as he approached the pulpit and rested his hands against it.

"Hello. I'm . . . well, I'm not much of a public speaker. But I do have a story to tell, and I hope it'll give you all some hope. Two years ago, I was in Venezuela on a mission trip. I was a doctor, and all I wanted to do was help people. But I hadn't been there very long when some guerrillas attacked the clinic I was working at.

"I intervened so that the guerrillas wouldn't take the doctor who ran the clinic. They took me instead. They threw me in a cage in the jungle and left me there." He wondered how much to say. "Some of this I haven't even told my parents or my friends, but there was another man there. His name was Joshua Omer, and he was my friend."

The auditorium was completely silent. He saw the surprise on the faces of Dean and Jolie, and of his parents and Wes. They'd all thought he'd been alone.

"Joshua and I, as you can imagine, grew pretty close over a year. But the day I escaped . . . he died. Joshua stayed behind and fought one of the guerrillas so that I could get away. He sacrificed himself.

"In the same way, we've seen people sacrifice themselves for this city in the past month. Some of you have lost family." The Jonson family sat near the back. "This city lost a great many police officers, as well as the Crusader, who—whether you agree with his methods or not—did his best to protect us.

"You see, whenever a crisis rises, God will always intervene, and He usually doesn't do it through some great lightning strike from the sky—He does it through His people. People like Joshua, whose last request was that I find his family and tell them about the love of Jesus. People like the Crusader, whose very symbol was that of the cross.

"People aren't perfect. We make mistakes, we fall short of God's love. But we can also be used by Him. And when we let Him use us, great things can happen. I'm here today because of Joshua Omer. Many of us are here because of the Crusader, or because of the police. We all have heroes. We all have people who protect us. And I encourage you: be that person. Be the protector. So when your crisis comes, people will remember your help for them, and they will help you, too."

Gideon stepped back from the pulpit and walked down to his seat. He didn't listen for the applause, though it was there. He'd said what he needed to say, and that was what mattered. But he still had a promise to fulfill.

* * *

Gideon's speech had been moving. The words *be the protector* rang in Wes' ears long after he returned home and dropped down on his bed. He hadn't found out until days later that the guy who had saved his family the day of the Uprising had been the Crusader's son—and that the real Crusader had died fighting to protect the bridge to the

Platform. Well, whether the younger man had been the actual Crusader or not, he'd proven his heroism.

Wes longed to do the same. He thought back to the moment when the house's door had blown in, when he'd been sure for a moment that they were all going to die. He didn't want to feel that way again. He didn't want to be helpless.

He sat up and looked his desk. A letter from Juncture City School of Law sat next to his laptop—he had gotten the acceptance letter the day before the Uprising. Being a lawyer was one way to help people. He walked over to the desk, picked up the letter, and weighed his options.

First things first. He had to finish undergrad school first. Then he could decide whether he wanted to go to law school . . . or if his best chance of helping others would be found elsewhere.

* * *

All in all, Edgar Sterling's sentence was not nearly as severe as it could've been. Dean suspected it was because of his wealth, but he would never accuse his father of that to his face. He knew his dad would never bribe a court of law—but his status might've influenced the decision, regardless. He had been sentenced to ten years at Stone Gate penitentiary with the possibility of parole.

At first, Dean wished the sentence had been worse. Life in prison, or something. But then he realized what that would mean for him— he'd never see his dad outside the walls of a prison again. No matter how angry he was with Edgar, he could never wish that on him. And he did seem truly repentant, and that had shown through in the court-room. Maybe that was why it had gone so well for him.

Dean sat across from his had in the visiting room, looking at him through the glass and wondering how he'd go ten years like this. He picked up the phone.

"Hey, Dad."

"Hello, Dean." Sterling smiled. "I'm glad you came to visit. Son, I am so sorry . . . "

"Dad. You've apologized enough." Dean tapped his fingers on the table in front of him. "I . . . one of my friends recently had to forgive something pretty big—a secret that had been kept from her by another friend and that she had every right to be angry about. But when she found out, do you know what she said? She said she forgave him, because if she didn't, it would only hurt her. So I forgive you, Dad. Because I don't want to hurt myself by holding a grudge . . . and I don't want to hurt you, either."

"Thank you, Dean." Edgar blinked rapidly. Tears formed in his eyes.

"Listen, I'll come visit you whenever I get the chance, okay? But I'm going to be busy. The board wants to make me acting CEO of Sterling Enterprises while you're in here. Ha! Can you imagine it? Me, a twenty-six-year-old dork. The CEO."

"You'll do well with it." Sterling wiped his eyes. "You are the company scion, after all. What other choice did they have?"

"I'll do my best. So, what about Serban and Monahan? Are they in there with you?"

"They are. They're in the maximum-security section, however; I'm in minimum security. They can't get to me."

"Good." Dean put his hand on the glass, and Sterling did the same. "I love you, Dad. I'll be praying for you in there."

"Thank you, Dean. I love you, too."

* * *

Jolie cuddled with Gideon on his couch. She gazed out the window at the sunset as it fell over the Brooks. Finally, that part of town was getting a little bit of peace and quiet. Things had been way different over the past month. Captain Cranston had replaced the former police chief and was cracking down on corruption in his ranks. The force was now divided much more evenly across the city. Andrews had been promoted to captain and put in charge of the twelfth precinct in Cranston's place. Pulaski, for his bravery in protecting the mayor, had been promoted to sergeant. Jolie herself had been promoted to detective. Someone had to replace the void left by Detective Walters—who was sitting in Stone Gate along with Serban, Monahan, and Sterling. Andrews and Cranston had agreed that, since Jolie had been so involved in exposing Walters, along with the rest of Serban's plot, she deserved the promotion.

"In other news," said the anchor on the TV, "the mayor held a press conference today, speaking about the actions of the vigilantes who many say saved our city on the night of the Uprising."

Jolie turned her attention to the TV. She felt Gideon perk up, too, and smiled.

"These vigilantes have, for months now, been persecuted and pursued by our own police like criminals," Mayor Crowe said. "And perhaps they were. But I believe they were something more: heroes. I have been informed that the Crusader, who watched over the Brooks long before we even knew of the danger that awaited our city, died while protecting the bridge to the Platform. One of the officers on the scene reported that this man singlehandedly took down dozens of criminals before he died. I don't know what to call that, if not a hero."

Jolie looked at Gideon. His jaw was set, and his eyes glistened with unshed tears. She put a hand on his cheek. He looked away from the TV and forced a smile. He felt responsible for Wyatt's death, because he'd convinced him to become the Crusader again; he had told her as much. But she knew it wasn't his fault. Even if he hadn't asked, Wyatt would've gone out there. It was a part of him.

And it was a part of his son, too. Jolie could see it in his eyes. Carter would take up his father's mantle full-time now. She hoped Gideon would be there to help him grow to be the hero that Wyatt had already known he'd become.

"And as for the Seraph," Mayor Crowe continued, "there is much that we don't know about this hooded figure. Where did he get his powers? Who is he? Of all the cities in the world, why did he choose to bless us with his protection? I don't know. But what I do know is that he saved my life. And not just mine—he saved all our lives. And for that, I formally recognize the Seraph as the honorary protector of Sojourn City—our Shining Knight. He is not a criminal. He is not a menace. He is our hero, our guardian angel."

Gideon turned off the TV. "Uh . . . wow."

Jolie sat up and turned to face him. "Congratulations."

"Thanks." He stared at his lap, and then looked back at her. "I know you never wanted this for me, but . . . "

"It doesn't matter anymore. I had one bad dream, and I was stupid to believe it could ever come true. And how could I ever want you to stop doing something that gives you so much purpose? I can see it in your eyes; this is your calling. You were meant to be a hero." She kissed him. "There's no one better suited for the job."

"Thank you." Gideon kissed her back. "I love you, Jolie."

"I love you, too, Gideon."

* * *

"So, what's the plan?" Dean asked.

Gideon stood looking out over the city from the living room window. He'd been asking himself that same question for a long time, and he still didn't have an exact answer. But then, he supposed he didn't need one. Plans seldom worked out the way they were expected to.

He didn't have to hide in the shadows anymore. He was an officially-recognized hero, a force for justice. But did the city still need him? With Serban and Monahan, and even Sterling, locked away in Stone Gate penitentiary, there was more peace, even in the Brooks, than there had been in years.

And then, of course, there was Jolie. Their relationship was blossoming. He was again beginning to consider when he could propose to her. He loved her, and he had every intention of marrying her.

But there was something else he had to take care of first.

"I'm going to go find Joshua's family," he said. "I've put that off for way too long."

"And then what?"

"Then . . . then I have a name." Gideon walked up the stairs to the lair, and Dean followed. "Ashcroft. He's the doctor who gave me powers, and I want to find out how he did it. Serban said there are more like me. If that's true, then I should find them, too. Some may be able to use their powers for good. Others . . . well, if any of them abuse their powers, they need to be stopped."

"What about Sojourn?" Dean asked. "Look, the city may be at peace right now, but there will always be crime."

Gideon nodded. "I think we should train Carter. Give him one of the spare sets of armor; let him honor his father by becoming the Crusader in his place. Let him have my staff; I don't need it anymore. He can protect the city in my absence."

"What about your suit? It got pretty beat up in the fighting."

"Repair it. But work on some updates, if you can." Gideon typed "Patrick Omer" in the lair's computer and searched.

"Got it. I'm thinking about doing away with the cape. It just gets in the way, you know?" Dean leaned against the computer. "Do you really think there are people out there with powers who'll use them for evil? Like, real supervillains?"

"I do. As long as there is power, there'll be someone who'll use it for right, and someone who'll abuse it for their own purposes." Gideon walked over to his suit, damaged as it was, and looked into the empty eye holes of the domino mask. "And as long as they're out there, the Seraph will be there to stop them."

"Uh . . . Gid?"

Gideon turned. "What?"

Dean pointed at the computer. While one window was running the search for Omer, Dean had opened the other to a news station. The blonde news anchor who'd questioned the Seraph's motives months ago was center frame, and in the top right corner of the screen was a photo of . . .

"Is that me?"

Gideon circled around to stand beside Dean. Dean tapped the screen and turned the volume up.

" . . . an anonymous source has delivered this image to the station today," the anchor says. "It provides definitive proof that the

Seraph's true identity is Gideon Turner, son of local megachurch pastor Matthew Turner."

"How did they get this?" Dean asked.

Gideon examined the image. Given the bruises and cuts on his face, it was probably the night of the Uprising—and the only time he'd removed his mask and hood that night was on the rooftop of Sterling Enterprises.

"The helicopter pilot. He must've taken this picture before he flew away."

"What does this mean?"

"Well . . . " Gideon looked at the Seraph suit again. "I guess it means you don't have to worry about designing a new mask."

COMING SOON

FREEDOM'S FIGHT

Since the defeat of Luca Serban and the outing of Gideon Turner's identity as the Seraph, Gideon has been focused on one mission: finding the man who gave him powers. In *Freedom's Fight*, Gideon, along with his best friend Dean, girlfriend Jolie, and sidekick the Crusader, look for answers surrounding the mysterious Dr. Ashcroft, and why new superhumans, heroes, and villains alike, are appearing. This is a mission that will take Gideon across the country, introduce him to new allies, and set a course for an inevitable encounter with Ashcroft.

For more information about
Jake Tyson
&
Vigilante's Light

please visit:

www.creatingforcreator.wordpress.com
www.facebook.com/jaketysonauthor96

For more information about
AMBASSADOR INTERNATIONAL
please visit:

www.ambassador-international.com
@AmbassadorIntl
www.facebook.com/AmbassadorIntl

*If you enjoyed this book, please consider leaving us a review on
Amazon, Goodreads, or our website.*